PRAISE FOR TAHOE BLUE FIRE

"A GRIPPING NARRATIVE...A HERO WHO WALKS CONFIDENTLY IN THE FOOTSTEPS OF SAM SPADE, PHILIP MARLOWE, AND LEW ARCHER" - *Kirkus Reviews*

"A THRILLING MYSTERY THAT IS DIFFICULT TO PUT DOWN ...EDGE OF YOUR SEAT ACTION" - *Elizabeth, Silver's Reviews*

PRAISE FOR TAHOE GHOST BOAT

"THE OLD PULP SAVVY OF (ROSS) MACDONALD...REAL SURPRISE AT THE END" - *Kirkus Reviews*

"NAIL-BITING THRILLER...BOILING POT OF DRAMA"
- *Gloria Sinibaldi, Tahoe Daily Tribune*

"A THRILL RIDE" - *Mary Beth Magee, Examiner.com*

"BORG'S WRITING IS THE STUFF OF A HOLLYWOOD ACTION BLOCKBUSTER" - *Taylor Flynn, Tahoe Mountain News*

"ACTION-PACKED IS PUTTING IT MILDLY. PREPARE FOR FIRE-WORKS" - *Sunny Solomon, Bookin' With Sunny*

"I LOVED EVERY ROLLER COASTER RIDE IN THIS THRILLER 5+ OUT OF 5" - *Harvee Lau, Book Dilettante*

PRAISE FOR TAHOE CHASE

"EXCITING, EXPLOSIVE, THOUGHTFUL, SOMETIMES FUNNY"
- *Ann Ronald, Bookin' With Sunny*

"THE LANDSCAPE IS BEAUTIFULLY CRAFTED... PACE BUILDS NICELY AND DOESN'T LET UP"

- *Kirkus Reviews*

"BE WARNED. IT MIGHT BE ADDICTING"
- *Gloria Sinibaldi, Tahoe Daily Tribune*

"OWEN McKENNA HAS HIS HANDS FULL IN ANOTHER THRILL-ING ADVENTURE"

- *Harvee Lau, Book Dilettante*

PRAISE FOR TAHOE TRAP

"AN OPEN-THROTTLE RIDE"

- Wendy Schultz, Placerville Mountain Democrat

"A CONSTANTLY SURPRISING SERIES OF EVENTS INVOLVING MURDER...and the final motivation of the killer comes as a major surprise. (I love when that happens.)" *- Yvette, In So Many Words*

"I LOVE TODD BORG'S BOOKS...There is the usual great twist ending in Tahoe Trap that I never would have guessed" *- JBronder Reviews*

"THE PLOTS ARE HIGH OCTANE AND THE ACTION IS FASTER THAN A CHEETAH ON SPEED" *- Cathy Cole, Kittling: Books*

"A FASCINATING STORY WITH FIRST CLASS WRITING and, of course, my favorite character, Spot, a Great Dane that steals most of the scenes." *- Mary Lignor, Feathered Quill Book Reviews*

"SUPER CLEVER... More twists in the plot toward the end of the book turn the mystery into an even more suspenseful thriller."

-Harvee Lau, Book Dilettante

"AN EXCITING MURDER MYSTERY... I watch for the ongoing developments of Jack Reacher, Joanna Brady, Dismas Hardy, Peter and Rina Decker, and Alex Cross to name a few. But these days I look forward most to the next installment of Owen McKenna."

- China Gorman blog

PRAISE FOR TAHOE HIJACK

"BEGINNING TO READ TAHOE HIJACK IS LIKE FLOOR-BOARDING A RACE CAR... RATING: A+"

- Cathy Cole, Kittling Books

"A THRILLING READ... any reader will find the pages of his thrillers impossible to stop turning"

- Caleb Cage, The Nevada Review

"THE BOOK CLIMAXES WITH A TWIST THE READER DOESN'T SEE COMING, WORTHY OF MICHAEL CONNELLY"

- Heather Gould, Tahoe Mountain News

"I HAD TO HOLD MY BREATH DURING THE LAST PART OF THIS FAST-PACED THRILLER"

- Harvee Lau, Book Dilettante

PRAISE FOR TAHOE HEAT

"IN TAHOE HEAT, BORG MASTERFULLY WRITES A SEQUENCE OF EVENTS SO INTENSE THAT IT BELONGS IN AN EARLY TOM CLANCY NOVEL"

- Caleb Cage, Nevada Review

"TAHOE HEAT IS A RIVETING THRILLER"

- John Burroughs, Midwest Book Review

"WILL KEEP READERS TURNING THE PAGES AS OWEN RACES TO CATCH A VICIOUS KILLER"

- Barbara Bibel, Booklist

"THE READER CAN'T HELP BUT ROOT FOR McKENNA AS THE BIG, GENEROUS, IRISH-BLOODED, STREET-WISE-YET-BOOK-SMART FORMER COP"

- Taylor Flynn, Tahoe Mountain News

PRAISE FOR TAHOE NIGHT

"BORG HAS WRITTEN ANOTHER WHITE-KNUCKLE THRILLER... A sure bet for mystery buffs waiting for the next Robert B. Parker and Lee Child novels"

- Jo Ann Vicarel, Library Journal

"AN ACTION-PACKED THRILLER WITH A NICE-GUY HERO, AN EVEN NICER DOG..."

- Kirkus Reviews

"A KILLER PLOT... EVERY ONE OF ITS 350 PAGES WANTS TO GET TURNED... *FAST*"

- Taylor Flynn, Tahoe Mountain News

"A FASCINATING STORY OF FORGERY, MURDER..."

- Nancy Hayden, Tahoe Daily Tribune

PRAISE FOR TAHOE AVALANCHE

ONE OF THE TOP 5 MYSTERIES OF THE YEAR!

- Gayle Wedgwood, Mystery News

"BORG IS A SUPERB STORYTELLER...A MASTER OF THE GENRE"

- Midwest Book Review

"EXPLODES INTO A COMPLEX PLOT THAT LEADS TO MURDER AND INTRIGUE"

- Nancy Hayden, Tahoe Daily Tribune

PRAISE FOR TAHOE SILENCE

WINNER, BEN FRANKLIN AWARD, BEST MYSTERY OF THE YEAR!

"A HEART-WRENCHING MYSTERY THAT IS ALSO ONE OF THE BEST NOVELS WRITTEN ABOUT AUTISM"

STARRED REVIEW - Jo Ann Vicarel, Library Journal

CHOSEN BY LIBRARY JOURNAL AS ONE OF THE FIVE BEST MYSTERIES OF THE YEAR

"THIS IS ONE ENGROSSING NOVEL...IT IS SUPERB"

- Gayle Wedgwood, Mystery News

"ANOTHER EXCITING ENTRY INTO THIS TOO-LITTLE-KNOWN SERIES"

- Mary Frances Wilkens, Booklist

PRAISE FOR TAHOE KILLSHOT

"BORG BELONGS ON THE BESTSELLER LISTS with Parker, Paretsky and Coben"

- Merry Cutler, Annie's Book Stop, Sharon, Massachusetts

"A GREAT READ!"

-Shelley Glodowski, Midwest Book Review

"A WONDERFUL BOOK"

- Gayle Wedgwood, Mystery News

PRAISE FOR TAHOE ICE GRAVE

"BAFFLING CLUES...CONSISTENTLY ENTERTAINS"

- Kirkus Reviews

"A CLEVER PLOT... RECOMMEND THIS MYSTERY"

- John Rowen, Booklist

"A BIG THUMBS UP... MR. BORG'S PLOTS ARE SUPER-TWISTERS"

- Shelley Glodowski, Midwest Book Review

"GREAT CHARACTERS, LOTS OF ACTION, AND SOME CLEVER PLOT TWISTS...Readers have to figure they are in for a good ride, and Todd Borg does not disappoint."

- John Orr, San Jose Mercury News

PRAISE FOR TAHOE BLOWUP

"A COMPELLING TALE OF ARSON ON THE MOUNTAIN"

- Barbara Peters, The Poisoned Pen Bookstore

"RIVETING... A MUST READ FOR MYSTERY FANS!"

- Karen Dini, Addison Public Library, Addison, Illinois

WINNER! BEST MYSTERY OF THE YEAR

- Bay Area Independent Publishers Association

PRAISE FOR TAHOE DEATHFALL

"THRILLING, EXTENDED RESCUE/CHASE" *- Kirkus Reviews*

"A TREMENDOUS READ FROM A GREAT WRITER"

- Shelley Glodowski, Midwest Book Review

"BORG OFFERS A SIMPLY TERRIFIC DOG"

- Barbara Peters, The Poisoned Pen

WINNER! BEST THRILLER OF THE YEAR

- Bay Area Independent Publishers Association

"A TAUT MYSTERY... A SCREECHING CLIMAX"

- Karen Dini, Addison Public Library, Addison, Illinois

Titles by Todd Borg

TAHOE DEATHFALL

TAHOE BLOWUP

TAHOE ICE GRAVE

TAHOE KILLSHOT

TAHOE SILENCE

TAHOE AVALANCHE

TAHOE NIGHT

TAHOE HEAT

TAHOE HIJACK

TAHOE TRAP

TAHOE CHASE

TAHOE GHOST BOAT

TAHOE BLUE FIRE

TAHOE DARK

TAHOE CHASE

by

Todd Borg

THRILLER PRESS

Thriller Press Revised First Edition, August 2013

TAHOE CHASE

This novel is a work of fiction. Any references to real locales, establishments, organizations, or events are intended only to give the fiction a sense of verisimilitude. All other names, places, characters and incidents portrayed in this book are the product of the author's imagination.

Library of Congress Control Number: 2013938829

ISBN: 978-1-931296-21-2

Cover design and map by Keith Carlson

Manufactured in the United States of America

For Kit

ACKNOWLEDGMENTS

Sometimes it seems that presenting a book to the world is a three-part affair.

The first impression for the reader comes from the cover. Luckily, the cover designer, Keith Carlson, produced yet another great cover. (Love the eyes!) People do judge a book by its cover, so I'm very fortunate to be in such good hands.

Editing is the next thing a reader notices. (Or, hopefully, doesn't notice!) Only when one has expert editing does the writing flow and not distract the reader with bad grammar, awkward punctuation, and sentences that trip up the tongue.

Liz Johnston, Eric Berglund, Christel Hall, and my wife Kit pulled off another miracle. They took the messy pile of words I handed them and scrubbed and polished it into something presentable.

Of course, after they fixed things up, I continued to make changes, which gives me ample opportunity to put mistakes back into the manuscript!

The third part of producing a book is the story itself, but I probably shouldn't comment on that other than to say it was great fun to write.

Thanks to all who helped produce this book. And thanks to you, dear reader, for your interest and support!

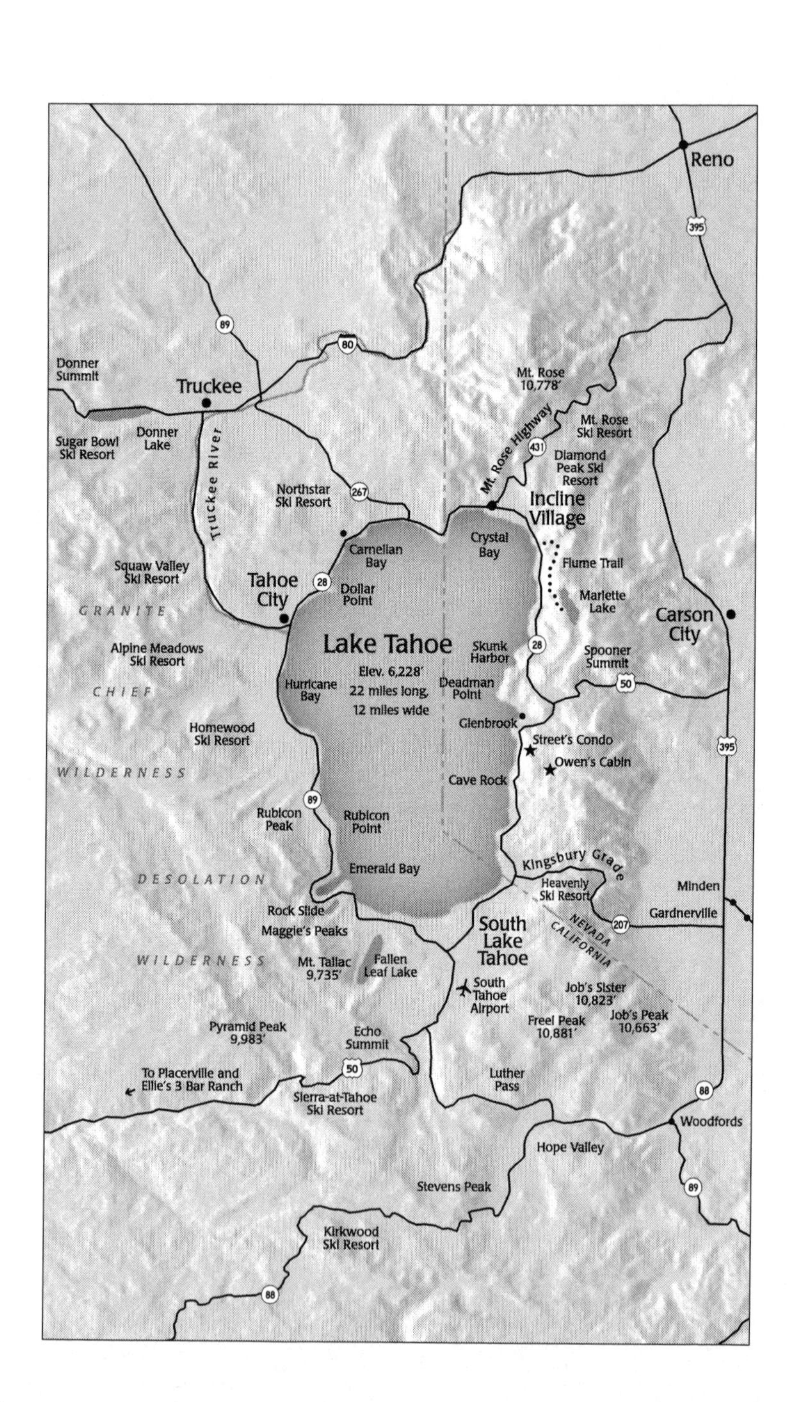
Reno
395
89
80
Donner Summit
Truckee
Mt. Rose 10,778′
Mt. Rose Highway
Mt. Rose Ski Resort
431
Sugar Bowl Ski Resort
Donner Lake
Truckee River
Diamond Peak Ski Resort
Northstar Ski Resort
267
Incline Village
Crystal Bay
Carnelian Bay
Flume Trail
Squaw Valley Ski Resort
Tahoe City
28
Dollar Point
Marlette Lake
Carson City
GRANITE
Lake Tahoe
Skunk Harbor
Alpine Meadows Ski Resort
Spooner Summit
Elev. 6,228′
22 miles long, 12 miles wide
Hurricane Bay
Deadman Point
50
CHIEF
Glenbrook
Homewood Ski Resort
Street's Condo
Owen's Cabin
WILDERNESS
Cave Rock
Rubicon Peak
Rubicon Point
Kingsbury Grade
Emerald Bay
Heavenly Ski Resort
Minden
DESOLATION
Rock Slide
Gardnerville
Maggie's Peaks
South Lake Tahoe
207
NEVADA
CALIFORNIA
WILDERNESS
Mt. Tallac 9,735′
Fallen Leaf Lake
South Tahoe Airport
Job's Sister 10,823′
Pyramid Peak 9,983′
Freel Peak 10,881′
Job's Peak 10,663′
Echo Summit
To Placerville and Ellie's 3 Bar Ranch
Luther Pass
Sierra-at-Tahoe Ski Resort
88
Woodfords
Hope Valley
Stevens Peak
Kirkwood Ski Resort

PROLOGUE

It was the softness of the metallic click that sounded dangerous.

Cynthia Rorvik was filling the bird feeder out on the deck when she heard a faint sound of metal on metal. Her heart thumped.

Maybe it was the latch on the deck fence gate, the whisper snick of spring-loaded bar as it was eased out of its cradle.

Cynthia inhaled a short, reflexive breath and held it, listening, her hearing one of the few things that still worked as well at 79 as when she'd been a teenager. She hadn't heard the doorbell, although the deck slider was shut and she'd been making noise with the bird seed bag. Maybe someone tried the door, got no answer, and came around the house.

Cynthia set the seed bag down in the fresh snow on the bench, walked over to the edge of the deck, and looked along the stone walkway that led to a gate in the fence. The gate was in the dark shade of the big California Red Fir trees. In contrast to the bright snow on the ground and tree boughs, it was impossible to see anything in the relative darkness near the gate. It looked like the gate was still shut. Or maybe it was open an inch. She couldn't tell. Cynthia stood silent, listening.

There were small cracks between the fence boards, but Cynthia could see no shape of a person through the cracks. She waited and watched. After several seconds of no other sound, she decided she must be mistaken.

She stepped back to the feeder and finished filling it. In the nearby Lodgepole Pines, several Mountain Chickadees fluttered in excitement, their quick-step, aerial dance moves too fast to see in detail. The birds came down to the feeder one at a time, then each flew off with a seed. They chirped and sang, a coffee-klatsch of busy birds trading gossip as they feasted.

Cynthia listened instead for the lonely chick-a-dee song from up in the tree off the corner of the deck. In a moment it came, the beautiful, three-note, minor-third music that was Molly.

Cynthia pulled several black oil sunflower seeds from the bag and walked over to the corner of the deck. She put the seeds on the palm of her gloved hand and held her hand out. The tiny, one-legged chickadee she'd named Molly swooped in and landed on her outstretched index finger. The bird never went to the feeder, perhaps unable to muscle in with the other birds. Balancing on her one leg, Molly hopped a step forward and picked up the seed. The bird cocked her head at Cynthia as if in thanks, then flew over to the closest tree. Molly landed on a short broken twig, and bent down to position the seed so that her single foot could hold the seed even as it held her perch.

As Cynthia watched, Molly used her beak to crack open the shell and eat the seed inside.

In a moment, the bird flew back to Cynthia's palm, grabbed another seed, and flew off. Molly disappeared into the forest canopy. In a few moments, she came back for a third seed, then a fourth and a fifth. Cynthia knew that Molly was stashing the seeds, adding to her winter food cache.

Molly came back, landing this time on the deck railing, hopping in the snow, cocking her head.

Cynthia liked to think that Molly enjoyed her company.

Then, in a flash of light and puff of snow, Molly seemed to vanish. The movement was so fast it was as if she were the disappearing bird in a magic trick.

Cynthia knew what it meant. She looked up for a cruising raptor, but saw none. A lurking cat? She glanced over the deck railing.

She sensed a sudden movement off to her side.

Cynthia's heart beat so hard that it hurt. She jerked her head to look and saw a person.

"Oh, thank God it's you," she said. "I saw movement and I..." She stopped talking to breathe. She put her hand to her throat. Fast breaths. In and out.

"I'm so sorry that I startled you!" the visitor said. "I thought I heard someone on the deck, so I came around the house."

Cynthia nodded. "Not to worry. Just let me catch my breath. Have you seen that hawk we talked about?" she asked.

"Yes! That's why I stopped by. It was flying down by Lake Tahoe Blvd. At least, I think it's the same bird. Quite a bit bigger than a crow. Dark on its back, light on its breast and under its wings. It was doing a swooping motion just in front of me while I drove! Then it made a big turn and came up the mountain. I followed it up Tahoe Mountain Road. I know you can't, you know, follow a bird. It's not like they stay over the roads. So I lost it. But I kept looking. Then it came back, diving like before, staying right in front of me. Then flew into these trees. I could see from the street." The person pointed and peered into the trees where the Mountain Chickadees had been, then walked over to the deck railing and looked down.

"There it is!"

"Really?" Cynthia hurried over to the edge of the deck. "Molly disappeared in a flash a moment ago. It must have been the hawk. Where is it?" Cynthia couldn't see anything from where she stood. Her house perched on the edge of the mountainside, and the deck projected out over the steep slope. Mt. Tallac loomed across the valley of Fallen Leaf Lake. The sun reflected off its brilliant snowfields. In the distance to the north, the vast blue of Lake Tahoe shimmered. There was so much light that Cynthia's eyes couldn't adjust to make out anything in the dark shade below the deck.

Her visitor pointed again. "Look! It has something in its claws. Or whatever they're called. Maybe you know what kind of hawk it is."

Cynthia shaded her eyes from the light off Mt. Tallac and studied the snowy rocks thirty feet below the deck. She saw nothing except movement to her side as the person pushed her against the railing. Cynthia grabbed at the deck rail, her teeth clenched in terror as her visitor reached down, lifted up on her ankles, and flipped Cynthia over the railing.

ONE

I'd just fired up the coffeepot in my office on Kingsbury Grade when Spot, my Harlequin Great Dane, lifted his head off the floor. His nose pointed toward the window and its view of Lake Tahoe in the distance and the snow-covered mountains beyond. But his gaze was vague. He was seeing something else. One ear swiveled left, then right, then both turned rearward. It was a sight I'd seen many times, my dog looking inward, focusing on a sound I couldn't hear.

Spot's nose twitched, big wet nostrils flexing. Then he cranked his head around and looked at the closed door. I still heard nothing, and I certainly didn't smell anything over the aroma coming from the gurgling coffee maker.

There was a soft two-rap knock, and the door opened.

An old man stood in the doorway. He was large of frame but bent a bit forward at the waist and showing favor to stiff joints. He was handsome despite the wear of years, his eyes as blue as those of a Husky sled dog. He wore a black watch cap, which he took off as he nodded at me. The top of his head was as bald as a cue ball, but the sides and back had a ring of white hair. Matching his hair were white eyebrows, thick and long but brushed and trimmed into submission. Above his upper lip was a small white mustache, cut very short.

The man made a little foot-stomp on the mat, shaking off the bits of snow left on his shoes after his walk up the stairs and down the hall.

As he walked through my office door, he seemed strong and well-balanced, yet he held his arms out just a bit, the watch cap wavering in his right hand. It made me think of how people walk when they are in an earthquake and know that the floor might shift at any moment. Probably, the ground beneath him had shifted recently.

Now that Spot saw our visitor, he got up to satisfy his olfactory curiosity. I grabbed his collar to hold him back. I gave a little tug, patted him on his rear, and he sat down next to my chair, his head over the top of my desk. He panted as he stared at the man.

The man looked at Spot, then turned around and glanced at the rest of my small office as if to make sure that we were alone. He took a step back to shut the door, then came toward my desk.

"My name's Joe Rorvik. I've asked around a little. You come recommended. Although it was hard to find you with that scaffolding on the building. It blocks the address number."

I nodded. "Sorry. They're making repairs." I reached out my hand. "Owen McKenna," I said. Rorvik switched his cap to his left hand, leaned forward, and we shook. I was careful not to squeeze hard on the man's swollen knuckles.

I'd heard the man's name before, but I couldn't place it.

I put my palm to the front of Spot's nose, a sign that means 'stay,' and I moved around the side of the desk, gesturing at the chairs behind the man.

"Get you a chair?" I said.

"Thanks, I'll get it," Rorvik said. He turned just enough to reach out and pull up one of the two chairs. He sat, grunting a bit with discomfort. He hooked the cap onto the arm of the chair.

The coffee maker did the spit and gurgle that meant it was through dripping. I reached for a mug. "Coffee?"

"Please. With cream if you've got it."

"I've only got these," I said, holding up one of the little plastic containers of pretend cream. "They might be out of date by a few years."

Rorvik frowned. "Black then."

I filled the mug, handed it to him, then poured my own and returned to my chair. I waited.

The man hesitated. He looked left, then right, the motion noticeable because of the intense blue color of his eyes. He radiated melancholy.

"I'm hoping you can help me," Rorvik said. He pulled out a handkerchief and wiped his lips, then sipped coffee, the actions in reverse order from those of most people. He moved his mouth and tongue like he was at a wine tasting, then swallowed. Maybe he was a coffee connoisseur. Then again, maybe his motions were those of distaste. I was pretty sure my coffee wouldn't rate higher than about seven on a hundred-point scale.

"What's your problem?" I asked.

"My wife is lying in intensive care in Reno. A coma. She's unresponsive and likely to die."

"I'm so sorry. What happened?"

The man swallowed. "She fell from our deck. The cops think it was an accident. I think someone tried to murder her."

TWO

When he said it, I recalled the story that had been in the news a week or so before.

"I remember," I said. "I was very sorry to read about your wife's injury."

Rorvik made a small nod.

The familiarity of his name came back to me.

"You're the ski racer Joe Rorvik," I said. "The Olympic medalist famous for the Rorvik Roar."

In Tahoe we get as used to seeing sports superstars as we do movie and TV celebrities. But Rorvik's racing career was long before I was even born, and his image was not common around the Tahoe Basin, so I hadn't recognized him.

Rorvik nodded. "My last race was sixty-one years ago this winter." He sipped more coffee, made more of the mouth movements.

"I think the paper said your wife's name is Cynthia?" I asked.

Rorvik nodded. "Rell to me."

"Rell?"

"Goes way back to when I met her. After I retired from ski racing, I was working a job near UC Berkeley. I was bored, so I took a theater workshop. Thought I'd try my hand at acting." He sipped more coffee, his eyes looking off at the memory.

"I quickly learned that ski racing skills don't translate to the stage. But I met Rell in that class. I couldn't keep my eyes off her. Not that she was a beauty queen or anything. She was actually somewhat plain-looking at first, tiny as a hummingbird and wearing frumpy, second-hand clothes. But I noticed her because she had a fire inside. So I asked her out to a dance and picked her up at her parents' house where they lived in Fremont. Her parents were grim, small-minded people who treated her as if they resented that a ski racer was paying her attention, as if I was going to take her away from them, out into the big world. Which of course is exactly what I did."

I understood that Rorvik's story was a way to avoid talking about the current situation. I didn't interrupt.

"After I got Cynthia out of that house and to the dance, she lit up. You know how an optical illusion does that thing where you see something one way and then it flips the opposite way and you can never see it the first way again? Well, that was Cynthia when we went on that first date. She was vivacious and charming, and she had a wicked-fun sense of humor. She suddenly went from plain to more beautiful than any other girl at the dance. She became my Cinderella. Pretty quick, Cinderella got shortened to Rell. Rell Rorvik after we married."

He paused.

"Any word on her condition?" I said.

"Worse and worse," Rorvik said. "They take these new pictures. Brain scans. Different areas light up. On the kind they showed me, red shows the most intense activity. Yellow for medium, and blue for the least intense. Rell's picture had little bits of blue here and there, areas that make the heart beat and such. But no color at all in most places. They say this is common with severe brain damage. According to the doctors, she's gone forever in every way that matters."

Joe Rorvik looked down at his lap, swallowed, then raised his head back up to me, his jaw muscles bulging.

"Rell and me had a deal," he said. His eyes held mine. No mist that I could see. Just pure blue in the irises and, in the whites, a red that had no doubt been building up for days.

He continued, "From the beginning, we always made agreements about most of the important things in life. One of them was that neither of us would let the other be hooked up to a machine if it was just prolonging an inevitable death. Of course, when we spoke of it, we were really talking about me, because I'm thirteen years older than her. Yet now it's time for me to pull the plug, as they say." He looked out my window, then looked at my dog who was still sitting obediently behind my desk.

"C'mere, boy," Rorvik said, and he patted his thigh.

Spot turned to look at me, looking for approval.

"It's okay," I said. I gave Spot a touch to let him know that he could move.

"His name is Spot," I said to Joe.

Spot stood, walked around the desk, and approached Rorvik slowly but with his tail held slightly up. Dogs sense more through tone and scent than non-dog people would believe, and Spot seemed to know that he should not be boisterous with the old man.

Rorvik reached out and put his hands on either side of Spot's snout, then rubbed up and over Spot's eyes and ears, and down his neck.

Spot was immediately smitten. He closed his eyes, lowered his tail a bit, then lowered his head to rest his jaw on the arm of Rorvik's chair.

Rorvik rubbed him several more times. Rorvik's frown was deep.

"The problem with disconnecting the life-support," he said, gritting his teeth, "is that I find that I can't let her go like this. I have to be able to tell her what happened. They say she can't hear, can't understand a thing. The hearing part of the brain is one of the areas with no color on the scan. But I still have to have a final talk. I suppose it's just for me. At any rate, once I can explain it to her, then I will have settled up my personal business between Rell and me. Then I can let her go and I can try to move on."

"What would you like me to do?" I asked.

"I want you to find out what happened."

"Mr. Rorvik, I take your concerns seriously. But the cops must not have found anything to raise concerns if they think that her fall was an accident. What would I go on?"

"Call me Joe. Yeah, that's what they think," he said. "And maybe they're right. But I don't think so. Rell is careful. She's not excessively cautious, but she's prudent. She wouldn't lean over the deck railing or do anything else risky. She must have been pushed."

"From what I read," I said, "it sounded like there was nothing missing, so she probably didn't interrupt a burglar."

"That's true," Rorvik said. "I checked the house. Nothing missing that I could see. I even had a spare money clip with five hundred dollars in it sitting in my desk drawer. It was still there."

"Yet you still think that someone pushed her. If there wasn't a burglar, then it would suggest that someone went to your house just to murder your wife. Why would someone want to murder your wife?"

"I can't imagine it. She's a sweetheart. Everyone loves Rell. No one would want to hurt her."

"You've stated two opposing views. She wouldn't fall accidentally. But no one would push her, either."

Rorvik looked at me for bit. "I know. It doesn't make sense. That's why I need you to figure it out."

"If someone did push her," I said, "that would mean that person had an enormous problem with your wife. Either the would-be murderer hated your wife, or he saw your wife as an obstacle to something he really wanted."

Joe narrowed his eyes. "Well, no one could hate my wife, I can tell you that. No one would even dislike her."

"Then she must have been in the way of what the murderer wanted."

Rorvik paused. "Give me an example of that."

"Let's say that Rell witnessed a crime. The perpetrator wants his freedom, but the only way to ensure that he gets away with the crime is to kill the witness before she can tell the cops."

Rorvik flinched when I said the word kill.

"Rell would have told me if she'd witnessed a crime," Joe said.

"Maybe it happened right before she was pushed."

"As best as the cops and the doctors can establish the time of her fall, I talked to her on the phone shortly before it happened. She didn't mention anything."

"Maybe she couldn't tell you because the killer was with her, preventing her from saying anything."

Rorvik didn't like that thought. His frown took over his entire face.

"Are you certain you made a thorough check of everything a burglar might take?" I said.

"Well, I don't know how one would tell. But I looked around. Everything seemed okay."

"Another possibility," I said, "is that a burglar came to your house to burglarize it. He thought no one was home but discovered that your wife was out on the deck. If she got a good look at him, he probably worried that she could identify him, so he pushed her off. Maybe the experience spooked him enough that he decided to leave without taking anything."

"It doesn't make sense to me," Joe said. "I think that any man bold enough to push a woman off the deck would take a quick look around and pocket the easy valuables. We have some valuables."

"Maybe the burglar wasn't spooked by pushing your wife off the deck," I said. "Maybe he simply heard a noise and thought that somebody else was coming. So he left without looking through the house."

Joe made a slow nod.

I saw in him the pain that so often accompanies the end of life. Even if you live a happily-ever-after life, it still has to end. Even the best endings are extremely painful for at least one of every pair. In Joe's case, the ending he was coping with was as bad as it gets.

We want to comfort people in these situations. But Rorvik didn't come to me for comfort. He came to me to learn what had happened, which would be an indirect comfort at best.

Spot tired of standing. He sat his rear down, moving awkwardly so that he could lower his head onto Joe's lap.

"Let's reconsider the possibility that her fall was an accident," I said. "Maybe no one came to your house at all."

"I can't see it." Rorvik looked out my office window toward the lake, but I don't think he was seeing the water.

"Maybe she had a little stroke," I said. "Got dizzy and lost her balance."

"I doubt it. She was a hiker. In great shape. She had no history of high blood pressure or any other health issues. She took no medications. So that is unlikely. And the doctors saw no evidence of a stroke in the X-rays. And even if she'd had a stroke, she's only five-two. That's not tall enough to accidentally fall over the railing."

Rorvik's arthritic hands gripped each other on top of Spot's head as if in a wrestling match. "Will you help me?" he asked, his voice plaintive, almost desperate.

"Joe, sometimes people get an idea that I can figure out exactly how something happened, and then they are disappointed when I can't deliver. Will you be disappointed if I find nothing?"

"Yes, of course. I want to know what happened. I owe it to Rell. But if you find nothing, I'll accept that I did everything I could."

"Then what?" I asked, wanting this sad man to face the possibility that I might not be able to tie up the loose ends of Rell's fall from the deck.

"Then I have my sit-down with Rell," he said. "I explain that the cops think it was an accident and that you were unable to find out anything more. Once she knows that I did what I could, then she'll accept it."

"Rell will accept it," I said. "But will you accept it? Will you find some peace after this?"

Joe's eyes filled with tears. "I don't know," he said. "But I'll still go ahead and let the doctors turn off the machines. Rell and me, we had a deal."

THREE

Joe Rorvik said that I could come out anytime but that sooner was better. Rell was waiting, he said. He gave me directions to his house, southwest of South Lake Tahoe, in the Angora Highlands neighborhood, up off Tahoe Mountain Road.

After finishing up some other business, I took Spot in my Jeep, went through South Lake Tahoe, and headed out of town on Lake Tahoe Blvd. I found the turnoff and climbed up the mountain to Angora Ridge and the Angora Highlands. Because Joe's neighborhood is closer to the Sierra Crest – the high mountainous ridge west of Lake Tahoe – there was much more snow than at my cabin on the east side of the lake. Even though it was still early December, the snow banks were already half way up to the street signs. The vertical snow walls that were cut by the giant rotary plows made the neighborhood remind me of a medieval walled city, but one where the fortress ramparts were made of white ice. Here and there, the walls were breached by driveway openings.

I parked in Joe's driveway at noon. His front door was set back under a large entry roof and nearly hidden from the street. Flanking the door were two, large, shiny metal sculptures, abstracts that could be, if one had an open mind, interpretations of ski racers.

A skinny young man in his middle twenties was stringing Christmas lights. He had one sculpture evenly wrapped and was working on the second one. In a glance, I could tell that he wasn't just hanging lights on them to get the job done, but cared a great deal about getting the placement exactly right. The bulbs seemed to be in two sets of parallel lines, each intersecting with the other at precise angles.

"Oh, hello," he said in a pleasant voice as I walked up. "You must be the private investigator. Mr. Rorvik said you'd be stopping by." He shifted the bundle of lights to his left hand, then shook my hand, his grip cold and limp. He had watery eyes that were overwhelmed by heavy black-framed glasses. His pimples and pallor made me wonder if he ever saw the sun or got any exercise or ate anything besides pizza and ice cream. He wore a thin red stocking cap from which spilled long messy hair so red it almost matched his pimples.

"I'm Dwight Frankman," he said. "I live down the street."

I introduced myself.

Dwight gestured at the lights. "I try to help the Rorviks now and then. They... They don't have any family, so I occasionally stop by to check on them."

"Nice of you to help out," I said.

Dwight made a little nod. "Mr. Rorvik is waiting for you. You can go right in." He opened the front door a few inches and called out in a high, soft voice.

"Mr. Rorvik? Mr. McKenna is here to see you." Dwight pushed the door open farther.

I thought it best to wait outside.

Joe Rorvik appeared in a few moments.

"I see you've met Dwight," Joe said. "Best neighbor two old people could have." He put his hand on Dwight's shoulder. "I told him I didn't need Christmas lights this year. Without Rell here to enjoy them, what's the point? But here he is, anyway, trying to cheer up an old man."

"Oh, Mr. Rorvik," Dwight said, "watch this, and you'll be glad I put up these lights." He walked over to the wall and flipped the switch on a power strip that he'd plugged into an outdoor outlet. The sculpture to the left of the door lit up. Although it was daylight, it was shaded under the door. A hundred points of light suddenly reflected in the shiny metal. "Now tell me that isn't worth the effort."

Rorvik looked at the lights and nodded. "You're right, Dwight. Very nice. I thank you."

"Don't let me interrupt your meeting," Dwight said. "I'll be through here in a little bit, then I'll head home."

Rorvik motioned me inside and shut the door behind me.

"Dwight lives a block away," Joe said as we walked toward a big room at the rear of the house. "He seems to like to help us. He says we're the grandparents he never had. What family he has is in the Bay Area, so we all benefit from the friendship." Joe stopped and pointed back toward the door. "I couldn't see your vehicle, but I wonder if you brought your hound?"

"Yes, actually. He goes most places with me."

"Then you can bring him in if you want."

I wasn't sure how sincere the invitation was. "When you came to my office, it seemed like you knew Great Danes," I said.

"We never had one, but we like them. Before we moved up to the lake, we lived in Danville in the East Bay, and our neighbor Sissy Lakeman raised them. We got to know all of them. Rell is pretty much afraid of animals, but she loves Great Danes. She says that Danes are sweet toy lap dogs inside guard dog bodies. Your guy's got some size on him. At your office, just having his head in my lap was heavy. What does he weigh?"

"One-seventy."

"Bring him in. Please. It will be a good distraction for me."

I went back and let Spot out of the Jeep. He trotted up to Dwight. Dwight backed up, fear on his face.

"Don't worry," Joe's voice came from the doorway. "He might be a giant dog, but he's friendly. I've already met him. He won't hurt you."

Dwight was up against the wall.

I held Spot's collar so he couldn't touch Dwight.

Dwight tried to relax, but the tension in his body was obvious.

Spot stretched his head toward Joe, who then pet him.

"See?" Joe said to Dwight.

Dwight made a little nod.

Joe was obviously Dane-fluent. He turned sideways, rested his hand on Spot's back and walked him through the open front door. Joe was stooped enough, and Spot was tall enough, that Joe could use Spot's back for support.

I watched them go. Spot held his tail high as always when he's happy and exploring. I followed and shut the door behind me, leaving Dwight safe from Spot.

"Get you something to drink?" Joe said when we were inside.

I hesitated.

"I'm about to have a beer," he said as if wanting me to join in.

"Sounds good," I said.

Joe walked Spot around the kitchen island to the fridge. Recognizing the implicit permission, Spot reached his nose deep over the kitchen counters, investigating food scents. If Joe minded a giant dog wiping the counters with his jowls and neck, he didn't show it.

The big living room projected out from the rest of the house. In the back wall, a sliding glass door opened onto a deck. Picture windows flanked the door. More windows on the side walls faced the forest on both sides of the house. Through the trees in one direction, I could see the vague shape of a neighboring house. In the other direction, there were only trees.

The large deck overhung the slope that dropped away below. It was likely the deck from which Rell had fallen. The slider and picture windows faced west and framed a grand view of the massive cliffs of Mt. Tallac. A thousand feet below the summit, a cloud roiled against the cliff face. Trailing below as the cloud moved north was a fall of snow. It looked delicate and light, but I knew that if one were in that snowfall, it would be a whirl of wind and cold and biting bits of ice and snow.

At the edge of the view, just visible through trees to the north, stretched Lake Tahoe, blue where the sun shone through and angry gray where the snow showers dotted the surface.

Out of sight, hundreds of feet below us, was Fallen Leaf Lake, the large scintillating body of water just southwest of Tahoe. Legend has it that it was formed when an Indian boy was chased by the devil. The boy had a magic branch with leaves that, when they fell off, instantly created lakes behind the boy, preventing the devil from catching him. I wondered if there was a devil someplace in Joe and Rell's life.

I wanted to investigate the deck but thought that I should wait a bit before we discussed the details of Rell's fall.

On a table near the picture windows was a pair of binoculars and a bird book. "Who's the birder?" I asked.

Joe came over and handed me a Fat Tire Amber Ale. "Rell's main focus is birding." Joe sat down on a chair, his breathing noticeable but not really strained. He took a sip of his beer. Spot lay down on the floor next to him.

"Was Rell trained as an ornithologist?" I asked.

"No. She's an amateur, but she's gotten more serious as she's gotten older. Her life list is up to five hundred sixty-something species. Her goal is to join the Six Hundred Club." He looked up toward the peak of Mt. Tallac. "I guess she won't make it. I didn't realize that until now." He turned away from me.

I drank beer, gave him some time, looked for a way to change the subject to something less sad.

The house design was Mountain Modern, post-and-beam and rustic touches combined with slick granite counters, slate floors, stainless steel appliances, and Scandinavian furniture. The view out the windows from the chairs was spectacular. As I glanced out, I thought I saw something move in my peripheral vision, moving fast.

Maybe it was a bear going through the forest. But it didn't seem like a bear. It seemed like a person trying to hide in the trees.

FOUR

I looked toward where I'd seen movement, but there was nothing to see.

I didn't want to scare away anybody watching us, so I turned from the windows and studied the room for places from which I could look outside without being obvious.

Spread through the living room were four tall, white sculpture pedestals. On each one stood an elaborate origami sculpture, white paper folded into a shape, detailed enough to be clearly recognizable. They were sizable works, each as tall as a wine bottle. One was an eagle, another an ice skater in a spin. The third was a dog leaping to catch a Frisbee. The fourth was a ski racer. Draped over it was a gold necklace. In its center was a small golden pair of skis.

Joe saw me looking at it. "That's my lucky necklace," he said. "I was wearing that when I won my Olympic medal."

"Wow. This is an important historical artifact," I said. "And these origami pieces are beautiful, too." I walked behind one so that it was between me and the windows. By looking just past it, I could see outside. Anyone watching might think I was looking at the origami. "Rell found time for several pursuits," I said.

"No, those are mine," Joe said.

I was surprised that the big ski racer of Rorvik Roar fame would create something so fragile.

"You have a serious skill with paper," I said. "How did you learn it?"

Joe smiled. "Lots of practice." Joe stood and walked over. He picked up the leaping dog and handed it to me. "It's kind of a combination of art and science," he said.

I turned it around, being as gentle as if I were holding a Ming vase. I held it up at eye level, which made it easier to disguise my real purpose of looking out the window. There was so much snow that anyone in the forest would have to be wearing snowshoes. In fact, it was probably too deep for bear until the thaw/freeze cycles firmed it up and crusted it over.

"Don't be timid with it," Joe said, pointing at the origami piece. "It's just paper. You can hold most pieces by any part. If you drop it, no big deal. Most of my pieces are pretty tough. They bounce."

"The art is obvious," I said. "Where does the science come in?"

"We start with a two-dimensional medium and turn it into three dimensions. Math meets art. Some of the best origami artists are top-level mathematicians."

I walked over to the pedestal that held the eagle. I picked up the sculpture and carried it over to the windows as if to get it into more light. By turning the origami, I was able to give the forest a thorough look. I saw nothing. I thought about Dwight. There was no car, so he'd walked up the street from his house. I saw no snowshoes, either, so if he were now out in the forest, he would have had to have brought his snowshoes and stashed them nearby.

"Joe, I can't remember if I shut the car door after I let Spot out. Give me a moment to check."

He nodded. I walked back to the entry, opened the door, and looked out. Dwight was still there, finishing the lights on the second sculpture.

"Oh, hi," Dwight said. "I'm just about done."

I nodded as I stepped outside and closed the door behind me. I walked away from the house as if to take in the lights on the sculptures. From where I stood, I could see no person in the trees and no tracks, either.

"Dwight, I thought I saw someone outside in the forest. Have you seen or heard anyone?"

He immediately looked worried and made a furtive glance out toward the street. "No, I haven't. The snow is deep. You'd need snowshoes or skis to get off the street. Plus the rotary walls are so high, it would be hard to climb up and over them."

"Right. Maybe let me know if you see someone?"

"Sure. But I'll be leaving in a bit." Dwight was holding a step ladder below the eave. A string of lights hung from his shoulder. He climbed up three steps on the ladder as I moved by. As he reached out to put the light string on the eave, I noticed his legs vibrating. I'd seen it before. Fear of heights can kick in just two feet off the ground.

"Here, let me steady the ladder for you." I held it firm.

"Thanks very much," Dwight said. His face went red with embarrassment. He hung the lights on hooks that were screwed into the eave. Now his hands were shaking. "Sorry," he said when he was done. He climbed back down and took a deep breath, calming himself.

"That ladder just doesn't feel right. And, well, I'm ashamed to admit that I've always had a little problem with heights. Dogs, too, for that matter. I have a recurring nightmare where a mountain lion jumps out of the trees onto my back and puts its jaws around the back of my neck. I see a dog as big as yours, and it makes me think of it."

"I understand," I said, even though I didn't.

We moved to the other side of the entry, and Dwight again climbed up three feet and hooked up the other end of the light string while I held the ladder. It must have helped because he shook a little less. When he climbed down, he glanced out toward the street. My question about a possible person in the forest had obviously made him worry.

He turned back to me. "Thanks again," he said, and I went back inside.

Joe was sitting in an upholstered chair. Spot was lying on the floor next to him, his head in Joe's lap, eyes closed, soaking up Joe's pets.

"Door shut?" Joe said.

"Yeah. You mentioned that origami is a combination of art and math," I said. "Is that your background? Mathematics?"

"No, not at all. I couldn't solve a quadratic equation if my life depended on it."

"I don't even know what a quadratic equation is," I said, "so you obviously know more about math than I do."

"Really, I don't," Joe said. "But part of a ski racer's job is to see a mountain slope – even the narrow path defined by the gates on a race course – and understand the nature of its shape, how its valleys and ridges connect and how to pick the fastest line through that landscape. Mountain valleys and ridges are not unlike the folds of origami."

"Cool linkage," I said, "ski racing and origami."

"Yeah," Joe said as if he'd heard it before. "In fact, origami artists refer to the paper folds as mountain folds and valley folds depending on whether the folds go away from you or toward you."

Joe sipped his beer, more relaxed now that we were talking about origami. "I love the concept of origami. Even though I made these myself, when I look at the finished work, I can't really see the original piece of paper anymore. The alchemy even works its magic on the alchemist."

I was struck by the old man's infectious passion. I picked up the ski racer, and carried it over to another window. "This stands over a foot tall," I said. "You must use large paper."

"Come, I'll show you." Joe gently pushed Spot's head off his lap, stood up, and led me through an opening to a study of sorts. Spot jumped up to follow.

There were bookshelves on the wall, filled with row after row of amazing paper sculptures, most white, some with colored and patterned paper. On another wall was a counter with a roll of what looked like white butcher paper in a dispenser. In the middle of that wall were two large windows that looked out to the trees.

In one corner was a large plastic garbage can. It was filled to over-flowing with small origami sculptures.

I strolled into the study and stepped to the side of one of the windows, somewhat out of sight from anyone who might be outside, but able to see if something moved.

"This paper is thirty-six inches wide," Joe said, unaware that I was watching the trees. He continued, "Usually we work with square pieces, but I can make the paper as long as I want. Tear off a piece and fold it into something, repeat a thousand times, and you'll get pretty good."

"Like skiing," I said. "I'd love to see it in action." I moved to the other side of the window and leaned up against the wall to make myself hard to see from outside.

Joe pulled some paper off the roll and tore off a piece about a foot and a half long. He sat down at a large table in the center of the room. There was a grid printed on the table. Joe lined the paper up on the grid and used the table edge to tear the paper. When he was done, he had a square piece 18 inches on a side.

Joe folded the sheet in half, then unfolded it and folded it in half at right angles to the first fold. Unfolding it again, Joe folded two corners over.

Using the crease marks as guides, Joe began new folds, some to keep and others to create more crease marks. I'm sure there were geometric principles behind his actions, but they eluded me.

I saw no more movement out the window. But I kept watching.

Joe worked fast and with confidence. In a few minutes, he stood up and handed me a sculpture of a tall man with a large head. The man was wearing a hooded cape and looked strong and intimidating.

"Amazing," I said. "It looks like Darth Vader's brother."

"Sort of," Joe said. "It's my interpretation of Erebus, God of Darkness."

"I'm sorry, but I'm new to Erebus," I said.

"One of the early gods in Greek mythology. Perfect subject for origami."

"Why is that?"

"Just because origami subjects are often light and happy. I suppose it's a match-up between subject and the lightness of the medium. Birds and flowers and ballerinas. You do see some large animals depicted, bulls and elephants, but they are rare. Erebus is all about dark power, a perfect counterpoint to a delicate art made of a delicate substance."

"I've never paid attention to origami. This can obviously be a..." Another movement outside? I focused on the place in the trees where I thought something shifted.

"This can be what?" Joe asked.

"Art. Origami can be a serious art medium."

Joe nodded. "The Chinese were folding paper over a thousand years ago during the Sung Dynasty. And Europeans sculpted with both cut and folded paper during the Renaissance. But it was seventeenth century Japanese artists who elevated folded paper to something serious, more than just pretty shapes."

"The math you referred to," I said. I stepped over to the other side of his table where I had a view out the other window.

"Yeah. Not only can you use math to broaden origami possibilities, but you can use origami to expand your math exploration. The study of the math of origami has led to lots of practical applications like how they fold airbags in cars."

It made sense as soon as Joe said it. "How to fit the bag into a small space and control the way it unfolds?" I said. "That came from origami?"

"Even more wonderful is what they now do in space. A Japanese mathematician named Koryo Miura used origami to figure out a way to fold and unfold giant solar panel structures so that they can take the folded structure out of the rocket or space shuttle and completely unfold it by simply pulling on two corners. It automatically assumes the correct shape. The huge solar panels that power satellites no longer have to be laboriously assembled by space-walking astronauts."

"Art powers science," I said.

"Yeah. It's pretty awesome," Joe said, sounding for a moment like a teenager.

I was beginning to think that if I'd actually seen any movement outside, it was probably just an errant squirrel moving in my peripheral vision. Nevertheless, I kept watching. I'd learned long ago that patience was often rewarded. Certainly, impatience rarely was.

I thought about the shortest path from the study to the front door, as well as to the deck slider, while I kept watch on the windows. I decided that the fastest route to intercept any trespasser would depend on which way the trespasser was going.

I gestured with the Erebus sculpture. "How do you figure it out? Are there books with folding diagrams?"

Joe nodded. "I started with some of those. Then I started inventing my own."

"Like the mathematicians?"

"No," Joe shook his head. "They use computers. Maybe blackboards, too, for all I know. They use equations to create complex shapes. I'm a fold-by-the-seat-of-my-pants guy. No equations in my art. I try different things, and the result is often unsatisfying or even stupid-looking. But I sometimes see a way to adjust it to make it better. It's like any art. You keep learning and improving your craft bit by bit."

I pointed to the garbage can. "Are these your rejects? There must be thousands of origami sculptures in that can."

"No, those are the entries in a contest that I ran last spring."

I was surprised. "Joe, you're not the kind to just kick back and relax, are you?"

"Well, when I heard the latest figures about how this country is getting more scientifically illiterate, I thought about encouraging would-be artists to see what they could do that might advance science. It was called the Art Meets Science Origami Contest. I wanted to see if any people out there had invented any designs that would advance science in some way."

"Like airbags and solar panels in space," I said.

"Yeah. So I offered a five-thousand-dollar first prize and four twelve hundred and fifty dollar prizes. Ten grand was enough to get the contest written up in several magazines and put on a bunch of websites. In addition to giving out prize money, I sent the five winning entries to the Massachusetts Institute of Technology. They have the foremost origami mathematicians there. I haven't heard back, yet, but I think that the one that I awarded first prize to is going to raise their eyebrows."

Ten grand was also enough to attract dirtballs looking for easy money. "How did people send you their entries?" I asked.

"Mail. UPS. FedEx."

"Did the contest publicity information have your home address?"

Joe gave me a worried look. "My home address is the only one I have."

FIVE

"No one would think that ten grand in prize money means I have ten grand in cash sitting around," Joe said.

"Probably not. But it does suggest that you have resources, resources that might show up in other ways that someone could steal. You also said that you had five hundred in a money clip."

"That they didn't take," Joe added.

I nodded. "Did you know or have you met any of the winners?"

"No." Joe shook his head. "At least I don't think so. I handled the judging and Rell mailed off the money. She would know the names. But I guess that means they're lost unless I can find them in her notes."

"We could find the canceled checks and get the names that way."

Joe frowned. "She got money orders from the Post Office. I forget why, but she had a reason." Joe paused, and looked off at nothing specific, his face sad. "I wasn't a good listener. She took care of so much. I didn't pay enough attention."

Joe's face went vacant for a bit. "Do you have a girl, Owen?"

"Yes. A good one. Her name is Street Casey. Maybe you'll meet her."

"Do you pay attention to her?"

It was a personal question that I wouldn't have liked from most clients, but I didn't mind it coming from Joe.

"Probably not enough," I said.

I turned back to the trash can full of origami sculptures. "Do you remember anything about the winners?" I asked. "Where they lived, for example?"

"Rell talked about it. Let me think. All over. I believe the winner was from Chicago. She might have mentioned Boston, too. I forget the others."

"You said you sent the winning entries to MIT. Any chance you took pictures of them?"

"Yeah." Joe walked into the kitchen, pulled out a drawer and brought me some photos. "I printed them on copy paper, so they are hard to see. But you get the idea."

They were worse than hard to see. I could tell that they were complex geometric shapes, but that was about it.

I took one of the sculptures out of the can. It was a type of ball made of many similar sides.

"That's a dodecahedron," Joe said.

"Sure, I knew that," I joked.

Another was a type of fan that expanded and contracted, snapping into each position.

"Not too many animals," I said.

"A few. But my instructions for the contest explained that we were looking for anything that could have an application in science. So there is a preponderance of entries that reveal controlled motion or geometric shapes that might be considered hard or even impossible to fold out of paper. Each entrant also had to include a short explanation of why they thought their creation had scientific merit. And of course they had to include folding instructions."

"Did the entry fee cover the prize money?"

Joe frowned. "There was no entry fee. The prize money was my contribution to art and science. A small price to pay in hopes of finding something of scientific value." Joe pointed at the can full of sculptures. "Also, I very much enjoy thinking about the thousands of hours away from the TV that these sculptures represent."

"Are you going to do it again next year?"

Joe smiled and shook his head. "No. I may be naïve, but I'm not stupid. I had no life for many months while I fielded questions and wrote emails and judged sculptures all day long, seven days a week. And when I found a piece that I didn't understand but could see that maybe it had merit, then I had to take photos from all angles and email them to origami mathematicians who were kind enough to give me an opinion. At one point, the project began to feel like I was living a nightmare that wouldn't go away. I also made Rell pretty miserable during those months."

Joe stood up as if even the memory of the contest made him weary.

I hadn't seen any more movement outside by the time we moved back into the living room. Joe's mood seemed better, so I pointed to the sliding glass door that led out to the deck.

"Is this the deck that Rell fell from?" I asked.

"Yes." Joe pulled open the door and walked out. Spot followed him. I trailed behind, casually looking around, my eyes turning farther as I tried to scour the forest without being noticed. Although Spot would struggle in the deep snow, I could send him on a search mission to "Find The Suspect." But even if a person was in the woods, that didn't make them guilty of anything. There was no cause to have Spot take them down.

The sun suddenly poked out and was surprisingly hot despite the cold air of December. Joe pointed over the railing.

"This is the spot," he said.

Hearing his name, Spot looked at Joe, anticipation on his face. He wagged a quick one, two.

I walked over, rubbed Spot's head. "He means place, your largeness, place."

My dog didn't understand, but he liked the attention. People were saying his name. He knew that was a good thing. Maybe it would lead to food. He kept wagging.

I looked over the railing where Joe indicated. It was a long way down. The snow-covered ground was lumpy, probably granite boulders. The area was shaded, protecting the snow from the sun's heat. The snow was tramped down and covered with footprints.

From nearby in a tree came the chick-a-dee call of a Mountain Chickadee. Over and over. I looked out but could not see any bird.

"That's Molly," Joe said.

I turned and looked at him.

"One of Rell's birds. The bird eats out of Rell's hand. But no more. I hear Molly every day. At least, I think it's Molly. She sounds lonely. I put out seed for her, but she doesn't come to eat."

I nodded. I didn't know what to say.

The railing was solid. It had balusters spaced every six inches. Rell couldn't have gone between them. She had to go over. I stepped back and tried to visualize a 5-foot 2-inch woman coming at the railing, striking it, and the inertia flipping her over.

Just as Joe had said, it didn't seem likely.

I turned to Joe. "Where were you when Rell fell?"

"I was in Reno at the doctor's office."

"When did you get back?"

"I got home just as it was starting to get dark. Maybe five o'clock. I spoke to her by phone right before I left Reno. That would have been about three-fifteen or three-thirty."

"You found Rell below the deck?"

"Yes." Joe swallowed. "I pulled into the garage and called for her when I walked into the kitchen. There was no answer. I opened the slider and called outside. Again, there was no answer. So I dialed her cell phone and heard the ring. I followed the sound and looked over the deck. I saw her lying on the rocks below." He made a little hiccup, turned away, and cleared his throat.

I gestured at the closest houses. "Do you know these neighbors?" I asked, as I shifted position to get a view of a different part of the forest.

"We've met and spoken, but no, we don't really know them well."

"Were they home?"

Joe pointed to the big tan house on the north side. "At first, I thought the neighbors on this side were home because I thought I saw him driving his car. After I found Rell and called nine-one-one, I knocked on his door. But the lights were off, and no one was home."

Spot turned his head and lifted his nose high, nostrils twitching. But he made no other motions that would indicate a person out in the forest. The wind was blowing toward us from Mt. Tallac. So any scent on the breeze probably came from a long distance. The scent of a nearby person would be moving away from Spot.

"What are their names?" I gestured toward the house that Joe had pointed to.

"The Howsers," Joe said. "They live in L.A. He's an entertainment attorney. They come up to ski during the holidays and spend the glory days here."

"Glory days?"

"The best of Tahoe summer. July Fourth through Labor Day."

"Have the Howsers been here recently?"

"No. It'll be hard to tell them about Rell. They like her."

"What about the other side?"

Joe gestured toward the stone and timber-frame house on the other side. "Melanie Schumann. She's a composer. Classical stuff for symphonies. I asked her if she was related to the famous Schumann. She said no. She said he did romantic stuff, whereas she writes postmodernist something or other. I forget her words. Something like ironic oratorio. She said it is like opera but without acting. Anyway, she's only here in the summer now and then. Lives in the Bay Area. I always thought that composers just wrote music. But apparently, that's just a part of it. They spend a lot of time working with orchestras and such."

"Is there anyone else in the neighborhood that you know well?"

"No. Dwight Frankman is the closest to a friend that we've got. A couple times a year, he hauls our bottles and cans to the recycle center. We have a service do the snow removal, but sometimes Dwight stops by with his shovel to do the walk when there isn't enough snow to send the service out. When you get older, these things make a big difference."

"Can you remember the names of any other homeowners?"

"Just a guy named Michael Paul. As you know, most houses in Tahoe are vacation homes. Empty most of the year. This neighborhood more than most. One of our vacation-home neighbors had a party one summer. He wanted all the neighbors to get to know each other. As far as we could tell, the only other person besides Dwight who lives in this end of the neighborhood full time is Michael Paul. Paul is almost as young as Dwight but much more mature. He started a tech company in Silicon Valley. I think he sold the company to one of the big banks a few years ago. Now he's a retired playboy. I think he still has a house in Mountain View, but he spends most of his time up here."

"How old is Michael?" I asked.

"I'd guess late twenties."

"Is Michael married? Does he have a family?"

Joe shook his head. "I don't think so. I've seen him driving with different young women in his car. I should say cars, plural. He drives a Ferrari in the summer and a Porsche SUV in the winter and a BMW spring and fall."

"Not your average vehicles," I said.

"Not your average girls, either. Expensive-looking girls. Paul even has a fourth vehicle for snowboarding, if you can believe that. It's a big black Range Rover with a snowboard rack, spare tire, and a gas can on the roof. He goes into the back-country to ski. Or I guess I should say ride."

"What about Frankman? What's he do?"

"Well, as you saw, Dwight's practically a kid. He does computer work. One of those telecommuting guys we hear about. Even though he's a computer guy like Paul, he's kind of the opposite in personality. Very quiet. Polite."

"Who does he work for?"

"He's self-employed. He writes software. He obviously does well because he bought a nice place down the street."

"Came here to snowboard like Paul?" I said.

Joe shook his head. "As far as I know, he doesn't do any sports. We've seen him walking on the local trails. But, as you could see, he's a skinny kid. It doesn't look like he gets any exercise. I think he just moved up here from the Bay Area for the peace and quiet. Tahoe's probably a great place to write computer stuff."

Joe paused. "At least Dwight isn't into tattoos."

"Michael Paul got himself tatted up, huh?"

"Is that the lingo, these days?" Joe shook his head. "Paul's got 'em all over his body. His friends have tattoos, too. They all wear shorts and sleeveless shirts to show them off. Although Paul's tattoos start below his neck and aren't on his hands. So if he wears long sleeves and pants, you might think he's normal."

"You don't like tattoos?" I said.

"No," Joe said. "But I'm a libertarian. You leave me alone to do my thing and I'll leave you alone to do your thing."

"Do you know if Dwight is married or has any family or relationships?"

"He's not married. Rell said that she asked him if he had parents or siblings, and he said not really, just a couple of aunts back east. I asked Rell, how can you 'not really' have siblings? Either you do, or you don't. But she thought maybe he did but was estranged from them. She didn't want to pry. Either way, Rell thought that was why Dwight's been nice to us, because he doesn't have others to turn to."

"So both Dwight Frankman and Michael Paul are well-off."

Joe nodded. "In my day, the guys with slide rules in their pockets were critical in manufacturing, but they didn't make that much money. Now the modern software engineer rules the world with binary numbers, and they can make a lot more money than the version from seventy years ago."

"Which helps in attracting expensive companions," I said. "Any idea if Dwight and Michael know each other?"

Joe seemed startled at the thought. "I don't know if they know each other well, but I often see them talking in the street. I never think about them in the same context, though, because they are so different other than their computer backgrounds. Michael's real athletic, the opposite of Dwight, who's kind of a wimp. Michael's got muscles. Not all bulk like a football player, but more like a..." he paused, looking for the word.

"Like a ski racer," I said.

"Yes," Joe said. "Fit and strong. Charming, too, in spite of the tattoos." Joe made a little smile. "Not that I was ever charming, although Rell seemed to think so when we were young."

"Does Rell know Michael or any other neighbors?"

"No more than I know them."

I about-faced and leaned my back against the deck railing, my elbows on the rail. I could see to both sides of the house. Nothing moved.

"I'm wondering if you've been able to think of anyone who may have had a disagreement with Rell?" I asked.

"No. I was serious when I said that everybody seems to love her. I'm not blind to what people think. I can see that they don't all love me. In fact, few do. But Rell is one of those people, kind to all."

A bird feeder hung from a pole that projected out from the deck. I pointed to it.

"It looks like Rell keeps the local bird population well fed."

"She did," Joe said. "A few days after her fall, I realized that it was empty. So I found a seed bag in the garage and filled the feeder. But the birds have left." Joe's voice was imbued with sadness.

"Is there a squirrel or something chasing them away?"

"I don't know. I probably filled the feeder wrong. We went from being a bird oasis to a bird desert. Maybe you can look at it. Does it look like I filled it correctly?"

"I don't know anything about bird feeders," I said. "I can see that there's seed inside and it comes out the bottom, so it looks good to me."

"Then the birds just left because Rell disappeared on them."

I walked across the deck, looked along the side of the house toward the gate. "Is that gate ever locked?"

"No," Rorvik said. "We always keep the deck slider locked so the gate need not be locked. That way the snow service can get in to shovel the deck." He looked off toward the forest. "Maybe that was a terrible mistake."

I walked along the house, opened the gate, and stepped through. There was a sudden sound of running footsteps, softened a bit by snow and ice, receding up the street. A car door slammed. A big, throaty engine started and revved.

I sprinted across Rorvik's driveway as tires made the rising, grinding pitch of spinning tread on ice. Then came a small squeak of rubber gripping asphalt as a vehicle raced away, not what you'd expect in an upscale neighborhood of mostly empty vacation homes.

Spot shot past me, excited by my sudden action. I got out to the street as another vague hint of movement – this time colored yellow – came from down at the far street corner. The engine sound continued to rise, then quieted as the vehicle turned another corner.

Up where I guessed the vehicle may have been parked, I saw short, darkish lines burned into the snow and ice on the street. It was one of the only locations with a sight line to both the front door and rear deck of the Rorvik house. There was also easy access to the forest at the side of Rorvik's house.

I yelled out toward the deck side of the house.

"Joe! I'll be back in a few minutes!"

SIX

I opened the rear door to let Spot jump into the Jeep. Then I backed out and raced after a vehicle the make of which I didn't know, but which may have been yellow.

There is one main road out of the Angora Highlands neighborhood and it was the route I'd driven up, Tahoe Mountain Road. There is also a narrow seasonal road that leads down to Fallen Leaf Lake, but it has no snow removal in winter. In the middle of December, the road to Fallen Leaf was already covered with two feet of packed snow. The only vehicles that could navigate it were snowmobiles.

I headed for the main road. There were two sharp corners I had to negotiate. I didn't want to spin out, so I took the corners at moderate speed. Then I sped up as I shot down Tahoe Mountain Road.

There are several places where you can see the road down below. I figured I'd get a glimpse of a speeding vehicle, but I saw none.

I pushed my speed fast enough to catch all but professional drivers and crazy drivers, but I appeared to be the only one on the road. When I got to Lake Tahoe Blvd at the bottom of the mountain, I saw no vehicle in either direction and no fresh tire marks, either.

Had the other vehicle pulled into a driveway to hide? Into a garage? Had I driven right past the person I thought I was chasing? Either that, or the person had driven down the mountain at insane speed and outrun me.

I drove back up the mountain and found Joe inside the house. I explained what had happened.

"Do you ever see anyone in the neighborhood who makes a habit of spinning their tires and driving very fast?" I asked.

Joe shook his head. "Everyone here seems to drive sensibly.

Even Michael. Which surprised me if you want to know the truth."

"Because of all his vehicles? Or his tattoos?"

Joe made a small embarrassed nod. "Both. I guess I'm old. Other than Michael and Dwight, most of the people you see in this neighborhood are somewhat mature. So the young computer men stand out. Michael especially. I would have guessed that he drove fast, but I've seen him driving several times. He's very reasonable."

"Are there any vacation rentals in this neighborhood? Where college kids might come up to Tahoe to party?"

"There is a vacation rental half a block down that way." He pointed the opposite direction from where the person I chased had done a quick start.

"None the other direction?"

Joe shook his head. "You think someone was watching my house?"

"Based on the position of the tire marks and the driver's behavior, it looks likely. Earlier, I thought I saw movement out in the trees. But I couldn't tell for certain. Now it would seem that the driver of the vehicle was watching us from the forest to the side of your house."

"I can't imagine why," Joe said. "The person who tried to murder Rell would know from the news that she was in a hospital, about to die. So there wouldn't be any point in watching me or this house, right?"

"Not that I can think of," I said.

Joe squinted his eyes as if thinking hard.

"Joe, what was your business after you retired from racing?" I asked.

Joe looked at me with a bit of a start, as if he'd forgotten that Spot and I were in the room.

"I had two different jobs working as a marketing executive for ski companies. Then I started my own company called Graphite Speed Sports. We started by designing and selling downhill skis, then expanded into cross-country skis, skates, bicycles, tennis rackets, golf clubs, you name it."

"All things you can make with graphite fiber," I said.

"Stronger, lighter, graphite speed," he said, repeating an ad phrase that sounded familiar to me. "We even showed how graphite snowshoes can make you go faster."

"Do you still have the company?"

"At my age? Oh, no. I sold it twenty years ago to an Austrian conglomerate. I'm pleased to say that they've done well with it."

"What was Rell's career?"

"She was an editor for a succession of magazines years ago in San Francisco. Then we moved from The City to the East Bay. She quit the last job and became a freelance editor when we moved up here. Kind of unusual considering that her training and education were in psychology."

"I know about freelance writing," I said, "but I didn't know about freelance editing."

"Most of her business was from her previous job. They'd email her projects for editing, and she'd email them back. She quit for good on her seventy-fifth birthday."

"How'd she get from psychology to editing?" I asked.

"I think she majored in psychology because she had a natural understanding of what makes people the way they are. She was good at psychology, and people always tell Rell the most amazing things. Her manner is so comforting and reassuring that having her around is like a truth serum. She would have done really well if she'd done clinical work in psychology."

"Then why editing?"

"You may think this a bit strange, but Rell didn't really like psychology that much. It was a case of being good at something that she wasn't fond of. Whereas editing was the area she loved."

I kept hoping that Joe was going to say something about Rell that would lead me in a promising direction regarding a would-be murderer. But Rell's life didn't seem to contain much useful material.

"Has Rell stayed in contact with her friends from work?"

"Rell isn't what you'd call chummy. She likes to spend time alone and with her birds, so she never made many friends at work. Her closest friend was Tanya Rodriquez from Walnut Creek. They met at a book club and got to know each other well. When Tanya died, that was a hard blow."

Joe paused. "An additional problem for her was me being older than she is. Our friends were mostly older than Rell. Several were even older than me. If you don't have kids, and your only friends are older, by the time you get to be eighty-five or so, your social contacts are gone."

"What about book clubs here in Tahoe?"

Joe shook his head. "Rell tried two different clubs, but the members were much younger. She felt like the token old lady."

"Do you or Rell belong to any other groups? Charity groups? Service clubs?"

"No. Rell prefers to spend her time with her birds, feeding her chickadees. In the old days, I used to have breakfast with some guys every other week. But you already know what happened to that group."

"Do you and Rell go to church?"

Joe shook his head again. "We actually talked about joining a church just for the community. Rell was more for it than I was, to tell the truth." He looked off into the forest. "I'm not much of a joiner. And religion for me is a private affair between me and my maker."

"Is there anyone else who Rell talks to? A person at a local business?"

"What do you mean?"

"Does she have a regular hairdresser? Does she have any regular acquaintances at the grocery store? The post office?"

"No, nothing like that. She goes to a hair salon, but she often tells me that they talk celebrity gossip, and she doesn't join in. The only other people she talks to are some fellow hikers who she goes hiking with once or twice a month."

"Does she consider them friends?"

Joe thought about it. "She speaks of them nicely. I think the only connection they have with each other is hiking."

"Maybe you could give me a list of names, and I'll give them a call."

Joe looked embarrassed and a little sad. "I'm sorry to say that I don't know their names. I suppose that reveals me as a real cad, indifferent to my wife's activities." He pondered some more. "Let me think about it. Maybe something will come to me." He paused. "The typical routine is that we'll be having dinner, and we talk about what we're doing the next day. I'll say what I'm doing – judging more of those blasted origami sculptures or something – and she'll say that she's going out with her hiking group. I'll ask where, and she'll tell me what trail they're taking and where they're meeting. But she doesn't mention their names."

"Where do they usually go?"

Joe spread his arms wide. "Everywhere. I don't think there's a mountain near Tahoe that she hasn't climbed. She takes pictures of the mountains with her phone and shows them to me. Beautiful places."

"Did you ever go along?"

Joe shook his head. "I used to do a lot of skiing, downhill and back-country. But I've got a bum knee, and it started getting worse thirty years ago. It dates back to my racing days. I can still walk just fine as long as I don't go over a half mile or so or go up or down a lot."

"The pictures Rell takes," I said, "do they show her fellow hikers?"

"No. She's interested in landscapes, in the natural world. For some reason, she never wants to document people, whether herself or others." He pointed at the couch. "We sit there, and she scrolls through the pictures on her phone. We have a little joke about it. When we're done with dinner after she's been out hiking, she'll say, 'Do you have a little time for some ooohs and aaahs?' Then she shows me her pictures from the hike that day."

"Does Rell see these people at other times?"

Joe shook his head. "I guess the reality is that she didn't see her fellow hikers as friends to socialize with, but more as healthy, able-bodied people with whom to hike up the mountains. It's also practical. When you take trails up into the wilderness, you never want to go alone. Too dangerous. If you twist an ankle, you could be in big trouble."

"How do the hiking people coordinate their meetings? Do they call on the phone?"

Joe frowned. "I don't know." He walked over to the kitchen, unplugged a charging cord from a phone, and handed the phone to me.

"This is Rell's phone," he said. "There's a way to look at the call history, right?"

I nodded. I turned it on and pulled up Rell's recent calls. There was only one number listed. I read it off to Joe.

"That's my number," he said. "That must be my last call to her. When she was lying on the rocks below the deck." He looked away.

"I'm sorry," I said. "She must delete her calls when she's done with them. What about email?"

Joe's frown grew. "I think she uses Gmail, but I don't know her password. She's probably told me, but I don't remember."

"If one of Rell's hiking companions calls, please get their name and number, okay?"

"Absolutely."

It was beginning to get dark outside. I stood up, walked over to the big windows, and looked out at Mt. Tallac, its snow-crusted hulk looming in the darkening sky, a deep gray-blue triangle that looked forbidding in the twilight.

"Do you ever have anyone over to visit?" I asked.

"No. We don't socialize. We don't have friends like that. I can't..." he stopped.

"What are you thinking?" I asked.

"I just remembered that there was one person. Not what you'd expect. And yes, she did come over to visit Rell."

SEVEN

"Who was it that visited?" I asked.

"A girl. Just twice, here, at the house. But Rell saw her some other times. I suppose she's a friend of sorts to Rell even though I don't think of her that way because she's so young. She's probably in her early twenties. Younger, even, than Dwight Frankman. Rell first met her when she ate at one of the breakfast restaurants in town. The girl was a waitress there. I think Rell and the girl have a kind of a grandmother/granddaughter relationship. From what Rell said, the girl – I suppose I should say woman – feels free to talk to her without worrying that Rell will judge her badly. In fact, Rell often makes a point about how we shouldn't judge other people because we don't know what they've been through."

"What's there to judge badly? Is this woman friend into something bad?"

"Not from what I gather. It sounds like she has an abusive boyfriend, and she's afraid to leave him. Apparently, he's violent. The girl's neighbors have called the cops a few times, but nothing's come of it. Rell has seen her with some bad bruises. Rell suspects that they're nothing compared to what's under the girl's clothes. Personally, I can't understand why the girl doesn't just leave him. If she's worried about what he'll do, then why not just slip out some time when he's at work and travel someplace else where he won't know to look? It can't be that hard."

"Usually, there are extenuating circumstances," I said, thinking back on my cop days. "Maybe she has no money. Or no transportation. Or she's convinced that she can't manage on her own. Abusers have many ways of keeping their victims dependent. It even has a name. Battered Woman Syndrome. It describes women who are so psychologically compromised by their domestic battery that they can't function well enough to leave their abuser.

Do you know the girl's name?"

"Yes, because Rell has talked about her at length. Simone Bonnaire. Rell said that she's originally from France and came here by way of Montreal. I understand that she wanted to pursue cross-country ski racing. Or maybe it was back-country skiing. It stuck in my mind when Rell mentioned it because, well, I still pay a little attention to snow sports. I don't know if Simone is intending to train for some kind of competition or what. But I saw that girl once when she came to our house, and I can tell you that she hasn't got what it takes. She has no discernible physicality. And anyone who doesn't have the fire to leave an abuser certainly doesn't have the fire to be an athlete. You can't compete in a physical sport if you're spineless."

"I've met abused women," I said. "They're not spineless. They're battered to the point that they can't function."

"You think my judgment of the girl is harsh."

"Yes."

"Okay," Joe said. "Maybe you're right."

"Have you ever gotten the idea that Rell might tell Simone personal things?" I asked.

"You mean like confiding in her? Something that could connect to Rell being assaulted on our deck? I don't think so. But she might have said a few things to make it seem like she's confiding in her so that the girl will feel freer to talk. Rell has worried about this girl a great deal."

"Rell must have felt a connection to her to invite her over."

"Yes. It almost didn't happen. Simone was worried that her boyfriend wouldn't approve. So Rell went and picked her up when her boyfriend would think she was at work. A secret visit, so to speak. They talked out on the deck. Later, they came inside, and I spoke to Simone a little bit. She is a tiny thing, smaller, even, than Rell, skinny as a cross-country racing ski, and timid as they come. She's also very pale, much more so than you would imagine for a person who supposedly skis and is out in the sun."

Joe got up and walked over to the fridge. "Would you like another beer?"

"No thanks," I said.

He pulled one out, opened it, and came back to his chair. He took a drink and made more of his mouth movements.

"A few weeks later, Simone and Rell got brave. Rell picked her up at her house when the boyfriend was supposed to be away. But it turns out that this boyfriend is very suspicious. He'd been watching. So he followed them to our house. When I heard a knock and opened the door, he pushed in and nearly knocked me over. He was like an angry bull, and about that size, too. He grabbed Simone's arm and dragged her out the door."

My vision darkened a little as Joe Rorvik talked. Back on the San Francisco PD, I'd seen insecure men who beat up on women and children. The mental image, and the disgust, never softens.

"Do you know the boyfriend's name?"

"No. But the cops must. I'm sure they would have looked it up because Rell went to talk to them. Oh, one more thing," Joe said. "The boyfriend forbade Simone to ever see Rell again. He even made her quit her job so Rell couldn't see her during her shift.

"But one day, Simone called Rell and told her that her boyfriend said she had to get a job on the other end of town where Rell wouldn't see her. So Simone got a waiting job at one of the Casino cafés. Rell has gone there a couple of times."

"You said that Rell talked to the police about Simone?"

"Yes, she did. After the boyfriend came to our house and dragged Simone out of here, Rell was so concerned that she went down to the South Lake Tahoe Police Department. She explained what she'd heard about Simone and her boyfriend and what she'd personally witnessed as well. The police said that there is a community women's organization that could help Simone find a safe house if she were willing to press assault charges. So Rell explained all that to Simone, but Simone was still unwilling to file charges. Simone says she'll be dead if she takes any action. In lieu of her pressing charges, I understand that somebody has to witness him assaulting her."

I nodded.

"One time," Joe said, "Rell went to Simone's house, but no one was home. So Rell talked to one of the neighbors. The neighbor told Rell that he'd seen Simone get beaten. But he was unwilling to testify because he also thought he'd get killed by her boyfriend. He was apologetic, but he said that he had a wife and two little kids to think of."

"Joe, you've probably pondered this at length, but can you see that guy coming over to teach Rell a lesson for talking to Simone without his permission? Can you imagine him throwing Rell off the deck?"

"Yes, I have thought about it. The answer is that I can certainly imagine that, but I don't think it happened that way. I'll tell you why. I have no doubt that this is the kind of guy who could kill an old woman. But a hothead like him exacts vengeance. He wouldn't just push an old lady over a deck railing. He'd hit her first. Probably multiple times. I talked to the doctor who examined Rell. He is confident that all of Rell's injuries came from striking the rocks."

"Good bit of deduction," I said. "You could be right." As I said it, I wondered if Simone's boyfriend would break pattern and simply toss Rell over the deck in order to disguise his involvement. But that would take some forethought.

"Simone's boyfriend," I said. "Did you get any sense of his smarts?"

"He just gave me the impression of a dumb thug," Joe said.

"Think about how he acted. Was he calculating?"

"He was like a wild animal. Feral."

"Smart feral? Like a wolf? Or stupid feral like a snapping turtle?"

"I see what you mean. Like a wolf. He had an evil self-awareness, like he wanted to be thought of as tough."

"Do you know where he and Simone live?"

Rorvik shook his head. "No. He drove this big pickup, all rebuilt except that it still needs bumpers. It sits up twice as high as any other vehicle. Rell said they live in Sierra Tract, so maybe you could drive those streets and look for the pickup. But I would warn you that you might get yourself killed. At my age, I've become quite a good judge of character. My sense was that this guy wouldn't hesitate to shoot you if he was mad at you. Or, more likely, he'd beat you up first, then shoot you. Although you don't look like you'd be too easy to beat up."

"Everybody can be beat up by somebody. I appreciate the warning."

I thanked Joe for his time. As he made a little nod, I saw a profound sadness in his face.

I felt bad leaving Joe, but I thought I should stop by to visit Dwight Frankman and Michael Paul.

"One more thing you can help me with," I said. "Do you have the addresses for your full-time neighbors Dwight and Michael?"

Joe looked embarrassed. "That would be obvious, wouldn't it? But no, I don't. I can tell you which houses they live in."

"That'll work just as well."

Joe walked over to the front door. When Spot realized where Joe was going, he got up and trotted over to join him. Doors always represent promise and excitement for dogs.

I realized that Joe wanted to point and such, so I opened the door and stepped outside.

Dwight was gone. The Christmas lights on the abstract sculptures were dramatic, and they lit up the entire entry.

"Do you see the reddish house with the big gable up the street on the right?" Joe pointed. "Just before where the street curves away?"

Spot looked where Joe was pointing, then turned toward me. Probably wondering if we were going to run again.

"Yeah," I said.

"Michael Paul's house is – let me think – one, two, three, four houses past it on the same side." Joe turned and pointed the opposite direction down the street.

"If you go down this other way and take the first two right turns in a row and drive down the hill a bit, there's a modern glass house on the right. The house right after it is Dwight's house. Kind of a greenish gray."

I was trying to visualize. "That would be down in the forest below your deck," I said.

Joe thought about it. "Yes, I suppose so."

"I'll be in touch," I said. Spot and I were half way to the Jeep when I realized that I had one more question. I went back and knocked again.

"You mentioned Simone's boyfriend's pickup," I said when Joe opened the door. "Do you remember the color?"

"Yellow," Joe said. "Bright yellow."

EIGHT

I drove to Michael Paul's house first. It was dark. Nevertheless, I got out and rang the bell.

There was no response. To be expected when the place was dark.

I tried again, waited again. Still no response.

I drove to Dwight's house. Light spilled out several windows.

He too had some Christmas lights near the front door, but none so high that he needed to risk his life on a step ladder to install them.

The wide entry door was made of beautiful wood with inset panels. Around each panel was a thin stripe of inlaid wood, darker, reddish. Rosewood, maybe. The door probably cost more than my used Jeep.

On the wall to the side of the door was a knocker made of a two-foot length of ski with a ski binding mounted on it. It was an interesting bit of ski country kitsch next to such an elegant door.

I lifted the hinged portion of the ski binding and dropped it down against the ski. It made a loud thwack. Three times was enough to wake any sleeping neighbors and send non-hibernating bears rushing back to their dens.

After a minute, I knocked again. There were no cars in the driveway, but the three-car garage could still allow for lots of people in the house.

In another minute I heard a faint noise. I smiled at the peephole.

"Who is it?" a tentative male voice said at a high pitch.

"Owen McKenna. I just met you at Joe Rorvik's. Wondered if I could ask you a question."

I heard the deadbolt turn. The door opened to the length of a door chain. Dwight looked out at me as the alarm warning started beeping. He shut the door. I heard faint beeps as he punched in the code to turn off the alarm. He unhooked the chain, and pulled the door open. He was wearing one long, blue, rubber glove. With his other hand he held a baseball bat. It was the junior size, made for young kids who need an easier bat to swing when playing t-ball. Around Dwight's neck was a dust mask, the white gauzy portion pulled down below his chin. On his feet were old-fashioned leather slippers.

"Sorry for the glove," Dwight said. "I was cleaning the sink. I'm sure I look like something out of a bad movie."

"You must be using strong chemicals," I said.

"Just regular cleanser," he said. "But that stuff is bad for you. It can get in your lungs and get absorbed through your skin."

I nodded. "Is this an okay time, or should I come back?"

Dwight's pause was probably long compared to how most people would react, but for someone who obviously spent time and energy considering the dangers of cleaning the sink, to be expected. "No, this is okay. Please come in." He pointed toward a large rubber tray next to the door. "You can put your shoes there. I don't think any of the slippers to the side are as large as your feet, but they're open-backed, so they should still work.

Dwight stepped aside. I walked past. I saw him look out the open door, turning to look both ways down the dark street. Then he shut the door behind me, turned the deadbolt and slid the chain into its holder. I stepped into the tray next to a pair of Hush Puppies and began removing my shoes. I'd often been to homes where shoes were discouraged, a fine idea in snow country. But Dwight went a step further. He didn't want my stockinged feet on his floors any more than my shoes. I found the largest pair of leather slippers and slid my feet into them. My heels hung out the back ends.

Behind the door were four pairs of skis hanging in holders mounted on the wall.

"You are an avid skier," I said.

Dwight shook his head in a dramatic way.

"Oh no. I bought this house furnished. I didn't want any of the stuff. But the sellers were getting divorced, and they said the low price was dependent on the buyer taking the house along with its contents. Apparently, they had been fighting about stuff and they both wanted to make their exit and start fresh without anything. But look at what I have had to put up with." He made a sweeping gesture at the living-dining-kitchen area. "Hard, Scandinavian furniture, sporting equipment, exercise bicycle, wine bar. My God, what would I ever do with all of that. And that door knocker. What were they thinking?" He pointed at the exercise bicycle. "I like to take walks. But not real long. And when the weather is nice. This stuff is so... so excessive. It just makes you sweaty. I believe in moderation."

"You could have a garage sale," I said.

"Absolutely. It's on the top of my list come summer. Once I get this place cleaned out, I can make it cozy and comfy." Dwight pointed toward the closed door. "Is it okay if I don't invite your dog in?"

"Of course. I would never expect that."

"I like dogs in principle," he said. "But the shedding and the dander, well, I'd have to pretty much wear this mask with my inhaler under it until I'd thoroughly cleaned the house."

He pointed toward the living room. "Please have a seat. I'll be with you in a minute."

I walked into a living room with maple furniture that looked stylish but had very little upholstery. I sat on an upright chair. Dwight went into the open kitchen. He laid the t-ball bat on the kitchen counter, then peeled off his glove. He tore off two lengths of paper towel, laid them on the counter next to the sink, then set his glove on the towels.

Dwight looked out the dark kitchen window just as he had the front door, then walked down a hall out of my sight. I heard water running in a bathroom. After a long time, he came back, waving his hands in the air, fingers spread wide. He saw me noticing.

"The only way to get them completely dry," he said. "If I don't, my skin gets very chapped."

I nodded.

Dwight sat on a chair across from me, perching on the edge, his knees together, hands folded in his lap. He was skinny and angular, like he was assembled of two-by-fours. Although he appeared tall, it was largely because of his narrowness. He was shorter than my six-six by a half foot and lighter than my 215 by

50 pounds. He glanced toward the windows.

I turned to look. The windows had sheer, white window coverings that allowed one to look out but would be impossible to see through from the outside during the daytime.

"Are you expecting someone?" I asked.

"I'm just..." Dwight swallowed. "Would you mind if I take a moment to shut the blinds? I was so busy in the kitchen that I didn't notice it had gotten dark. It won't take me but a moment."

"Of course. Want help?"

"No, thank you." He stood up and went around the living room pulling on cords to drop custom blinds.

"Thanks for waiting," he said when he sat back down. "I'm sort of paranoid about people seeing into my house at night."

"Understandable after what happened to Rell. I'm curious, Dwight. You are, frankly, very young. How do you happen to have such a nice house? Or does it belong to your parents?"

Dwight shook his head. "I never knew my parents. I was raised by my great aunt Vera on my mother's maternal side. Whenever I asked about my parents, she would say that she was my parent. As I got older, I came to realize that I was born out of wedlock and handed off to aunt Vera. We lived in her apartment in Redwood City. She was poor, but I never lacked for anything important. Vera died when I was seventeen, the same day I got accepted to Stanford. I've been on my own ever since."

Dwight seemed to relax a little as he talked.

"Luckily, I got through Stanford on a couple of scholarships and some student loans. Fortunately, I've done well, so I'm in good shape financially. I bought this house three months ago."

"Didn't you come to Tahoe to ski?"

"No. I'm not into sports. But it's a beautiful place and much safer than the communities where I could afford to live in the Bay Area. I'm pretty security conscious as you can probably tell."

"Joe says you work in computers like Michael Paul down the street."

Dwight frowned. "Well, I'm a software engineer. I specialize in nano-structure computer modeling. Michael was an entrepreneur, more of a money guy. He put together a startup, then sold it."

"He didn't write code," I said.

"He obviously knows his way around code, and that helped him with his venture. But he's more of a businessman, not a geek like me."

"What is nano-structure computer modeling?"

Dwight made a little sigh. I took it to indicate that once again he was going to have to explain a tech field to a naïve layman, and that frustrated him. He took a little breath.

"Have you heard about nanotechnology?"

"Not really," I said. "Techy small stuff? Super small stuff?"

"Yes. Super small would be an appropriate description. Nano design is working at the molecular level. The atomic level. A nanometer is one billionth of a meter. To put that into perspective, a nanometer is to the head of a pin as a small boat is to the Pacific Ocean. When you work with something that small, the effects of quantum mechanics intrude on your device, whatever it is. And if you know anything about quantum mechanics, we're talking about some really weird effects."

"Sorry," I said. "Quantum mechanics is something I've heard of, but it is obviously over my head."

"No problem," Dwight said. He was more relaxed now, finding comfort in talking about something in his area of expertise. "Suffice to say that we're now designing useful materials made up of nanometer-sized pieces. As scientists design these things, they need to model them in computers. That's my specialty. I write custom software that predicts how certain materials behave in certain environments. All at the nano level, of course."

"Of course," I said. "And you do this from here?"

He nodded, still sitting primly in his chair, his hands folded on his knees.

"I assume this work pays well," I said.

Dwight's face reddened a bit. "Yeah. It's kind of embarrassing. There is a group of professors at Berkeley who use me now and then. We have a little joke about money. Our unit of currency is the nano GDP."

"Let me guess," I said. "A billionth of the Gross Domestic Product."

"Right. The GDP of the U.S. is about fifteen trillion dollars. Which makes a nano GDP a billionth of that, or about fifteen thousand dollars. So they'll call me up and outline a project they'd like me to do. Then they'll say, 'What do you think? Will it come in under a nanoGDP?' And I say, 'maybe,' or 'yeah, just barely.'

"So they send me the specs. I write the code and send it back. It usually takes me about five or six days. Sometimes a week."

"You make fifteen thousand a week."

Dwight nodded. "But not every week."

"Stanford turns out students who do well," I said.

Dwight nodded. "I pretty much spent my childhood working with computers while the other kids played ball. When I started at Stanford, their computer courses seemed pretty remedial to me, so I got the department head to let me into some grad-school courses, and I began to focus on nano design modeling in my freshman year. After school, I worked at a couple of startups, then went out on my own as a consultant."

"You met Joe and Rell after you moved here?"

He nodded. "They're pretty much the oldest people in the neighborhood. I saw them on my walks. We talked. Rell especially. She's very nice." He made a little smile. "Actually, I sort of forced myself on them. I could see that they could use help now and then. And outside of my work colleagues, I don't have friends. They've been very nice to me."

"Do you think that Rell could have fallen by herself?"

"I don't know. If you asked me before her fall, I would have said no. Rell is not uncoordinated and, considering her age, very steady on her feet. But after her fall, I thought about it, and I can't imagine anyone pushing her. She's so sweet. So it's a conundrum."

"Your neighbor, Michael Paul. Do you know him well?"

"Not well, but yeah, we talk in the street. He's often polishing one of his cars when I walk by. So I always try to say a few things. I don't want him to think I'm weird or anything."

"What's Michael like?"

"He's kind of a glam boy." Dwight's tone was pejorative.

"You don't like him," I said.

"No. It's more like I don't understand him. He seems to care about style more than substance."

"Meaning..."

"Everything about him is shallow. He puts a lot of energy into how he looks and sounds. You know the cliché, 'clothes make the man?'"

"Yeah," I said.

"That's Michael. Appearance rules. He has several cars, and they are always washed and polished. He has several girlfriends, and they always look like models. His house has lots of mirrors, and I've watched him check himself out in them."

"He's into clothes," I said.

"Yeah. And his tattoos. He's got them all over like he's a walking art project."

"Joe told me that he didn't like tattoos. Sounds like you and Joe have that in common."

"No," Dwight said, shaking his head. "I like tattoos when it is a personal expression of individuality, when it's a small thing like a hair style or a different kind of earrings. But when a person makes their tattoos their brand, like they are a product and the tattoos are their packaging, then it's distracting. I don't think there is anything wrong with it." Dwight pinched his lips. "You must think that I'm a really conservative conformist. And maybe I am. But I'm sure you've had this experience. You meet someone, and you talk a little, and you each find that the other person is intriguing. It's always a nice discovery to find another person who is interested in the same parts of the world as you, whether it's poetry or Nascar racing or Middle Eastern politics or rock and roll. But if that person sports a big nose ring or has a purple mohawk or their entire body is covered in tattoos, their looks hijack the conversation. A certain level of conformity allows us to concentrate on substance over style. But in-your-face nonconformity gets in the way. No matter how important anything is to that kind of person, it is a lower priority to them than how they look."

Dwight's sudden, thoughtful analysis surprised me. "And Michael is like that," I said.

"Yeah. He's still a nice person, but his style gets in the way of communication."

"When you've talked to him, has anything ever come up about Joe and Rell?"

"Not that I remember. The only things we've ever talked about are computer hardware and software."

"Joe said that Michael's retired," I said.

"Yeah. He's real smart. He quit college at nineteen when Oracle made him a good offer. Then a couple of years later, he quit and started a company that produced finance software. He sold the company to American Bank Central. So he's set for life." Dwight made a little jerk of his body, raised his eyebrows, and said, "I should have asked you if I could get you a drink or something. I'm so bad at social things. I have tea and sparkling water."

"Thanks, but I'm fine," I said. "Let me change the subject. Even though you think Rell is sweet, in your talks with her, have you ever heard anything that would suggest that anyone had a problem or disagreement with Rell? Or Joe, for that matter?"

Dwight shook his head. "Not really."

"I'm looking for anything. Think back on your conversations. Life is not always smooth, not even for the kindest of people. I need to know about the bumps that Joe and Rell experienced."

Dwight looked puzzled. "Once or twice I saw Rell and Joe get upset with each other. But it was nothing. Joe's kind of a hermit, and I think that got on Rell's nerves. Not that she's a social butterfly or anything. She's pretty solitary, too. But I've seen her express her frustration that Joe never wanted to go out and see people."

"Did either of them ever say anything about other people?"

"Not specific people."

"What does that mean?"

"Just that one time I was in their garage carrying their recyclables out to my car. I could hear Joe through the kitchen door. He was raising his voice saying something about how some of the people in the group were idiots."

"Did he sound mad?" I asked.

"No. I thought maybe it was about a meeting. You know how meetings can be frustrating? Well, it was like Joe was just being a curmudgeon who was ranting about having to participate at all."

"Did he say what the meeting was?"

"No."

"Any other thoughts about what happened to Rell?" I said. "I'm interested in anything at all, no matter how unlikely the connection might seem."

"No. Sorry. But I'll call you if I think of anything."

I stood up and handed him my card. "Thanks, Dwight."

Dwight stood and walked over to the door, undoing the chain and deadbolt. "If someone did push Rell off their deck," he said, "I'd do anything to catch him. If not, I'd still do anything to help ease Joe's pain. I know it is hell for him to have her in the hospital like this. I can see it on his face."

I nodded. "I'm curious about one thing."

"What's that?"

I pointed over toward the kitchen counter where the t-ball bat lay. "What's the bat for?"

Dwight looked embarrassed. "I told you that I was a bit paranoid. The bat's for protection. I used to live in a bad neighborhood. Things happened. So when I hear a knock at the door, I get scared."

"Is there anything in particular that gives you reason to worry about your safety?"

"Just me and my neuroses," he said.

I thanked Dwight and left. I heard the deadbolt and the chain slide behind me.

NINE

Spot and I headed back through the dark town of South Lake Tahoe as the intermittent snow showers grouped together into a comprehensive blanket of steady, silent snowfall. The flakes got bigger over a short period of time, and soon the air was filled with huge light flakes, drifting down so slowly it was as if they were weightless.

I turned off Lake Tahoe Blvd onto Sierra Blvd and drove through the Sierra Tract subdivision. Although Sierra Tract has its share of vacation homes, it's a working class neighborhood, with many year-round residents who teach at the schools, work for the Forest Service, or run South Shore businesses.

Except for the perimeter streets, most of the streets are laid out on a grid pattern. I cruised the up-and-down streets first, looking for a bright yellow pickup. Then I toured the back-and-forth streets.

I saw two pickups that qualified as yellow, but they were old, darkened yellows. Joe had said that Simone's boyfriend's truck was bright yellow and very tall, and nothing I'd seen fit that description.

As the snow increased, the traffic diminished. By the time I'd driven all of the neighborhood roads, some of the streets were swaths of untracked powder four or five inches deep, glowing white in my headlights. Snow is the ultimate sound absorber, and all noises other than the Jeep's defroster fan and the windshield wipers disappeared as I glided on the hush-soft carpet of white back out to Lake Tahoe Blvd. I turned right, drove through the quiet town that would be inundated with holiday traffic in a little over two weeks, and headed up the East Shore.

I hadn't noticed how much the snowfall had increased until we entered the Cave Rock tunnel and were plunged into sudden, snow-free darkness. Immediately, I was aware of the tires on wet asphalt, the splashy noise reflecting off the tunnel walls. A few moments later, we popped back into the world of white silence. A couple of minutes later, I turned off the highway and drove up the private drive that I share with my vacation-home neighbors. With all four tires churning under four-wheel-drive, we ground up one thousand vertical feet, and I pulled onto the parking pad in front of my little log cabin.

As I got out of the Jeep, I heard from up the street the shrill, eerie voice of Mrs. Duchamp floating through the quiet snow, falling so thick that I couldn't even see the lights of her house, the closest house to mine.

"Treasure! Oh, Treasure! Come to mama right now!"

I let Spot out, and he galloped toward Duchamp's, looking for his Toy Poodle friend. As he disappeared into the whiteout of giant flakes that filled the sky, I could imagine Mrs. Duchamp – the only woman in Tahoe who apparently wore a housecoat and strapless heels 24 hours a day – quivering on her front doorstep, petrified that her precious little dog had run into the snowy night and been consumed by a waiting pack of coyotes.

Then came, "Oh Treasure! Don't you let that big dog hurt you! Treasure, I can't see you in the dark! Treasure, I'm afraid." I knew that with Spot cavorting in the darkness as Treasure traced circles around him, the little dog would be safer than at any other time in her life.

I left Spot and Treasure to cope with Mrs. Duchamp while I went inside, opened a Sierra Nevada Pale Ale, and called Sergeant Bains of the El Dorado County Sheriff's Office.

"McKenna calling," I said when he answered.

"Wow, calling during the wine hour," Bains said. "I didn't know you private cops worked so late. I'm guessing you're calling about Joe Rorvik."

"You're practically a psychic," I said.

"I use the same technique. Deduce something logical about my mark, then reveal it as if it came from psychic powers."

"I'm your mark?" I said.

"Sure. Except I forgot to get your credit card number."

"How did you deduce that I was calling about Rorvik?"

"Partly because I'm the one who recommended you to him.

But more so because he called me an hour or so ago to ask if I had any news about our investigation of the assault on his wife. In the process he told me he'd hired you and that you just left his house."

"Did you have any news for Rorvik?" I asked.

"Unfortunately, no evidence means that we still think it was an accident. What do you think about Mrs. Rorvik's fall?"

"No idea, yet," I said. "Joe told me that his wife had a young waitress friend who's been over to their house."

"The abuse victim," Bains said.

"You know about it," I said.

"It probably came up the same way it did with you."

"Any idea what the abuser's name is?" I asked.

"He was a logical look-up, beating on his girl the way he does. Never know what other craziness he's into. His name is Nedham Theodore Cavett. Goes by Ned. Works at an auto parts store. I found out that he's taking up more than his share of space in the computers at the Inyo County Sheriff's Office. Of course, juvenile records are sealed. But I spoke to a Sergeant Gramercy. He's known Ned since he and his brother were little boys. Ned was the sick and twisted one, the other was normal. Said they grew up in a single-wide out on a patch of desert scrub at the southern end of the Sierra Nevada. The mother beat on them, especially Ned, and she started calling the cops on him when he was about eight. So all the deputies got to know Neddy Teddy."

"Neddy Teddy," I repeated.

"That's what mama called him. Can you imagine her calling him Nedham Theodore Cavett? So she'd call nine-one-one and say things like, 'Neddy Teddy came home with a new F-One-Fifty pickup last night.' Sergeant Gramercy and his buds'd go out and collect the truck and return it to its owner. Young Ned spent a good part of his youth in Inyo County Juvie. Then his mom died, and he went to foster care, then to L.A., then eventually ran away to Nebraska."

"The dream of young men everywhere," I said.

"He met an Omaha gang leader who was recruiting in L.A. where Neddy had tried pimping. Ned didn't have pimping skills, so he followed the gang leader to Omaha. He used a knife to jack a

Mercedes from a little old lady, then hustled it to a chop shop. For that he enjoyed ten years getting three square a day on the Bureau Of Prisons expense account."

"And then he came to Tahoe," I said. "Lucky us. What happened to the brother?"

"Once a cop, always a cop, eh? I wondered the same thing. A good sibling can be a good handle on a degenerate. So I asked Gramercy if Ned was close to his brother. Gramercy said that Peter William Cavett was in fact close to Neddy Teddy when they were very young. They were good athletes, played ball together. He said that Peter also went into foster care after the mom died. A couple of years later, he disappeared. They never knew where he went. Gramercy's read on it was that Peter wanted to get as far away from Ned as possible."

"By their names, it sounds like mom dreamed of aristocracy."

"Yeah," Bains said. "Didn't quite work out that way."

"Any idea where Ned's girlfriend came into the picture?"

"Simone Bonnaire? No. I assume the usual applies. Introverted girl, probably an abuse victim as a child, falls for a handsome guy who knows exactly how to control her and take over her life. If she strays from his rules, the punishment is severe."

"Do you think Ned could have assaulted Joe's wife?"

"Sure. But I still think her fall was an accident. I have no evidence to suspect otherwise. I could come up with a pretense to go roust Ned out of bed, but he lives in the city of South Lake Tahoe. I wouldn't want to interfere on Commander Mallory's territory."

"El Dorado County, too, sergeant," I said. Once in awhile, cops want to take on matters that could be handled by another agency with the same jurisdiction. More often, cops want to let the other agency handle it. Rare is the case that makes a cop feel great.

"You got Ned's descriptors?" I asked.

"Six-three, two-twenty, brown and brown, medium mustache, mono-eyebrow. Think Clarke Gable with muscles. Even his mug shot makes him look like a model."

"Rorvik is also confident that Ned is capable of murder," I said, "but he doesn't think Ned pushed his wife off the deck."

"Hmmm," Bains said. "I never thought to ask him that. What's his reasoning?"

"Joe thinks Ned couldn't just kill somebody. He'd insist on beating the victim first. The doc says Rell wasn't beaten, so by Rorvik's logic, Ned didn't do it. I think Rorvik may have a valid point."

"Rell?" Bains said.

"Sorry. Cynthia Rorvik. Rell was Rorvik's nickname for her. Short for Cinderella."

"Got it."

"Did you interview the neighbors?" I asked.

"Yeah. I sent two deputies through the neighborhood two different times. No hits, no runs."

"They find anybody home?"

"A geeky kid named Dwight Frankman and a tatted-up playboy named Michael Paul. Paul claimed to be gone when Mrs. Rorvik went over the railing. Frankman claimed to be home watching a DVD of – get this – a nano-modeling lecture."

"You don't believe that?"

"Do you?" Bains asked.

"After meeting him, probably. You have Ned's address?"

"Gimme a sec." The phone was silent for half a minute. "Got a pen?" Bains said. Then he read off the address. "You going to pay him a visit?"

"Yeah. I'll let you know if I find out anything illuminating."

"Illuminating," Bains said. "I love the way you private detectives speak. Does that come from wine? That's probably the biggest difference between you and me. Maybe I should learn to drink that stuff."

"But I'm working," I said. "I would never drink wine while I'm working."

We said goodbye, and I drank the rest of my beer.

TEN

The next morning, I called Street Casey.

"Early in the morning for you to call," she said.

"Never too early to ask you out on a date."

"A date? That takes your wanna-do-cheeseburgers-tonight-routine to a new level," she said. "Do you have a time in mind?"

"Tonight?" I said. "I could tell you about my new case."

"Impress the girl with your detecting skills?" Street said.

"Yeah."

"You detected something? Wow."

"Well, not yet, but I will eventually."

I gave her a summary about Joe and Rell Rorvik.

"I'll have to let you know about tonight," she said. "I have a lot of work piled up. Can I call you back this afternoon?"

"Sure."

Spot and I left early and drove back to the South Shore. I wanted to have a chance to see Nedham Theodore Cavett's pickup before he went off to work at the auto parts store that Sergeant Bains mentioned. If I got familiar with his truck, I'd be able to identify him from a distance.

Because the snow had stopped for a moment, I rolled down one of the rear windows. Spot had his head out the window, tongue dangling in a heavy pant in spite of the winter weather. Judging by his focused attention, the snow-covered world from a moving Jeep was utterly captivating.

I glanced at the address Bains had given me and turned down the street. Many of the house numbers were not obvious, but Ned Cavett's pickup might be visible. It could be in a garage, but if it stood as tall as Rorvik had described, it would probably only fit in an RV garage. Chances are it was parked outside.

After several blocks I came to a small cabin with a steep-sloping, green metal roof. The cabin had a small wrap-around porch and what looked like a single upstairs bedroom with a ceiling that angled four ways.

Parked in the street, its front wheels high up on jack stands, was a brilliant yellow pickup, a Chevy from the middle '70s. The truck was missing a grill and front bumper. Parked at such a steep angle, it looked vaguely like a huge, chinless, tropical fish.

To one side of the cabin was a newer double garage nearly as big as the cabin itself. The garage probably qualified as detached, but it looked like the door at the rear corner met up with the front corner of the cabin. In front of the garage was an older model Toyota Corolla with a dusting of snow on it.

The garage door was up, revealing the standard detritus that collects in garages along with several pairs of skis and one unusual item. At the back of the garage was a half-sheet of plywood mounted on the wall. Laminated on the plywood was a circular bulls-eye pattern. In the center of the bulls-eye was a square piece of paper on which was written the name of a famous politician. Sticking out of the politician's name were eight or ten throwing knives.

I parked in front of the yellow truck, walked up to the door and knocked.

Noises like bear grunts came from inside. The door jerked opened. Revealed in a sleeveless shirt, Ned was as advertised, mid-30s, muscular, and beyond ordinary handsome. With a modicum of skills and attitude, he could have been an A-list movie star.

"Wha'dya want," he said, no doubt recognizing me from his Rorvik spy mission but not wanting to reveal to me that he was the spy. Even his voice was rich with depth. I could visualize him yelling, 'Stella!' in Streetcar.

"Looking for Simone Bonnaire," I said.

"She's not in," he said. "Wha'dya want with her, anyway?"

"Just talk."

"What about?" His voice hissed with anger, and he smelled like old meat and stale beer.

"That's between her and me," I said.

He stepped forward, his face in mine. He was almost as tall as me and a bit heavier.

"I don't like a smartass," he hissed. "And no one talks to Simone without me there," he said. "Understand?"

"Sure, pal." I turned to leave.

"Be careful you don't bump my truck when you pull away."

"That yours?" I said pointing. "Nice paint job."

He softened. "I know some guys with a shop in Carson City. This is a new color they're working on."

"Looks like a tropical fish," I said. "Or daffodils."

I glanced at him. Ned was pink, on the way to crimson.

"Hey, you weren't up at Angora Highlands yesterday, were you?" I said.

"I don't know what you're talking about." He turned into the house and slammed the door behind him.

I saw movement over by the garage. A tiny woman was brushing snow off the old Toyota. I walked past my Jeep where Spot still had his head hanging out. I gave him a quick rub, then continued on past the fish truck to the garage. The woman was as skinny as she was short. As Joe said, she looked too meek to do anything on skis other than shuffle along.

She wouldn't even look at me.

"Simone?" I said. "I'm Owen McKenna. I'm a private investigator looking into Rell Rorvik's fall from her deck. You probably know that she is now in a coma at a Reno hospital. Her husband Joe tells me that you were her friend."

Simone glanced up for a brief moment, then looked down. Her head movement was just enough for me to see the bruise on the lower edge of her jaw, an ugly purple smudge that reached back toward her ear.

"I wonder if I may ask you some questions about Rell?"

She shook her head with a kind of desperate fear.

"No. Go away!" she said. She spoke in a harsh whisper with a hint of French accent, but her voice was so soft that I could barely hear her words.

The inner door of the garage opened. Ned rushed out into the garage, took fast steps to Simone, and grabbed her by the upper arm in a grip that might break bones.

Simone shrieked.

"You will never talk to this man, you understand?" he yelled.

Simone's face was filled with pain as the man lifted up on her arm, wrenching her shoulder joint.

It took great self-control to keep from jumping him. But I was in his garage. Unless Simone requested help, I was on bad legal ground.

"I can stop him," I said to Simone. "You want me to stop him? All you have to do is nod."

She shook her head, frantic, panicked. I understood the reaction. Despite her current pain and humiliation, if I got involved, she would suffer a future beating much worse.

Ned had something like flames in his eyes as he stared at me. If he hadn't been holding Simone by her arm, he probably would have charged me.

Ned dragged Simone into the house and slammed the garage side door just as he had with the front door. I heard him yelling. Simone screamed. I felt pushed to the point of explosion. Her scream was right on the edge of the legal footing necessary to go in on a no-knock entry to save her.

But I knew what would happen. She'd have another bad bruise but no broken bones. I'd be charged with a home invasion at the least and get shot to death at the worst.

Fearing for her life, Simone would refuse to testify.

Without her testimony, the jury would convict me. I might be sentenced to prison, while Simone would continue to face continuous beatings until she either died from her injuries or summoned the wherewithal to kill her tormentor. If instead she finally decided to leave him and get a restraining order, he would, likely as not, kill her. I'd seen it too many times to hope for any other result.

The current laws are insufficient to protect battered women. And there was no way I could help Simone unless I was fortunate enough to catch him beating her out in public. Only then could I intervene in any meaningful way. Unfortunately, the cowards who prey on women and children do it in the privacy of their homes where the man's-home-is-his-castle laws help perpetuate the torture.

I drove away, my heart pounding, blood pressure threatening to blow a pipe in my brain.

ELEVEN

To try to calm down, I drove to my office. I sat in the parking lot for fifteen minutes, breathing hard. Gradually, I focused on other things.

I let Spot out of the Jeep, and we went under the scaffolding to the front entry. I stepped on something hard. It was a rusty bolt. As I picked it up, I saw another one a few feet away. I picked that one up as well and in the process noticed two more bolts some distance away.

Looking up, I saw two men on the scaffolding boards about twenty feet up. "Hey guys, looks like someone dropped a bag of bolts. I'll set them here by the door."

"Okay, thanks," one of them called down.

Spot and I walked up the stairs to my office. I checked the phone machine for messages. No blinking light. I turned on the computer and checked for email. There wasn't even any spam. I checked the floor near the door in case someone had slipped a lavender-scented note under the door. There was nothing, reminding me once again that, except for the lavender, other people get all this stuff remotely on their smart phones. Maybe the lavender, too. But I was suspicious of smart phones' tendency to use up what little spare time people had left. Thus, I was the world's slowest technology adopter.

Spot looked around and, like me, also found nothing. He lay down in the exact same place as during our last visit. Sighed. Flopped down onto his side. Appeared to go to sleep.

I didn't know Street Casey's schedule, so I called her cell.

"Hello?" she answered, the warm harmonics of her voice ratcheting up my heart rate a notch.

"Street, my sweet," I said. "I came to my office and there were no messages from you. I was hoping for a lavender-scented note. I'm distraught."

"Sorry. I remembered your date request, but I've had no time to call."

"What do you recommend?" I asked.

"Well, one option would be to go down the hall to the restroom and take a nose-hit on the liquid soap. It's not lavender, but with your aroma detection skills, you probably won't notice the difference."

"What are my other options?"

"Go home and take a cold shower?" Street suggested.

"How about the option where we have wine and an early dinner followed by post-prandial exercise?"

"Oh, that option. How did I forget? A restaurant date would probably run too late for me. Maybe you should just come to my place. I'll cook."

"And you'll be my after-dinner entertainment," I said. "My kind of date."

I called Joe Rorvik and asked if I could stop by. He said yes.

Spot and I were up at Angora Highlands a half-hour later. Spot was excited to come back to Joe's expansive and fancy home. Probably the granite counters.

Joe tried to be pleasant, but I could see that he'd had a hard night. The circles under his eyes were deep and dark.

When we were sitting in his living room with Spot prostrate at Joe's feet, I said, "I'm not certain, but I think that the person watching from the woods yesterday was Simone Bonnaire's boyfriend, Ned Cavett. You've already stated that you don't think he tried to murder Rell because you felt he would have smacked her around as punishment, and the doctors found no such bruises. I'm inclined to agree because I met Cavett this morning and witnessed his sadistic abuse toward Simone."

"Did you teach him a lesson?" I was pleased to hear a little venom in Joe's voice. Passion of any flavor is an antidote to old age.

"I wanted to, but he's clever. He did nothing that gave me a technical reason to intervene. It would be counter-productive for Simone if I tried to insert myself into the situation and was prosecuted for assault and possibly convicted."

Joe scoffed, "They wouldn't really do that, would they?

Everyone in local law enforcement must know that Ned is a walking bomb."

"True. But the system has rigid rules. A DA who doesn't follow them can find himself or herself in trouble. Anyway, can you think of any reason why Ned would be watching you?"

Joe shook his head. "No. I would assume he was watching you. Maybe he worries that having a detective on a case that touches Simone, even if in a distant way, puts him and his abuse under the spotlight."

"It doesn't make sense to me. But maybe you're right. Please pay attention to your surroundings and let me know immediately if you sense anyone near your house or anything else out of the ordinary."

Joe nodded.

"Another question," I said. "I know you said that most of your social circle was made up of people who have died. You told me about Rell and Simone and Rell's hiking group. But there must be some people that you speak to now and then, your acquaintances, if not close friends. Even if they don't know Rell, they still might be useful for me to talk to. For example, of all the people you know, who, after Rell, are you closest to?"

"The first person that comes to mind is Manuel Romero. He's a young man like you. A year ago, after the paper did a little thing on me for the anniversary of my Olympic medal win, I got an invitation to a breakfast get-together every other month. Because it wasn't too frequent, I decided to give it a try. There are four other men besides me. Manuel is the one I've most connected with. If I'd ever had a son, I would have wanted him to be like Manuel. In fact, Manuel once told me that he considered me to be one of his best friends. I was surprised and flattered."

"Does he know Rell?"

"He doesn't know Rell very well, but he's met her on several occasions."

"You have common interests?"

"Nothing specific. He's done some skiing and is interested in my ski history. Mostly, he is the only person in the breakfast group who treats me like a regular guy. The other men are very nice, but I grow weary of the constant references to my age and my

Olympic history. They refer to me as the sage and the chief and the champion. They're all respectful, but it's tiresome. Manuel just treats me as Joe Rorvik, no roar attached."

"Any idea what things Rell and Manuel ever talked about?"

"I have no idea. But they've met at several social functions, and they seem comfortable around each other. A few months ago, she sat next to him at a dinner for the Heavenly Race Team fundraiser. I imagine that their conversations were just typical social niceties. Weather and town politics and such. But, of course, you could ask Manuel what they discussed."

"What kind of work does Manuel do?"

"He's an environmental scientist for UC Davis. He's worked on a variety of issues for them. As you probably know, UC Davis has done the main research on the decline of the lake's clarity. A year ago, they got a grant that allowed them to have Manuel move up from Davis and work at the lake full time."

"What is his focus?"

"I'm not clear on that. I think he called it social environmentalism, a recognition that saving the lake is not going to happen just through big policy changes, but through shifts in personal attitudes. He wants to convince people that individuals can make a difference."

"I would have thought it was primarily the big stuff that mattered."

"Me, too. The only specific thing that I remember about Manuel's program is that he's trying to get Central Valley farmers to not plow their fields when it's windy. Apparently, a big source of the silt clouding up the lake comes from those farms a hundred miles away."

"Ironic that after he moves up here, he's trying to work with valley farmers."

"Yes. That's why it stuck in my mind. But the farmers respond better when they learn that they're talking to someone who lives in Tahoe. He seems less like an ivory-tower scientist and more like a Tahoe local who is passionate about a local project.

"Manuel also has what he calls his weekly monitor route around the lake. There are a number of devices all over the basin that collect air and water samples, and Manuel monitors the results. They're trying to discover where pollution inputs are increasing and where they are decreasing. It goes into what he calls a pollution source map. Not only that, but he has isolated some of the dust collected from his devices, and he's demonstrated that it came from Central Valley farms. Something to do with the fertilizer they use. He carries the evidence with him to show the farmers. It's very convincing."

"I should talk to him. Do you have his number?"

Joe nodded. "Hold on. I'll get it."

Joe walked down a hallway, then returned a minute later and handed me a Post-it note with Manuel Romero's name and number on it.

"Any other people I should check with? Anyone who has spoken to Rell recently?"

Joe shook his head. "Rell knows Simone, and I know Manuel. That's pretty much it. Oh, I forgot Jillian. Her last name starts with an O. Oesska. Or something like that. It'll be in Rell's book."

Joe stepped over to a small desk that was built into the kitchen, and he looked in an address book. "Here it is. Oleska. Jillian Oleska." Joe came back and handed me another sticky note with Jillian Oleska's number.

"How does Rell know Jillian?"

"She met her at one of those book clubs that Rell gave up on. I believe they still speak on the phone now and then."

"About?"

Joe frowned. "I have no idea. I think Jillian is an event planner. Perhaps Rell was interested in one of her events. Or maybe Jillian needed some editing on her promotional materials."

"Where do Manuel and Jillian live?" I asked.

"I haven't been to Jillian's house, but I think Rell said that she lives on the North Shore. Manuel lives in the Keys here on the South Shore. I remember how he said that it's part of his job to confront the worst environmental mistake ever made at the lake."

"Interesting choice," I said.

"It gives him credibility to live in and be invested in the area where they dredged out water-purifying wetlands. He can take people on a tour and point to all the nasty details and the ongoing detrimental effects on the lake. People think that if this Tahoe

Keys homeowner feels this way, it must be a serious problem."

"Do Manuel and Jillian have families?"

"I have no idea about Jillian. Manuel is married and has two daughters in college. The younger one is here at the community college. The older one was here, too, but she transferred to UC San Diego this fall. Manuel is very proud of his kids."

I thanked Joe, let Spot into the back of the Jeep and left.

Because I was once again close to Michael Paul's house, I stopped by and pressed his doorbell. Once again, he was either out or he was not answering the door.

I looked at my phone and saw that, despite the high elevation of Angora Highlands, I had poor reception. So I drove down Tahoe Mountain Road and headed toward town, glancing at my phone now and then. When I had good reception, I pulled over and dialed Manuel's number.

The phone rang many times. Five or six rings after a typical answering machine or voicemail service would have picked up, someone finally answered.

"Hello?" the voice was female and very soft.

"Hi, this is Owen McKenna calling for Manuel. May I speak to him, please?"

There was a short pause. "Tell me who you are again?"

"Owen McKenna. I'm a friend of Joe Rorvik. Joe gave me this number and said I could reach Manuel. We had a question about Joe's wife Rell, and Joe said he thought that Manuel could help. If this is a bad time, I can call back. Or perhaps you could have Manuel call me?"

This time, the pause was much longer. I heard breathing, short pants.

"Hello?" I said. "Are you still there?"

"I'm sorry, but Manuel is dead."

TWELVE

Sometimes you get presented with a big, negative surprise, and you roll with it. Other times, it renders you speechless and confused.

After a long moment, I said. "I'm so sorry. Maybe I called the wrong Manuel. Is this Manuel Romero's number?"

"Yes."

"I was under the impression that Joe had been in recent communication with Manuel."

"It just happened. Last night. A car accident. We only just found out this morning."

"Are you Manuel's wife?"

"Yes. I'm Lucy."

"I'm very sorry, Lucy. You have my deepest condolences. I'm sorry to have bothered you."

I waited a bit, heard no other words, and hung up.

I called Sergeant Bains.

"I just spoke to Lucy Romero, wife of Manuel Romero, who lives in the Keys, and she told me that Manuel died in a car accident last night. Any chance it happened in El Dorado County and that you've heard of it?"

"We're at the scene as we speak. The guy cruised off one of the switchbacks at Emerald Bay with enough speed to launch off the mountain and pancake his Toyota Prius a few hundred feet down. We got the body out and removed it a couple of hours ago. Now a wrecker is pulling up the vehicle carcass. Quite the trick, because they have to chainsaw out the Manzanita that's in the way."

"Okay if I come by?"

"Yeah. I'll tell the deputy to look for your Jeep."

When I came to the four-way intersection called the "Y," I turned north on Highway 89 and headed out past Pope Beach, through Camp Richardson, past Kiva and Baldwin Beaches, through Cascade Properties, went around the first switchback, and crawled up toward a group of El Dorado County patrol units with two CHP units mixed in. The northbound traffic lane was blocked, and they were alternating both northbound and southbound traffic flow through the southbound lane. I rolled down my window when I got to the first deputy directing traffic.

"I'm Owen McKenna. Sergeant Bains said he'd notify you."

He nodded and pointed. "Pull over there. Stay outside of the cone perimeter."

I nodded and did as he said.

They'd set up some orange roadwork cones to mark an area of vague skid marks mostly buried in fresh snow. I walked around them and found Bains with some other officers near the wrecker truck, which was backed up to the edge of the shoulder where the mountain pitched away. The cable stretched down the mountain. Two men with chainsaws were working above the wreckage, tromping on snowshoes through deep snow, cutting away the obstructions. Their saws made the gurgle-cough of small engines backfiring on idle. When they revved them for another cut, the whine smoothed out as it went up in pitch. One of the men on the saws had a radio, and he and the truck operator coordinated how much cable the machine could reel in before more saw work was necessary.

I found Bains.

"What's your interest in the car crash victim?" Bains said.

"I asked Joe Rorvik who had spoken with Rell recently. He could think of just a few people. One was Simone Bonnaire, partner of the abusive Ned Cavett. Another was Jillian Oleska. The third was Manuel Romero, perhaps Joe's best friend."

"Now I really feel sorry for the old man," Bains said.

"I see that you're protecting some skid marks. You think he woke up and hit the brakes at the last minute?"

"Maybe. The marks could just be someone else who came after the accident. They could have seen something, or they could have just pulled over to check their email. It's hard to do road-and-tire forensics anymore, now that most cars have anti-lock brakes. Romero could have stood on that pedal, and all we'd have as indication are some vague marks in the snow at the edge of the road. Never did like that whole trend of letting computers override what the driver is trying to do. Like those fly-by-wire passenger jets. Something about it just isn't right. If I wanna stomp on my brakes, that's what I want, brake-stomping, not some micro-chip intervening and deciding that what I really want is super fast brake-pumping."

I nodded. Hard to argue with Bains's logic even if the statistics sing the benefits of anti-lock brakes. I also realized that Bains was trying to put his mind on thoughts other than his current task.

"Who found the accident?" I asked.

"A bakery truck driver was down below, heading north to Tahoe City, coming around the curve from the Cascade Properties area. He said he saw a sudden bright light arcing through the sky and forest on the mountain above him. Then the light turned into two lights before it disappeared. He said that he would have thought it was a UFO because it looked just like a UFO, except that he doesn't believe in UFOs. So then he thought it was some kind of meteorite that split into two. It wasn't until he climbed up to the second switchback that he had the idea that it might have been a runaway vehicle shooting off the mountain. So he stopped and looked over the edge. He couldn't see anything, but he could smell stress in the air. So he dialed nine-one-one. He was still here when we arrived. He left an hour ago."

"What's that mean, 'stress in the air?'"

"That's what I asked him. He said that the air had a crinkly, disturbed feel to it. Those were his words. He couldn't explain it more than that. If I had to guess, I'd say his sense came from the mixing of smells that you don't normally find together."

"Ah," I said. "Forest air at night with snow and sand and dirt and exhaust thrown into it."

"And ripped foliage and broken trees," Bains said. "One time a windstorm blew down a pine near our house. I went out right after I heard the crack and boom. The piney turpentine scent coming from that broken pine was powerful, like it was calling out its distress. Right up there with the scent you get out of a wood chipper eating pine branches." Bains gestured at the trees below. "Now that I think of it, it may be that these smaller broken trees are actually firs – I'm not much of a tree guy – but the scent is pretty much the same."

Bains pointed down at the wreckage, a bit of blue mixed into the green and brown and snow-white forest. "You mentioned exhaust smells. Not that it matters, but a Prius like that maybe wasn't making exhaust. Those things can go pretty fast on just their electric motors without ever turning on their gas engines, especially when they're coming down a steep road like the one above this switchback."

"Good point. Any chance the bakery trucker noticed the time?"

At that moment both chainsaws revved up loud and Bains had to nearly shout in my ear.

"The nine-one-one call was logged in at four-forty-three this morning. Our first deputies on the scene could find nothing but the marks in the snow at the edge of the drop-off. They even shined a searchlight, but all they saw in the dark was a mess of broken trees and shrubs. It wasn't until morning light that they were able to hike down and find the wreckage. It took two more trips up and down to lower a rescue toboggan and the pry bars they used to bust out what was left of the windshield and remove the body. The slope is so steep and the snow so deep that they hooked the wrecker cable to the toboggan and one guy on each side guided it up the slope while the wrecker pulled. Afterward, they hauled the wrecker line back down to repeat the process with the vehicle."

The chainsaws dropped back to idle, and the wrecker reeled in more cable.

"You get a coroner's report yet?"

Bains shook his head. "No, but I saw the body, so I know it will say blunt-force trauma as cause of death."

"Under the influence?" I said.

"I doubt it."

"Why?"

"You ever seen a druggie drive a Prius? Priuses are the granola crowd. People who get their buzz from green tea. I'd be surprised if we find out he was on anything more powerful."

"You're probably right," I said.

The wreckage was now just one hundred feet below us. From

the condition of the car, I could already tell that Manuel's death was probably an instantaneous one.

Behind us, two deputies were taking pictures of the vague skid marks. One had the camera. The other held a big floodlight despite the cloudy daylight. They moved to different positions for each of several sets of photos.

I'm not an expert in skid marks, but even I could see that what visual evidence there was would reveal very little under any analysis. Manuel was going much too fast, skidded, and went off the mountain. Not much more information could be squeezed out of the snow.

Fifteen minutes later, the wreckage was up to the edge of the drop-off. It looked like someone had ground up the Prius in a giant eggbeater, then stomped on it until it was mostly flat.

The wrecker driver got in the cab and pulled forward enough to drag the Prius carcass onto the flat ground behind the truck, just to the side of the cone perimeter around the skid marks. Then the driver tilted the cargo bed of the truck back until the trailing edge touched the ground.

Bains waved at the driver, who stuck his head out the window.

"Hold up a bit until we can look at the wreckage?"

"Sure, man, but I'm on a clock. Longer it takes me to get back to the garage, the more likely I'll miss other calls."

"We'll be quick," Bains said.

Bains came back, and we both studied the wreck. I walked around and looked at it from all angles. The only way it could have been more smashed would have been to put it into one of those giant auto compactors. There was no part of the vehicle with any smooth metal. Every window was broken. The passenger compartment, designed to hold four, was squeezed nearly flat.

I looked inside. Take away the splattered blood and broken glass, the interior looked to have been clean when the car went off the mountain. There was a jacket crammed under the crushed dashboard. Loose in the vehicle, but crushed flat, was a metal thermos, the kind that was considered indestructible. The driver's door panel was stained dark as if with coffee. If Manuel had traveled with a briefcase or any other items, they had been ejected from the car.

Other than the crash debris, the only items that seemed out of place were a mangled cigarette pack and a crumpled piece of colored glossy paper on the rear floor, just visible under the edge of a pancaked seat. I could see them, but I couldn't reach them.

I pointed them out to Bains.

He leaned to the side to see into the narrow space. "Funny," he said. "Seems like this guy is fastidious. The rest of the car is clean. Stuff would fly around in this kind of crash. But that looks like the paper was crumpled up in someone's hand and tossed on the floor. And the cigs don't make sense."

"Because people who drive Priuses don't smoke," I said.

"Right."

I stuck my hand partway into the wreckage, assessing whether or not I could reach the paper and cigarettes.

"You'll cut yourself if you try to reach past all that ripped metal. I checked and found that there are no warrants on Manuel. Not even a speeding ticket. He's clean as they come. So all I want is the registration."

Bains reached through the broken passenger window to the glove box. It was obviously jammed, but he tried wiggling it anyway.

"Looks like we'll need a pry bar." He walked over to one of the patrol units and came back with a pry bar. He worked it into the glove box seam, levered it up and down. Plastic broke with loud snapping sounds. Bains repositioned the bar and jerked it back and forth.

Bains lifted up his foot, got it in through the opening, and started kicking, over and over. He pulled his foot out and began working once again with the pry bar. This time he made a stabbing motion. Eventually, he pulled out the vehicle manual and registration and held it up, victorious.

"You're sweating like a gladiator," I said.

"Working like one," he said. Bains walked around to where the rear hatchback had been and absently lifted up on the crushed metal, knowing that it wouldn't budge.

"If we want to get into any of the other crushed spaces, we'll have to borrow the Jaws-of-Life cutters from the fire department.

I'll check with Manuel's wife and see if there's anything she's missing that might be under that hatch. Otherwise, I'm done with this."

As he spoke, I walked around to where he had attacked the glove box. I reached into the cup holders and other compartments. All were clean. If there was an ashtray, I couldn't find it among the broken metal and plastic.

There was a stiff stick about three feet long that had gotten stuck into a crack in the wreckage as it was pulled up the mountainside. I jerked the stick out and used it to reach through a torn opening in the crushed metal car body and fish out the crumpled paper. It didn't want to come. Eventually, I got the paper ball lined up just so, and I stabbed the stick through the paper. I slowly pulled the stick out from the wreckage, careful not to bump the paper off. Next, I reached the stick back in, got it into the open end of the cigarette pack, and pulled it out. The pack was empty.

Bains watched as I opened the crumpled paper and smoothed it out on my thigh. The paper showed a picture of a skier with a very blue Lake Tahoe in the background below. The skier was catching some air off a lip of snow, flakes spraying into the sky, sparkling in the sunlight. The paper was heavy-weight stock, like a magazine cover. The right edge was torn leaving three letters showing. STE. I turned the paper over. It showed another picture, two young couples at a restaurant table. They were well dressed. The table was elegant, with candles and large wine glasses. If this side had any writing, it had been on the left and was torn off.

I looked at Bains. "So Manuel had a picture from a brochure or something," he said.

"Why would a fastidious guy crumple it up and toss it on the floor of his car?"

Bains shrugged. "No crime here that I can see. You can have it if you want." He turned and signaled the tow truck driver. "Okay, Grady, all yours," he said.

The driver winched the wreckage up onto the cargo bed. There was nothing left that resembled four normal tires on wheels, so the scraping and screeching of metal on metal was severe. Once in place, the driver leveled the cargo bed and secured the wreckage with cargo straps that were tightened by ratchets.

One of the deputies came up. “Sarge, we’ve got pics from pretty much every angle.”

“Did you check to see if the snow tracks had enough shadows to be easy to see?”

“Matt held the big light down low just to make shadows. See what you think.” The man held up the camera so that Bains could look at the screen. He pushed a button to scroll the photos.

“Looks good,” Bains said. “Okay, let’s gather up the cones and turn this land back over to the public.”

THIRTEEN

I stuck the ski photo and cigarette pack into my pocket and got back in the Jeep. Spot was subdued. As always, the lingering scent of deceased human was hard for him.

I often think of how hard it must be for Ellie Ibsen, the search-and-rescue trainer, and her dogs. To have a job finding missing persons would be great when the people turn up alive. But many times the dogs are brought in too late. In that situation, the dogs still perform the miracle of finding the victim, but the victim is dead. It's the worst reward for a job well done.

The body had been removed before we arrived. Yet, even Spot's limited experience with the smell of death made him sad. He leaned forward from the back seat, sticking his nose onto my clothes and the back of my neck, reaching down toward the pocket with the cigarette pack, perhaps looking for a scent that would suggest a happier ending. But he didn't find it. As I drove back toward town, he lay down on the back seat and sighed, deep and long.

I didn't want to give Joe Rorvik the news over the phone, so I headed back to his house. I let Spot out of the Jeep, thinking that he might be needed. As I knocked, I hoped that Joe wasn't taking a nap. He answered after just a few seconds.

"Sorry about not calling first," I said.

"You found out something."

"Yes," I said. "Okay if I come in?"

Joe nodded, once again put his hand on Spot's back, and walked him into the living room.

When we were seated with Spot lying on the floor next to him, I said, "I'm sorry to tell you that Manuel Romero died early this morning."

Joe jerked as if I'd hit him. His skin lost its color. His forehead wrinkled with stress. It was a moment before he spoke.

"How?"

"A car accident. He skidded off one of the switchbacks at Emerald Bay and went some distance down the mountain."

Joe was shaking his head before I finished the sentence. "I don't believe it," he finally said.

"What don't you believe?"

"That it was an accident." Joe's shock and pain were obvious. He was trying to focus on cause, pushing away the effect for a bit.

"I was there when they pulled up the car. It would be hard to imagine anyone surviving that kind of wreck. There was no other vehicle."

"Somebody must have forced him off the mountain."

"Why do you think that? Had Manuel been threatened or something?"

"Not that I know of. I just know that Manuel was too focused and careful to drive off a mountain. You'd have to be going fast, right?"

"From the distance the car went down the mountain, I think so, yes."

"Manuel was not a reckless driver. He would never be so careless as to drive fast on those switchbacks. He was... I'm not sure how to describe it. The opposite of absent-minded."

"Mindful?" I said.

"Yes, that's it. He paid attention to everything he did. I played golf with Manuel. Not that what I did could be called playing. I puttered. He played. And I never saw anyone who had greater powers of concentration. Manuel wasn't a scratch golfer, but for someone who was quite short and had an old arm injury, he was amazingly good. That didn't come from any natural talent but from his ability to concentrate. So I can't see him driving off the road."

"Even focused people can get distracted when they are driving," I said. "Or fall asleep at the wheel. The cops said the crash happened in the middle of the night."

"So that naturally makes you and the cops think that he fell asleep. But I knew him. He wouldn't do that. He was the kind of man who was always in control. If he planned to drive in the middle of the night, he would make certain that he'd gotten enough rest. He'd bring a thermos of coffee."

"Yes, he did," I said. "A thermos, anyway. It was probably coffee. Joe, when you suggest that someone arranged Manuel's accident, that is an extreme thought. Was there something about Manuel that might create a serious enemy?"

"No. Manuel was as careful and tidy with his relationships as he was with his physical life."

I pulled the empty cigarette pack out of my pocket and held it out. "I found this on the floor of Manuel's car."

Joe moved his hand through the air in a dismissive wave. "It didn't come from Manuel. He didn't smoke."

"How do you know he didn't smoke? Did he tell you that?"

"No, he didn't need to. I never saw him smoke, I never saw any evidence of smoking, and most of all I never smelled smoke on him. I can tell that you don't smoke either, even though we've never discussed it."

"Then how do you imagine a cigarette pack got in his car?"

"Someone must have put it there."

"Did Manuel pick up hitchhikers?"

Joe shook his head. "I doubt it. I think he would consider that a risk. He was very focused about the welfare of his wife and children. And yes, it is an extreme thought to suggest that it wasn't an accident." Joe held my eyes. "But it is certainly possible, right? Maybe someone followed him and rammed him from behind at the right moment. It would be relatively easy to do that to someone, wouldn't it? One of those switchbacks would be a perfect spot for it."

As before during our previous visit, Spot lifted his head and raised his nose toward Joe's face. Joe looked at him and frowned.

"His name," I said. "He thinks you were talking to him."

Joe looked confused, then said, "Oh." He rubbed Spot's head. After a moment, Spot rested his jaw on Joe's lap.

Joe said, "It would be easy to push someone's vehicle from behind, especially if you were coming down the mountain, because gravity would be on your side. You could get your victim going much too fast. Then, if you stepped on the brakes at just the right moment, you would have enough road to stop, but your victim would not."

"The roads were covered with snow. It would be very tricky to control it as you say," I said.

"Slippery snow just makes it so you would have to brake much sooner. Still possible. I know something about snow."

"Yes, you do," I said. "More than almost anyone."

"Another possibility is that some oncoming driver came toward Manuel. To avoid being hit, Manuel might have swerved off the mountain."

"You sound pretty sure about this," I said.

"I'm certainly not sure how it happened, but I'm sure that it wasn't an accident. As I've said, I'm a good judge of character."

I got up and walked over to look out at the deck where Rell fell. Rorvik was confronting two separate accidents that happened to people close to him. Apparently, after Rell, Manuel was the closest person to Joe. Both were victims of what seemed like obvious accidents. Manuel died, and Rell was near death. Although there was no evidence to suggest otherwise, Joe believed that both incidents were intentional.

I turned back to face Rorvik.

"Have you met Manuel's wife and kids?"

"Yes, once. On the way to one of our lunch meetings, I picked Manuel up at his house. I believe his wife's name is Lucy. I don't remember his daughters' names. Nice kids. That was last summer."

"Do you remember anything else about them?"

Joe shook his head. "Just that Manuel was crazy about them. He told me that the rest of his family is in Mexico. Lucy's family is from Philadelphia. And because they recently moved up from Davis, they don't have friends here to speak of. I suppose that's why Manuel was willing to spend time with me."

We sat in silence for a bit.

"Joe, after Rell's fall, you said that you didn't think there was a burglar in your house because nothing valuable was missing."

"Correct."

"How did you determine that?"

Joe frowned as if he didn't understand why I would ask. "I just looked to see if our valuables were still here."

"So you didn't make a rigorous search of the house."

"No. Why would I look in the towel drawers or the coat closet?"

"No reason," I said, "as far as valuables go."

"Is there another reason?"

"It's possible that someone was looking for something other than valuables."

"You mean something personal?" Joe asked.

"Maybe. I don't know. As an investigator I always look for things that I don't expect to find."

"Give me an example of what I wouldn't expect." It was a phrase he'd used before in talking about Rell.

"The nature of the unexpected is that you don't know what it is until you experience it. In your house, the expected are those things you know. You open the glass cupboard and see the glasses. That's expected. But if you look in your coat closet and find the garbage, that's unexpected."

"Got it. It sounds like you think I should go through this house and see if anything unexpected happens."

I nodded. "Probably nothing will turn up. But it doesn't hurt to look."

"You think this will help you find out why someone threw Rell off the deck?"

"If something unexpected turns up, yes."

I said goodbye, and Spot and I left.

FOURTEEN

The winter sun was setting, bringing on the fast, hard, winter night.

I knew that I should reconnect with Manuel's wife Lucy. This was the first evening on the day Manuel died. I didn't know if she had local friends. Joe had said that their relatives were in Mexico and Philadelphia. And Manuel and Lucy had just moved up from Davis. I knew nothing about coping with the loss of a spouse, but I did know that what Lucy needed was reassurance and help. I also knew that if you call the same day someone dies, people will say, no, it's not a good time to come over. No, I'm too upset. No, I have to deal with my kids. No, I don't trust you not to try to sell me something. No, I'd rather be alone.

Or they won't even answer the phone.

You have to show up on their doorstep, preferably with food.

I dialed Street to tell her about the sudden change of plans.

She didn't answer her lab or her cell or her home.

We'd made a date, and Street was the most reliable person on the planet. That meant she was either driving or in the shower.

I didn't know what to say on her voicemail, so I didn't leave any messages. I drove to her condo.

I saw the peephole darken after my first push of the doorbell. The door opened.

"Owen, you're early. What's wrong?" Street had her hair in a towel. She was fresh out of the shower and wearing the big, peach-colored terry cloth robe. Women don't come more attractive. Her skin glowed in a way that harmonized with the robe.

"Remember my client Joe Rorvik?"

Street nodded.

"Joe's best friend, Manuel Romero, died this morning in a car accident at Emerald Bay. One of his daughters goes to UC San Diego. I don't know what can be done about that right now. But

I'm thinking that maybe Manuel's wife and their other daughter could use a stabilizing presence. From what Joe said, they recently moved up from Davis, and they don't have any family members close. They haven't lived in Tahoe long enough to have much in the way of friends."

"You want me to go there with you."

"Yes, please."

Street nodded. It was a sudden, major adjustment in her evening plans.

"Okay," she said. "I'm in."

"One more thing," I said. "Have you made food arrangements?"

"You mean, did I plan for dinner? Yes. I roasted a chicken and veggies. It's all ready to pop in the oven to warm up."

"Can we bring it?"

"Of course."

I called Joe Rorvik and told him about our plan. He agreed to let us pick him up. Next, I called my buddy Diamond Martinez, sergeant with the Douglas County Sheriff's Office, told him about Manuel, and explained that I was putting together a small party to help distract Manuel's wife and daughter.

"I thought someone with your gravitas would be a helpful presence. Plus, we're bringing some food. Not much, but Street cooked it."

He said he'd join us.

An hour and twenty minutes later, we rang Lucy Romero's doorbell in the Tahoe Keys. Street was dressed in jeans and cotton shirt and over it she wore a shiny leather jacket. Casual, but nice enough to show respect. Lightweight, too, but Street has a metabolism to rival the boiler on a steam locomotive. Joe wore a sport jacket over dress pants and dress shirt. He looked elegant even with his bent posture. Diamond had switched from his uniform to his civvies. He looked good in navy slacks and navy sweater. I had on my work clothes, jeans and flannel shirt and down vest. Functional to a fault.

I carried Street's large covered pan. Leaving Spot in the Jeep, we four stood on Lucy's doorstep for two minutes before the door opened a little.

A woman peeked out. She was large and pale and pretty, and her eyes revealed that she was as emotionally ripped apart as people get.

"Hello?" she said in a small voice.

"Hi, my name is Owen McKenna. I spoke to you on the phone this morning. I'm the guy helping Joe Rorvik regarding his wife's fall." I moved my head toward Joe. "You've met Joe, of course. Manuel was his closest friend. This is my girlfriend Street Casey. And this is my friend Diamond Martinez, all-around good guy and friend and sergeant with Douglas County. We brought you and your daughter some dinner."

Lucy didn't react and didn't move except for her lower lip, which started quivering. The quivering turned into a small facial earthquake, and then her body started to sway and melt as she let go of the door.

Street was smart enough to figure it out before I did. She pushed forward and grabbed Lucy Romero in a bear hug, steadying herself against the door frame.

When Lucy got her blood pressure back, she stood up on her own, wiped her eyes with the back of her hand, and said, "Please come in." She turned, and Street took her elbow and walked her up the stairs.

Many houses in the Tahoe Keys are built with the bedrooms downstairs and the living room and kitchen on the second floor, the better to take in the views of the lake and mountains. Joe and Diamond and I stepped in and followed up the stairs. Joe didn't hesitate at the effort.

Upstairs, I walked into the open kitchen. I looked around and sniffed and decided that Lucy had made no plans for dinner. Following Street's instructions, I set the oven for 325 degrees, put the big pan in, then turned on the timer for 30 minutes.

I turned back toward the living room and saw that Street had maneuvered Lucy onto the big couch. Next to them was a girl of high school age. Beyond them was the fireplace mantel and on it pictures of the family. Manuel was a handsome guy with a strong nose and thick black hair.

Street sat on the other side of the girl. She held hands with the girl. The girl was speaking, answering Street's questions. How a bug scientist can work such magic with people is a mystery. Street was not what people think of as a naturally warm person. But she can be the kindest person in the room.

Joe was in one of the arm chairs. Diamond took one nearby. I pulled over a bar stool from the kitchen counter.

"Owen," Street said. "This is Katia." She turned to Katia. "Owen is my boyfriend."

Katia looked at me. I gave her a little wave.

The girl stopped talking for a moment. The silence in the room was uncomfortable.

A very small orange cat watched me from behind the end of the couch.

"What's your cat's name?" I said. I pointed at the cat that was behind the girl.

"Tiny Scared," the girl said.

"Boy or girl?" I said.

"Girl."

I was thinking about what would change the evening from one of mourning to one of comfort. Diamond beat me to it.

"Owen has a giant dog that would like Tiny Scared," he said.

The girl shook her head. "Tiny Scared is petrified of dogs."

"She's only afraid of dogs that would threaten her," Diamond said. "But not Owen's dog. He likes cats. So cats are not afraid of him."

The girl shook her head. "They could never be friends."

More silence. Lucy looked like she was about to collapse in grief.

Joe spoke up, "I've met his dog. His name is Spot. Diamond's right. If he brought Spot in here, your cat would probably crawl on top of him."

The girl's eyes widened a bit. She turned to me. "Did you bring Spot with you?"

I nodded.

"Mom," the girl said. "Mr. Owen brought his dog Spot. Can he come inside?"

Lucy was staring at the wall.

"Mom," the girl said again.

Lucy slowly turned her head and looked at her daughter. "Whatever you want, Katia," she said, her voice like a robot.

"You want to come with us to get Spot?" I said.

Katia nodded.

Katia, Diamond, and I went down the stairs and outside to the Jeep. When Katia saw Spot get out of the Jeep, she stepped behind me.

"Don't worry, he's friendly," Diamond said. "In fact, he wants to meet you. Spot, sit." He sat. "Katia, stand in front of him, and he'll shake hands."

She moved toward Spot with great care.

"Spot, shake."

He pawed at the air. I caught his paw. "Here you go, Katia."

She took his paw with both hands, gave it a shake. "Whoa, his paw is heavy."

"Yeah, it is," I said.

"Can I pet him?"

"He'd love it."

She reached out, slow but steady, and touched her hand to the top of his head.

Spot began panting.

"Oh my God, look at the size of his tongue."

"Come on," I said. "Let's introduce him to Tiny Scared."

We walked Spot into the house. Katia, like Joe, rested her hand on his back as they walked up the stairs. In a near-silent whisper, Diamond said to me, "I hope I'm right that your hound won't decide he wants a kitty dinner."

"He won't," I said.

At the top of the stairs, I took Spot's collar before he could frighten Lucy. When she saw him, she inhaled. I had Spot lie down. Katia sat on the floor next to him. She wanted to know all about him. I answered her questions. She pet Spot, leaned on him and wrapped her arms around him.

A few minutes later, Tiny Scared walked out from under the couch, strolled over to Spot, and sat down in front of his head. Katia gasped. The cat stretched her head out and sniffed Spot, nose to nose. Spot, whose head was bigger than the cat, didn't budge beyond flexing his nostrils.

"That's unbelievable," Katia said.

The timer buzzed. Street said, "It's time for dinner."

I stood, leaving Katia in charge of dog and cat. Street found plates and glasses and silverware, and Diamond set the table and put water in the glasses.

Street took the lid off the big pan to reveal the chicken and potatoes and squash and green beans. Instead of much excess food for two people, we had a small amount for six people. I ate a small part of my normal portion, which left a decent amount for all the others.

We never spoke about Manuel during the evening. I didn't know if that was good or bad, but I took my cues from Street. If she wanted to push conversation one way or the other, she would have. I assumed that our only goal was to make things a bit easier for Lucy and Katia.

After dinner, Lucy and Diamond ended up sitting at the dining table talking while the rest of us retired to the living room and watched Tiny Scared as she discovered that Spot's prostrate body was a soft warm playground. First, she explored the little gap between Spot's throat and the floor, and she jabbed her paw into the space as if to catch a critter. He never raised his head. Then she crawled up his bent rear leg and slowly walked up his back to his neck. When she saw his rhinestone ear stud bobbing and flickering, she leaped and attacked it. Spot lifted his head and shook his ears and Tiny Scared did the kitty-cat slingshot disappearing act.

Katia called her for a bit and then said she must have gone under one of the beds, not to come out until morning.

When we were leaving, Lucy gave Diamond a big hug, then took me aside.

"You and I should talk."

"When is good?" I asked.

"Tomorrow morning. After Katia goes to school."

"Should I come here?"

"Yes."

FIFTEEN

The next morning, I was at Lucy Romero's house at 9 a.m. Katia had gone to school. We sat at a small table in the kitchen. Lucy looked like she was in shock. Her eyes were red and puffy, and her hair wasn't brushed. She stared vacantly at the salt and pepper shakers.

Lucy's black hair was cut straight and short and was as thick as the hair of a horse's tail. She had sapphire eyes that shimmered against skin as white as marble. I guessed her to be classic Black Irish. Probably had an Irish maiden name.

"How is Katia?" I said.

"She is devastated, of course. We were both up most of the night, crying, coming apart. But having you visit helped a lot. And Diamond knows what it's like to find one's way in a new country. Manuel never spoke of it, but I could sense the struggles. It helped me to talk to Diamond, to know that Manuel wasn't alone in that. Thanks. Oh, and you should know that Katia now wants a dog like yours."

I smiled.

Lucy said, "This morning, I told her that she could stay home from school. I was thinking about distractions. I told her that she could go online to look up Great Danes. But you know what she said? She said it would probably be better if she went to school. It would force her to continue on. How is that for maturity? She is stronger than I am, a hundred times."

"I understand that you are relatively new to Tahoe," I said. "Up from Davis in the last year or so, right?"

She nodded.

"If you need anything, I probably know people who can help."

Another nod. She started to speak, then stopped.

I waited.

"I want to tell you something," Lucy said, staring down at the table surface, "but I'm worried that you'll think I'm crazy, like I can't accept Manuel's death."

"You can say anything you want. I won't judge."

Lucy jerked her head to look straight at me. "That's what Manuel says."

"What?"

"He always says he won't judge. It's a thing with him. That we shouldn't judge others."

I nodded. "I guess it depends on the circumstances. What did you want to say?"

Lucy clenched her jaw. "The cops think that Manuel's death was an accident. Of course, they would think so. It looks like it in every way. But I don't think Manuel's death was an accident."

When Joe had said it about Manuel, I thought it was an overreaction based on what happened to Rell. To have Lucy say it was a surprise.

"Why?" I said.

"Because Manuel wouldn't accidentally drive off the road. He was a careful driver. A slow driver. So slow that my nickname for him was Pokey."

"It was the middle of the night. Couldn't he have fallen asleep?"

"Manuel could barely fall asleep in his own bed."

"You don't think it's possible that he could fall asleep driving?"

Lucy shook her head. "In all the times I've ridden with him, he never once got drowsy. The car was his thinking time. Once, when the girls went on a sleepover at friends, I rode with Manuel on his night route. It was like being with a young scientist all excited about his discoveries. He was so engaged, so involved in this project."

"What is this project, this night route?"

"It's part of Manuel's job with UC Davis, studying Lake Tahoe. He has pollution monitors around the lake. He collects samples twice every week. Once during the day, and three and a half days later, at night. It turns out that day pollution is a little different than night pollution. Manuel has made some discoveries about this. And when we went, he was excited like a kid. He talked about it continuously. No way would he fall asleep."

"Then what do you think happened?"

"Somebody must have caused him to crash."

"Caused in the sense of a purposeful crash?" I said. "Or caused it accidentally?"

"I have no idea how something like this could happen. I just know that Manuel would not drive off the mountain. The policeman told me that his car was a long way down, that he was going fast. That's not Manuel. Not Pokey."

"Then how could he be driving fast enough to go far down the mountain?"

"Somebody must have made him go fast."

"Lucy," I said slowly, "what you're saying implies manslaughter, or even murder. Have you considered that possibility?"

"No. The very idea of murder is ridiculous. No one would want to... to kill Manuel. He was good to everybody. I'm only looking at the situation. Manuel wouldn't have driven off the mountain, and he wouldn't have driven fast. If that means murder, then it must be murder."

"Did you tell this to the police?"

"No. I only realized it last night when you were here. Yesterday, I was in such shock that I couldn't think." Lucy stopped for a moment. "You know how you can get a sudden idea in the shower? Something about disassociating yourself from what you've been concentrating on? Well, when Street served us dinner, I was able to step back a bit from the situation. I'd been so focused on what I needed to do next that I hadn't thought about the big picture. Suddenly, I realized that Manuel's accident didn't make sense."

"What would you like me to do?"

"I don't know. I haven't thought about it. I just wanted you to know."

We sat in silence for a minute.

"Did Manuel have any enemies?" I asked.

"Of course not."

"When he last got promoted, was there anyone who wanted the job he got?"

She shook her head. "It was a new job. Created out of the blue just for him after they got the big grant. And Manuel wrote the grant application. It's possible that someone else would be envious, but they wouldn't feel cheated."

"Did Manuel have any disagreements with anyone?"

"No. He got along with everyone."

I thought about the familiarity of what Lucy was saying. Her words about Manuel were a repeat of Joe's words about Rell.

"Was Manuel a smoker?" I asked.

Lucy scrunched up her face as if the question were ridiculous. "No. Why do you ask?"

"There was an empty pack of cigarettes in his car."

"That's not possible. It must be a mistake."

"I was there when they pulled the wreckage up the mountain. I'm the one who first saw the cigarette pack. It was on the floor."

Lucy was shaking her head.

"Maybe someone dropped it into his car at an earlier date," I said. "Where are these pollution monitors that Manuel used?"

"In the woods. They are mounted in places where people wouldn't normally see them."

"What if Manuel found a pack of cigarettes near one of his monitors. He would pick it up, right? He wouldn't leave it in the woods."

"True, but he wouldn't toss it in his car. He would put it in his pocket. That's what he did with car trash. He didn't like a trash container in his car. Too messy. He was very neat."

"Besides his work and family, what else did Manuel do with his time?"

"Our girls were his life. Between them and his job, he had little time left."

"What did he do with his little time?"

"He skied a little. He hiked. And he golfed. He was a very good golfer. Joe Rorvik could tell you. Manuel golfed with Joe sometimes. As you know, they were good friends. Sometimes they ate lunch together."

"Anything else?"

"Not really. His job had him involved in a few different groups. He served on several boards. I asked him not to because they take up time he could spend doing more fun things. But he said he had to because of his work. It was a way for him to test-drive his social environmental principles."

"What are those?"

"He's been developing some new ideas about how to change people's attitudes about pollution and development. It goes back to his masters thesis on social environmentalism."

I remembered Joe mentioning it.

"Which boards was Manuel on?"

"Ski and golf. We had a joke. Everything in life outside of work came down to skiing and golfing. Of course, hiking was important to Manuel, but there are no hiking boards. It didn't matter whether the subject was helping lake clarity or going out to have fun. The answer was always ski and golf. So let me think, the main board was for the local race team foundation. Raising money and such. Then there was the ski resort development board. And there was the one about golfing and water quality impacts. There's a fourth, but it escapes me for the moment."

"Did you ever visit any of those meetings?"

"Oh, no. You must know that they are the most boring things on earth. Even Manuel thought so."

"Did Manuel ever talk about friction on any of these boards?"

"No. The thing to know about Manuel is that he got along with everyone. And if ever there was a problem with bruised egos, Manuel was the one who smoothed things out."

I thanked Lucy, told her that I'd be in touch.

SIXTEEN

From Lucy Romero's house in the Keys, I drove down Tahoe Keys Blvd, took a left on Lake Tahoe Blvd, and drove toward Stateline.

Joe Rorvik had told me that Rell first met Simone Bonnaire at a breakfast café on the southwest end of town. Then, when boyfriend Ned forced her to quit, Simone found a new job waiting tables in one of the hotel cafés.

I cruised the big hotel parking lots, hoping that Simone was working. There were lots of cars, tourists in town to ski. I wondered where anyone would park when the massive holiday crush of tourists arrived.

Employees are usually told to park in the far lots to leave the closer spots for customers. I found Simone's old Corolla at the rear of the lot behind Harrah's, parked under some big Jeffrey pine trees. Several pine cones were scattered on the icy pavement around her car. Some locals avoid parking under the trees because the big cones will put a serious dent in your vehicle. But it wouldn't matter to Simone's tattered Toyota. It already had several pine cone dents.

I parked nearby. It was noon.

Simone came out at 2:10 p.m. I got out and met her as she approached her car.

"Hi, Simone. I'm sorry if my presence yesterday caused you stress."

Simone looked shocked and worried as she realized who I was. She looked around, searching the parking lot for danger signs. She did a double take, then stared at a treed area at the edge of the parking lot.

She crouched, looked both ways, then ran around the far side of her car as Ned came running from the trees.

I stepped forward to intercept him. I thought of letting Spot out of the Jeep, but I worried that Ned might have a gun.

"That's right, Mr. Detective!" he yelled as he got close. "I was staking you out just like you were staking Simone out."

He carried a large pipe wrench, and threaded onto his belt was a leather knife holster with five throwing knives.

Ned stopped ten feet from me, the wrench out and waving, ready to cut my head off. The man was panting from his run and his adrenaline, but he looked in good shape with hard muscles layered over harder muscles. His run didn't slow him down. He feinted right and left, then did something I didn't expect. He sprinted a wide arc, went around the Corolla behind me and grabbed Simone. She screamed.

He held her with one hand and brandished the wrench with the other. He was giving me my opening to engage. But he might kill one or both of us if I attempted to intervene.

He yelled at Simone, "I told you, bitch! I told you not to talk to him! I told you why. But you didn't listen. You never listen. You're going to pay the price as soon as I'm finished with this jerk."

Simone's terror was complete. She twisted in his grip, but he held her tight.

Ned advanced on me, dragging Simone, his wrench held high. He telegraphed a deadly earnestness as if he wanted to kill me, as if he needed to kill me.

I didn't know how to play it. A strong man with good coordination is unlikely to miss with a metal club. My best and most reasonable choice was to keep my distance and hope any witnesses were summoning the cops. But Ned shifted his arm around Simone's neck. She began choking.

I bent a little at the waist like a shortstop ready for the pitch. There was no easy way to miss a club swipe, even when it is wielded by a man holding a woman. The best I could do was try to misdirect him and dodge the result. Maybe I could get him to make a stupid move.

He came toward me. Simone was gagging, choking, desperately trying to dig her fingernails into Ned's arm. Her eyes were beginning to lose their focus. I backed up. Saw a Jeffrey pine cone to my side. The cone was fresh and heavy with resin, maybe a pound. At eight or nine inches in length, it was too big to throw easily or accurately. But it was all I had.

I ducked and spun, grabbed the pine cone, ran a circle around the man.

"Hey, Neddy Teddy! You get your kicks beating up Simone? Hitting a little woman makes you feel like a big man, right?" I wanted to throw the cone, but Simone, trapped in front of him by his necklock, was a bigger target than he was behind her.

Ned looked psychotic when I called him Neddy Teddy. His eyeballs appeared to shake. He lurched forward, dragging Simone. He took a hard, awkward swipe with the wrench. I sprinted away before he could connect. I did a quick stop and spun. He was twenty feet from me, bent forward, swinging the wrench back and forth the way I imagined the cave men swung a club in front of an advancing pack of hyenas. His face was purple with rage. Simone's face was blue from lack of oxygen. I saw an opportunity that might work or might get Simone or me killed.

I took a three-step sprint directly toward him, winding up with the cone. I was close enough that he could easily take a step toward me and cut me in two with the wrench. But he was startled, hesitating at my bold move. He turned so that his body was a bit sideways to me. For the first time, he presented a bigger target than Simone.

I let go with the cone. If it hit Simone, it was heavy enough that it could kill her if it struck her head or throat. But I focused on Ned.

He made a sudden ducking motion.

The cone caught him behind his ear. He jerked, a bit stunned, then turned, anger radiating from him like a burst of fire. His eyes widened at my charge.

I kept up my forward momentum, plunging forward, and hit him on the shoulder as I grabbed the wrench from him.

The blow made him loosen his grip on Simone. She pulled away, gasping for breath. She staggered, then broke into a run.

I tossed the wrench far across the parking lot.

Ned's hand went to his throwing knife holster. But he must have been too tempted by his rage and my proximity. He took three running steps toward me, then leaped as if to tackle me.

It was the strange, irrational move of a brawler who'd never had any professional fight training.

I flashed on a memory from decades before when a sergeant who knew some judo taught moves to us rookies.

"If you deal with an enraged thug," he said, "you will sometimes get some amazing opportunities." He then proceeded to teach us the clown toss, so named because circus clowns do it for laughs.

The goal is to grab a charging attacker by the front of his shirt, then drop down onto your butt pulling him with you. Using his momentum, you roll backward as you raise your knees and get your feet into the attacker's gut. Then it is a simple matter of kicking out hard as you continue pulling him over your head. With some practice and a lot of luck, the attacker is launched through the air like a clown.

My grip on Ned's jacket wasn't good, and when I dropped to my butt, I hit at an angle, sending shocking pain up through my back. But I was able to get my shoes up against his hard, six-pack stomach, and I kicked out hard as I continued my backward roll.

My body was a little turned, and Ned didn't come off my feet in a straight line. But the less-than-perfect angle of launch was more than made up for by my lengthy legs.

I kicked up hard.

Ned went into the air on a rising arc, his trajectory impressive in both its height and length. He did a slow flip over his head as if to land flat on his back. But because of my angled launch, he also performed a half twist so that his front side faced the ground.

He hit in a feet-first belly flop. Although he must have been disoriented, he got his arms most of the way out in front of him to cushion the fall like the down-motion in a pushup. Nevertheless, his chin slammed into the pavement, his head bouncing a little. Then he was still.

I pushed up, electric pain shooting down my left leg. I did a rotating stretch, trying to realign my back and hip bones. When the pain lessened a bit, I hobbled over to where Ned lay, still breathing, but unmoving.

I grabbed his belt and rolled him over onto his back. He groaned but made no resistance. His chin was badly scraped and bleeding. I knew that his jaw could be broken, but I didn't care.

He was wheezing the tiny breaths of an unconscious person whose wind had been knocked out from a blow to the solar plexus.

I unbuckled Ned's belt and pulled it off. The knife holster came loose, and I tossed it and the belt a good distance away, out of his reach.

It took only a moment to pat him down, checking for other weapons. There was nothing but the usual keys and wallet, which I left in place. I took off his shoes, then unsnapped the front of his pants, pulled down his zipper fly, and jerked his pants down. With another jerk, they came off his feet. I tied his shoes together by the laces, then tossed them and his pants up toward the lowest branches of one of the smaller Jeffrey pines. The shoes stayed but the pants came back down. They stayed up on the second toss, his keys still inside the pockets.

A groan came from behind. I turned. Ned was trying to move but without much success. He hissed at me.

"You're a dead man, McKenna."

I grabbed one of his arms and pulled until he flopped back onto his stomach, his other arm tucked underneath him. Then I squatted down, putting my knee and shinbone across the back of his neck. I gave it some weight, grinding his bloodied face down into the asphalt.

Ned tried to scream, but the sound came out garbled.

I leaned over and whispered in his ear.

"You hit Simone again, you're the dead man."

I stood up and walked back to pick up his belt and knives.

I turned to scan the parking lot.

Simone was nowhere to be seen. Nor was her Toyota.

I could call the police, but there were no witnesses other than Simone. In fear for her life, she would refuse to testify against Ned, and instead, she would dispute my account of Ned's attack.

SEVENTEEN

Spot sniffed me all over when I got back in the car.

"Unusual odor, huh, Spot? That's what a homicidal idiot smells like."

I was stiff and sore, but I thought I could still be productive. I drove to Ned and Simone's house to see if she was there, but her Toyota was gone. So I headed back up to Angora Highlands, to try Michael Paul's house once again.

His Porsche SUV and Range Rover were in the drive, so I parked in the street.

He answered the bell so fast, he must have been on his way out. I knew it was Michael because he was wearing shorts and flipflops and a sleeveless shirt. He had a pair of sunglasses on the back of his head, the bows coming forward through thick hair that came down over his ears. Except for his hands, every inch of visible skin from his shoulders down was tattooed. The current weather was cold enough to freeze him to death in 30 minutes if his car should break down. But why pay attention to winter weather when you have body art to show the world?

I thought I'd try an approach that assumed that Rell Rorvik's fall was no accident.

"Hi, I'm Detective Owen McKenna, investigating the assault on your neighbor Mrs. Rorvik. Are you Mr. Paul?"

"Yeah. Good to meet you," he said in a voice so raspy that it made me want to clear my own throat. He shook my hand. "Hey, man, that whole fall-off-the-deck thing was terrible. I couldn't believe it when I heard it. Now you're saying it was an assault, not an accident? That just blows my mind. Do you have a suspect? I'd like to take my shot at him."

"May I come in and ask you some questions?"

"Sure, man. I was just heading out to go pick up my dinner date. She wants to come back here for chicken stir fry, but my cellar is totally set up with beef vintages. So I need a few minutes to get the right wine. But I can chill for a bit." He lifted his arm to look at his watch, a huge techy-looking slab of metal that he wore on the inside of his wrist. "I could probably do ten minutes of Q and A. Come on in." He turned and gestured for me to walk past him.

I stepped into a wide entryway, walking slow to favor my pinched nerves, wondering what kind of pad such a hip, tatted-up, beach dude wannabe would have in Tahoe.

His house was done up in Bachelor Black. Black leather furniture, giant black TV, black surround-sound speakers. The walls were gray in both the living room and kitchen. The kitchen appliances were stainless steel to match the gray walls, and the counters were black granite. The only warmth came from the oak floors, but they were mostly covered by expensive black rugs.

"Have a seat wherever you like," Michael said.

I walked toward an articulated chrome-and-black-leather chair that probably was the tech version of a recliner. With arcing, silvery tubes, the chair looked part robot. I decided that I shouldn't submit my sore back to such a contraption, and I sat on a rounded, black hassock, thinking that it was unlikely to fold up on me.

Michael sat on a couch and took another look at his watch.

"Sergeant Bains told me that you were out of town the day of Mrs. Rorvik's fall."

"Right," Paul said absently. "I was in the Bay Area. I keep a place in Mountain View. When the weather here sucks for back-country turns, I hang in the valley. It's good to nose around, see what's going down."

"You mean, Silicon Valley."

"Right on, man. SOMA, too. There's a new world being made in the whole South-of-Market area in The City. The best VC opportunities are found by watching the kids."

"VC?" I said, thinking that this was a kid referring to even younger kids.

"Venture Capital. We go where the kids go. Be there when they hatch a new golden egg. The first adult on the scene can make real bank by just being there, answering questions, providing the capital. Young brains are where the ideas grow. And for the near future, the kids are hanging in SOMA." He looked at his watch again. Maybe it was a teleprompter.

"How long have you known the Rorviks?" I asked.

It was like jerking him out of a dream. "Oh, awhile, I guess. Three years? Maybe more."

"Have you spoken to Mrs. Rorvik much?"

"Look, Owen, you know what they're like, right?"

"The Rorviks? Not really. I've met Mr. Rorvik. I haven't met Mrs. Rorvik. I'd like you to fill me in."

"Well, ol' lady Rorvik is sweet. She's into birds, and all I know about birds is they chirp and they fly and they make a hell of a mess up under my eaves. Anyway, it's not like there's much I could talk to her about. We're cordial. We say hello and goodbye. That's about it. It's different with Mr. Rorvik. He's a world builder like me. He built an impressive company same as me. Sold it like me, too. We talk shop, business, the markets, trends, government interference. He's actually quite philosophical, which is good for me because I'm probably too focused on making a buck. He connects me to larger issues."

"What was your business?"

"I wrote software for investment companies. It's boring, to tell the truth. But it was a market-driven and sales-driven venture from point A. So I never stressed about it not being fun."

"I'm sorry, I think I'm missing something," I said.

"Look at it this way. Typically, a guy writing an app, or even a team working on a big project, will think up something that could be innovative or sometimes even fun. They produce the app, it works great, but then they realize that there are very few potential customers for it. Or there are lots of customers, but they don't have money to spend on such a program. I took the other approach. First find a bunch of customers who have a lot of money and figure out what they want to buy."

Michael gave me a big grin. He was obviously proud of his business savvy.

"It worked," I said.

"You bet. I looked at banks and investment houses and found that they generally presented their proposals to customers in a way that frankly looked bad and was hard to understand. So I designed a pretty package and added some effective sales features. It sold very well at a good price. I was already making good money when I approached American Bank Central. They didn't just want the software, they wanted my whole company. They offered me seventeen million. I would have been a fool to turn that down."

"Joe Rorvik was impressed. He said you retired at a seriously-young age."

"Well, I'm not that young. And I'm not really retired. I've just shifted to VC work. It would be fun to find the next Apple or Google, huh?" He grinned again.

"Yeah," I said.

"My dad always said that the world is created by dreamers and that we have a responsibility to dream up a better future. I kind of worry that I haven't made anything better in the world. But now that I have some capital, maybe I can be more like what my dad talked about."

"Back to the Rorviks, if I may," I said.

"Of course. I didn't mean to take over the conversation."

"Did you ever hear anything or witness anything that would suggest why someone might toss Mrs. Rorvik off her deck?"

"God, no. When Joe first said that, I thought, what would be the point? Who would benefit? Then the cops asked me a bunch of questions. So I started to think that maybe they had some kind of evidence. Then again, maybe it's just my tats."

"You think you get questioned because of your tattoos?"

"Not think. Know. If I put on long sleeves and pants, cops never notice me. If I go out in shorts and sandals and muscle shirt, I get looked at with scowls. I even get pulled over by cops."

I stood up and handed him my card. "If you think of anything, please call. I hope I haven't delayed your date."

Michael shook his head, looked again at the watch so massive that checking the time was exercise, and showed me out.

I drove down the block to Joe's house.

"Can you tell me a little more about Manuel?" I asked after Spot and I were inside and sitting down. "What you talked about? What kind of person he was?"

Joe took a moment. "The best way to describe Manuel is to say that he is virtuous. Was virtuous. God, it will be an adjustment for me to think of him in the past tense." Joe paused. "Maybe virtue is an old-fashioned concept. Either way, Manuel might be the most virtuous person I know. In fact, I think he is the only person I know who looks at every decision as a choice where the task is to identify the best choice and to always make that choice. Manuel says that to make the wrong choice as a result of misinformation is ignorant, but to make the wrong choice as a result of selfish desire is immoral. His words have stayed with me ever since he said them."

"Sounds like he had high standards."

"The highest." Joe pet Spot, thinking, remembering. "Manuel sometimes talked to me about the decisions that a father has to make. Manuel described tricky situations such as when to protect a daughter from the world and when to allow her those experiences that teach her about responsible independence. Manuel was thoughtful and caring."

"You were probably a mentor for him."

"He asked for my advice at times, but I always thought that my judgment wasn't sufficient. At his young age, Manuel had always thought through any subject far more than I had. In fact, the only subject where I could offer him any expertise was in the world of sports and sports equipment."

"That seems an unlikely area for an environmental scientist to have questions. Were his daughters into ski racing?"

"His daughters ski, of course, just like most young people in Tahoe. But they weren't racers. Manuel's interest in my sports advice was about the Steven's Peak Resort proposal."

"What's that? I haven't heard of it."

"You haven't?" Joe sounded surprised. "You must know the mountain."

"Isn't that down Christmas Valley?"

"Yeah. The huge mountain at the end. If you're leaving Tahoe by way of Echo Summit, you stare right at it as you drive up the cliff edge. An investment group out of San Francisco, RKS Properties, has plans to develop it into a resort. Of course, the Tahoe Regional Planning Agency and the Forest Service have to approve it. And there are already three lawsuits trying to stop the process, one of which UC Davis is connected to. Which means that Manuel was involved in some fashion. But this development group has some legal rights to the land as well as a great deal of money to defend those rights, so the assumption of some people that the resort won't go through is premature."

"Manuel came to you for advice on it?"

"Yeah. He found out that I sit on the Steven's Peak Resort Commission, so he wanted to pick my brain a little."

"What does the commission do?"

"The Forest Service decided to put together a commission to look at all of the information about the proposed resort and make a recommendation. There are nine of us representing a wide range of viewpoints. Our decision will be a non-binding recommendation, but the Forest Service also has made it clear that they are giving great weight to what we decide."

"I've read that this country has too many rules for a new ski resort to be built. Is that not true?"

"No, it's not. There have been several new resorts in the last two decades, and there is an entire law written to outline and shape the process. It's called The National Forest Ski Area Permit Act of Nineteen Eighty-six. The main constraint on resort development isn't environmental concerns, as everyone seems to think, but simply the belief in the investment community that new ski resorts won't produce enough business to make the investment pay off. The numbers of skiers and riders is not expanding. So a new resort has an extremely difficult time bringing in enough business. In many ways, it's a parallel to golf course development. A static customer base means that for any new development to survive, it has to take customers away from existing venues."

"It sounds like the developers believe differently?"

"Actually, everybody involved believes differently, both those for and those against the idea."

"Why?"

"There are several reasons. They have plans to run large, free introduction-to-skiing seminars in the Bay Area, which will produce new ski customers. And, no doubt, investors also think that the Stevens Peak Resort will draw many skiers away from other existing resorts. Another reason is the mountain. It's huge. It has massive terrain for every kind of skiing. Treeless bowls and cirques, steep chutes, meadows and glades, and gentle, treed slopes. The acreage available alone would make it one of the biggest resorts in the country. And the best slopes face north and northeast, so the snow quality wouldn't be degraded by sun exposure. The area is also easy to access. There's already a highway right to the base. Like all Tahoe resorts, Stevens Peak Resort would be easy to get to for ten million Bay Area and Sacramento-area people. Outside of other Tahoe resorts, no other top areas in the country have population centers that big and close. Another draw is that the mountain gets massive snowfall just like all of the other areas on the Sierra Crest. Last, there is a large flat area that is perfect for putting up base operations, hotels, restaurants, parking, etc."

"Really?" I said. "I think of Christmas Valley as being quite narrow at the end."

"It is. But what gets overlooked is multiple meadow areas to the south of Christmas Valley, just five hundred feet up from the valley floor along the Upper Truckee River. It's not as large as the floor of Squaw Valley, but it's close. It would be easy to put a wide road up in there to access the entire resort."

"Isn't that whole area protected?"

"That's what everyone thinks," Joe said. "It's called the Meiss Meadows Roadless Area, and it's being promoted for Wilderness designation by Congress. But when the last ranchers moved their cattle out, and their old leases were canceled, there turned out to be some gray area in the legal wording. RKS Properties says they have purchased the rights to those canceled leases. I don't know the details. I just know that they're throwing a lot of legal firepower at it. If they prevail, and if they fulfill the other requirements set out in the Ski Area Permit Act, we're going to have another ski resort whether people want it or not. Of course, it is obvious that skiers and riders will want it. It's a dream mountain."

"You sound like a proponent."

"In general if not specifically. I'm frank about my perspective. I believe that a good ski mountain is a benefit to the country. Yes, there is an environmental price to pay, but it's relatively minor. In fact, the Upper Truckee River drainage is, by virtue of the lay of the land, the best kind of drainage to have because environmental mitigation could be installed to easily filter all of the water that would drain from the ski resort.

"In return, we would get an enormous infusion of exercise into the population, and, if it's done right, booming economics. I could show you a giant amusement park built on an ancient wetland. It's an environmental catastrophe, and its customers get no exercise at all. And from my reading, amusement parks get no scrutiny compared to ski resorts. Which is better for society? A resort that produces exercise? Or a playground that doesn't?

"If, however, I learn things that make me think that the Steven's Peak Resort is poorly designed in any way or even poorly capitalized, then I will vote for no recommendation."

"What did Manuel think about the resort?"

"He's an environmental scientist. His default position is that all development that uses land is bad until proven otherwise. And his standards of proof are nearly impossible to satisfy."

"It sounds like you and Manuel disagree about this."

"We just come from a different perspective."

"How often do you have meetings of the Steven's Peak Commission?"

"Once a month. The last one was a few days after Rell fell from the deck. Do you think this could have something to do with Rell?"

"I don't know. How does she feel about the resort proposal?"

"She's against it. She thinks we have enough ski areas, a point I agree with. But I don't think that's germane to whether or not the developers should be allowed to build the Stevens Peak Resort. I think it's an issue of law, of development rights. Not the personal preferences of Rell, me, or anyone else."

"So both Rell and Manuel were against. And both of them could potentially influence you."

"People may think that," Joe said. "But I pride myself on making my own decisions based on my own research and information. Do you really think that someone might try to kill Rell and Manuel to prevent them from influencing me?!"

"I don't know. But Manuel's wife Lucy said the same thing that you did. She can't believe Manuel's death was an accident. If Manuel was murdered, there must be some reason why."

EIGHTEEN

When I was back in town and had cell reception, I dialed the number for Jillian Oleska, the event planner who had met Rell in a book club.

It rang several times, then was answered by a breathless, husky, female voice talking loud over background noise.

"Hello, this is Jillian."

I introduced myself and explained that, at Joe Rorvik's request, I was looking into Rell's fall. "I'm wondering if we can talk."

"Uh, yes, of course. Hold on a sec, will you?"

I heard clattering and voices and what sounded like someone blowing air into her phone. Then the phone went silent.

"Sorry about that," Jillian said. "I'm walking through the Fresno airport. This place is really crowded. Fresno. Who would have thought? Okay, now I'm in a quieter place. Yes, I'd like to talk to you about Rell. I've been very uncomfortable about her fall. I can't stand the idea of her lying in a hospital, in a coma. I want to visit her, but I don't want to invade Joe's space."

"He'd probably welcome it," I said. "Is there a time I could come to meet you when you're back in town?"

"Let me pull up my calendar. I'm doing an on-snow event tomorrow at Northstar, and I'm buried the next three days. Wait. Here's an idea. Why don't you meet me on the mountain during lunch? I'll be doing recon, but you can come with me, and we can talk on the chairlift."

"Tell me where you'd like to meet, and I'll be there," I said, wondering what recon was. Probably event-planner speak.

"Top of the gondola, one o'clock. My ski suit is a pink Descente with white trim, and my hat is pink."

"I'll be the tall guy in black, suit and hat. See you tomorrow."

NINETEEN

When I got home, I called Diamond at the Douglas County Sheriff's office and got his voicemail.

"Hey sarge, gimme a buzz," I said at the tone.

My phone rang five minutes later.

I told Diamond about Nedham Theodore Cavett. "Ned lives on the California side in Sierra Tract, so he's Mallory's problem in the main, but my little altercation was on the Nevada side of the state line, so he's your problem now and then."

"Sounds like instead of running away from an obvious threat, you busted him up pretty good. Almost like that vigilante justice stuff we got laws against."

"Yeah," I said. "It could probably be read that way."

"Good," Diamond said. "But don't quote me on that."

"Hey, you're just looking out to conserve precious county resources."

"Let me guess why you didn't want me to bring him in," Diamond said. "He'd get someone to bail him out, and then he'd be that much more likely to beat on the girl."

"My thought, exactly. This way he's been put on notice. Maybe he'll think twice before he grabs her again. Not that I'm confident about it. Also, he'll be in too much pain to do anything for awhile."

"He will hit her again, though," Diamond said. "Again and again. It never stops. You know that, right?"

"Yeah. But I'm hoping to come up with an idea for how to get her out of there."

"She doesn't want to go?"

"Wants to, no doubt, but is afraid to. Same old situation. You get a thought on it, let me know. In the meantime, I confiscated his weapons. Thought I should turn them in to the proper authority."

"I'm up at the lake, and my shift goes 'til midnight. You want me to stop by?"

"That'd be great."

"Proper authority," Diamond said. "Never been called that before." He hung up.

I was in the rocker, the wood stove fired up on high, when Spot lifted his head, looked at the door and thumped his tail on his bed.

"Come in," I said before Street knocked.

The door opened. Street walked in. Spot jumped up and trotted over to her, his tail on high speed. "Did you know it was me?" she said.

I nodded.

"How? I was silent."

"I have a special delectable-woman detector."

Street leaned over and hugged Spot. "I bet you're his special detector, huh, largeness?"

Spot wagged.

I was going to say something, but Street was wearing tight jeans tucked into tallish black boots, and when she bent to hug Spot, my brain went blank.

"At least Spot gets up to say hi to me," Street said.

"Sorry. But I'm in therapy for a sore back."

"Thus the heat?" she said. She looked at the wood stove, then waved her hand in front of her face as if to cool off.

"Yup."

"You take anything for pain?"

I held up my Sierra Nevada Pale Ale.

"What's wrong with your back?"

I told her about Ned Cavett the abuser and the diminutive woman named Simone Bonnaire, who bore the brunt of his abuse. "He must have been watching her. I went to the casinos to talk to Simone. He ran out and jumped me, and I responded, and it gave me a sore back. As soon as my medicine takes effect, my muscles will loosen up."

"You say you responded. Does that mean Ned has a sore back, too?"

"Probably. And a sore jaw."

"You hit him on the jaw? That can break hand bones, you know." Street's tone wasn't exactly scolding, but it wasn't far from it.

"The parking lot hit him."

Street frowned. Spot turned back toward the door. Diamond walked in. He looked at us.

"Am I interrupting?" he said.

"No," I said. "We're just discussing medical treatment breakthroughs for wounded warriors."

"Self-medicating again, are you?" Diamond stepped over to Street, gave her a kiss on the cheek, then saw the throwing knives on the little kitchen table. He walked over and pulled one out of the holster, turned it over, felt its weight and balance. "Nasty," he said as he slid the knife back into the holder.

"You can have the belt, too, if you want."

Diamond picked it up, held it around his waist. "Looks like it would fit. This Ned guy is built just like me?"

"Exactly, except he does have an extra forty pounds or so of hard beef on his frame."

Diamond made the smallest of smiles. "After I talked to you, I called Sergeant Bains over at El Dorado County. He told me Ned coulda been a contender in the movie star world but for a missing charisma gene."

"Missing charisma," I said. "My first thought."

"Keep in touch," Diamond said. He gave Spot a pat, and left with the knives.

"Did you learn anything more about Manuel?" Street asked.

I told her that Lucy didn't think his death was an accident and that her words mimicked Joe's skeptical words about both Rell and Manuel. I also explained about the proposed ski resort for Steven's Peak, as well as Joe's position on an advisory commission that the Forest Service put together to study it.

"You think that the ski resort commission could have something to do with Rell and Manuel?"

"I don't know what to think."

"What's next besides going easy on your back?" Street asked.

"I have a ski appointment tomorrow with another woman who knows Rell. An event planner named Jillian Oleska. She's got something going on at Northstar. She says she's doing recon on her lunch break, and we can talk on the chairlifts."

"Recon?"

"I'll find out tomorrow. In the meantime, I have ribeye steaks and a Bogle Petite Sirah. Can I talk you into dinner?"

"Are you okay cooking with a sore back? Your oven is down low. You'd have to bend."

"Actually, I would need to loosen it up before I start bending over to work the broiler. Maybe we start with the wine, then do a little gentle exercise. That should do the trick."

"Gentle exercise? I didn't bring any exercise clothes," Street said.

"Exactly what I was hoping for," I said.

TWENTY

The next morning when I struggled out of bed, I could barely bend to put on my socks. Street already had the coffee brewed. She didn't stay long because she had a mentoring appointment with a young female student at the Environmental Center at Sierra Nevada College in Incline Village.

"You're going to teach this girl about bugs?" I said.

"Yeah. It's so rare that a woman pursues entomology, that I feel an obligation."

We said goodbye. I was sad to see her go.

I spent some time doing stretches, trying to get my body back to pre-clown-toss condition. When I could once again bend a bit, I ate, gathered my skis and boots and poles, walked Spot, and, after telling him to be good, left.

The drive up the East Shore, through Incline, and on to Kings Beach was spectacular. There was just enough breeze to build a color-intensifying chop on the water. Waves make the lake such a deep blue that tourists have a hard time convincing their friends back home that their photos aren't Photoshopped. In the winter, the blue contrasts with the snow-capped mountains to make every glance at the landscape a postcard view.

The high temps had stayed under freezing for the last ten days – a serious cold spell by Tahoe standards – so the snow everywhere had the micro sparkles that come from individual flakes. And most nights produced another inch or three. The skiing was probably amazing.

In Kings Beach, I turned north on 267 and climbed up to Brockway Summit. Of the seven routes in and out of the Tahoe Basin, Brockway Summit is the steepest. The snow in the night meant they would have put on chain-up requirements, so the truckers along with the unfortunate tourists who'd rented two-wheel-drive cars were forced to put on chains and crawl at slow speed up the steep highway. We locals, most of whom have all-wheel-drive, were allowed to proceed without chains.

Partway down the north side of the pass, I turned off toward Northstar. It was a weekday before the holiday tourist rush had started, so the resort was uncrowded. I parked in the lower lot, walked up to the pedestrian village, bought a ticket, and got on the gondola.

The trip up to the day lodge at mid-mountain is a gentle ride, floating through the tree tops. The snow was heavy on the conifer branches. I was in a gondola cabin with a family, two parents and three boys from Orange County. They had a condo at Northstar and were familiar with the routine.

At the gondola top station, we got out. I said goodbye to my fellow passengers and pulled my skis from the gondola rack. I carried them out onto the snow, tossed them down, and clicked into my bindings. I looked around for Jillian. There were several women in pink ski suits, and a couple of them had pink hats. One stood out over by the Arrow Express Quad chairlift. She was scanning the crowd. I raised my hand to see if she would notice. She did and waved.

I pushed off with my poles and skated over to her.

"Owen McKenna," she said.

"Jillian Oleska," I replied.

"You skate well on those boards," she said.

"You put in enough hours on the slopes, even a klutz like me gets the hang of it," I said.

"Okay if we ride up here?" she asked. "Then we could catch the Comstock Express to the top of the mountain."

I nodded. I pushed with my poles, made a quick turn to face the same way as she was facing, and followed her into the lift line, sliding alongside on her left. The line moved fast. We merged with two guys coming in from our right, and we four pushed forward onto the loading ramp and were ready when the chair came up behind us. We all sat in unison as the chair moved slowly forward. At the end of the loading ramp, the chair accelerated and then locked onto the cable. Our skis separated from the snow as we lifted off into the air and glided at high speed up the mountain, our path well up in the trees, and our skis dangling 50 feet above the ground.

Jillian had a small fanny pack that she pulled around from her back to her lap. "Lunch on the go," she said. She took off her gloves, tucked them and her poles under her thigh and reached into the pack. "I have cheese and crackers and Heinekens. Want some?"

"Sure," I said. I slid my poles under my leg to free up my hands.

Jillian handed me two beers. Then she pulled out a pack of crackers and a pack of cheese. "Dig in," she said, setting them between us. "We've got a touch over three minutes before we land."

I popped the tops on the beers and handed one to her.

She took it and drank while I piled cheese on crackers and stuffed them into my mouth.

"On the phone, you said that you were here doing recon," I said as I ate. "What's that mean?"

"It's about the Stevies. I don't think it's sufficient to just send them out onto the mountain. They should know where to go, how to gauge their impact, what approach provides the most exposure. I'm doing mountain traffic studies to better assess where they should spend the majority of their time." Jillian put a cracker and piece of cheese into her mouth.

"Back up, please. What are the Stevies?"

"Oh, I thought you knew." Jillian chewed and swallowed. "Sorry. The Stevies are a concept I created for the new Steven's Peak Resort proposal. They've gotten quite a bit of press, so I stupidly assume that everybody knows about it." She drank some beer. "The whole reason that the Stevens Peak Resort people contacted me was that they wanted to seed the local resort communities with information about their development. They especially wanted skiers and boarders to know that there was going to be a new, awesome resort coming. It will take at least three years before the resort is ready for its first customers, but they want their future customers to know all about it, to be anticipating. So when they hired me for the early PR, I dreamed up the Stevies. What they are is a small army of excellent skiers and boarders. They ski and ride all of the Tahoe resorts. They wear the Stevies outfit of blue and gold, and they talk up the future of the Steven's Peak Resort. They also hand out save-the-date invites to Youtube resort-launch videos. They let people know about the website and the early options on timeshares, condos, and vacation home investment opportunities. The Steven's Peak Resort has a data assessment group that is already reporting huge early engagement."

"You mean data mining?" I said.

"Well, yeah, data mining is another way to describe it."

"You talk about this like the resort is a foregone conclusion."

Jillian ate more crackers and cheese and smiled as she chewed. "Well, I wouldn't be doing my job if I were putting out the qualifier that the resort isn't a done deal. So I approach this with a positive attitude about it coming to fruition." Jillian looked up the mountain. "Ten seconds," she said. She zipped the crackers and cheese back into her little pack and picked up her gloves and poles. I did the same.

Our chair rushed up to the offload ramp, slowed dramatically as it disengaged from the cable, and, with each of us holding our beer in one hand and our poles in the other, we skied off, along with the other two riders.

Jillian took the lead, skating, without using poles, toward the next lift while she still held her beer. I followed, impressed with her skill. She was obviously a pro.

We were in line at the Comstock Express in a few moments, and up on the lift shortly after that.

The breeze in our faces was bracingly cold as we gained elevation. But veteran skiers all appreciate colder temperatures for the way they preserve the powder snow.

Jillian once again pulled out the crackers and cheese, and we continued our lunch.

She suddenly pointed up the mountain. "Look, here come the Stevies. They work in pairs. That's Jason and Lena. This is why I'm doing recon. They should only be skiing the lift line when it is over an open trail where there are lots of skiers. But where the lift goes through the trees, like where they're catching those bumps right now, they should leave the line and head over to the open trail."

"At least a lot of chairlift riders will see them," I said as I ate.

"Yeah, but no one will be able to talk to them. And chairlift riders rarely twist around on the chair because of the risk of falling off, so they won't see the Steven's Peak logo on the back of the jackets."

I nodded. We ate and drank as Jason and Lena got closer. As always, when good skiers ski the lift line, the chairlift riders are riveted. It is a close-up view unlike any other. First, you see them from below as they drop down the mountain above you. Then, you rush up above them as they race past and plummet below you.

Jason and Lena looked like professional models who were also expert skiers, their upper bodies flowing smoothly while their legs pumped, absorbing moguls, making little jumps, alternating between quick, skidded, windshield-wiper turns and longer, carved turns. As they got closer, their faces came into view. With tousled golden hair and happy, white-teeth smiles, they were a picture of beautiful people having a great time cruising the mountain. Jason was in the lead, showing off, but no doubt aware that Lena was close behind and matching him turn for showy turn. We could hear them breathing hard as we watched their infectious grins.

It was clear that Jillian's concept was genius. If these young people had even a fraction of the charisma while talking that they displayed while dancing down the slopes, it would be a powerful, subliminal endorsement of the Steven's Peak Resort. People would instinctively want to go and check out whatever resort gave birth to these perfect-looking ski ambassadors.

"Nice moves," I said as they flew past us.

"All Stevies candidates have to apply as if for any other job. If they get through the interview cut, then they have to do an extensive onslope audition. They have to ski or ride by us on the bunny slope, on the steep moguls, and in deep powder. We've since learned that a majority of those who get chosen to be Stevies have professional ski or boarding backgrounds. Many have worked as instructors at major areas across the West. Many have race backgrounds from the time they were little kids. Some were freestyle competitors. We even have two ex-Olympians. An even dozen Stevies have endorsement contracts from ski and clothing manufacturers. And one of those clothing companies designed and produces the Stevies uniform. It's actually kind of thrilling to see Stevies on the slopes and hear people call out their names as they recognize them from race posters and ski magazine ads."

"How did you get these kids to sign on as Stevies when some of them are already making a good living as professional skiers?"

"Two things. One, we pay them a ridiculously high fee to simply ski and be ambassadors for the coming resort. Believe me, it was a battle to get the development bean counters to go along with it. But I knew what would happen. As soon as the word started getting out in the professional skier community that these positions were high-paid, everyone began to think that the job was the coolest thing going. The spin-off from that was huge. Young professional skiers tend to come from families who introduced them to skiing and boarding at a young age. Those families are heavily invested in snow sports, both psychologically and financially. The people who own the vacation homes and businesses at the major resorts across the country tend to be connected to each other. They are also the investors in the resorts. So once you create the buzz, large numbers of people in that community are practically lined up, ready to invest in the next big resort."

Jillian drank the last of her beer, and put the can back in her pack. I took my last swallow, and she reached for my can as well.

"I'm not privy to the financial side of the Stevens Peak Resort," she said, "but I've heard some things here and there, especially from one of the Stevies' fathers. It sounds like people with money want in. They want to buy condos and build ski-in, ski-out vacation homes. And the people with a lot of money want in on the development end. RKS is a private equity group, and they don't release their numbers. But this one father – who is some kind of big shot in Hollywood – made it sound like RKS isn't going to have to put up much money to build this monster resort. The package looks so good that investors are lining up."

The offload ramp at the top of the mountain was approaching. Jillian and I pulled our poles out from under our legs and were ready as the chair slowed. We skied off. I followed and stopped at the edge of a clearing where Jillian had stopped.

"Should I just follow you?" I said.

"If you can," Jillian said with a grin. Then, "That was a joke.

I'm sure you'll be waiting for me at the bottom."

"Which run do you want to take?"

"This morning I cruised the front side of the mountain and had my meeting. So I can free-ski for the rest of the day. I'd like to do the backside this afternoon. It's mostly Black Diamond, though. There's even a section I like that approaches Double Black Diamond. Are you okay with the steeps?"

"I'll give it my best," I said.

"Great. Let's start with Burnout. It's usually good for turning my thighs into rubber."

I nodded. "I'm curious what your mission is and if I can be of help."

"Actually, you can. As you ski, think about the Stevies and how other skiers will see them. What I want is to find the terrain with the most exposure where the greatest number of other skiers and riders will see them. Of course, that suggests that the Blue Square intermediate runs on the front of the mountain are where to go for an audience because that is where the greatest number of people are.

"But I also want the kind of challenging terrain where the Stevies can really show their stuff. It's a display, a performance, and Black Diamond runs are the best for that. But if they're mostly deserted, then they do us no good.

"So keep your eye out for where the skiers are and where the challenging slopes are. If we can find the best intersection of those two concepts, then we have Stevie heaven." Jillian winked at me, reached up to pull her goggles over her eyes, and pushed off with her poles.

I followed.

I'm a decent skier, somewhat expert but not great. I never bomb the slope but usually keep some pretty good speed onboard unless the moguls are big. I thought I'd have no trouble keeping up. But Jillian dropped down Burnout like a cannonball. I stopped carving big turns and took the fall line, making only slight turns in my effort to speed up. By minimizing how much I used my edges, my speed increased until I was up near my limit in just five seconds. Yet Jillian's distance from me grew fast.

She wanted me to observe the slope for both challenges and

other ski traffic to judge what size audience any given skier would have. But I had all I could handle just concentrating on my line. I was going fast enough that if I caught an edge, I would make a spectacular fall.

I went through a transition that compressed me down, making my thighs burn. Then came a lip. I couldn't see what was below. I tried to pre-jump it to minimize how much it would toss me into the air, but I misjudged and came down too early, my skis slamming onto the top side of the lip. It nearly crushed me, but I managed to keep my balance. The lip sent me airborne. I landed going fast. Too fast. There was a smooth patch where I thought I could turn. I edged hard to the left, slowing dramatically, then found a perfect, low mogul and used its lift to put me into a right turn, carving through some junk snow. When I came to an open area, I did a hard, skidding stop and came to rest at the edge of the trail.

My lungs were heaving, my heart protesting the sudden extreme exercise.

As Jillian skied down below me, her pink cap bobbed and danced and then disappeared as she went around a curve in the trail.

When I caught my breath, I resumed my descent, going slower this time, threading my way through moguls, picking my line with care.

When I finally got to the bottom, Jillian was waiting. She seemed to examine my suit, no doubt looking for, but not finding, snow patches that would reveal a fall and explain my delay.

"How'd it go?" she asked.

"Great," I said, trying to muster enthusiasm. "But I found out that there is no point in trying to keep up with you. You're amazing. So 'fess up. Where'd you get your chops?"

She smiled. "I grew up in Colorado. We skied nearly every weekend in the winter. I tried racing here and there. Not enough to get good, but enough to get hooked. In high school, I read an article that said that Sierra Nevada College was the number one ski racing school in the country. A dozen Tahoe resorts within an hour's drive. Diamond Peak was five minutes from campus, Mt. Rose fifteen minutes, and this one, Northstar, twenty. So

I came west for school and eventually won a couple of NCAA championships. But that was as far as my racing career got. Now I just ski for fun. I like to take it easy and enjoy the scenery."

"Taking it easy?" I said. "That was my last thought as you shot down the mountain and disappeared into the mist your skis kicked up."

"So what do you think? See any good spots to direct the Stevies?"

"Any place but Burnout," I said.

"Then how 'bout we try Polaris?"

"Sure." As I said it, I knew that it would be every bit as difficult as Burnout.

Jillian skied over to the Backside Express. I followed. We were on the chair a minute later.

A few runs later, my thighs began to get shaky. Following Jillian was one of the more difficult things I'd done in years. I found myself stopping more often and watching her go, taking no rests. She skied with an economy that revealed her race background. Her turns were carved, not skidded. She had no wasted moves. She was not a showy skier like the Stevies. Every move Jillian made led to speed.

Once, as I stood at the edge of a trail, trying to catch my breath, I noticed another skier behind her and to the side. He wore a white suit and had a white knit cap. When he was away from the trees, he blended into the snow and became hard to see. He was obviously a very good skier, not as clean of line as Jillian, but able to ski hard and fast. He wasn't a showy skier, but he caught my eye because I realized that I'd seen him near Jillian on the other trails.

I pushed off and tried to ski fast. When I got to the bottom of the run, Jillian was waiting as before, but the man in white was already on the chairlift, well up the mountain. I looked up to see if his face was visible, but he was too far up into the trees and facing upslope, away from me.

Jillian and I got on the lift and rode in silence. When we got to the top, the man was gone.

Two runs later, came a repeat experience. I was catching my breath, watching Jillian disappear down a mogul field, when I saw the same man. He appeared at the side of the trail, skiing fast, staying behind Jillian and nearly matching her moves.

Sometimes, an aspiring skier will choose a better skier and follow that person down the mountain as a learning device. If the following skier doesn't get too far out of their control zone, it can be very instructive to try to keep up and match the moves of the lead skier.

It seemed like the man in white had chosen Jillian. It was obvious that she was one of the best skiers on the mountain.

Yet something about his actions seemed different. He didn't telegraph student learning from the master. He telegraphed wolf chasing prey, gauging its speed, its stamina, its strength.

When I got to the bottom, he was gone. I decided that I was over-reacting to something that goes on constantly at every ski resort, so I didn't say anything about it to Jillian. I didn't want to alarm her.

We skied the rest of the afternoon, taking in most of Northstar's back side and finished the day with a beer in front of an outdoor fire at the pedestrian village.

"Where else do the Stevies do their thing?" I asked when I had my boots off and my stockinged feet up near the flames.

"All of the major destination resorts. Sugar Bowl, Squaw, Alpine, Diamond Peak, Mt. Rose, Northstar, Homewood, Heavenly, Sierra, Kirkwood. It's been so successful that we're considering putting teams out at the major Colorado areas."

"They ski every day, these Stevies?"

Jillian nodded, obviously proud. "Yeah, we have eighteen teams of two. Two main teams for each of the areas. They rotate so that every major area has seven-day-a-week coverage. Because Squaw is bigger than most of the other areas, we have two extra teams there. Heavenly gets even greater treatment because of its huge size and because it's close to Steven's Peak. We know that many of the future customers of Steven's Peak are currently skiing at Heavenly. So we have two main teams on the California side, one for the lower mountain and one for the upper mountain. Another two teams cover the upper and lower mountain on the Nevada side. Teams five and six rotate in to handle the sixth and seventh days of the week."

"Impressive," I said. "Sounds like a good plan."

We watched the people ice skating on the rink at the center of the plaza.

"I wanted to ask you something about Rell Rorvik," I said, changing the subject.

"Yes, of course! That's why we met in the first place! How is she doing?"

"Not well. I contacted you because Rell's husband Joe isn't sure that her fall was an accident."

Jillian's face darkened. "You mean to say that someone made her fall off the deck?! My God! That is a horrible idea! I can't believe that someone would push Rell!"

"It's not proven, yet. I'm sorry to be the one to tell you about it."

"I was so sad about her fall," Jillian said. "So sad. And now... to hear that it might not be an accidental fall, that makes it so much worse."

"How well did you know Rell?"

"Well enough that we felt very comfortable with one another. But not well enough that we ever told each other secrets."

"She didn't confide in you?"

Jillian shook her head. "But I sort of confided in her. She was very easy to talk to. Rell had a gift. She made you feel like you could say anything."

"Did you confide anything that could have distressed her?"

"No nothing like that. I can't even remember what I said. But I talked to her a little bit about some problems I've dealt with over the years."

"Can I ask what kind of problems?"

"Just personal stuff. Family stuff. Relationship stuff."

"I think Joe said that you and Rell met at a book club?"

"Yes. It was an on-again, off-again group. One of the regular women apparently knew of Rell and invited her. Another member did the same with me. Rell and I got along very well. But both of us only went to one more book club meeting. It wasn't very organized, and both Rell and I are organized and focused. Neither of us has time for chit-chat over snacks."

"Did you ever see her or talk on the phone after you left the book club?"

"Yes to both. She called me one day to catch up, as she called it. Then she asked me if I wanted to go hiking. I said yes. So we met at a trailhead near the Desolation Wilderness and hiked up to a couple of the lakes. There were some other people along. It was a good hiking group."

"Did any of the others make you uncomfortable? Or did anything happen or get said that would suggest that Rell might have disagreements with anyone?"

Jillian paused, then shook her head.

"Do you know the names of the other people in the hiking group?"

"No. It wasn't like that. We were all just hikers. It wasn't about us, it was about the mountains."

I got out my card and handed it to her.

"Will you call me if you think of anything that could pertain to this?"

She nodded.

We finished our beers. "Time for me to go home and rest my sore muscles," I said.

"Me too," Jill said. "Maybe we can ski together again sometime. Maybe do some back-country descents."

"That would be fun."

"By the way," she said, "when I said that I was just cruising that first run? I was kidding. Truth is, I did push it a little. I wanted to see how you would handle it."

"Did I pass?"

"Yeah. Lots of guys make excuses if they can't keep up with a girl. It's pathetic. But you were honest. I like that in a man."

"I'll remember that when I can't get out of bed tomorrow morning."

TWENTY-ONE

Spot was excited to see me when I got home. As always when I've been gone, he pushed his nose hard into my clothes, sucking air through the fabric, teasing out hints of where I'd been and what I'd been doing. I let him outside, and I stood in the open doorway for a moment as he raced around. Spot seemed puzzled when I went back inside, chunked some food into his bowl, then popped an aspirin, sat down in the rocker with a beer, and barely moved.

I called Street and told her about my day. Then I finished my beer and went to bed without eating. Wrestling with Ned Cavett was hard on a body. Trying to ski with Jillian was worse.

When I heard Spot's nails click on the floor, I rolled over and saw him standing in the dark, staring at me, wagging his tail. It was his come-and-give-me-some-attention posture. The red numbers on the clock said 7:30 p.m., the normal hour for a long pre-dinner walk and snowball fetch.

"Sorry, largeness. I'm beat. See you in the morning."

I went to sleep.

The clock said 7:30 a.m. when Spot woke me up by sticking his cold, wet nose in my face. It took me a minute to realize that it was exactly twelve hours later.

He was standing in the same place, wagging as before.

"You been there all night?" I realized that he was thinking the exact same thing. "Okay," I said.

My leg and back muscles were so sore from skiing that I was barely able to move. I did some slow stretches, made coffee, played with Spot in the snow, fed us both breakfast, and was about to call Street when the phone rang. It was Diamond.

"The Rorviks have a neighbor named Dwight Frankman."

"Yeah, I've met him," I said. "What's up, Sergeant?"

"About an hour ago, he was in a head-on collision with a tree. He's alive but a little confused. Says someone ran him off the road. He thinks it was on purpose, but he's a little paranoid, if you ask me. They just carted him off to the hospital."

"Where'd it happen?" I asked.

"On the highway near Spooner Summit. His Chevy Tahoe went off the road, slid down the snowy bank, and did a face plant on a Jeffrey Pine. The pine is okay. The Chevy is pretty banged up. Airbag deployed. We might not have found him until spring, but for the kid happened to have a flare gun."

"Flare gun," I repeated.

"Sí. He fired several rounds until a lady going by noticed and called it in. Dangerous stuff, those flares. Burn at three thousand degrees for eight or ten seconds. If they land on something flammable, they'll start a fire fast. But maybe they saved this kid's life. He couldn't get up the steep slope in all the snow. Anyway, after the whole Manuel Romero thing, driving off the mountain at Emerald Bay, I thought you'd want to know."

"Thanks," I said, again trying to wake up, trying to make my sore body move. "I'll check it out."

I put Spot in the Jeep, drove to the South Shore and over to the hospital, parked around back, and walked into the ER.

"Any chance Doc Lee is in?" I said to the nurse on desk duty. She was tall and blonde and so focused that I thought it must be a new job for her.

"He's with a patient," she said with a slight accent.

I gave her my best smile. "Please tell him that Owen McKenna is here to see him."

"Yes, sir." She went back to typing at her computer.

I waited. She didn't call Doc Lee.

I waited some more. She moved her computer mouse, typed again. The phone rang. An ambulance drove up. Two paramedics brought a patient in on a gurney. Two nurses met the patient and wheeled him through the wide door. Someone shouted. A doctor I didn't know came out, talked to the desk-duty nurse, then left.

Then Doc Lee walked out. We shook and clasped left hands to shoulders without speaking.

"Did you just happen to walk out? Or did you know that I

was here?"

"I knew."

"I don't get it." I watched the nurse on desk duty. "The nurse never called you."

"Trade secrets," he said.

"Got a call from Diamond about an accident victim named Dwight Frankman. Did you see him?"

Doc Lee gestured toward the door, and we went outside into the cold winter air.

"You know Dwight Frankman?" he said.

"Met him," I said.

Doc Lee nodded. "I've been sitting on him a bit. I wanted to see if he settles down. Is he always so paranoid?"

"Got me. I've only spoken to him twice."

"Could be he's just dazed. He took an airbag in the face. That can shake you up. It's like a bomb going off twelve inches from your nose."

"What's the paranoia?" I asked.

"Someone has been following him. Someone ran him off the road. Someone's trying to kill him." The air outside was cold enough that Doc Lee's breath was visible.

"You going to keep him for observation?" I asked.

"No. Ula or Inge or whatever her name is on the desk was making some calls to see if she can find him a ride."

"Ula or Inge?"

"Yeah. The woman you saw on desk duty. She's new with us. East European or something. I forget where. Anyway, maybe you could take Dwight home."

"Maybe I could."

I thanked Doc Lee for his time, and walked back inside with him. He went on through the wide interior doors, back to his job. I stayed with Ula or Inge. "Doc Lee says Dwight Frankman could use a ride," I told her.

Ula/Inge nodded, looked at her computer, typed a few words, and hit enter.

"He'll be out in a minute," she said, her accent a bit more noticeable.

TWENTY-TWO

Dwight walked out a few minutes later. He looked frantic with worry. He shook.

"Hey, Dwight, you're okay. I talked to the doctor. He says you'll be fine with a little rest."

"Will you take me home? I'm scared!"

"Easy, Dwight. Don't overreact."

I guided him outside.

"You don't understand," Dwight said. "He came right toward me. It was either run off the road or get hit head-on! I could have been killed!"

"But you weren't, Dwight. You did the smart thing. It saved your life. The other driver was probably falling asleep."

"I don't know. I saw his headlights coming down the road perfectly straight. On his side of the line the whole time. Then, at the last moment, he swerved toward me. It looked like he was trying to hit me."

"Could you see his eyes? His face?"

"No, it was early morning. Still dark out."

"Did you see what kind of vehicle it was?"

"No. All I could see were the headlights. It was big, and it looked black."

"Could it have been yellow?"

"I don't know! I don't think so. But it was dark out, and the headlights were in my eyes. I've never been so scared. I jerked the wheel to the right. There was a big snowbank but my car just went through it and down below the highway. I stepped on the brakes, but there was a tree, and then the steering wheel exploded. I was in a haze for a bit. Then I tried the door, and it was jammed. So I climbed out the window. But it was too steep to get up the bank. So I fired flares until a lady stopped and looked over the bank to see me waving. Eventually, the cops came, and the ambulance, and they put me on a stretcher and got me up to the highway."

"You just happened to have a flare gun in your car?"

"Yeah. I bought my Chevy Tahoe at an estate sale, and it came with the flare gun and a whole box of flares. They were old, but they still worked. Lucky thing, too. I could have been down in that snowbank for days. I would have died."

We got to my Jeep, and I opened the door for him. Dwight stared at Spot, whose head was reaching forward, panting.

"He'll sniff you, but he won't hurt you." I reached in and put my hand to Spot's nose. "Pull back, Spot," I said. Then I walked around and got in the driver's side. Dwight was still standing outside. Again, I pushed Spot back. Dwight bent down to look in the Jeep, hesitated further. He saw me holding Spot back. He got in and shut the door.

I started the engine and drove off.

"Dwight, where were you going when the accident happened?"

"I was going to meet a business associate."

"Who?"

"I don't actually know. A man called last night. He said his name was Robert Carter and he had talked to the professors at Berkeley, the guys I do programming for. They recommended me, and he had a business proposition. He said he was in Carson City. So we agreed to meet at Comma Coffee."

"Do you think this person was connected to your accident?"

"I don't know. Maybe. On my way to meet him, the guy called me and asked what kind of car I was driving so he could watch for me to pull up. So I told him I had a blue Chevy Tahoe."

"It would be hard to tell it was you," I said. "From the front, a Chevy Tahoe looks like a Chevy pickup."

Dwight ignored my comment. "The name Robert Carter is probably made up," he said. "How many Robert Carters must there be in this country? Thousands, no doubt."

"Dwight, did anything else happen before you went out? Any other unusual phone calls? Emails? A person outside of your house?"

Dwight shook his head. "Wait, there was one thing. I was originally going to take my Subaru because it's a better snow car.

But when I went out to my Subaru to go meet Carter, it had a flat tire. So I called Triple A to come fix it. I didn't have time to wait, so I took my Chevy Tahoe. That was probably a bad idea because it doesn't have good tread. But it's not like I had a choice. And even if I'd been driving the Subaru, the guy still would have run me off the road."

"Was your Subaru in the garage?"

"No. The Tahoe was in the garage, but I usually leave the Subaru out unless we're getting a big storm. The Subaru is the car I use the most. God, maybe Carter came in the night, let the air out of my tire, forcing me to take the Tahoe! Maybe he's been watching me and knew that my Tahoe didn't have good tires. Maybe he planned it that way so that I'd be more likely to slide off the road!"

"Maybe," I said in a low, soft voice, hoping to calm Dwight down. He could be right, but he was cranked up and sounding paranoid.

"Let's just say that this person targeted you," I said, "and he tried to run you off the road. Can you think of a reason why?"

Dwight shook his head. "I can't imagine it. I've never hurt anyone in my life. I respect everyone. I don't even hurt bugs. I carry the spiders outside."

"Dwight, do you know about the Steven's Peak Ski Resort commission that Joe serves on?"

He nodded fast, still agitated. "Yeah. We talked about it. I told him I thought he should vote it down."

"Did you get the idea that Joe was interested in how you came to your opinion?"

"Yeah. He asked me why I thought the resort shouldn't be built. I told him it was bad for the environment. And it's not like we don't have enough resorts already."

"Has anyone else ever talked to you about it?"

"No, why?"

"I'm wondering if someone might have thought you have influence with Joe."

Dwight paused. "You mean I was run off the road so that I couldn't influence Joe on the resort?! That's terrible! But I bet there's big money behind that resort, isn't there? Maybe an investor is trying to kill off the people who would have Joe vote no!"

"It's a far-fetched idea, Dwight, but yes, that's what I'm wondering. If you think of anyone who's talked to you about Joe or about the resort, let me know, okay?"

He nodded again, multiple times.

I drove him home. His hands gripped the armrests the entire trip.

Dwight's Subaru was in the driveway. On one side of the car, there were lots of boot tracks in the fresh snow near one of the tires.

Once inside Dwight's house, I said, "Do you want me to stay for awhile?"

Dwight seemed to have calmed. "No thanks. I'm going to take an Ambien and go to bed."

TWENTY-THREE

After dropping Dwight off, I paused to think about what he'd said. His crash seemed like an accident. But Manuel's death looked like an accident, too. As did Rell's fall. Dwight exhibited all the signs of paranoia. And the recent events fed that. But someone could still have tried to run him off the road.

I cruised by Simone and Ned's house. Ned might recognize my Jeep if he paid attention, but Spot's head hanging out the window would be an advertisement he couldn't ignore. So I kept the rear windows up. Spot, frustrated, hung his head.

Neither Ned's truck nor Simone's Corolla was at the house. So I headed over to Stateline and drove to where she'd parked before. No Corolla.

I crawled through all of the hotel lots in case she'd parked elsewhere in an effort to avoid me. Still nothing.

So I tried to think like someone who was desperate to never see Owen McKenna again.

I wouldn't just park someplace else. I'd park where you couldn't even see my car. In the far corner of an upper floor in one of the ramps.

It was better to forget about her car and explore the cafés nearest to where she'd parked before. I started in the casino hotels.

Casinos are designed to make it hard to understand the layout, the better to keep people at the slots and tables. It had been a few years since I'd wandered the spaces. They all looked different. Cafés were hard to find. The big name restaurants were hard to find. The bars and nightclubs were hard to find. But the slots and gaming tables were ubiquitous. Probably, the rents paid by restaurant owners were nothing compared to the take on gambling from an equivalent square footage.

But even the most dedicated gamblers need to eat, so the food vendors were still a necessary part of the casino equation.

I was in my third casino, looking into its fourth restaurant, when I saw Simone. All the waitstaff were women. All wore the same orange uniform with white accents on the shoulders and the cute white apron. The other women filled out their clothes. But Simone was so tiny that her uniform flapped. They probably gave her the extra small, but her 95 pounds were still lost in swaths of fabric.

Seeing her again without winter clothes on gave me two immediate thoughts. Like Joe Rorvik had said, I couldn't imagine her in an athletic pursuit. She looked like physical activity would break her in half. Yet, she supposedly skied in some capacity. My second thought was that she was so small, the idea of Ned beating on her seemed that much more unfair.

Of course, no woman of any size should ever have to endure a man's assault. Yet Simone's diminutive size put her closer to the category of children. My blood pressure rose thinking about it.

I walked over to the little podium near the door. A woman wearing the same orange outfit but without the white accents and apron approached me, smiled, reached a menu off the stack, and said, "Table for one?"

"Yes, please. May I have Simone as my waitress? Last time, she was so charming that I came back for a repeat meal."

The woman frowned. "Charming," she said in a flat voice. She glanced over at Simone, working across the room, and frowned harder. "I believe I can find a table for you."

She took me to a small table next to a little railing that separated the restaurant from the casino floor. It came up just above table height, ensuring that I would never be very far from the excitement of the slot machines beeping and chirping and making robot noises just six feet away. It was obviously one of the least desirable tables in the restaurant, punishment for my requesting the waitress the hostess liked least.

I sat down, and she handed me the menu and said something I couldn't hear above the cacophony of the slots. I smiled and looked at my menu. The menu selections were standard diner fare but in a restaurant without the diner charm.

I sensed a person walk up to my side.

"Are you ready to order?" she said in a small voice with a slight

French accent.

I kept my head down and told her eggs, scrambled, sausage links, and hash browns. At the last moment, thinking about Street's recent remarks about healthy eating, I added, "Whole wheat toast. Dry."

"You mean no butter?" The small voice revealed disbelief.

"No butter," I said, thinking that this would give me ammo in convincing Street that I ate healthy. I could get some doughnuts later.

I looked up at the waitress for the first time. She was so short that her head wasn't much above mine.

Simone recognized me and gasped.

"What are you doing here?!" Her voice was part hiss, part fear.

"Hi Simone."

"You came here because of me! You're going to get me killed!" Her voice was loud. "You're going to get yourself killed!"

"Probably the opposite," I said. "I might save your life."

"No! You're just like all men. I hate men! I hate you!"

"Why me? I'm trying to help you."

"No, you're not. You're disgusting. You men prey on women. You prey on anyone smaller than you. The whole world is like a jungle. The bigger you men are, the more people, the more women, you can beat up on. You big men prey on other men, too. You make us all do whatever you want."

I noticed that she had a bruise on the inside of her forearm and another just poking out above her collar.

"Not all men are like Ned." As I said it, I realized that her previous reaction had been so broad that Ned was probably not the only abuser in her life. "Neither are all men like your father or your stepfather or your uncle or your neighbor or any other men who have assaulted you."

Simone's face was red with anger and hate and frustration. She stared at me, frozen in place.

"Simone, I'm going to tell you something that you might not believe, but it's true. I have never struck a woman in my life. Not even a slap. Not even when I was a kid, although I suppose that if I'd had a sister, I might not be able to say that. But I didn't, and so it is. Yes, I've said many things that I regret, said them to both women and men. And, yes again, I've struck men. Almost always it was necessary. But I've never had physical contact with a woman that wasn't affectionate or at least caring. There are lots of men like me."

Simone looked at me, not hearing. She looked a bit like a cartoon figure. Her eyes weren't clamped shut, but they were narrowed almost the same. She had a set to her face as if nothing could get in. Then, without uttering a word, she turned and walked away at high speed, the little white accents on the shoulders of her orange uniform dancing in sequence, left, right, left, right. She rushed across the restaurant, through the door to the kitchen, and disappeared.

Maybe ten minutes after I should have gotten my food, she came back, her eyes red and puffy. She pulled out the chair across from me and sat in it. She looked down at her lap.

I waited.

Her tiny shoulders went up and down with her heavy breaths. A minute went by. Her breathing slowed. Then she looked up.

"Do you swear that you're telling the truth? That you've never hit a woman? Because I don't believe it. I wouldn't believe it of any man."

It was hard to hear her doubts because of the implication.

"Yes, it's true," I said.

Simone's nostrils flared. Her eyes twitched and watered. She looked down and sideways. I couldn't see her hands below the table, but I could tell that she was getting some isometric arm exercise.

"Then why do other men hit women?" She looked up at me. Her eyes were wet and wide and red and very sad.

"I don't know, Simone. I think it's because some emotionally-immature men have never felt that they are in control of their world. They feel powerless. If those men weren't raised with any clear sense of right and wrong, then they lash out without thinking. As they grow up, they realize that if they lash out at other men, they eventually get themselves killed. So they go after women and children. I'm sure that psychologists have complicated explanations for it, but that's my simple explanation."

Her eyes teared further, and her mouth started to shake. “Then why have I always been around men who hit?! Why?” Her voice was suddenly loud. “What does that say about me?!” She was shouting. “What is wrong with me?!!”

The nearby diners were all staring, their faces showing shock and distaste.

“There’s nothing wrong with you, Simone.”

The woman who brought me to the table rushed over.

“Simone!” she shouted in a loud whisper. “Shut up! You’re making a scene. I want you to leave right now!”

“No,” Simone said.

“Yes. You’re disturbing the other diners. If you don’t leave, I’m going to let you go.”

“Look, ma’am,” I said in my calmest voice. “Please understand that Simone is upset. She is trying to cope with something bad that happened to her. I’m sure you understand what that’s like. She is calmer now. She won’t raise her voice again.”

“Who are you, anyway? Her father? And Simone, where is his meal? What is going on, here? I have a restaurant to run, and you have neglected your customers. Either you get back to work right now, or you’re fired.”

I stood up. “Ma’am, I’d like to explain. But this is uncomfortable. Please let me talk to you for a moment.”

The woman suddenly went from looking mad to looking fearful. I was afraid I had made things even worse. I stepped away from her to give her space, turned and smiled, waiting, trying to put an expectant look on my face.

She came over.

I spoke in a soft voice. “I’m Detective Owen McKenna. I’m investigating domestic abuse. Simone has a bad situation at home. You’ve probably noticed the bruises. Local law enforcement has a plan to arrest her abuser. But until that happens, I’d like to ask you to go easy on her. Battered women undergo stress unlike anything we can imagine. I understand that this little scene has made other diners upset.” I pulled out my credit card. “Please charge all their meals to me. Then you can go around and tell them that their meals are on the house.” I stuck my credit card into her hand. She reluctantly took it.

"Simone will get past this," I said, "if you can give her a little flexibility and understanding."

The woman looked at me for a few seconds, then walked away, gripping my credit card. If, in fact, she charged the meals to my card, it wouldn't amount to a great deal. And it would go on Joe Rorvik's bill, anyway.

I went back to my table. Simone was standing behind her chair.

"It's okay," I said. "Sit down." I sat.

Simone seemed to think about it. Then she sat.

"What did you tell Marilyn?" she asked.

"Your boss? I just asked her to give you a little space. I told her that things would be calm from now on."

"And she believed you? She just walked away?"

I nodded.

Simone looked at me, then at the table, then at her hands, which were red and still shaking.

"I'll go get your meal."

She left, came back a minute later with my plate. The food looked a little dry but otherwise okay.

I ate. Simone sat across from me.

After a moment, she said, "You think that Rell Rorvik's fall off the deck wasn't an accident?"

"It's not clear. I have doubts."

Simone chewed on her lip, swallowed, looked around the room as if she was avoiding looking at me. Finally she spoke. "I don't think it was an accident, either."

"Why?"

"Because Ned has a side job as a spy, and he is paid to spy on Joe Rorvik."

TWENTY-FOUR

Simone looked across the room with concern. "I have to get back to work. I need this job."

"When do you get off?"

"The lunch shift goes until two. I usually have to stay another half hour for cleanup."

"I can pick you up."

She began shaking her head.

"We need to talk. You can pick a place where Ned won't see you," I said.

She looked doubtful. "You talk like you're trustworthy. Maybe you are. But I don't really know, do I?"

"I understand. The other men sounded trustworthy, too. You tell me how we can meet. I need your help. If I'm going to find out what happened to Rell, I need to know more about her. Do it for Joe, please."

"I don't like Joe. He's patronizing. He's condescending. He treats me like I'm nothing, like I don't have dreams, like I'm a loser for being with Ned." Simone sucked her left cheek in between her teeth. "I guess I am a loser."

"No, you're just trapped. I can help get you out of that, if you let me."

"Oh, like you're the white knight or something?" Simone's tone was scathing, her French accent stronger than before.

"I want to help. I'm sorry if that makes you unhappy. But I'm glad to see you angry."

"Why? Is that another twisted thing that men like?" Her voice hissed.

"No. I'm glad because it's better than seeing you fearful. Anger is the first step out of bondage. It shows that your captor hasn't completely destroyed you."

Simone went silent for several long seconds. "He's almost

destroyed me," she said. After another silence, she said, "There is a little coffee shop that Ned doesn't know about. It's in the basement of Harvey's, not far from the tunnel from Harrah's. I'll meet you there at three. But when the auto-parts store is slow, they let him off early. Sometimes he comes here. If that happens before I leave, then I'll have to go with him."

"I understand. See you at three."

Simone stood up and carried my dishes back to the kitchen. I thanked Marilyn for her understanding. She handed me my card and a slip to sign. I was pleased to see the large bill. That meant it was more likely she'd go easy on Simone.

I was in the coffee shop at three. I'd figured out the stealthiest route that Simone could take from the café. I was pleased to see her arrive from the opposite direction. It trumped my expectations and showed a good sense of psychological cunning.

We got our coffees and sat in a corner behind a support post. Even if Ned walked by outside, he wouldn't see us. He'd have to come in the coffee shop and look into the corners.

Simone seemed edgy, like she was suspicious of me.

I waited for her to talk.

"You said you wanted to help me," she said. "Why?"

"Its a worthy thing to do. If you find that unbelievable, then consider that I'm being paid by Joe Rorvik to find out what happened to Rell. You may as well benefit. Anything Rell cared about falls under the umbrella of my job."

Simone dipped a spoon into her coffee, lifted the spoon up and slurped the coffee off the spoon. Then she looked up at me, doubt still on her face.

"You want a third reason? I'm an ex-cop. Twenty years in San Francisco. I bought into all the clichés about protect and serve. I still feel that mission. During those twenty years, I had to engage with wife beaters on many occasions. I saw how that kind of domestic abuse usually ends." It was a harsh statement, but I've learned that you can't be too harsh with the truth if you want to motivate an abused woman to save her own life.

Simone took a few deep breaths and closed her eyes.

I decided to press on and let the abuse situation simmer while we talked. "You said that Ned is paid to be a spy," I said.

Simone nodded. She looked around, fearful, worried. "I know it sounds ridiculous, but it's true. I don't know the details. But a man comes to the house about every other week. Ned turns on music in the living room and tells me that I can't turn it off. Then he and the man go up to the bedroom and shut the door. I can't overhear what they say. Ned is clever that way." Simone spooned more coffee into her mouth.

"If you can't hear them, then how do you know what's going on?"

"Because I'm clever, too. I've spied on Ned when he's spying. I've seen him go up to Angora Highlands and watch Joe's house. I've also seen him follow Joe when Joe runs errands. Ned is so focused on not letting Joe discover him that Ned doesn't realize that I'm following him."

"Why do you think that Ned's visitor is connected to the spying? It could be drugs or something."

"I think it because every time after the man leaves, Ned has extra money, and he spends it in ways that are noticeable. It's almost like he's flaunting it because it reminds him that he's doing something exotic. I know the money doesn't come from his paycheck because I've been with him many times when he deposits his check at the drive-up bank machine. I pay the rent and other bills, and we barely get by. So I know that Ned isn't taking the money out of the bank."

"Sounds like you have good reason to think that Ned gets cash from the man," I said. "But you have no direct evidence that it's payment for spying on Joe."

"Yeah. But it's still indirect evidence. There are two strange things in Ned's life. Unexplained money that follows the visit from the man, and unexplained spying. It makes sense that they're connected. Am I wrong about that?"

"Probably not." I drank coffee, holding the cup to my lips longer than normal so I could look around near the front of the coffee shop without being obvious. I saw nothing of concern.

"You've clearly thought a lot about what the purpose of the spying might be," I said. "Have you come up with any answers?"

"No," she said, spooning more coffee. "I can't dream up any

reason why someone would pay Ned to spy on an old man."

"What about Rell?" I said. "Do you think Ned pushed Rell off her deck?"

She hesitated. "It's very hard for me to think straight about Ned. He's a hothead. He's crazy. He's threatened to kill me many times, and now he says he's going to kill you. So yeah, he could certainly throw Rell off her deck. But Rell never gave him any reason to do such a thing. Rell was always civil to Ned the few times she talked to him. I know she worried for me a great deal. If Ned had known that she talked to the police about him, then I could see him exploding in rage. But he's never found out."

"How do you know?"

"Because Ned can't know something distressing without talking about it. He can't keep something inside. He obsesses. And when he obsesses, he stomps around and hits things and talks about it incessantly."

"I understand that you're afraid to leave Ned. But..."

"He'll kill me if I do," she interrupted. "Simple as that."

"You didn't see any hint of that side of his personality when you met him?"

"Here's where I should get angry and say of course not. But the truth is that I did sort of see it coming. I have no excuse for being so stupid. But men like him pull you in gradually. Ned can actually be charming, believe it or not. And because of my past, I stupidly thought that a big strong man like Ned would protect me from any other potentially abusive man. So I ignored the early signs. It didn't help that he's gorgeous. It made me blind. Then, after he and I moved in together, everything changed. He took possession of me. I became a material object, a robot to wait on him and do whatever he said. If I ever protest, he hits. When I protest the hits, he hits harder. One time, when I threatened to call the cops and press charges, he went very cold and calm. Like ice. Like an ice cold killer. He said, 'Do that and you're dead.' I knew he would do it even if he ended up back in prison."

"After he came at me the other day, did he punish you?"

"Just one hard slap on my face. Then he took to focusing on you. He got drunk and was mumbling and swearing and pacing around. He moved like he was sore, like he got hurt. But I got the sense from his mumbling that what really upset him was something about his pants. I don't know what you did, but you should know that he is going to kill you unless you stop him first. It's not an idle threat. It's real. That's why I eventually came back out of the restaurant kitchen. I knew I had to warn you."

"I appreciate that. Can you tell me about Rell?"

"First, is she still alive?" Simone asked.

I nodded.

"Good. I've been so worried. Is she going to be in the hospital for a long time?"

"Probably. She's in rough shape. It's not looking good."

Simone's face shifted away from fear and anger to sadness. It was a bit before she spoke.

"What do you want to know?" she asked.

"How you met her. What you talked about. Anything that might help me understand why she was pushed off the deck."

"You don't think her fall was an accident?"

"I don't know. I'm still trying to get a picture of her life. What I learn will probably tell me if she was pushed or not."

Simone looked into her coffee. "Rell is my best friend. Maybe my only real friend."

She paused. I waited.

"She came into the breakfast café where I used to work. I waited on her a few times before we talked much. She would say a few things, just being nice, and I found myself talking to her a lot. I said things I would never normally say. She is so easy to talk to. She makes you feel safe."

"Joe told me that Rell really cares about you. He thinks she feels closer to you than just about anyone."

Simone looked up at me, her eyes wide with astonishment. "Really? Did he really say that?"

I nodded. "Yes. He was sincere about it."

"Oh, I never..." Simone stopped. "That's amazing. That's wonderful. I love that woman."

"Rell told Joe that Ned made you quit your job and go to work someplace where Rell couldn't find you."

"He did. He's the biggest jerk. So controlling. I can't believe that I thought I liked him once. He's made my life hell." Simone took another spoonful of coffee.

"So I got a job at the other restaurant you came to. First chance I got, I called Rell and told her. So she started coming there. We saw each other maybe three times a week. She was like the grandmother I never had. The mother I never had. No one has ever cared about me the way she does. She even brought me little presents sometimes."

"What did you talk about?"

"Anything. Everything. Hopes and dreams. My life has always been drudgery. Work and survival. Rell wanted me to believe that it could be something more. So I told her my secret dream. I assumed she would think I was ridiculous. But she didn't. She believed I could do it."

"If she believed you could, then she's probably right."

"I don't know if she's right. But it's nice to have someone think it. After she said that, I actually thought that maybe I could be more. That maybe I could make something of myself. That was the first time in my life that I ever thought that. But I'm such a chickenshit. I'm afraid to try anything."

"Maybe that's because Ned has scared you."

"Yeah. Ned and the other men."

The way she said it sounded a little pregnant, like she wanted me to ask about the other men. But it seemed like dangerous territory, especially for an ex-cop. A trained psychologist can explore treacherous country. Maybe Rell could, too. But I might make things worse by what I said or didn't say.

I went back to her previous subject. "What is your dream? I realize that you might not want to tell me. But I'd like to hear."

Simone frowned, worried, probably, that I would not give her a good reaction. She ate another spoonful of coffee.

Simone hesitated. "It's probably ridiculous, but I'd like to do the Tahoe Randonnée Extreme Challenge."

"What's Randonnée?"

"It's a kind of back-country skiing that originated in the Alps. I didn't learn about it until I came to Tahoe. You've probably seen it. Randonnée uses that special ski and binding that allows you to lift your boot heel up and down for touring, prop it up high when you're climbing a slope, and then lock it down in the normal position for when you ski down, similar to downhill skiing at a resort."

"Yeah, I have heard of that, but I didn't know the name. You use skins on the bottom of your skis to grip the snow on your ascents, and then you take off the skins to ski down, right?"

"Yeah," Simone said.

"But what is the Tahoe Randonnée Extreme?"

"There's a guy who writes a blog about it. He's kind of a back-country legend. He's set several records for back-country treks. You've probably heard of the one where you ski the high country from Tahoe to Yosemite. Well, he's been promoting a trek that sort of follows the Pacific Crest Trail from Donner Summit on Interstate Eighty all the way south to Carson Pass on Highway Eighty-eight. But his trek veers away from the PCT to bag a bunch of peaks along the way."

"You climb the nearby mountains on your skis."

"Right. Over twenty peaks." she said.

"And after you bag the peaks, then you ski down them."

She nodded. "But on the steepest ones, you have to take off your skis and pack them up and down."

"Kind of dangerous," I said.

"The participants prefer to think of it as challenging instead of dangerous."

"Is it a race?"

"No. It's enough simply to complete the challenge. The way it works is you hold your phone out and take a picture of yourself at the top of every peak. Then, when you finish the route, you upload the photos to this website. It's still new. Not many people have done it. I want to be one of the first women to do it."

"From Donner to Carson must be forty miles. Several days what with climbing the mountains. Plus, you would have to bring a full range of winter camping gear and all your food."

She nodded. "We can stay at the Benson Hut or the Bradley Hut on the north end of the expedition. And there's the Ludlow Hut about midway. But the rest is all camping."

"Are those the huts the Sierra Club maintains?"

"Yeah."

"The rest of the time you're sleeping in a tent in the snow."

She nodded.

"Putting up with whatever storms come through."

Maybe I sounded doubtful because she said, "You don't think I could do it?"

"No, didn't mean that at all. I was just cataloging the challenges. I'm sure you could do it."

"Don't say that." Simone gave me a stern look. "Almost for sure I couldn't do it. But I want to try. It would be the most amazing experience of my life."

"You go on the buddy system?"

"They recommend it for safety. But I want to do it solo."

"Because then it would be a greater achievement."

"Right," she said.

"Have you been training for this?"

"Trying to. But it's hard to find the time."

"Does Ned know you want to do this?"

"Of course not. He would forbid it. That's why it's hard to train. If I go out too much, he gets suspicious."

"Why would he forbid it?"

"Because he thinks I'm his property. Anything that I do on my own is something where he is not in control of me. And he needs to control me at all times." She spooned two quick spoonfuls of coffee into her mouth.

"Simone, let me ask you another question about the earlier subject."

Her face went from excited to dark.

"The man who visits Ned every other week and pays Ned to spy," I said. "What does he look like?"

"Just...I don't know. He's a regular guy. His hair is long and brown, and his eyes are brown. He's a big guy, not as tall as you but bigger around. A bit like Ned but without so many muscles."

"His clothes?"

She shook her head. "Nothing noticeable. Not nice, not grubby. Decent pants. A flannel shirt. Except he wears a sweatshirt from a bar. What kind of guy would want to advertise that? Everything is solid colors. High ankle shoes for snow. A brown ski jacket. He looks nice like he's at work."

"What about him is different from everyone else? Something

he says, some way that he moves?"

Another head shake. "The only thing that comes to mind isn't something he did but something Ned said about him."

"What's that?"

"One day, after the guy left, Ned left too. Later that night, when Ned came home he mentioned something about a boat. He kind of mumbled it and then shut up on the subject. But I got the sense that Ned followed the guy. That would be just like Ned."

"Ned mumbles a lot."

"Yeah. It's how he processes."

"And he mentioned a boat," I said.

"Yeah. Nothing specific, but I got the feeling that the guy got on a boat. Or lives on a boat. I don't know if you can even do that in Tahoe. But it was something about a boat."

"When did this visitor last stop by?"

"Let me think. I was watching my favorite show when he came. I remember because after Ned turned up the music, I had to sit right next to the TV to hear the sound. But I've seen the show once since then, so it had to be the week before. That would make it twelve days ago."

"Thanks, Simone. Can I drop you at your car?"

"No." She looked alarmed. "I can't break my pattern. When I come home later than normal, I always say it's because I had to work late to clean the kitchen after my shift. But sometimes he's watching when I leave. There's a way I can walk there from here where he won't see me until it looks like I'm leaving the restaurant."

"Got it," I said.

TWENTY-FIVE

I called Street and asked if she would join me for dinner. She said yes. My heart made some extra beats.

"Any news on the Rell Rorvik situation?" she asked when we were eating. The little candles on the vinyl fold-up table in my kitchen nook made her eyes sparkle. It was hard to concentrate on what she was saying.

"A bit," I finally said. I told her about Joe's neighbor Dwight Frankman, and his car crash, and how he thought it wasn't an accident.

Street said, "Joe thinks that both Rell's fall and Manuel Romero's crash weren't accidents, either. And Lucy Romero agrees with him about Manuel. Add in Dwight, and you've got quite the accident pattern. What do you think?"

"I tracked down Simone, Ned's live-in punching bag. She says that Ned is being paid to spy on Joe."

"Are you going to ask him about it?"

"I'd like to, but Simone says that Ned won't be forthcoming. He's angry at me for rejecting his advances in the casino parking lot." I decided not to tell Street that Ned wanted to kill me.

"Maybe you could find the guy who is paying Ned," Street said.

"My thought, too. He's supposed to come around again in a day or three. I was thinking about staking out the house and intercepting the visitor."

Later, I sat in the big chair in front of the woodstove. Street sat scrunched in at my side, half on my lap.

"Warm fire," Street said.

"You could take off your clothes to cool off."

"Not that warm," she said.

"I think I should go back and hit the slopes, track down some Stevies, and see what I can learn from them. Want to come along?"

"When?"

"Tomorrow."

"Let me look at my calendar." Street picked up her phone, moved her finger around and said, "I have to make a call in the morning, but that's my only commitment. So if we don't leave too early, I can join you."

"Perfect," I said.

Street moved her finger some more, then set the phone down.

"Seems like your whole life is in that thing," I said. "What if you lost it?"

"Then I'd be in big trouble. I wouldn't even know where to start or what to do."

"We'd have lots more time to get exercise," I said.

"Skiing?"

"Well, that too."

Street turned, sat on my lap face-to-face, her knees straddling my thighs.

"If all I did was exercise," she said, "I'd really develop my technique."

"If you develop your technique any more, I'll have to be hospitalized for exhaustion."

The next morning, I slept in. Street and I had decided on a half day of skiing, and the weather was supposed to be less breezy and warmer than the day before. They were also forecasting sunshine, so I brought Spot along. The solar heat would keep him comfortable inside the Jeep.

We picked up Street and her gear at noon. She was wearing her silver stretch pants with her silver jacket. The jacket was unzipped, and I got a glimpse of her snug black sweater underneath. No wonder so many men are slow at learning to ski. There are too many distractions on the slopes.

"We never decided where to go skiing," I said as I backed out of her condo parking lot.

"Wherever the Stevies are, I guess," Street said.

"Jillian said they're at all the areas."

Street thought about it as I turned onto the drive and pulled up to the Highway 50 stop sign. I waited.

"Let's do Alpine," Street said. "I love that place, and I haven't been there in a couple of years."

I turned right and we headed north around the lake, past the turnoffs to Diamond Peak and Mt. Rose ski areas, past the Kings Beach turnoff to Northstar, and headed on to Tahoe City.

In Tahoe City, we went straight through the stoplight near the dam. The water was flowing well, making strong eddy currents. The top six feet of Tahoe's water is used like a reservoir, storing an enormous amount of water and letting it out as needed. We drove out of town on 89, heading down the valley alongside the Truckee River where Tahoe's water coursed with gentle rapids on its way to Truckee and then down the big canyon to Reno. A few miles down the road, before we got to the Olympic Rings of Squaw Valley, we turned at the River Ranch restaurant and headed up the steep road into Alpine Meadows. It is a spectacular valley with a ring of mountains at its end.

There were some clouds when we parked, but we cracked the windows for Spot in case the sun came out for any length of time. The main base lodge was a bit of a hike from our distant parking lot, but we had our half-day tickets and were in line at the Summit Six-pack chairlift in a few minutes.

"How do we know when we see the Stevies?" Street asked.

"Based on what I saw and heard at Northstar, we just look for blue and gold ski suits, expert skiers who also happen to be young and beautiful."

"Is that all," Street said. "And what is your plan when we find them?"

"Chat them up. Pick their brains. Learn the secrets to the Steven's Peak Resort universe."

The lift line was long, crowded with skiers heading back up the mountain after lunch. We shuffled ahead as we talked.

"All of this focus is because of the Steven's Peak Resort commission that Joe serves on," Street said.

"Yeah. If Manuel's death and Rell's assault and Dwight's crash aren't accidents, then I need to look at some connection between them. Joe might be the connection. So I'm looking at all aspects of

Joe. The part of his life that is connected to the most controversy is the Steven's Peak Resort Commission. Joe said that he was inclined to vote in favor. Manuel and Rell and Dwight were all against it."

"You think someone may be trying to influence the outcome of Joe's vote?" Street asked.

"It's worth looking at. Joe respected both Rell's and Manuel's opinions. Maybe Dwight's opinion, too. With them out of the picture, someone might think that Joe would be more likely to vote for the development. Then again, if Joe thinks someone is doing something so outrageous as trying to influence his vote, he would likely vote the opposite way to spite them."

"In other words," Street said, "if these deaths are actually murders, the perpetrator could be trying to prevent the development."

"Right," I said.

"You think the Stevies might know something about any of this?"

"I doubt it," I said. "But they are probably smart people. Never know what I might learn."

"That's curious."

"What?" I said.

"That you categorize them as smart without having met even one of them. Why?"

"Well," I said, "I once read about a survey of professional ski instructors. It said that a quarter of them had graduate degrees and ten percent of them had written screenplays and were shopping them in Hollywood."

"You think writing screenplays indicates smarts?" Street joked.

"Good point," I said.

The lift line had moved us over to the left. The four other skiers next to us all came together in a kind of slow compression as we approached the loading ramp and sat on the chair six abreast. In moments, we were riding up the ramp, and we lifted off into the air as the chair locked onto the high-speed cable.

"The woman you skied with, Jillian, what is her connection to the Stevies?" Street asked.

"She invented them. She's a public relations consultant and

event planner. She formulated the concept, set up the hiring, and is still directing the Stevies. The other day when I skied with her, she was scoping out the best places for them to put on their show."

"Sounds like you could get whatever info you need from her."

"Maybe. But unlike Jillian, who is working as an independent contractor, the Stevies are employees of RKS Properties. They might have a different, insider's view of things."

"How do we find them?"

"I don't know. Ski around the mountain and look."

"Do they ski the blues or the black diamonds or what?" Street asked.

"Probably all, but we have to stay with the blue runs. We can scan the black diamonds from the chairlifts."

"Why do we have to stick with the blues? I like black diamonds."

"I know you do. But my legs are still beat from the other day. You have to go easy on me."

"Skied too many bumps?"

"Too many bumps, too many steeps, and did it all too fast and for too long."

"We could have gone to Squaw. They've got that great huge bunny area at the top of the cable car."

"I think I can do more than green circle bunny slopes. Blue squares would probably be okay."

Street had pulled a trail map out of the dispenser box when we were in line. She spread it out on her thighs as we lofted our way through the trees.

"Okay, here's a plan that even you will love." She pointed to the map. "When we get to the top, we'll head down Sun Spot, then take that down to Rock Garden."

"Quite the name for a ski trail," I said.

"No doubt the rocks are covered with six feet of snow. From there, we'll head over to Firing Line." Street turned and grinned at me.

"Don't my legs just love the sound of that run," I said.

Street bumped her elbow against my side. "Easy, boy. Stay

with me until you understand my concept."

"I should have brought a wineskin to fortify myself."

"For a high enough fee," Street said, "you could maybe get the Ski Patrol to take you down on their toboggan. Anyway, Firing Line drops us down to the Roundhouse quad chair. Once we take that up, we work our way over to the Alpine Bowl chair. See the pattern? Gradually, we'll work our way across the mountain. Once we've sampled the front side, we head over to the back side. If we ski fast and hard, we'll cover bits and pieces of the entire resort before they close."

"It's the fast and hard part that has me worried."

"But you must agree that this gives us a good chance of seeing the Stevies, wherever they are."

"Agreed," I said.

The offload ramp at the top of the chair was approaching. We lifted our ski tips and touched down onto the snow as the chair disconnected from the high-speed cable. In a moment, the chair crested the top of the ramp's arc, and we pushed off and skied away.

"I'll follow you," I said, "if you keep your speed under the sound barrier."

Street grinned. She pulled her goggles on and did an accelerating skate toward the Sun Spot run, pushing hard with her poles. As she approached the lip at the top, she did a pole plant, and, just for show, lifted her ski tails into the air a few inches, then carved a long, hard turn as she dropped out of my view, her silver outfit describing a silver streak.

I skated and poled and did my best to follow, but she was like Jillian. In the interest of keeping my body intact, I kept my speed down and made a controlled descent. At one point, I realized I was approaching a mogul field, so I made a hard carve to the side and found a line without too many bumps.

Street was waiting down below, just as Jillian had two days before.

"No Stevies," she said as I did a skidding stop next to her.

"Not that I would know," I said. "It took all of my focus just to stay upright and keep you in view."

"Too fast for an old guy?" she said.

"Next time you wonder about those guys who take up with the ski bunnies who can't even walk their skis across the flats, it's because those ski bunnies make us feel competent."

"False modesty!" Street hit me with a light slug to my shoulder. "You ski as well as most anyone on the mountain."

"Hard to know when my first and second days on the slopes are with Jillian and you."

A woman in a puffy pink suit skied by doing a shaky snowplow, her speed about half the rate I use shuffling from my bedroom to the coffee maker in the morning.

Street leaned sideways and whispered, "There's your girl! Go get her! She'll make you feel like a mountain stud!"

I looked at the woman, then turned and looked back at Street. My eyes went down to her stretch pants, tight around her hips.

"But I'll learn more watching you," I said.

"Not watching me there," she said.

"I wasn't talking about learning skiing," I said.

Street pushed off and skied away. She had classic ski posture, knees bent, butt low, back nearly straight, arms reaching forward as she picked her pole plants, made quick precision turns, her boots and skis going up and down over the bumps like she had shock absorbers in her legs. As the terrain varied, her upper body traced smooth arcs, left and right, up and down.

It was the kind of show that thrills onlookers as much as the skiers themselves, a captivating, enthralling dance.

Street came to a junction and carved off to the left. I understood that she was heading down Firing Line. I pushed off to follow.

We continued the pattern of moving across the mountain until we rode over to the back side. The Sherwood Express took us to the top of the back side. As we were getting off the chair, Street said, "There they are."

I turned to look where she was pointing. Two matching skiers dropping down into the trees.

Street pulled out her map. "They're heading for Sherwood Forest. Follow me, I'll catch them." And she was off.

I tried to follow, but by the time I was part way down the trail, I realized that I'd lost them all. So I took the fall line, ended up on what seemed like a Black Diamond run, and, thighs screaming, picked my way down the mountain.

"Owen!" came Street's shout as I approached the bottom of the chairlift. She was gesturing for me to come over to the outdoor deck. I skated over.

"The Stevies stopped. Looks like they're taking a break." She pointed.

Two matching skiers, a man and a woman, had gotten coffee and were walking to the sun deck. They sat down at a table.

I kicked off my skis, walked over to Street, and we headed over to the deck.

"You two are the Stevens Peak Resort ambassadors, right?" I said.

They both nodded. "They call us Stevies," the woman said. "I'm Debbie, and this is Kevin."

"Owen and Street," I said, and we shook all around.

Like the pair I'd watched with Jillian at Northstar, this couple were young and attractive, but dark-haired instead of blond. But the biggest difference was their mood. At Northstar, they grinned like movie stars. These two were glum.

"Mind if we join you?" I said.

"Not at all," Kevin said. "Pull up a chair," he said to me as he stood up, grabbed a chair, and held it for Street.

"Wow," Street said. "Chivalry lives. Are you noticing, Owen?"

The younger guy flashed a small grin, then stopped.

"We've heard of you guys," I said. "It's a great marketing plan, sending you out to all the ski areas to talk up the new resort."

"Yeah," Debbie said. "But there's good days, and there's bad days."

"Sounds like this is a bad day," Street said.

Both Stevies nodded. "Our boss had an accident," Debbie said.

"Would that be Jillian?" I asked.

The woman nodded. She frowned with what seemed like physical pain. "Jillian did a back-country descent yesterday. On the mountain above Sand Harbor. She hit a tree and died."

TWENTY-SIX

We were stunned. None of us spoke for a moment.

"How did she hit the tree?" I asked.

I got a call last night from a fellow Stevie named Howard," Kevin said. "He was pretty broken up about it. He just said that he and Gigi and Jillian picked a good line with enough trees to protect the snow from the sun and wind but not enough trees to be crowded. He didn't see any reason that Jillian would be cutting close to the trees. They were all together as they went down most of the slope. But you know how it is when you're tree-skiing. The powder flies up in your face and you have to concentrate to see where you're going. So it's not like you can be watching your companions all the time. Sometimes the only way you know where they are is by listening to their shouts and yells."

We nodded, looked at him, waited.

"Anyway, Howard said that he and Gigi pulled up for a rest on a knob. They couldn't hear Jillian anywhere. So they started yelling. Then they called Jillian's cell, but there was no answer. They yelled some more, but got no response."

"All three of them wore beacons and the new avalanche vests," Debbie said. "But they had no signal from Jillian's beacon, so they knew she was either too far away or the signal was blocked by the terrain. They traversed back and forth, looking for tracks. Unfortunately, quite a few other skiers had been down the same way, so there were too many tracks to suggest where she might be. Howard said they debated whether they should call nine-one-one and get a SARS team sent out."

"Search-And-Rescue," Street said.

"Right," Kevin said. "It's a hard decision, trying to decide when to put out the call. She could have been in a slide, but they saw no slide residue. You know how it is when you fall down a tree well and it takes you twenty minutes to get your skis off and climb out, pulling yourself up the snow walls. You'd feel bad if the county had mobilized a SARS unit and avalanche dog and it was a false alarm. But eventually, they did call nine-one-one. While they waited, they kept searching. Howard thought that he'd been in the lead at the last point that he heard both Gigi and Jillian. So he wanted to search upslope."

Kevin slurped coffee. "Of course, side-stepping up a steep slope is nearly impossible when the snow is deep, so he and Gigi put their skins back on their skis, and they traversed up, zig-zagging back and forth so that they didn't get too far from the line. As they went up, they eventually got a signal from Jillian's beacon. They found her about two hundred yards up. She was lying several feet above the tree. But they could tell from her tracks that she'd hit the tree and bounced back. No pulse, no breathing, blood pooled in her mouth. Howard said he knew she was gone, but he started CPR just in case, while Gigi phoned in their GPS coordinates and the physical description of their location. Then they both worked on her, one doing heart compressions, the other breathing."

Telling us about it made Kevin breathe hard.

"They got a call back from the SARS team saying that it was too steep to get snowmobiles up from below, so they were going to drive around and up to Mt. Rose Meadows and try to come down from above, the same way that Jillian and Gigi and Howard had skied in. That meant the SARS team wouldn't get there for two hours minimum. They asked if Howard and Gigi thought it was possible for a chopper to land or if a chopper could lower a medic on a cable. Howard told them not to take risks and not to bother with a chopper, either, because Jillian was dead. Howard is a Ski Patrol at Heavenly, full certified PSPA and First Responder. He said when he first saw her, he recognized severe trauma to the face and chest. And when he tried heart compressions, her chest sunk in, so he knew her sternum and ribs were crushed. He said he figured she had crushed her heart."

Kevin drank the rest of his coffee and crushed the cup in his fist as if he were crushing demons.

"We're so sorry," Street said. "What a tragedy."

"Do you know if Jillian's family has been notified?" I asked.

"Gigi said, yes," Debbie said. "Jillian was single, no kids. So there was only her mother in Marin to contact."

"What will you do now?" I asked. "Who takes over for Jillian?"

"No idea," Kevin said. "I guess RKS Properties will appoint someone. We'll just keep doing what we've been doing until we hear."

"Did you know Jillian well?" Debbie asked us.

I shook my head. "I just met her two days ago. Her work for RKS intersects with a job I'm doing, so we talked shop while we skied at Northstar. I liked Jillian. She seemed like a very nice person. Great skier, too. I couldn't keep up."

"That's what bugs me," Kevin said. "I don't see Jillian hitting a tree."

"Really? What do you mean?"

"She was a professional skier. Grew up racing. Won a couple of championships. That's part of why us Stevies all respect her so much. When we interviewed for our jobs, we had to do onslope auditions. Jillian would take us up and ski with us. And frankly, we're all good skiers. We've raced and performed and been in the ski world our entire lives. So it gave us a bit of a chip on our shoulders. When Jillian first took us up the mountain, we were all kind of skeptical, especially us guys. I mean, she's a girl, and..." Kevin reached out and touched Debbie's arm, "I don't mean to sound sexist, but let's face it, it's hard for girls to keep up with the best guy skiers. Also, Jillian's pretty old. She must be thirty. But we get up on the slope, and it turns out she's hot on her boards. I mean, of course we could keep up with her, but you just don't expect an older lady to kick ass like that.

"Anyway, I'm rambling. But what I'm trying to say is this. After you ski with Jillian, you just can't see her hitting a tree. She's a professional. She was free-skiing. It's not like a race where you're pushing yourself to the max, punching sixty, seventy miles per hour on ice, skiing close to the gates because you have to. This is casual skiing, good snow conditions and good light, and there is no pressure to take unnecessary risks. Howard said that the area wasn't tree-crowded." Kevin shook his head as he stared at the distant snow, seeing a different slope on the other side of the lake.

I said, “When I skied with her the other day, I also got the impression that she was a real pro. That she'd never make an avoidable mistake. But it still seems like mistakes are possible, even for the pros.”

Kevin was still shaking his head. “Pro guys take dumb risks. Maybe it's testosterone or something. I've seen it many times, a guy who knows better getting air when he doesn't know the landing. Or a guy who cuts close to terrain hazards just for the rush. But I haven't seen pro girls do that.” He turned to Debbie. “Have you, Debbie?”

She looked down at the table, made a little head shake. “No,” she said. “It's true. Women are just more sensible. We sometimes really push it, but we rarely take unnecessary risks.”

“Debbie,” I said, “what's your ski background?”

“I grew up in SoCal,” Debbie said. “My parents were ski hippies, and they packed me and my sister into the VW Micro-Bus every weekend. We'd go up to Big Bear outside of L.A. and ride the terrain parks on our snowboards. My dad works remodel construction, so he can usually find jobs wherever we go. My mom works escrow for a title company. One day she got transferred to Placerville.

“So we moved and started constantly going up to Tahoe. My mom was able to get a four/ten schedule, giving her three-day weekends. After a couple of years, they bought a tear-down cabin on the South Shore. Of course, they didn't have money to tear it down, so my dad fixed it up. Right about then I switched from riding to skiing, and I took up racing. I practically grew up at Heavenly and Sierra and Kirkwood. Then I went to Sierra Nevada College and raced in their program. That's how I met Jillian. She was a mentor to us because she's an alumna. And when she started the Stevies, she called me.”

“So you have basically been a professional skier most of your life.”

“Yeah, I guess you could say that.”

“Do you think you could ever hit a tree?”

Her head shake was immediate. “Never. We grow up learning never to come close to trees or lift towers or any other solid object. Even in snowboard class as a little kid, we always heard the phrase,

Trees always win. You hear it enough that it is engraved in your brain. Trees always win."

"Assuming that Jillian is the same as you that way, how could she hit a tree?"

"I have no idea. No idea at all. It doesn't make sense."

"But she did, so imagine what it would take for you to hit a tree."

"Someone would have to push me. It would have to be a good-sized person compared to me, and they'd have to ski next to me and hip-check me hard when I came near a tree. That's the only way it could happen."

I thought about the man in white following Jillian down the ski runs. In a misguided attempt to keep her from worrying, I decided not to tell her.

Now she was dead.

I tried to shake the thought, tried to keep my focus on the current task.

TWENTY-SEVEN

"Debbie, I'm sorry for all of these questions, but I have a reason to ask. I'm a private investigator. I met Jillian because she was friends with a woman who may have suffered an assault. I was talking with Jillian to learn more about the woman."

Kevin interrupted, "What does that mean, may have suffered an assault?"

"She had a bad fall, and she's in a coma. The doctors say she suffered severe brain damage. So we can never ask her. The nature of the fall sounds like Jillian hitting a tree. The people close to her can't believe it was accidental."

"Let me get this clear," Kevin said slowly. "You're a detective and you're investigating an attempted murder?"

"Yes."

Kevin stared at me like I had suddenly become an alien.

I turned to Debbie. "I have one more question for you, Debbie."

She nodded, her forehead wrinkled with worry.

"You said that for someone to hip-check you into a tree, they would have to be a fair amount bigger than you. I'd like you to think about when you're skiing along at a pretty high speed. You're an expert skier, stable and solid, and you have the ability to adjust and react to changing conditions as quickly and as well as any skier out there. Can you estimate how big a person would have to be in order to hit you so hard that you couldn't arrest yourself and keep from hitting a tree?"

Debbie thought about it. "Well, if you want my guess, I'm a hundred fifteen pounds, so I'd guess the person hitting me would have to have a good thirty or forty pounds on me. So maybe one fifty or so would do it."

"Kevin, what do you think?"

He pushed his lips out, then pulled them in. "Yeah, I think Debbie's probably right."

"So we're talking about either a somewhat large woman or most any man."

Both Kevin and Debbie nodded.

Before we left, Street had the sense to ask them for phone numbers including Gigi's and Howard's. Debbie pulled out a brochure on the proposed Steven's Peak Resort and wrote on the blank spaces. We thanked them for their time and thoughts and left.

It was a long, quiet drive through the basin and down the East Shore.

I dropped Street at her condo and drove with Spot to my office. I was still wearing my ski suit, but I didn't intend to be long.

I took the Steven's Peak Resort flyer as I stepped out of the Jeep. Two workmen were just coming down from the scaffolding as Spot and I approached the building. One of them called down to me.

"Hey, you were right about the scaffolding bolts. There were quite a few of them. We picked up all we could find, so hopefully no one will slip on them."

"Thanks," I said.

When I got inside, my phone machine was blinking. I pressed the button and looked at the Steven's Peak Resort flyer while I waited for the recording. One of the pictures looked familiar. A restaurant scene. It was the same one on the torn piece of brochure that I'd found in Manuel's crushed Prius.

"Owen, this is Joe," the voice on the machine said. "I found something you should see."

I called Joe, and he said I could come by anytime, so I headed to his house.

When he let us in the door, Spot was excited to see Joe. In contrast, Joe seemed imbued with melancholy, and he dragged his feet as we walked into his house.

"Remember you said that I should be aware of anything unexpected, something out of place?"

"Yeah," I said.

Joe walked over to the counter, picked up a bent cigarette pack, and handed it to me.

"I found that in my desk drawer. Like what you found in Manuel's car, right?"

"Yeah. And like Manuel, you don't smoke," I said.

"Right." Joe shook his head twice, slow and solemn.

"How do you think the cigarettes got inside your desk?" I asked.

"The burglar. The person who threw Rell off the deck."

"You haven't opened that desk drawer since Rell's fall?"

"No. It's the lower left one. I keep insurance papers in there. I only opened it because I got to thinking about what you said about the unexpected. So I opened every cupboard in the kitchen, every cabinet in the bathrooms, every drawer in my desk. And there it was."

I wondered if it had any prints on it, but whoever placed it in Joe's desk had probably wiped it clean.

"Why do you think Rell's assailant would leave a cigarette pack in there?" I asked.

"I think it's a message."

"In what way?"

"I think it's about my involvement with the Stevens Peak Resort Commission. I told you that I was somewhat inclined to vote in favor of the development. Rell was against it. She's in a coma. Manuel was against it, and he's dead. My neighbor Dwight Frankman is an even more committed environmentalist than Manuel was, and he was just run off the road. He could have been killed. It would seem that someone is telling me to not let these people influence me. That I should vote in favor."

"What do the cigarettes mean?"

"When the commission was first formed by the U.S. Forest Service, the Steven's Peak Resort Association, and the Tahoe Regional Planning Agency, there was an initial meeting. Those of us chosen for the commission made short statements. Several members of the press were there including one who had written a story about my past and how I used to smoke cigarettes back when I was a ski racer. Before I retired from ski racing, I had begun to lose ski races. At the time, the press said it was my cigarette addiction that was destroying my fitness. They were correct of course, and I quit smoking soon after I announced my retirement.

"Now, I have a bit of a reputation as a curmudgeon. So I tried to lighten things up with a little self-deprecating humor. I said that considering all of the efforts to protect Tahoe's environment, the forests and lakes needed another ski resort like a ski racer needs cigarettes. I intended the joke to poke fun at myself."

I nodded.

"The joke was also intended to show that I was open-minded on limiting resort development because I also have a history of being pro-development. Now it appears that someone is referencing my past smoking or at least my comment about smoking."

"Who could be doing it?"

"Anybody who wants the resort to go through and who knows of me because they were at that meeting. Or anybody who read about the meeting in the paper. For that matter, they could have just read the minutes of the meeting, which were also in the paper."

"If this is true," I said, "it's a threat or blackmail. Do you think the other commission members would be targeted in a similar way?"

"I doubt it. From my sense of the makeup of the group, my vote will probably be the deciding vote. I'm like the swing vote on the Supreme Court. The others look to be set in their opinions, and they make an even split."

Joe looked stressed. I felt stressed. Even Spot turned from me to Joe and back, his ears up and forward, his brow wrinkled.

"Joe, you told me about Jillian Oleska. Did you ever talk to her about the resort?"

"No. But it's funny that you ask because Rell said that even though Jillian is working for the resort people, and she acts like a huge cheerleader for it, she has some doubts about it."

"Really? Then she's a good actor."

"Does her job well," Joe said.

"Yeah. Did you ever feel that Jillian's position on the subject could influence you in any way?"

"No, of course not. But indirectly, who knows? Rell influences me, and Jillian might influence Rell. Why do you ask?"

"Because I just found out that Jillian died yesterday in a ski accident."

Joe looked like he'd been struck by lightning. He staggered back. I was about to rush forward and grab him when he suddenly sat down in his chair.

"My God! They're killing everyone I know!" he said.

"It's officially an accident. It has all the characteristics of an accident."

"You wouldn't refer to it that way if you believed it was an accident. And I don't care what they officially call it! I don't believe it. What if everyone you knew died?! What would you think? You'd think that it was a grand scheme directed at you! You'd think it was designed to unravel you, to make you go unhinged!"

"If these deaths are in fact not accidents," I said, "it seems an extreme way to reduce your exposure to any anti-resort influence."

"Of course, it's too extreme. It makes no sense. And I'm going to lose what sanity I have left because of it." Joe's eyes were red and moist like he was about to cry. "Murder to limit influence over me is counter productive. If I lose everyone close to me, and if I have any sanity left, and if I believe that these deaths are connected to the pro-development block, then I'd vote against it just to spite them. Why not? I have nothing more to lose?"

"I agree with you that murder is a counter-productive way to influence you. A more reasonable way to look at it is that you might vote for the resort simply in hopes that this slaughter would stop. If in fact it is a slaughter. They could all still be accidents."

"Except for the cigarettes," Joe said. "You're right. I can't reconcile accidents with the cigarette packs. I'm at my end, Owen. I can't take this anymore. I have no more purpose in a life where everyone I know is dying. Next thing I know, you'll be next."

His words hit me hard when I realized that, if Ned has his way, they may be true.

"I'm sorry I called you, Owen. I should never have gotten you involved. There is something really evil out there, and it's targeting me. Maybe you. All because I called you."

Joe bent his head, chin against his chest. He remained in that position for a long time. Eventually, he lifted his head. His eyes were swollen and red.

"I'm going to have my talk with Rell, then I'm going to have them pull the plug. And when I leave the hospital, I'm going to figure out how to pull my own plug."

I couldn't breathe. I couldn't swallow. My heart felt like it was banging against my ribs. "Joe, I don't have any good words to change your mind, except please don't. Please give me some time. I need you to have more staying power and let me finish what you asked me to start."

"What I asked you to start is creating death all around me. Rell is still alive. Sort of. But since I called you, two people have died. Who's next?"

Joe stood up. I realized that he wanted me to go. He walked over, opened the front door wide, and held it there. The cold night air rushed in. Snow blew off the eave above the entry and swirled down into the house, the flakes hitting the ceramic floor tiles and melting into water drops.

"This isn't a life I want," Joe said. "Please leave."

I stood still.

"Leave, Owen! Please!"

A sharp headache grew behind my eyeballs as I walked out, Spot at my side, head hung low. I was helpless, feeling that my choice of words, my presentation, was pushing Joe over the edge. But worse than the thought that I'd gone about it the wrong way was the thought that someone else was ruining Joe's life, making him so miserable that he was ready to be done with this world.

I was desperate for something to say that could make it better. But there were no words.

Joe shut the door behind me. I hesitated on his entry step, wondering what I could do differently. I could force myself in and restrain him. I could call a judge, get a doctor, try to convince them to intervene. He would fight at every step as we forced drugs into his system, drugs that would sap his will and take away his last sense of self-determination. Doing so might make him live a little longer, and yet it would be the cruelest crime of all.

Diamond often talks about the philosopher John Stuart Mill and how he said that the principle right of any human is the right to be left alone. Anything that I could do would be interfering with that right, intruding against the explicit wishes of the man. To step in against a person's will – a person who isn't hurting anyone, not even himself yet, a person who by any measure has lived a very successful life, a person who is in full command of his mental faculties and has explicitly and clearly articulated his wishes – to force yourself on him and make him do things my way would be a crime nearly like murder, because I would be taking away his life as he wants it and remaking it in my own arrogant, condescending, and self-righteous way, treating him like a child who doesn't know any better.

If you respect the individual, you respect the individual's desires as long as those desires don't directly wound others.

From that perspective, I couldn't force myself through Joe's door. I couldn't make him do and be the way I wanted him to be. I had to let him do what he wanted to do.

As Spot and I got into the Jeep, the Christmas lights on the sculptures went out. Then the lights coming through the windows went out, one by one until everything was dark. I sat there feeling like I had turned out Joe's last light and, in doing so, had darkened my own world in a way that I could never restore.

TWENTY-EIGHT

I drove back through town, crawling along with no sense of purpose, no desire to move forward, only regrets. Everything was wrong, and I was at the epicenter, the cause. Without seeing it coming, I had become the new agent of Joe's misery.

When I came to the red light at Sierra Blvd, I remembered what Simone said about Ned's visitor, the man she believed was paying Ned to spy on Joe. The man had been coming at night every two weeks or so, and she thought that the last time had been about twelve days before.

Maybe this time he'd come a couple of days early. Maybe I should be watching. Having failed to bring Joe the tiniest bit of comfort, I had nothing else to do.

I turned right, headed over to where Ned and Simone lived, and stopped a block short. I parked where I had a sight line to their house. I turned off the lights but left the engine running so the defroster could keep the windshield from fogging up in the cold, winter night. Street's binoculars were still under my seat. I didn't remember why I had them, but I did remember that the last time they were used was when the illegal alien kid Paco Ipar looked through them and identified the bad guys who were chasing him.

When I looked through the glasses, it was obvious that Paco's eyes were much different than mine. I had to spin both knobs to bring Ned and Simone's cabin into focus.

The downstairs lights were on, upstairs lights off. Simone had said that when the mystery man came, Ned took him upstairs to the bedroom.

I could barely see the front door. If I missed seeing the man drive up, and if I missed seeing him go through the door, I would still notice when the upstairs light went on.

I sat in the dark, watching for a vehicle or any other movement. Nothing happened, and I couldn't stop thinking about Joe and his distress and my misery over it. I knew that I hadn't created the situation in the first place, but my self-critique was nevertheless relentless.

I'd arrived at Ned and Simone's house about 6:30 p.m. By 9:30, I decided that the likely window for an evening visitor was closed. So I drove home to my little, lonely cabin and was miserable there instead.

The next morning, I decided to go to the office to do desk work. But first I parked in one of the big hotel ramps, far from where Ned had watched me a few days ago, and walked to the café where Simone worked.

The hostess named Marilyn came up to me, alarm on her face.

"Don't worry, I'm not going to eat, and I won't distract Simone. I just need to ask her a question."

Marilyn seemed to ponder it. "Just one question?"

"Yes. You can even ask it for me, if you prefer."

"Okay, what is the question?"

"Does Ned ski, does he know a Jillian Oleska, and where was he two days ago?"

"That's three questions," she said, her face serious.

"You're right. Sorry. But they kind of go together, so I thought of it as one question."

She hesitated, then said, "Wait here."

She walked back to the kitchen. I expected Simone to come out. But a minute later, Marilyn returned. "Simone said yes, of course, Ned skis. She added that he's a very good skier. She has no idea whether or not he knows a Jillian Oleska, but she's never heard the name, if that makes a difference. And she has no idea where Ned was two days ago. He was gone all day. He wasn't at work, and he wasn't at home."

"Thank you. I'm sorry, but I forgot one more question. Can you please ask her what color are Ned's ski clothes?"

Marilyn stood there staring at me. I was a pest, and she didn't know the best way to get rid of me. She glanced at the other diners, then walked away.

She was back in a minute. "White jacket, white warmups. Now will you please go away."

I got the message. I thanked her and left.

The workers were back on the scaffold at the office building, installing some kind of mesh on the outer wall to support a new layer of stucco.

Once my coffee maker was done and had stopped making its loud noises, I called the numbers for Jillian's ski companions Gigi and Howard and left messages for both. I pulled out the sticky note on which Joe had written Jillian's number and dialed it just in case someone else was at Jillian's home. Her machine answered. In the hope that someone else who knew Jillian would call me, I left a message with my name and phone number.

Then I called RKS Properties in an effort to learn who was now in charge of the Stevies. I worked through multiple voice menus and eventually got a young male secretary who wouldn't give me any information about Jillian or her ski accident or the Stevies or the name of any RKS managers or managing partners. I said it was important, but he would only take my name and number and pass it on. When I hung up, I realized I was going to have to resort to subterfuge if I wanted to speak to anyone.

Next I called Diamond.

"Sergeant Martinez," he answered.

"You sound very official," I said. "Stern almost."

"Sí. Intimidates bad guys. Is it working?"

"Yeah."

"You calling on official business? Or did you need help eating another pumpkin pie?"

"I'm trying to eat more vegetables, so I better save it all for myself," I said. "The official word is that your county neighbors to the north had a back-country ski accident in their territory day before yesterday."

"Sí. Washoe County. A woman hit a tree about a thousand feet above Sand Harbor. The way you say 'official word' makes it sound like there is a differing, unofficial explanation."

"According to an expert skier who knew Jillian well, yes."

"What's the unofficial explanation?"

"This expert says that Jillian wouldn't have hit the tree by accident, therefore she was pushed."

"And this has to do with Rell Rorvik falling from her deck,"

Diamond said.

"I know it sounds like a stretch, but yeah. The ski victim, Jillian Oleska, was one of Rell's friends."

"Like Manuel Romero," Diamond said. "Like Dwight Frankman."

"Yeah. I'm wondering if you have a contact you recommend I call at the Washoe County Sheriff's Office. The last Washoe County guy I knew well retired."

"Try Sergeant Cal Kimmel. I've got his number in my phone."

"Am I the last guy left using Post-it notes?" I said.

"Yeah. Here's the number." Diamond read it off. I wrote it down.

I thanked Diamond, hung up, and dialed Sergeant Kimmel.

"Cal, here."

I introduced myself and explained how I got his number. "Diamond said that you handled Jillian Oleska's accident."

"Yeah, what a mess that was. Getting her body off the mountain was a trick in itself. Trying to boost morale after two of our younger guys saw the body was like being a dad all over again. That tree pancaked that poor girl. Broke most of her ribs. I just spoke to the Medical Examiner. He said her aorta didn't just rupture, it exploded. He said it looked more like spaghetti than like an artery."

"I spoke to a friend of the victim. She said that Jillian was an expert skier, ex-racer, etc. It's the friend's belief that Jillian wouldn't have hit a tree by accident."

Kimmel guffawed. "Oh, that's a good joke. The young lady was up on the mountain with two friends. Their stories are consistent. They were skiing and noticed that Jillian hadn't kept up with them. So they hiked back up the mountain and found her dead. How is that not an accident?"

"I don't know. Were you at the scene?" I asked.

"No, I was down at Sand Harbor when the SARS team brought the body down on a toboggan."

"Any chance the rescue crew mentioned ski tracks near the accident?"

"No. But even if there were, what would that tell us? That

entire mountain is a popular back-country descent. There are ski tracks all over it. Is there some other reason you're calling? You got motive or something?"

I didn't want to get into a discussion of other accidents that may not have been accidents, so I said, "No, just expert opinion that Jillian Oleska was unlikely to have that kind of an accident."

"Expert opinion of a friend," Kimmel said. "And friends are always crystal clear thinkers when their buddies die."

"Right," I said. "Thanks for the info."

"Any time."

We hung up.

The phone rang immediately.

"Owen McKenna," I answered.

"Owen, Joe. Something happened. I think I need help."

"What?"

"I got a call from the hospital in Reno. Where Rell is. They had some incident early this morning. Some unknown intruder was in the hospital. A nurse was struck and hurt. The intruder was in Rell's room."

"Was Rell hurt?"

"Not that they can tell. The intruder ran out. I want to go down there, but I'm pretty shaky. Can you drive me?"

"Of course. When can you go?"

"Now."

"I'll be there in twenty minutes."

TWENTY-NINE

I got to Joe's house a few minutes faster than I anticipated. He must have been watching, because the door opened and he came out before I could ring the bell.

Spot wagged like a puppy when Joe got in the Jeep, and I had to push his head back several times to keep him from being too boisterous.

"Who called from the hospital?" I asked as we headed down Tahoe Mountain Road.

"I forget how she introduced herself. Something like the hospital security officer."

"She said that an intruder had been in Rell's room," I said.

"Yes. A nurse surprised him. He knocked her down, and he ran out."

"Anything else?"

"Not that I can remember. I said that I was on my way, and she said she'd talk to me when I arrived."

We rode in silence for many minutes. I tried to imagine what had happened. Every thought I had was ugly.

We took Highway 50 through town, went up the East Shore and climbed up Spooner Summit. As we crested the pass, Joe spoke.

"She's helpless," he said. "Her brain is mostly gone. She's a shell of a person, a body utterly dependent on others to care for her. It's not possible for a human to be more vulnerable. So what kind of a person would go into her room and do something? Is it possible that the person who pushed her off the deck came back to finish the job?"

"Hard to imagine," I said. "But yes, it's certainly possible."

"If that's the case," Joe said, "then it makes me really angry. I'm going to find out from the hospital if they think someone chose Rell's room at random, or if there is some indication that the person was looking for her room. If the latter, then I will do whatever it takes to bring that person to justice."

"I'm glad to hear that, Joe. I believe you have a lot of fight left in you."

Joe didn't respond.

A few minutes later, I said, "I've read about the Rorvik Roar," I said to make conversation. "Something you did back when you raced. What was that about? Was ski racing like a fight? Was your roar a kind of intimidation like the roar of a lion?"

In my peripheral vision, I sensed Joe turning to look out the side window. In time, he turned forward.

"Maybe my roar seemed intimidating to others, but that wasn't what it was about. It was about fear."

"Making other racers fearful?"

"No. Coping with my own fear. Ski racing can be terrifying. You rocket down a mountain at high speeds. Outside of falling from a balloon or a tall cliff, skiing is the fastest way a human being can move without motorized help. Back when I raced, we didn't go as fast as they do now. But we didn't have the control of modern equipment, either. You carve your way down steep ice and snow at sixty or seventy miles per hour and try to hold it together. Maybe you hit eighty in a downhill race. There is nothing that keeps you in the course and out of the trees except your guts and your skill. The tiniest mistake, a misjudgment that only lasts a hundredth of a second, and you lose control. If you hit an obstruction, you can be torn in two. If you don't, the smallest mogul or bump or ridge can still toss you into the air. A skier making a yard-sale crash at high speed is a frightening thing to simply witness. But when it is you tumbling down the mountain like a cartwheeling gymnast, the power of the shock will surprise you. If you live to consider it, that is."

"So your roar was...?"

"A push-back at my fear. I discovered that if I roared, it helped me to not succumb to the fright."

We came down to the valley at the bottom of Spooner Summit and turned north toward Carson City. After a couple of miles, and a jog to the east, we connected with the new I-580 freeway and headed north toward Washoe Valley and Reno beyond.

"Ski racing always seems glamorous," I said. "Up on the mountains, in the sun, in the clouds. Spectacular vistas. People watching, amazed at what you do."

"It is glamorous," Joe said. "That's part of the pull of ski racing. It's not an ordinary sport like hockey or bowling. Ski racing is more like driving race cars or racing horses. But glamour goes hand-in-hand with fear. You step out in front of a world that expects you to be part sports star and part celebrity. The pressure to perform is huge. And if you fail by falling, you can get banged up in a big way."

"When you mentioned falling, you referred to a yard-sale crash. Does that happen often to racers?"

"Often enough that it stokes your fear. After a bad, high-speed fall, your equipment ends up scattered all over the mountain. Skis, goggles, helmet, hat, gloves. Maybe even some of your clothes get ripped off as you slide over frozen debris at seventy. The result looks like a yard sale of junk gone bad."

I nodded. "I've done that a few times myself," I said.

After a moment, I said, "Did Rell ever ski?"

"No. She was afraid of speed. She was very delicate. Like a flower. I often called her my hummingbird."

"She didn't do any sports?"

"No. She often said that sailing looks so beautiful, but when people would invite us out on their boats, she'd decline. She'd tell me, 'Your little hummingbird is afraid of the wind and water. I'll have to go sailing in my next life.'"

We pulled into the hospital parking lot a few minutes later.

"I can drop you at the door and then go park," I said.

"No. I'll walk from the parking lot like anyone else. If I didn't walk, how would I stay in shape?"

"I just thought you might be in a hurry," I said.

"I am. I'll walk fast."

I parked, and we left Spot in the Jeep. I had to walk at a good pace to keep up with Joe. When we got inside, I thought that if Joe was too upset, I could be his interface and spokesperson, but it was a foolish notion.

"My name's Joe Rorvik," Joe said as he walked up to the

counter. "My wife is Cynthia Rorvik, and she is in a coma here in this hospital under your care and protection, and I got a call from your security person saying that someone violated that protection and accessed her room, for what nefarious purpose I cannot imagine. Please have someone take me to her room." His impatience was palpable.

The woman behind the counter was visibly shaken and had no doubt been informed of the situation.

"Yes, Mr. Rorvik, I'll have someone here in a moment." The woman picked up her phone, pressed some buttons. "Mr. Rorvik is here," she said, and hung up. She looked up at Joe. She was obviously intimidated by him. "Ms. Morrison will be here in a minute."

Joe nodded, turned, and looked around as if he expected the woman to be there already.

When a woman walked up a minute later, he started walking in the direction from which she'd come before she could even introduce herself.

"Hi Mr. Rorvik, I'm Jeanine Morrison." She began to reach our her hand, but had to do an about-face. She began walking next to Joe. "I'm so sorry about this trouble, but I want to reiterate that your wife is okay. I mean, the intruder didn't do anything to her. Her doctor, Dr. Wells, will be joining us. Oh, Mr. Rorvik, the elevators are this way, please." She pointed to the left. People were getting off one of the elevators. Joe pushed in to their side. Jeanine Morrison and I followed.

"Hi Jeanine, I'm Owen McKenna, a friend helping out."

She turned and shook my hand.

"I can't remember her floor," Joe said, his voice stressed. "I can't seem to think."

"Five," Jeanine said. She reached over and pressed the button.

Jeanine spoke as we rode up several floors.

"The intruder came at four a.m. The nurses on duty were Gail Prescott and Marie Rodriguez. Gail and Marie heard a noise like someone bumping into a cart. They looked down the hall, and saw movement at the doorway of Mrs. Rorvik's room. The hall lights were on the low setting, and the main light in Mrs. Rorvik's room was off. All visitors coming from the elevator have to go by the nurse's station, so they knew that no one other than another patient could legitimately be in that part of the floor.

"Gail ran down to the room while Maria dialed security. As Marie watched, Gail went to the doorway. There was a thudding noise. She fell to the floor. A man in dark clothes stepped over Gail and ran to the exit stairwell, presumably the same way he accessed the floor."

"Rell is okay?" Joe asked.

"Yes."

"Is Gail okay?" Joe asked.

"She has a nasty bruise on her face where the man hit her, and she is a little dazed, but she'll be okay."

"Did Gail or Maria get a look at the intruder?" I asked.

"No. They both just said that he wore dark clothes. Neither of them got a look at his face."

"Was anything disturbed in Mrs. Rorvik's room?"

"Nothing appeared to have been touched including Mrs. Rorvik. Gail is a fast runner. She got there in time to scare him off."

The elevator came to a stop. When the door opened, Joe recognized his surroundings and immediately began walking fast. We matched his pace, Jeanine struggling in her pumps. A man and a woman at the nurse's station watched us go by.

Joe seemed to accelerate until he got to Rell's door. He came to a quick stop as he turned and looked in. He walked into the room and shut the door behind him. We came up behind him.

Jeanine turned to me. "He's very stressed," she said.

"He's got a good reason."

"He walks fast. Faster than young people."

I nodded.

"He really loves his wife, doesn't he?"

"Yeah, he does."

"How long have they been married?" Jeanine asked.

"I'm not sure. Around sixty years."

"Wow," she said.

We waited in silence. We could hear nothing through the thick door.

After a long minute Jeanine said, "I've burned through two

marriages. Twelve years on the first, and six on the second. I'm too old now to have a long marriage even if I found the right guy."

I didn't know how to respond.

"Of course," she continued, "maybe the problem is that I'm not the right girl. I'm pretty self-focused. My career. My friends. My travel plans. My movies. My restaurants. My home decorating preferences." She looked at the closed door. "Sixty years. She was obviously the right girl."

A man in a white coat came down the hall. Under the coat, he wore a purple dress shirt and a blue tie.

"Mr. Rorvik is in the room with his wife, doctor," Jeanine said.

The man glanced at Jeanine and turned to me. "I'm Tom Wells, Cynthia Rorvik's doctor."

"Owen McKenna," I said. "I'm a private investigator Joe has hired to look into Mrs. Rorvik's injury."

Wells stared at me, his eyes intense. "Which suggests that her fall may not have been an accident? Does that mean that our intruder may have been targeting Mrs. Rorvik?"

"Yes," I said.

The door opened, and Joe came out.

His agitation seemed gone. Spending a few minutes alone with Rell had helped. "She seems the same as before," he said. He looked at the three of us. "Hello, doctor. Am I interrupting?"

"We were just discussing what you and I talked about earlier," the doctor said. "Mr. McKenna says that there is a possibility, however remote, that the intruder in Mrs. Rorvik's room could be the person who pushed her off your deck."

"And?" Joe said.

"The assumption being that the intruder may be thinking that Mrs. Rorvik could come out of her coma and identify him."

"What is your thought?" Joe asked.

Wells looked uncomfortable. "Perhaps you and I should discuss this in private."

Joe said, "Please say what you think. I want Owen McKenna to hear what you have to say."

"Then let's go to my office." He looked at Jeanine Morrison. She smiled and left.

We walked the other direction, went through a series of doors, and entered a small office messy with books and periodicals and multiple computers and other specialized equipment I didn't recognize.

When we were sitting, Joe said, "A week or so ago you told me about Rell's injury. You were being gentle and you talked about it in generalities. Obviously, you know from experience that spouses do not take these things well. I've had some time to adjust. I'd like you to tell me again with Owen here to hear it. Please give me the details."

Dr. Wells took a deep breath as he rubbed his eyes. It was the kind of moment that made me thankful that I was not a doctor.

Wells began, "People who have miraculous recoveries from persistent vegetative states or even comas always have some higher brain function. We often believe that these people will never recover, and usually we are right. But sometimes they do, and we are as pleased and mystified as anyone else.

"Unfortunately, Mrs. Rorvik doesn't have the type of brain function she would need in order for us to even hope for such a recovery. She scores a three on the Glascow Coma Scale, which is a basic kind of measurement of how comatose patients respond to stimuli. Three is the lowest score and means that she has no verbal, motor, or visual activity. Her lack of brain function is consistent with the scope of her trauma, skull fracture, massive intracranial hemorrhage, brain edema, and brain shift. Her EEG also shows little activity. She exhibits several of the other characteristics that we look for on the brain death exam such that I and my colleagues expect her to progress to brain death. In short, eventual recovery from a deep coma is very rare, but there is no potential recovery from brain death."

"How is it that her heart is still beating when she can't breathe?" Joe asked.

"It is common in these situations. Heartbeat is controlled by the brain stem. It is one of the last things to go."

Joe said, "What is the brain death exam?"

"I already mentioned the EEG, the electroencephalogram. Brain activity is manifested by electric signals between the cells. An EEG shows whether or not the basic function is there. There are also a variety of other tests we do that reveal whether or not a person's brain is functional at basic levels, even if the person is in a deep coma."

"Such as," Joe said.

"Vestibulo-ocular reflexes, for example." Wells paused as if searching for an easy way to explain something to a layperson. "People have a built-in system that keeps our eyes moving opposite to the rotation of our heads so that we can focus on an object. For example, when your head turns to the right, your eyes tend to automatically turn to the left so that you can keep focusing on whatever you're looking at. If I look at you and shake my head left and right, my eyes keep looking at you. This is so important for basic activity, that it's hard-wired in the brain."

"A person in a coma has the reflex?" I said.

"Yes. If you shake their heads, their eyes move opposite to the shake. Even in the dark. If a person doesn't have the reflex and their eyes stay fixed in their head, we say they have doll's eyes, and it suggests severe impairment of the brain."

"Rell doesn't have it," Joe said.

"No, she doesn't."

"What else?" Joe asked.

"People in a coma respond to cold water in their ears. Their eyes turn toward the cold. Such patients also react to direct touch on their eyes. If you touch a cotton swab to a comatose person's corneas, they respond. People in a coma also show significant activity on their EEGs. Your wife has lost all these brain functions."

Joe looked down, then raised his head again to look at Dr. Wells.

The doctor said, "I can't tell you how sorry I am about this, Mr. Rorvik."

"Understood. Thank you."

"We will beef up our security," the doctor said. "Jeanine is putting a guard on this floor. He will be stationed near your wife's room all night long."

"Thank you," Joe said. "I will be in touch with you in the next few days regarding disconnecting the life support."

The doctor nodded, his face long and solemn.

We left.

"I'd like you to meet Rell," Joe said when we were back in the hallway.

"I'd like that," I said.

Joe led me into her room. "Rell, this is Owen McKenna. I've hired him to find out who pushed you off the deck. He's a good man, and he's making progress."

I looked at Joe. He gestured toward the bed.

Rell Rorvik was as tiny as her friend Simone. She lay under a white blanket. The hospital bed was tilted up at an angle. A breathing tube was inserted at the base of her throat, and the sheet curved around it and went up to cover shoulders that were as thin and narrow as those of a child.

Rell's eyes were closed. There was no movement except the soft rise and fall of her chest as the machine air was pushed in and out of her lungs.

Her skin was almost as pale as off-white wall paint, and it appeared to be paper thin as it stretched over prominent cheekbones and eyes that were pronounced in their sockets.

She had a high forehead, with soft, straight white hair that flowed down the sides of her face. It was thick enough that I imagined her to be one of those women who can proudly wear a pony tail all of their lives. On the upper left side of her head was a large bandage where they had probably operated. Below the dressing was a blue-brown bruise seeping under the skin of her temple.

In spite of the bruising, she was beautiful, and the lack of extra flesh on her face made me think that she was like an elegant bird, regal in life and graceful as she approached death. Joe's little hummingbird.

I'd seen many dead bodies during my cop career. As I walked through the door, I expected that seeing Rell would be another one of those experiences. But it was different in a significant way. Her brain might be nearly dead, and when it was, she would be declared legally dead. But having her living body before me gave me a sense of the Rell that once was.

There was a chair next to her bed. Her arm stretched under the covers so that her hand, still under the blanket, was close to the chair. I imagined that Joe had held her hand.

So, for Joe's benefit, I sat in the chair and reached under the edge of the blanket. As I wrapped my fingers around her tiny, warm hand, I felt a profound connection to the woman. I had been talking to Joe and Simone and others about her. I'd been learning something of her life. Now, holding her hand, I felt something of her spirit, a woman who fed the birds and searched out and befriended the abused girl, a woman who possessed a kind of magic such that everyone I had met said they felt they could say anything to her.

It is a strange connection we make between the personality and the vessel in which it resides. I knew her brain was gone, which meant her personality was gone. And yet, as I held her hand I could sense something of the woman who'd once existed in the body before me.

In many ways, touch is the greatest sense, the most intimate sense, the truest sense. Rell was mostly gone, but we shared touch.

After another minute of silent touch, I let go of her hand and turned to Joe.

He had left the room and shut the door without my knowing it.

I turned back to Rell Rorvik. "I'll do right by him, Rell. And by you." I stood up and joined Joe out in the hallway.

THIRTY

We were quiet on the drive back up to the lake. It was dark by the time I dropped Joe off at his house.

"I'm glad I got to meet Rell," I said as he got out of the Jeep.

"Me, too."

"I'm learning some things on this case. I'll call as soon as I know more."

He nodded, closed the door and went inside. I waited until I saw lights go on, then left.

"I know you're hungry, largeness, but hang in a bit longer, eh?" I said, reaching into the back seat to rub Spot's head.

Once again, I turned on Sierra Blvd, parked a block down from Ned and Simone's house, got out the binoculars and settled in to a boring evening of watching.

It was the same as the previous evening. Lights on downstairs, dark upstairs, no movement outside other than the occasional vehicle going by. At one point, I was getting drowsy, and I set down the binoculars to turn on the radio. When I raised the glasses back to my eyes I saw a person moving in the street in front of Ned's cabin. The darkness obscured any details, but the person looked to be male. He was thin and appeared to be wearing baggy jeans that bunched up around his shoes. It's one of the more reliable qualifiers. You see baggy gangsta jeans with the waistband hanging at the bottom of their butt, you know it's a guy between the ages of twelve and twenty-eight.

Gangsta-wannabe turned into a different driveway, shuffled up to the door, knocked, and someone let him inside. I went back to watching Ned's house.

Simone's Toyota was in the drive in front of the garage, which had its door lowered. Ned's tropical fish truck was at the end of the short drive, parked in the street, blocking Simone's car so that she couldn't leave without his permission and help. His truck was still sans bumper. This time, it wasn't up on jack stands, so its roof was only eight feet high.

I imagined them in the cabin, Ned sprawled on the couch watching a game, the volume turned up high, beers lined up on the couch arm, periodically shouting for Simone to bring him food or more beer, smacking her if she didn't jump fast enough. Simone would be in the kitchen, maybe reading a magazine or cooking a pie so that Ned would be so stuffed with food that maybe he'd hit her just a little bit less.

The evening rebroadcast of Fresh Air on NPR came and went. Then came an hour-long jazz program with the über-laid-back announcer periodically talking about the other side of Coltrane, whatever that was. Next, we were plunged into the classical triumphs of the Baroque period, too stuffy and formal for a romantic guy like me. When the news break came, I decided it was once again getting too late for Ned to have a visitor.

I turned on the lights, put the Jeep in drive, and cruised on past Ned and Simone's. A casual glance in my mirror showed a vehicle come down a side street, pull in front of Ned's place and turn off the lights.

I drove around the block, parked in the same place where I'd just spent three hours starving both Spot and myself. Looking through the binoculars, I saw that the car was a cab. Its lights were off, but I could see the silhouette of the driver.

The house showed no change. Whomever was visiting was already inside.

The upstairs light turned on. I couldn't hear the music, but I assumed, based on Simone's report, that it was playing loud downstairs.

Ten minutes later, the upstairs light went off. In little more than the time it would take to walk down the stairs, the front door opened. A man walked out and got into the cab. The cab's lights came on, and it pulled away.

I waited until it turned the corner, then I started up, turned on my headlights, and followed. Although it is hard for someone to detect a tail in the dark, I stayed back. Two turns later, the cab pulled out onto Lake Tahoe Blvd heading northeast. A few blocks down, the cab turned left on San Francisco Avenue and drove into the Al Tahoe neighborhood. Despite the snowy streets, I stepped on the gas and got to the intersection just before a knot of traffic would have cut me off. I braked, skidded into the turn, and went through the intersection.

The cab wasn't far ahead, so I slowed to let it gain some distance on me. When the cab was a block down, I sped up and followed. The cab drove all the way to the end of San Francisco before its brake lights lit up. It came to a stop. I kept going until I was a block behind the cab, then pulled over and parked.

Through the binoculars, I could just make out a dark shape getting out of the cab. The cab turned around and drove back toward me. I ducked down as it went by.

I told Spot to be quiet, knowing that it was a command that he wouldn't obey if he didn't feel like it. I got out of the Jeep, eased the door shut, and walked down the edge of the road in the dark.

San Francisco Avenue is lined with houses, most of them modest in size and style. Many are remodeled cabins from decades ago. At this time of night, most were dark on the street side. A few had lights on over their doors or garage doors. But it was not enough to see my mark. When I got near the end of the street, I tried to see tire tracks or footprints, but it was too dark.

I listened for any sound that might indicate which house my man had disappeared into. There was nothing. Two of the houses at the end of the street had no lights on. If he'd slipped into one of them in the dark, there was no way for me to know.

The road ended at the Truckee River Marsh. Although it was a cloudy night, the snow cover glowed a dim white. I was looking for a trail around the last house when I sensed a flash of light.

I turned to look, but there was nothing but snow-covered meadow interrupted by stands of meadow grasses that had somehow stood up through the snow. Well out into the meadow was the Truckee River, dark undulating shapes as the water meandered toward the lake. In the distance was the black water of Tahoe.

As if I were doing a grid search, I looked over the landscape in a regular fashion, taking care to study each part of the meadow whether there was something interesting to see or not. Nothing appeared to move. The flash of light had not been significant. I assumed it was someone walking their dog, using a flashlight intermittently to look for obstructions and hazards. But if that were the case, the dog would have been obvious in the night, a darker shape running around, silhouetted against the snow.

Seeing no dog made me more interested in finding the source of the light. I found a little trail in the dim light of night and walked down it a hundred feet or so, wondering if I should explore the meadow or go back and look in house windows. I was about to give up when I saw a flashlight go on farther out, over by the shore. The beam silhouetted a man. I couldn't tell for certain that it was the man at Ned's house, but I assumed it was.

I jogged out onto the marsh, going as fast as I could on uneven, frozen snow that had a thousand holes punched into it by walkers.

As I ran, the man's flashlight beam illuminated an object at the edge of the water. It was light in color and was about the size of a small rowboat. It was an unusual shape. The man bent down and appeared to lift up on it.

I trotted farther out the trail, then stopped and raised my binoculars.

The man had a type of boat I'd never seen before. It looked like an inflatable of some kind, but it looked high tech, with a center console that held a steering wheel. He pushed it into the water and jumped on. I heard the soft crank of a starter followed by an engine starting, an engine I couldn't see. Such a small boat would typically have an outboard motor, but this was some kind of a quiet inboard contained within the center console. It was one of the smallest inboard boats I'd ever seen.

I jogged down the trail hoping to get closer before the boat took off. The footing was uneven. My foot landed at a sharp angle, tempting a sprain. Then I slipped off the firm prints of people who'd come before me, and my leg sank deep into the untrampled snow at the side of the trail.

The engine revved a bit. It had a hint of lower harmonics in its sound. A four-stroke with some power. When he gave it a touch of throttle, the sound of thrust was like that of a jet ski. No propeller on an inflatable hull meant that it was a very low-draft boat. Drive it up onto the beach. Drive it away with no fear of a prop strike.

The boat cruised away, angling to the northeast.

I ran until I got to the shore and raised the binoculars.

He cruised without running lights, a violation of the law. I was breathing hard, and the image in my glasses jumped around. Eventually, my breathing calmed. With the image in the glasses steadied, I saw where he was going.

In the distance beyond the inflatable, was a large dark boat with dim light coming from some windows down near the waterline. Even in the darkness, I could see that the boat, while big, was sleek and pointy. I guessed it at fifty feet or more, constructed like a very modern cabin cruiser built to look like a race boat.

As the inflatable got farther from me, it was harder to see details in my binoculars. The inflatable slowed as he approached the big boat's stern. The man jumped out onto a tender deck, pulled on some kind of line and appeared to attach it to the bow of the inflatable. Then he stepped forward and reached for something.

A second later I heard the sound of a motor whining. At first I didn't know what it was. Then the inflatable lifted up onto the tender deck, and moved forward as if it were being pulled into a cavity of some kind. The motor sound quit. The man used both arms to pull on something above the boat. The vague picture of the inflatable boat disappeared as a white partition blocked my view.

I finally realized what I'd seen. The inflatable was the yacht's custom tender boat, a small, high-tech inboard designed to ferry people between the yacht and the shore. But unlike a dinghy towed behind or lifted off the water by a pivoting davit, this tender was simply winched into its own garage. With the garage door shut, no one could even tell the tender existed.

In a few moments, the deep rumble of the yacht's engines started. Running lights turned on. I heard the RPM shift as the props were engaged, and the yacht headed away.

I watched through the glasses for fifteen minutes as the big boat motored at no-wake speed out into the lake. The dark shape on dark water soon disappeared.

I walked back to the Jeep where Spot, no doubt hypoglycemic from lack of food, showed little enthusiasm at my return.

THIRTY-ONE

Early the next morning, Diamond stopped by my cabin. "Buenos días," he said when I opened the door.

Spot was at the door with me, wagging.

I motioned for Diamond to come in. "Coffee's still hot," I said.

"Stuff you made?"

"You're too picky to drink mine?"'

"No," Diamond said. "I just want to prep myself. Got doughnuts?"

"Nope."

"Hold on." He walked back to his Douglas County Patrol Unit and came back with a bakery bag. "Doughnuts," he said, as he opened the bag.

"Makes my coffee a little more palatable?"

"Sí." He held the bag out to me, holding it from the bottom.

I reached into the bag, pulled out a doughnut, and tossed it to Spot. It disappeared with one chomp and one swallow.

"That was a perfectly good doughnut," Diamond said, pulling one out for himself.

"I wouldn't have given him one if I thought otherwise. You're the one who introduced him to Danishes."

Diamond shrugged. "He's a Great Dane."

Spot stared at Diamond's doughnut bag. He carefully ran his tongue around his upper lip, starting all the way back on the left side, around the front, and back to the rear of the right side. He took a quick glance at me, then focused again on the doughnut bag.

I took another doughnut and ate it as I poured Diamond a mug of coffee.

"The throwing knives you gave me?" Diamond said. "Thought you'd want to know that they were made by Veitsi Mies."

"Who's that?"

"A metal-folding bad ass in Omaha."

"Nebraska," I said, remembering that Ned Cavett had gone there when he was a kid and ended up spending a long time in prison.

"Sí."

"What's a metal folding bad ass do? Duct work for buildings?"

"Different kind of metal folding," Diamond said. "Kind where they make super strong swords. Layers of steel, layers of nickel, tungsten, chromium. Heated up, folded, hammered, heated up, folded again. Like Damascus steel. Guy's a swordsmith. Got some Finnish in his background, thus his chosen name Veitsi Mies. Finnish for Knife Man."

"What's it mean to you that Ned Cavett is carrying Veitsi Mies's throwing knives?" I asked.

"Just that Ned has some association with someone who's way over on the dark side. Veitsi Mies makes the ceremonial swords for the Canyon Brotherhood."

"The methhead bikers."

"Yeah. Ned isn't in their league. But good to be aware that Ned was probably exposed to stories from Veitsi when he was inside. Could give him an out-sized sense of bravado. Bravado can make even a dirtball like Ned more dangerous."

"Good to know," I said.

Diamond bit off more doughnut and, chewing, said, "Making any progress with the accidents that might not be accidents?"

"Some," I said. "On a tip from Ned's girlfriend Simone, I've been watching their house. Around ten-ish last night, Ned had a visitor. Likely a guy that the girlfriend believes pays Ned to spy on Joe Rorvik. The visitor came and left in a cab. When he left, I followed him over to the Al Tahoe neighborhood. The guy got out of the cab and walked over the Truckee Marsh to a boat he'd beached there. It was quite the little tender."

Diamond looked blank. "I grew up in Mexico City," he said. "Not the first place you think of for learning about boats."

"Sorry. I don't know much about boats myself. A tender is a small boat for ferrying people to and from a large boat. If there is no dock, the large boat anchors offshore and people come to shore on a tender."

Diamond nodded. "Like tying up your cruiser or sailing yacht to a buoy at Sunnyside, and they bring you in to the restaurant on the little dinghy."

"Exactly. And big boats often have a low deck on the rear for carrying the little boat. It's called the tender deck."

"McKenna's boat university," he said.

I ignored him. "Anyway, this tender was small and wide with an inflatable perimeter, an inboard engine, and jet propulsion."

"An inflatable Jet Ski?" Diamond said.

"No, this was an actual boat you step into. Looked like it could hold four people. But it was light enough that the guy could push it off the beach by himself. He drove it out to a sizable yacht. An interesting detail is that the tender slides up into its own garage at the rear of the yacht. Probably, even in daylight, you can't even tell that the big boat has a small boat hidden in its belly."

"Any idea who the big boat belongs to?" Diamond asked.

"No. Thought I'd look online today. See if the search gods know anything."

Diamond ate the last of his doughnut, and, as he finished his coffee, he made a tongue-smacking noise and looked into the cup as if there were a bug in the bottom.

"You gonna live?" I said.

"Remember that Thoreau said that the mass of men lead quiet lives of desperation? Gotta be the only reason why you would drink that stuff."

"You think I'm desperate?"

Diamond was at the door. "Must be," he said. He pet Spot and left.

I got on the computer and began poking around. I typed "tender boat hides in big boat garage" into Google. I got nothing. I typed "new yachts on Lake Tahoe," and "Tahoe cabin cruisers with inflatable tenders."

I got nothing of relevance.

Like an aimless, wandering dog, I expanded my search to "Nedham Theodore Cavett domestic abuse."

Nothing.

I typed in "Veitsi Mies throwing knives" and got hundreds of hits. Ned's knives were a big deal, but none of the hits was about Ned.

I typed in "tender boat with inboard engine."

This time I got a couple of interesting search results. Up popped some Zodiac-style inflatable boats that had center consoles that did double duty as steering wheel mounts and housings for small inboard engines. The boats were similar to, if not the same as, what I had seen. Finally, I had learned something, but it didn't get me any closer to finding Ned's spymaster.

After an hour or more, I decided to have lunch. We had what was supposed to be a short break between storms. I fired up the barbecue, put on several brats to the side of the coals so they wouldn't burn, and carefully laid a bunch of fries perpendicular across the grill so they wouldn't fall through. When the food was done and we were eating, the phone rang.

"Yeah?" I mumbled, mouth full. Spot and I were out on the deck, enjoying high-altitude December sun. Maybe the air temperature was only 30, but the sun was like a broiler on medium-high.

"You're eating lunch," Street said.

"Street, my sweet, so nice to hear the mellifluous harmonics of your voice. We are, yeah."

"What's on the menu?"

"Barbecued brats and cheddar cheese on Kaiser rolls, fries, Ketchup, and Sierra Nevada Pale Ale," I said.

"What's Spot eating?"

"Barbecued brats and cheddar cheese on Kaiser rolls, fries, Ketchup, and Sierra Nevada Pale Ale," I said. I dipped a fry in Ketchup and tossed it to him. He snapped it out of the air with a click of teeth. His tail was on medium speed. If I picked up another brat, his tail would go into the red-line zone.

"You know that's bad food," Street said.

"I ate broccoli at your house the other night."

"So?"

"They cancel out," I said.

"You think that eating a little good food means you can eat

bad food with impunity?"

"Of course. Check marks in the credit column cancel out check marks in the debit column," I said.

"I don't think so," she said. "Anyway, why not just eat food that's really good for you?"

"Because really good food tastes bad, and really bad food tastes good. The whole point of eating broccoli is so you can eat brats. It's the broccoli-to-brats equation. This is cutting-edge nutrition stuff. I thought all scientists were familiar with it."

"I'm not familiar with much of your world."

"Is that why you won't marry me?" I said.

"You never formally asked."

"What if I formally asked right now?" I said.

"Well," Street paused, "your diet might be a sticking point."

"I'd let you eat all the broccoli you want. Tell you what, you want to come over and join us? You could bring some broccoli. We could test-drive eating separate meals together."

"Thanks, hon. It's a sweet offer. But I better get back to work."

"Truth be told, I'd turn it down, too," I said. "It would be hard to watch us eat brats while you're picking broccoli out of your teeth."

"And after the brats, you'd probably eat a bag of doughnuts for dessert," she said.

"Actually, we already had the doughnuts an hour ago with Diamond."

THIRTY-TWO

After lunch, I began calling Tahoe marinas, starting at Kings Beach – which would be noon on the lake clock – and working my way clockwise around the lake.

"Hi, this is Tommy John Smith from Tom's Craft Brews over behind the Timber Cove pier," I said when they answered. "Hey, we had this guy come down the pier a few days ago and pick up a case of our TJ Smith Mountain IPA. It kind of stood out, you know, what with it being winter and there aren't a lot of boats out. Anyway, after he left, we noticed that he left his sunglasses on our counter. They're prescription Persols and look pretty pricey. So I wanted to return them, but I don't know his name or number. So I'm calling marinas to ask you if you've seen his boat. It's one sweet ride, probably over fifty feet, real pointy looking like a combo cigarette racer/cabin cruiser. And it's got an inflatable tender that parks in its own garage at the back of the big boat. I figure I've been exposed to most of the boats on the lake, but this one is bigger and faster-looking than most Tahoe cruisers I've seen. Any idea whose boat that is?"

"Nah. Sorry I can't help you," the first guy said.

I repeated my call at the next marina and got roughly the same answer. I dialed my way through Incline, down the East Shore, across the South Shore, and on up the West Shore. It wasn't until I'd gotten around to Tahoe City at ten o'clock, that someone knew what I was talking about.

A woman who introduced herself as Shirl said, "She hasn't stopped here, but I saw her cruise by a few months ago. It would have been around Labor Day. She was about a hundred yards out, so I didn't get a real good look at her. But from what I saw, that baby is pure boat candy. Like you say, I could tell she was fifty-plus feet if she's ten. She has a black hull and white topsides. Looks real James Bondy. So I grabbed the glasses to check it out. Dear

God, lemme step aboard, spend some time, have a gin and tonic, and lounge in my silk robe! Innaways, I didn't see any tender, but I took a zoom pic with my phone just to use for reference, and in my free time the rest of that afternoon, I poked around on the computer looking at boat pictures, and guess what?"

"What?" I said.

"I found it!" Shirl said. "She's a Predator Fifty-Four, built by Sunseeker Yachts. Turns out she's pushing sixty feet. And she's got this Oh-My-God layout. In the lower cabin, you've got your saloon with your entertainment center, dining, and full-on galley. Then there's the master stateroom with en suite bath. 'Course, in this business, I've seen that before. I even learned from a French tourist how to pronounce it. The EN in en suite is like the word On, but you kinda drop the N. Almost sounds like you're grunting. Innaways, in addition to all that, there's two more staterooms and a whole other head. So she can sleep six. Now topside, you've got your aft sundeck and cockpit and lounge and wet bar with a hydraulic skylight roof so, rain or shine, you're stylin'. There's also a forward sundeck. And the tender deck has a swimming platform and a hot and cold outdoor shower for when you come out of the water. We're talking a fifty-nine-foot-long, three bedroom house that goes thirty-three knots, and it looks like it goes a hundred and thirty-three knots. Can you believe it?!"

"Hardly," I said. "But no tender garage?"

"Oh! I forgot to tell you. You're exactly right. The tender has its own bay, and it's the cutest little thing. I saw on the computer how it works. If you're looking at the stern, the tender deck has two stairways, starboard and port, that lead up to the lounge and cockpit and sundeck. And right between the stairways, pretty much hidden like a secret door, is the garage door. It lifts up, and inside is the tender and your various boat toys, scuba gear and such. Close that baby, and no one knows it's there." Shirl finally stopped to breathe.

"Any idea whose boat it is?" I asked.

"Nope. I even asked some of the yachting types who've come in since. They've never heard of it. I mean, sure, this lake is big, but how you gonna hide a yacht like that? You'd think most people in those circles would know about it. It's kind of a phantom lux-yacht, probably hiding in some boathouse most of the time. And with the black hull, it look's like something in a movie, like a vampire yacht. Hey, that would be a cool idea for a movie, huh? A vampire yacht?"

"Yeah," I said. "That would be cool. Thanks so much for your time. And Shirl?"

"Yeah?"

"I don't know how much you like your current job, but I'm betting that Sunseeker Yachts would hire you as a salesperson."

"Oh, my God, are you serious? That would be, like, a dream job! Wouldn't that be a dream job?"

"Yeah, Shirl, it would definitely be a dream job. Keep it in mind."

I hung up.

Like Shirl, I found the Predator 54 on my computer, and her over-the-top description was perfectly apt for the futuristic, floating, speed machine.

Armed with the name of a boat model, I renewed my online search, typing all the stuff I tried before but with the addition of the words Predator 54.

Fifteen minutes later, I found what I was looking for.

It was on a woman's personal blog dated the previous July.

> Roughing It in Tahoe – Boat Camping!
>
> Last week, Jim and I were at an outdoor party at Jarrett and Suzanne's in Los Altos Hills, but it was so hot that you had to either be in the pool or, as soon as you dried off, you had to go inside. So the conversation turned to going up to Tahoe to cool off. Then Bob (RKS Properties for those of you who aren't up on the happening crowd) said he was going up that weekend, and he invited all of us to come up and ride on his new boat. Of course, most people had plans. But Jim and I went along with Jarrett and Suzanne. Bob and Tricia were the perfect hosts, and so was their dog Pretty Girl! And their new Predator 54 – named Beats Working – is the perfect boat!

The blog showed a bunch of pictures of the three happy couples on the boat. Some had been taken from way down a dock and showed the entire boat. In two of the pictures, the prominent subject was a beautiful Greyhound, its leash held by a middle-aged man who was dressed like a model, his clothes freshly-pressed and looking very suave.

As Shirl, the marina lady, had described, the boat had a black hull and white topsides, and it looked very fast. I wasn't certain that it was the boat I'd seen in the dark, but it looked like it. Mostly, the connection to RKS Properties and the Steven's Peak Resort was too much of a coincidence, so I assumed it was the boat I'd seen.

Most people leave their boats in dry dock over the winter because winter in Tahoe is brutal on boats. The snow melts on the warm days and runs into pieces of equipment and into drainage channels. When it refreezes and expands, it can cause major damage. And if you have a boat with indoor heating, that exacerbates the problem. The only way a boat can be out and about in the winter is if it is out of the snow during storms. The "Beats Working" was too big for most dry dock storage. So either it was kept in covered wet storage by a marina, or it had its own boathouse to keep it free from the onslaught of winter weather.

I'd just spoken to nearly every marina, and I felt like someone would have mentioned it if the boat was in their care. The reasonable conclusion was that the boat was kept in its own boathouse.

If I could find that boathouse, I could find Bob. At least, when he was in town. If I could find Bob, I could learn what Ned's spymaster was doing.

So I began another internet search, looking for Bob Somebody of RKS Properties. Real estate records are public. I spent some time searching online databases. I was looking for a lake shore address owned by Bob and Tricia, but with no last name, I had no luck.

Although not all Tahoe property records are online, they can all be obtained by personal visits to the county courthouses. That would take a lot of time. Another more likely problem was that Bob and Tricia's Tahoe home might be owned by a Limited Liability Corporation. Sometimes people do that for tax purposes.

Sometimes they do it to keep their addresses out of the public eye. It would be difficult and time-consuming for me to find Bob's house if it was owned by an LLC, even if he owned the LLC. And Bob and Tricia might keep the Beats Working in the boathouse of a friend, in which case I might never find it.

Now that I knew that RKS Properties was run by a guy named Bob, I thought I'd give the phone approach another try.

So once again I went through the multiple voice menus at RKS, got to an actual human secretary, and did my best performance of a guy who was one of Bob's old friends. Best old buddy. I was at his wedding. We got drunk together in college.

It didn't work. At the end, the secretary was so frustrated that he threatened to hang up on me.

So I hung up first just to show that, like Bob, I was a guy who was used to being in charge.

I realized that the easiest approach for me to find Bob might simply be to drive a boat around the shore of the lake and look for the Beats Working. The boat might be locked up in a boathouse. But because the water level was down several feet from the high-level mark, I could look under the lower walls of most boathouses. A black hull wasn't easy to see in the shadows. But it was unusual, so it would be relatively easy to identify the correct boat. Unfortunately, it was a 75-mile trip around the lake. But maybe I'd get lucky and find it before I had to make the entire trip.

And I knew someone who would loan me a boat, my patron Jennifer Salazar.

THIRTY-THREE

I dialed Jennifer's cell number.

After four rings, she answered, excited and breathless as only a kid can be.

"Owen!" she said, "I'm so glad you called! Where are you? How is Street? Is his largeness still catching bad guys? Is it snowing in Tahoe? Do you need a boat or something?"

"Jennifer, such enthusiasm makes me think you were expecting a boyfriend to call."

"Actually, I was. But I'm glad to hear from you, too!"

"You have a boyfriend? But I wasn't consulted. Don't I have approval privileges? If not, I still have approval responsibility."

"Well, I want your approval, but I'm almost seventeen years old. I have to grow up sometime."

"You grew up in the brain department about eight years ago. You're not allowed to grow up in the sex department for another six years. There are rules about these things."

"More of Owen's precepts?" she said. "And who said anything about sex, anyway?"

"Where I come from, a boyfriend means sex."

"Owen, you're so parochial."

"Parochial precepts might save you. And shouldn't you be in school instead of talking to me on the phone?" I added. "That's the first thing boyfriends do, you know, convince you to skip school and change your major to amore."

"I am in school. I was in a lecture class on Descartes when you called. Anything for a break from that. Of course, he's pretty important, but to call him the father of philosophy... gimme a break. Your call is a welcome relief. I sit in the back of that class hoping for a reason to leave prematurely."

"Why would you want a break?"

"The class is boring. Tedious. It stretches credulity to attach so much importance to this guy. It's not like he's the Einstein of philosophy. Not even the Newton. He's like the Jiffy Lube of philosophy. He came up with a couple of good concepts and wrapped it up in a clever marketing package. To ascribe all future philosophical insights to a Descartes foundation would be like saying that the robot missions to Mars were only possible because of the lubrication business model laid down by Jiffy."

"But I thought all classes at Harvard were exciting."

Jennifer burst into guffaws and shrieks and giggles. "That's good. That's funny. Wait 'til I tell that to my friends."

"You will of course exclude my name when you quote any of my pronouncements that they might think dumb?"

"Ha! The marquee at the Harvard Comedy Club will read, 'Jennifer Salazar performs Owen McKenna, Boston Native And Harvard Apologist.' I'm going to change my major to performance art. There's money in standup comedy, you know."

"But you already have four hundred million."

"Not if I keep lending you boats, which then get destroyed."

"Speaking of which..."

"You DO want a boat! I knew it!"

"I just need to make a little trip around the lake and look for a certain boat that's involved in a spy network."

"Spies in Tahoe! Wow! The most excitement we ever get at Harvard is when someone is late returning a library book."

"Libraries are a critical part of the foremost learning institution in the world," I said.

More guffaws and giggles. "Okay, do you want to use the runabout or the cruiser or the sailboat? Oh, wait, the sailboat is the one you sunk."

"Ouch, that hurts," I said.

"So the cruiser it is, then. Do you remember her name?"

"I don't think I ever knew."

"Babar's Mistress," she said.

"Because of your elephant project. I like it."

"I thought you would."

"How are the elephants, by the way?" I asked.

"Not good. Habitat destruction is still rampant. But worse, ivory poaching remains so severe that elephant survival in the wild is very tenuous. When I was young and naïve, I thought I could just use my money to buy more land in India and Africa and set up protected wildlife havens."

"But now that you're old and wise?"

"Now I know that bad people will come onto land, private or not, and kill the elephants anyway. And do you know what terrible euphemism the sympathizers use to minimize public perception of elephant poaching? Resource extraction. Can you believe it?"

"That is disgusting," I said. "What are you going to do?"

"The key is worldwide education. People need to understand that to buy something made of ivory is to kill more elephants. We're looking at the very real possibility of the extinction of elephants. It's so heartbreaking that I sometimes lose hope."

"Hang in there, Jennifer. The elephants need you."

I heard a sniffle and cough on the line, and I realized that Jennifer was losing her innocence at a deep level.

"I'll call my caretaker and let him know you're coming," she said, her voice a bit brighter. "When shall I say?"

"Tomorrow morning?"

"Will do. Just one question," she said.

"Yeah?"

"Not that I can't afford it, but what are the chances that this spy mission will result in Babar's Mistress being blown up or sunk or riddled with fifty-caliber bullet holes?"

"Less than ten percent for any single one of those. Chances of all three happening at once are miniscule."

"Okay. And one request?"

"Name it," I said.

"Will you take Street and Spot? I'd like to have that image in my mind. You're like the perfect family."

"Except that Street doesn't eat brats. She even disapproves of me and Spot eating brats. What kind of perfect family can we be with such a bratwurst divide?"

"Okay, she's flawed but she's worth it," Jennifer said.

THIRTY-FOUR

The next morning, Street and Spot and I drove down the East Shore and turned in at the big gate with the Tiffany lamps. I pressed the button and identified myself to the caretaker. The gate opened, and I drove the Jeep along the winding drive through the Jeffrey pine forest. The snow-covered ground looked clean and spare and uncluttered white. The tall trees had all been trimmed of dead branches up to about 60 feet, which made the landscape look like an abstract, high-mountain version of a Roman colonnade with huge columns of wood instead of marble, arrayed in a random layout instead of in regular rows.

I pulled around the curve at the end and parked in front of the 40-room, French Renaissance mansion, the personal lake estate that Jennifer Salazar called the Mausoleum ever since she was nearly murdered two and a half years ago. Although she was and still is a minor, the courts and state legislature took note of her excessive precociousness – and the sizable chunk of her inheritance that she decided to invest in Nevada – and made an exception to the laws. Ever since, Jennifer is the only Nevada resident under 18 who is considered an adult and doesn't need a legal guardian.

Street and I got out, and I let Spot out just as the caretaker walked out of the garage, which looked large enough to hold ten vehicles. As Spot ran up to him, he raised his arms in the air and froze. He didn't project fear as he held his arms up, but simple practicality. He didn't want his hands mangled by a dog.

"Spot, no," I said. Spot ignored me and sniffed the motionless man all over. I had to walk up and pull Spot away from him.

"Sorry," I said.

The man lowered his arms. "Dog's bigger than a mountain lion," he said, glaring at Spot. The man had a grizzled face, hard edge of jaw and nose, and red gray hair the texture of wire.

"Randall, right?" I said.

"Wow, good memory."

When I got close to the caretaker, I understood Spot's interest. The man smelled of fish.

The caretaker must have seen me sniffing the air.

"I've been cleaning fish in the garage. Miss Salazar allows me to fish off the dock when I have the time. Our arrangement is that half of my catch goes into the freezer for her, and I get to eat the other half."

"I wouldn't think that she's home enough to eat her share," Street said.

"No, she's not. So she has me drive her share to the local kitchen for the homeless, and she gives it to them. Let me give these mitts another go in the wash, and then I can take you to the boathouse. I'll be right back."

He went back into the garage. In a minute he returned, drying his hands on a towel, smelling no different. "You'll be taking out the big boat, then?" he said as we walked around the house on a flagstone path.

"Yes, please," I said.

He looked up at the sunny sky. "Nice day for a winter ride."

"Actually, we're just looking for a boat. Maybe you've seen it. A fifty-nine foot cruiser called a Predator Fifty-Four."

"White top, black hull?" he said.

"Yeah," I said, surprised that he would know it.

"I'm a bit of a boat fancier. Sometimes I use the binoculars to watch boats. After my chores, of course."

"Of course," I said.

"I've seen the Predator several times since it first appeared last summer. A standout craft by any measure. I think her home port is someplace a few miles north of here. She always comes and goes at an angle that indicates where she usually docks. I'd guess Cave Rock or thereabouts."

"Thanks. Good tip."

He took us into the boathouse. Babar's Mistress rocked gently. Lapping sounds filled the space as small waves bounced off the boat's side.

"Didn't there used to be two slips in here?" I asked, thinking back to the time Street and Spot and I rescued Jennifer from her would-be killer.

"Yes. The runabout was here," the caretaker said, pointing. "But Babar's Mistress is too big for easy dry dock, so Miss Salazar had the boathouse renovated and the roof raised to fit it. The runabout is in dry dock instead. In the summer, the runabout goes onto the boat hoist."

"Hey, Spot, wanna go for a ride?"

Spot has been on many boats, so it was familiar territory. He followed Street onto the boat, wagging with enthusiasm even though some of his boating experiences had ended badly.

The caretaker followed us onboard and gave us a quick tour. The boat had features similar to the Predator 54 but without such slick styling. I suffered a brief pang of envy when I saw that Jennifer's cruiser was two staterooms bigger than my log cabin, and it had an automatic dishwasher.

We went up to the upper cockpit, and the caretaker gave us basic instructions on running the bilge pump, starting the engine, shifting and steering and working the lines, running the computer and the radio.

"You've piloted big boats before, right?"

"Sure," I said, thinking back on the time I got in a canoe and remarked on how much bigger it was than the kayak I'd ridden in a year before. "What's the displacement on this ride?" I had to look away from Street who was distracting me by rolling her eyes as if they were loose in her skull.

"Forty-eight thousand pounds," he said. "So you have to go slow when you ease up to a dock or bring her back into this boathouse."

"No problem," I said.

"In case you have any questions, I've typed up some checklists here." He pointed to a three-ring binder in which were several pages in Mylar sleeves. "And if you have trouble, we have the latest marine radios, which I'm sure you're familiar with. Do you need anything else?" he said in classic butler style.

"No thanks. I think we're good."

He nodded at Street, kept his distance from Spot, and left.

I hit the transmitter button to roll up the big boathouse door. Then I studied the checklists.

"Are you not a confident sea captain?" Street said.

"I'm just checking to make sure he got his information correct," I said.

In my peripheral vision, I saw Street look at Spot, point at me, and make a little questioning shake of her head.

Spot glanced at me, then turned back toward Street and wagged. Maybe he was showing confidence in his master. Or maybe he was laughing at me, too.

I sat in the captain's chair on the bridge. With the checklists as my guide, I got the boat started. Street took care of the lines, I shifted into reverse, and we backed out of the boathouse.

Street came up to the cockpit and sat in the port-side captain's chair. It felt like we were sitting 12 feet above the water.

When we were well back from shore, I shifted into forward and cranked the wheel.

"You're pretty sure you know how to run this thing?" Street said. "He made it sound like its excessive size makes it take a long time to stop or turn. I'd hate to hit other boats or run aground." Street said.

"Your question reveals your confidence in me. I love that."

"Actually, it looks pretty easy," Street said.

"You need to remember that I take my responsibilities as boat captain very seriously. There's a lot involved."

"So I see."

I kept it at idle as we motored north slower than Spot swims when he's taking it easy.

"Do you need me to navigate?" Street said.

"I'm just heading toward Cave Rock like the caretaker suggested."

"And you know the direction," she said.

I pointed at Cave Rock, which stuck up from the shore in front of us. "I thought I'd just aim the boat toward it. Do you think that will work?"

"Probably," Street said. "But you've got so much to keep track of, being captain and all, I thought maybe you needed to plug coordinates into the computer."

"To enhance our adventure, I think we'll just do it the nineteenth century way."

"What shall we look for?" Street said.

"A big, sleek boat. But it will likely be hiding inside a boathouse."

"Hiding," Street said. "Because it's wondering if you're looking for it."

"Right."

"How will we find it when it's hiding?"

"Most boathouses have walls that start somewhere above the waterline. Because the lake level is down, I'm hoping we can see underneath those walls. If so, the hull will show. It's black, and that's unusual. So that should make it easier for us."

Street nodded.

We motored north.

Spot got tired of looking out the side of the lounge area behind the cockpit. He walked over to one of the curved seating areas and looked at the cushions.

"Spot's looking at the settee," Street said. "You think it's okay if he lies on it?"

"Jennifer would say yes," I said.

Street walked over, patted the cushion and said, "It's okay, Spot."

He jumped up, lay down, stretched out his jaw between his front paws. The sun coming through the vinyl windows of the removable canopy was warm, and he went to sleep. Behind him was the deep blue of the lake and the mountains beyond that.

The East Shore has lots of boathouses. We cruised by at a crawl. Street found the binocular stowage and focused a pair of them on the shore.

"Any luck?" I said after we'd gone a few miles.

"No. Lots of boats, but every one has a white hull."

"Cave Rock is coming up," I said. "I'd hoped we'd find it by now."

"Sorry," Street said.

We cruised by the last house south of Cave Rock. Then we came to the state park and the boat launch. Cave Rock loomed above. I looked up at the vertical wall of rock where Ryan Lear's friend and business partner had fallen to his death while making an illegal free-climb the previous summer.

"No black-hulled boats," Street said. "There are houses north of Cave Rock. You want to keep going?"

I nodded. "It would be worth it to go all around the lake to find out who is behind Ned Cavett's spy mission."

"Did it occur to you that we might not find the boat? It could be in a boathouse where we can't see under the walls."

"Yeah, it occurred to me. I've seen boathouses that are set into the shoreline and nothing is visible. But I have nothing else to go on."

"Just checking," Street said.

We went around Cave Rock. The shoreline curved to the northeast. The highway was well above the shore. There was a row of houses tucked in below, accessible by a narrow road that switch-backed down from the highway.

"Several of these houses have boathouses," Street said. Then, "Stop! Stop the boat!"

"What?" I said as I pulled the throttle back and shifted into neutral.

Street had the binoculars to her eyes for a long time. We coasted to a near stop, then rotated to port even as I cranked the wheel to starboard. No steering without forward motion.

"That's gotta be it," Street said. "Under the edge of that gray boathouse is a very long black hull. Do you see it?"

"I see the boathouse. It's too far away to see without the glasses."

Street handed them to me.

I refocused them and studied the shore. There it was, a dark hulking shape under the side of a long boathouse with gray clapboard siding.

"That must be it," I said. I shifted back into forward, left the throttle at idle, and we eased toward it.

I trained the glasses on the house behind the boathouse. It was a large modern design that stepped up the slope like boxes stacked on one another, each one above stepped back to match the angle of the mountain. One of the levels was all glass, and it blazed with light in the middle of the day.

It was a good sign because it meant someone was home.

As we cruised closer, we came into view of the end of the

boathouse. The door was open. The "Beats Working" Predator 54 floated in the serene protection of its shelter. Even from the rear, it was vaguely like looking at an F-16 fighter jet sitting in a hangar.

"I want you to drop me off," I said.

"What?!" Street said. "I can't do that!"

"Sure, you can. We'll just ease up to the end of the dock, I'll jump off, and you'll back away."

"You're crazy! I don't know how to drive this boat."

"Sure you do. You told me a few minutes ago that it looks easy. So you put it in forward or reverse, steer it like a car, and take it back to Jennifer's boathouse."

"You don't want me to pick you up?! What will you do?"

"Someone is home at that house. I'll ask them to talk to me. This is the break I need. When I'm done, I'll call you, and you can pick me up in the Jeep." I fished in my pocket, pulled out the key fob, and handed it to her. Then I steered toward the dock of the Beats Working.

"This is dangerous, Owen," Street said. "This guy may have killed multiple times. You'll be defenseless. He could shoot you, take you out into the middle of the lake, and sink your body."

"He could, but he won't. Even if he's the killer, he's gone to considerable effort to make the deaths look like accidents. This guy has to maintain his facade of a businessman who is simply trying to develop a ski resort. He may decide he wants to kill me, but he won't do it at his house or on his boat. He'll wait until I'm not on or near his territory, and then he'll arrange another accident."

"What about Spot?" Street said.

"He'll stay with you. Help you drive the boat."

"He'll help me swim to shore when I crash this thing into Jennifer's dock and sink it."

"You'll be fine, my sweet." I shifted the boat into neutral as we got close to the dock.

"I'm going to go out on the bow. When we get closer, shift it into reverse to slow our momentum. When we get close enough to the dock, I'll jump off, then you back it away. I'll call you later."

I got out of the captain's chair.

"But I..."

"No buts, hon, you'll do fine." I gave her a kiss and hustled my way down the stairs to the deck. Holding onto the railing for support, I walked the narrow passage to the forward sundeck. Spot joined me, looking toward the dock, turning and looking up at me. At the bow, I lifted my leg over the railing and waited as we coasted toward the dock.

We got closer, but we weren't slowing down. I envisioned what 48,000 pounds of ship would do to the dock. Without turning my head, I started waving frantically to Street up on the bridge, my palm out in a stop motion. I leaned over, wondering if I could lesson the blow. I waved more, a gesture of panic.

We were about to hit. I leaped down to the dock, turned to put my hands on the hull, and push. In a moment, the engine roared. The cruiser slowed. Just before it hit the dock post, the boat stopped and then moved backward. Relieved, I stepped back a bit.

The boat retreated at a faster crawl. Suddenly, the prop wash came toward me, a large churning, bubbling mass of water. I jumped back, worried that the swell of water would come over the dock. It didn't, and I relaxed.

Jennifer's boat continued to accelerate rearward. When it was well away from the dock, I heard the engine RPM drop.

Street was probably trying to calm herself. It was a close call, but nothing was damaged.

The boat's RPMs revved once again. I stared, feeling ill-at-ease. As the big boat came forward, it made a fast, sweeping turn. It curved away from the dock and boathouse where I was standing, and it then arced off toward the center of the lake and turned back south toward its home.

As I watched, stunned at Street's chutzpah, the aggressive, curving wake came toward the dock, hit the posts hard enough to send ice water spray into the air, soaking me.

The last thing I saw as they cruised away was Spot standing at the stern, looking at me, wagging hard.

THIRTY-FIVE

The Predator's boathouse was so big that it enclosed the 59-foot boat with room to spare. There was a roll-up garage door like the one on Jennifer's boathouse. The door was up. The boat inside glowed from the light coming through skylights in the roof. With its black hull and pointy lines, the small ship looked sinister.

There was a dock walkway along the inside of the boathouse. The dock, like the boat itself, did not extend to the end of the boathouse, so that even though the roll-up door was open, one could not walk into the boathouse from the end.

I walked down the dock and tried the side door of the boathouse. It was locked. Someone had at least made a pretense of security. I went back to the open end of the boathouse, wondering if anyone up in the house was noticing. I was in full view if anyone happened to look out the windows.

As I looked in the open rear of the boathouse, I could visualize where the boat's tender bay lay between its rear stairways. But it was very well hidden. The door was the same smooth material and color as the rest of the boat, and its edges were the natural lines of the boat. Without knowing about it, one would never imagine that it existed.

I gripped the rear wall of the boathouse and leaned out over the water to look inside. About five feet above the level of the dock was a metal electrical conduit. It passed through holes drilled in the metal wall studs. It wasn't much, but it was all I had.

I knew that if I hung from the conduit, my feet would be in the water, but thanks to Street's boating prowess, my feet and lower legs were soaked anyway. I grabbed onto the conduit and lowered myself down off the dock.

As my feet entered the icy water, I had a brief thought about how my body would provide a well-grounded electrical passage should any of the wires in the conduit have frayed insulation and – because of my weight pulling on the conduit – bump bare wire to metal. Metal conduit is not really strong, so I tried to grab it next to the studs as I went hand-over-hand down the wall. I figured it would have less chance of bending or breaking.

I came to the inner dock without experiencing electrocution. I stood on the dock until my shoes and pants drained some, then I stepped onto the tender deck of the Beats Working.

I walked up one of the rear stairs to the lounge and cockpit level. I sat down on one of the leather settees in the diffused glow from the skylights in the boat's ceiling, which in turn got its light from the skylights in the boathouse roof.

To one side was a wet bar with a nice selection of liquor bottles but no beer. I pulled a heavy lowball glass from a rack, poured a couple of fingers of Macallan single malt Scotch, and brought it over to the large, leather captain's chair. I sat down and took a sip.

I noticed the key in the boat's ignition. Lake shore dwellers often think of security in terms of protecting against riff-raff who come by highway. Rarely do they consider access from the lake. But I wasn't here to steal a one-point-five million dollar boat. I just wanted to get its owner to talk to me.

It took a minute to figure out what switches ran what. When I had the accessories battery turned on, the music panel over by the liquor sideboard glowed with blue back-lighting.

I got up and played with it. I'm not tech-fluent, so it took some experimenting to make the music come on. Push some buttons, tap on a touch screen, follow a menu within a menu, move a virtual volume slider, and piano music began playing through unseen speakers. The bass notes were rich and deep, the mid-range tones clear, the treble sharp and crisp, Tommy Flanagan playing big chords on a jazz standard, running up and down the keyboard using all five fingers on each hand.

Bob from RKS might not share my taste with his plan to reconfigure a beautiful mountain wilderness, but he shared my taste in music. The drink wasn't bad, either.

As I listened, I tried more switches and learned which ones worked which lights. Eventually, I had some good mood lighting, simulating a romantic twilight outing on the yacht inside the boathouse during the middle of a sunny day. Hidden cans made glowing ellipses on the carpeted floor. Blue glow came out from under the settees and from behind the edges of windows and fixtures and the opening to the companionway to below decks. Even the stairway going down below decks had light flowing from under the railings and the leading edges of the steps. It created a strong flavor of Vegas, which contrasted with the sophistication of the music and the single malt Scotch.

Despite my activities, no one came running. If the boat was alarmed, the alarm was off. I decided to take a tour of the boat.

Below decks was as advertised on the Sunseeker website, large spaces, luxurious appointments, top-quality fixtures, exquisite design. The carpets were thick. Every other surface was either upholstered leather, gloss-varnished birds-eye maple, or stainless steel. And everywhere, the lighting was such that you couldn't see the light source. All you could see was that the surfaces glowed.

After inspecting the staterooms and galley and saloon, I went back up the companionway and headed for the stern to satisfy my curiosity about the tender garage.

It took me awhile to figure out the mechanism. When I did, the door rose silently, revealing the tender boat inside. No doubt, like the rest of the yacht, there were lights in the tender garage as well, but I couldn't find them. Nevertheless, there was enough ambient light coming in the open boathouse for me to see a soiled mark on the tender's wheel and engine housing. It looked like a smeared hand print.

Partly, it seemed out of place because everything else I'd seen on the boat was spotless and clean. Mostly, it was notable because the mark was dried blood.

THIRTY-SIX

Dried blood is not a crime, even though it seemed like a crime to smear blood on a piece of equipment as nice as the Predator. Nevertheless, I figured that the blood might be significant.

Time to talk to Bob or his representative.

I'd already tried the polite way on the phone, and that wasn't effective. I had a better idea of how to get attention.

Without starting the engines, I turned on the ignition and tried a quick beep on the horn.

An amazing, deep, resonant honk shook the enclosed boathouse space. So I blasted out a Shave-and-a-Haircut-Two-Bits rhythm. It was like a ship's foghorn, painful to my ears. In a moment, an echo came back from the mountains, and in another moment, another echo. It was so loud that I'm certain that Spot's ears were twitching miles to the south.

While I waited for a response, I sat down on one of the settees and dialed Diamond.

"Sí," he said.

"Got a crime in your territory," I said. I sipped some Scotch.

"You call nine-one-one?" Diamond asked.

"Not that kind of emergency. This requires more finesse, somebody with your sense of nuance."

"You want me to respond personally," he said. "Why?"

"Because I'm the perpetrator. I've trespassed on Bob's boat, which is inside his boathouse."

"Bob...?"

"Bob with no last name. Bob from RKS Properties. Same Bob who wants to turn a wilderness mountain into a cash machine."

"That Bob," Diamond said.

"So I bumped the boat's horn. I'm expecting someone to arrive shortly. I figured that Bob and company might put in a courtesy call to the sheriff's office and inform them of interlopers in Douglas County. I thought that you might want to come and make an appearance, especially considering that if I'm arrested, it would have substantial negative implications for Bob."

"You're holding some cards that Bob wouldn't want you to play," Diamond said.

"They might lead to his arrest on murder charges."

"Sounds like a good hand. Property address?"

"I don't know. I came by sea. It's the first set of lake shore houses north of Cave Rock. The one you want is a modern arrangement of box shapes that step up and back."

"And you're currently on his boat."

"Enjoying his single malt Scotch and his jazz," I said.

"Taking a man's Scotch is a serious transgression some places."

"This is probably one of them."

I heard the sound of fast footsteps coming down the dock.

"Someone coming, gotta go," I said and hung up.

The footsteps stopped. There was a faint sound of a key sliding slowly into the boathouse door lock. I wasn't certain, but I may have heard a door open. Then came silence. The person who came through the door was being stealthy, worried about being tripped up by a burglar.

I called out in a loud voice, "No need to sneak up on me. Owen McKenna here, topside, on the settee in the lounge. No weapon, no threat. Enjoying your booze. Come and join me."

More silence. Tommy Flanagan had moved to a syncopated, uptempo number. Between the chords, I heard a creak of dock boards, felt the faintest of boat motion as if someone of size had come aboard on tiptoes. Movement on the port side aft stairway. I turned and saw the round eye of a gun barrel rise up above the stairway. The gun was followed by a large man dressed in jeans and blue sweatshirt with the logo of a local bar on it.

"Hands in the air," he said.

I raised my hands, looking up to make sure that I didn't spill the precious Scotch.

"Now stand."

I stood.

"Turn and put your hands on the bar rail, legs spread."

"I'll have to set down the Scotch," I said. I set the glass onto the bar, then assumed the position. In my side vision, I saw him approach. His gun looked to be a Beretta 92A1. Seventeen 9mm rounds in the magazine. Bob's guys didn't fool around.

He came up behind, patted me down, pulled out my wallet.

"Sit," he said.

I sat and watched the man.

He was a big guy, around 30 years old, not my height, but wider and heavier just as Simone had described Ned's night visitor. He was classic ugly, bad skin, bulbous, pock-marked nose, big hair brushed back and down and held in place at the back of his head by a thick layer of goo. Small eyes set way back. Heavy brow, receding chin. His left hand was bandaged. Perhaps the source of the blood on the tender bay, perhaps cut by one of Ned's fancy Veitsi Mies throwing knives. The thought gave me a small shot of empathy for this guy. Maybe he was Ned's spymaster. Or maybe Bob was Ned's spymaster, and this guy was just the courier bringing money and marching orders. Either way, he was the physical opposite of handsome Ned. When the ugly guy gets cut and the beautiful guy is unscathed, it reinforces my There's-No-Justice view of the world.

But Ned telegraphed feral smart, which equals stupid in the land of humans. This guy telegraphed real smart. In my experience, it was better to be real smart than pretty any day.

The man glanced at the companionway and backed away from the opening. No doubt wondering if I had backup lurking in the bowels of the ship. He kept the Beretta on me while he used his left hand to flip open my wallet. He looked at my licenses, then pulled out his phone and dialed.

"Got one Owen McKenna, private dick, drinking your Scotch." Pause. "Okay."

He put the phone back in his pocket.

"Private dick?" I said. "You time travel from Al Capone's gang?"

"Shut up," he said.

He was focused. His attention never wandered. I had a momentary thought of trying to distract him and then disarm him, but it did not seem like a reasonable idea. Besides which, having a gun trained on me gave me the kind of moral authority we attach to the underdog.

We looked at each other. I smiled. He scowled.

In a couple of minutes another man came up the starboard aft stairway. He had a large Greyhound on a leash. The dog was a beautiful tan and, like many Greyhounds, appeared to have little interest in people. It ignored all of us, looking instead, no doubt, for smallish animals to chase and eat.

"Bob," I said. "You're a hard man to track down."

He was a mid-fifties, business-executive cliché with thin-soled Italian loafers, high thread-count gray slacks, light gray V-neck sweater over gray shirt, and matching gray hair. He was thin like his dog.

"Who are you, and why are you on my boat?" he said in a soft voice. Too soft. Like a threat.

"Owen McKenna, working for Joe Rorvik, looking into the probable assault of his wife Cynthia Rorvik. One of the suspects is Ned Cavett, a wife-abusing dirtball whom you have hired to..."

I was interrupted by the sound of the boathouse door opening and closing.

The ugly man stepped behind me, put the gun to the back of my neck, and pressed the cold barrel against my skin.

"No movement, no talk," he whispered in my ear.

His angle was such that his gun would be pointing toward any person coming onto the boat. He could shoot me, or he could shoot the intruder by shifting his gun a few inches to my side. Or, aiming through my neck carefully, he could shoot us both with one bullet.

Diamond appeared, coming up the starboard stairway. He was wearing his uniform and his equipment, but his sidearm was snapped into its holster, and his hand was nowhere near. It was classic Diamond, casual, confident, relaxed. Although he obviously knew that I was there, and he must have deduced that the man behind me had a gun, he didn't even glance our way.

"You must be Bob," he said. "I'm Sergeant Martinez, Douglas County Sheriff's Office." He reached out his hand.

Bob seemed both surprised and wary. He shook Diamond's

hand.

"I understand that you have an intruder on your boat," Diamond said.

"Yes. I want you to arrest that man." Bob turned and pointed at me.

"I know McKenna," Diamond said. "He might be a pest, but he's not dangerous. Tell your man to put his weapon away."

Bob hesitated. He looked Diamond over as if trying to gauge the chances that Diamond had stolen the uniform and was impersonating an officer.

"Put it away, Benjamin," Bob said.

Benjamin stepped away from me, holding the gun down. He decocked it, which is always an adrenaline boost when you realize that the guy with a gun on you really did have a round in the chamber. Benjamin reached behind his back and put the gun into his concealed-carry holster at the small of his back.

Bob said to Diamond, "How did you know McKenna had broken into my boat?"

"He called and told me. Let's talk," Diamond said. He walked over and sat on the settee opposite me. He gestured at Bob and Benjamin.

Benjamin watched Bob. Bob walked over and sat down. His dog lay down next to him. Bob looked at Benjamin and pointed at the settee next to him. Benjamin sat down.

I looked at Diamond as I pointed at Benjamin. "The man's hand wound looks serious. Do you think that could have been one of the knives that Veitsi Mies gave Ned?" I saw Bob shoot a look of surprise toward Benjamin.

Diamond nodded. "Ol' Ned hangs with Veitsi and the Canyon Brotherhood. If the Brotherhood found out that Neddy had a disagreement with Ben, that could be serious. Story like that could be expanded into a rumor of something more serious. Like maybe Ned went down at the hands of Bob's enforcer."

Diamond turned to Bob. "All the law enforcement in Tahoe wouldn't be David against Goliath if the Canyon Brotherhood came to town to exact vengeance for what they think is a fallen brother. It wouldn't matter whether or not Joe votes for the Steven's Peak Resort if the Canyon crew takes out Ben and you. I don't know for sure, Bob, but it looks like you've maybe got some problems coming from multiple directions. Not sure if arresting this McKenna guy is going to improve things."

"Why are you here?" Bob said.

"First things first," I said. "What is your last name?"

Bob hesitated, thinking over how he should respond and whether he needed to respond.

"Hinton."

"And Benjamin?"

"Prattel."

"And your dog is Pretty Girl."

More surprise in his eyes. "What's my dog got to do with it?" he asked, suspicious, like I was playing with him.

"Polite conversation," I said. "Dog's part of the group. Maybe I want to say something to her."

Bob made a little head shake like he thought I was ridiculous.

Unlike Spot, Pretty Girl didn't turn at the sound of her name.

"Good. Now that we all know each other, we can talk about why I came to chat with you. Your man Benjamin Prattel, here, has been paying Ned Cavett by bringing late-night cash drops to Ned's house. Since then, Ned has been seen spying on Joe Rorvik's house. Joe's wife has been assaulted and is near death in a Reno hospital. Joe's best friend Manuel Romero is dead. Jillian Oleska is dead. All three were against your proposed resort development."

"That's ridiculous. Jillian worked for me. She was a tireless proponent of the Steven's Peak Resort."

"A tireless proponent who, according to Mrs. Rorvik, was having second thoughts about it. And, like Mrs. Rorvik and Romero, she was in a position to influence Joe's vote."

"I don't believe that for a moment."

"I don't expect you to. But there it is."

"You can't prove anything," Bob said.

"Not yet. But I won't need much more evidence than I already have to put you in the electric chair. Separate from that, I don't need to prove anything to kill your resort. If I suggest to Joe that the assault on his wife may be traceable to you, he'll vote against your project."

Bob did a good job of hiding his discomfort, but it showed in the tensing of his legs, the clenching of his toes, visible through the thin leather of his expensive shoes. He glanced at my glass of Scotch, then swallowed.

"RKS Properties is a large, serious business," he said. "Like any business, we occasionally hire lobbyists to look after our interests."

"You're claiming that Ned Cavett is a lobbyist?" I said, trying not to sound too scornful.

"Joe Rorvik's vote is important. So we looked at his associates. Mrs. Rorvik was spending an inordinate amount of time with a young French girl. We realized that her boyfriend had, in a manner of speaking, access to Joe Rorvik."

"So you hired the idiot dirtball to represent the interests of RKS Properties. Brilliant business decision." This time I couldn't hide my scorn.

"Cavett didn't present himself badly at first. In retrospect, perhaps he wasn't the best choice. I admit that. But we committed no crime. We simply put him on a bi-weekly retainer and gave him the goal of increasing the pro-resort influences on Mr. Rorvik and reducing the anti-resort influences. Benjamin provided Cavett with a detailed plan of how this would be accomplished. It was straightforward. There was no reason for Mr. Cavett to become..." Bob hesitated.

"A wild card," I said.

"Yes, I suppose that word would apply."

"In addition to the retainer, did you offer a bonus if the result was successful?"

Bob swallowed again. I could see that he was considering the implications of telling the truth versus obfuscating it. "We told Mr. Cavett that he would be paid ten thousand dollars if Mr. Rorvik voted for the development. That is standard procedure with lobbyists, only a much smaller payout than is traditional in these situations."

"Like putting a gerbil in front of a greyhound," I said. "Smaller than a bunny rabbit, but it produces the same prey drive."

Bob looked over at Pretty Girl. She appeared indifferent.

I stood up. "I might be calling you for more information. I'll need your number."

"I don't give out my private number."

"Which is why I had to break in here."

Bob thought about it. He reached into his pocket, pulled out a card, and handed it to me. "I've done nothing wrong, committed no crime."

"Right," I said. "You are a paragon of moral fiber."

Diamond stood up. He and I walked down the starboard aft stairway to the tender deck, and left.

"A paragon of moral fiber?" Diamond said as we headed up Bob Hinton's lawn.

"New phrase I learned. Sounded pretty good, huh?"

"Yeah," Diamond said.

"Bob knew we were bullshitting him about the Canyon Brotherhood," I said as we got into Diamond's patrol unit.

"Yeah. But he also knew that we're onto Benjamin bringing Ned cash. He's smart enough to understand how that would look to a jury."

"You think there's any possibility that they hired Ned to take out Rell and Manuel and Jillian?" I asked.

"If he knew that Jillian was rooting for the other team, maybe that would be enough to send Ned after her. So, yeah, the possibility exists. More likely that Ned got the brilliant idea himself, though. Probably thought it was a great way to earn the ten thousand bonus."

"Makes sense," I said.

Diamond drove me back to Jennifer's mausoleum, where I picked up Street and Spot.

THIRTY-SEVEN

That night Street had one of her stress dreams. They are infrequent, but when they happen, the pattern is regular. She whimpers while she turns back and forth. She grabs the sheets and twists them into knots, and she attempts a mangled, strangled cry of fear.

Long ago, I learned that my impulse to wake and comfort her is not always the right thing to do, because the interruption causes her dream to stay with her for hours or even days.

When the next nightmare struck, I sat on my hands and gritted my teeth and winced at every sound she made. In time, the dream passed, and she settled back into a calm sleep. The next morning, she awoke in a cheerful mood and betrayed no hint of the stress from the middle of the night.

So when she started up the bad sequence this night, I clenched my jaw, made my hands into fists, and waited it out.

When morning came, she was not cheerful.

"You seem in a dark mood," I said. "Anything I can help with?"

"No, thanks. I just had a bad dream."

"Are you okay now?" I asked.

"I'll be fine. It's just that certain childhood memories sometimes come back. I guess you never completely put these things to rest."

I wasn't sure what to say. "Simone's situation reminds you of your brother."

Street looked at me and nodded. The pain in her eyes was obvious. "I'm plagued by the if-onlys. If only my brother had been gone that night my dad came home late. If only my dad had just beat on me instead of my younger brother. If only my brother had run out the door the moment he saw that my dad was in a black mood. If only my dad had been one of those no-show dads. We'd have been infinitely better off if we'd never had a dad at all. The memory of my brother still hurts a great deal."

Street had never spoken much about it. I think she wanted me not to attach such dark thoughts to her.

"You once told me that the talk therapy helped," I said.

She shrugged. "You spend enough hours talking to a shrink, it helps, yes. But I found the promise of therapy to be overblown. Speaking for myself, no amount of talking can make the wounds heal beyond raw scars. And some therapists made it worse. The one who said I needed to forgive my dad in order to find comfort was the worst. His arrogance still burns. Maybe others can forgive. But the beating-death murder of your own son is an evil that I can never forgive. I can understand showing mercy to him, not wanting him to die with pain. I believe in the notion of getting on with life, of accepting that evil things happen, that justice fails us in those moments. But to pardon the perpetrator? To cease to feel resentment for the murder of my brother? Not possible. He took the life of an innocent boy, and he did it with malice and viciousness. I will resent it always."

"And Ned is doing a similar thing with Simone," I said.

"Yeah. And with many of these men, it never ends. I think that's what terrifies me about Simone. She's going to die by that man's hands. I can tell. It might not happen for some time, but the pattern is clear. He hates the world, and he channels that hate into Simone."

"I've tried to get her to leave him," I said, "but she won't hear of it. She says she'll be dead the moment she tries to leave. It sounds like Rell Rorvik also tried to convince her to leave. From what Joe Rorvik told me, the South Lake Tahoe Police offered to help find Simone a safe house. I haven't spoken to Mallory about it, but I know he would help. The women's center is very active and offers the exact kind of support that she needs. But Simone still has to decide to try. Unfortunately, she believes that any move in that direction will write her death sentence. And there are uncountable examples of domestic violence deaths that suggest the truth of her fear."

"If she did decide to leave him and press charges," Street said, "what do you think her chances would be?"

"Hard to say. I would try to stay in contact with her and be a liaison between her and the police. I could help see her through the turmoil and stress during Ned's prosecution. But it all gets down to her resolve. It takes a great deal of staying power for abuse victims to live in hiding and not communicate with anyone who could inadvertently reveal their location. Just testifying at the trial is too much for many, knowing that their abuser is flashing them the look that means he's going to kill them the first chance he gets. In the case of Ned, he's a particularly powerful and evil abuser. Having spent time in prison, he's likely to think that if he has to go back inside, he may as well kill her first. A good lawyer can often get such a person out on bail. All Ned would need to do is track her down before he's convicted and locked up."

Street stared into her coffee. "It doesn't look good, does it?"

"It never does," I said. "But a possible severe result from her leaving and pressing charges is – at least to my way of thinking – a much better option than the certain severe result that will come from staying with him. She's already experienced terrible beatings. Any number of them might have been fatal if his hand had struck her ear and temple or her throat instead of her jaw. Likewise, his punches to her body could have killed her if he'd hit just over her heart or caught her abdomen in a way that would rupture internal organs. He's smart enough to strike the big muscles or to use open-handed blows that bruise and hurt but don't kill as long as they are well-aimed."

Street winced at the image, and I was immediately sorry that I'd spoken of details.

"I have a question I want to ask," I said, "and I understand if your answer is no."

Street looked at me and made a little nod.

"I wonder if you'd sit down with Simone. Let her know that you understand abuse, that you survived abuse."

"I only survived because I ran away," Street said.

"Exactly. If you told that to Simone, it might make a huge difference. I think she's a classic victim in that she feels powerless. She thinks she's the only person around who has to endure this. She's embarrassed about it and is afraid to talk about it."

Street thought about it. "How do you think I should approach her?"

"I'd go to the café where she waits tables. If you sit in her section, you'd have at least a little opportunity to talk to her. Beyond that, you would know a hundred times better than I would what approach might work best. If you think it would serve the situation, you can of course tell her that you're my girlfriend and that you know about her situation."

"Let me think about it." Street sipped coffee.

I thought back to my childhood, which was blissfully free from abuse. I grew up never even imagining that men could ever beat on children or women. The time that I was first exposed to it was a disappointment larger than nearly any I had experienced growing up.

"Do you think she's working today?" Street asked.

"I don't know. I'd be afraid to call the restaurant to find out because word might get to her and make her run. Best to just show up and hope to catch her shift. When I saw her there before, it was morning, so she likely works the morning shift."

"I think I'll go give it a try. But it is a little scary."

"Because of the memories it conjures up," I said.

"Yeah."

I gave Street a hug. "Thank you for the effort. You want me to drive you? Wait for you in the car?"

"No. I think I better do this by myself."

That afternoon, I went to Joe's and gave him a full report. I hoped that Joe would think my meeting with Bob Hinton of RKS Properties was progress, but I don't think he was fooled.

That night, I went to bed feeling like I'd gotten nowhere. Since Joe had called me, two people had died, Simone had endured multiple beatings, and I still had little idea of what was going on.

THIRTY-EIGHT

The next morning my office phone rang at 11 a.m. I answered.

"Owen!" It was Street, breathless. "Owen, my God, Simone's been hurt! Ned beat her up. I called nine-one-one!"

"Where is she?"

"They took her to the hospital. I followed. I'm in my car, outside the Emergency Room."

"Where is Ned?" I asked.

"I don't know. The police went into his house with him. Maybe he's still there. Or maybe he's nearby watching me."

"The police didn't arrest him?"

"I don't know. It was my fault for being here!" Street nearly shouted in my ear.

"What happened?"

"I went and talked to Simone at the restaurant. She told me things. You let me know that her situation was very bad. But it was even worse than I thought based on what you said. After a short while, she said she had to go home. I feared for her life, so I followed her home and got out and spoke to her before she could get into her house. Just then, Ned came home. He shouted at me, then dragged Simone into the house. In a moment, I heard her screaming, over and over. So I called nine-one-one.

"The police came to their house. Ned came out and acted very concerned. He told them that Simone had fallen and hit her head. I spoke up and said that he dragged her into the house and beat her. So the police asked me if I was inside, if I'd seen him beat her. Of course, I said no. But I told them that I'd seen him grab her arm and drag her inside and that her screams started immediately."

"Did Ned get a good look at you?" I asked.

"Yes. Now you think I'm in danger, don't you?"

"Maybe," I said. "I'll come down to the hospital and find you.

Promise me that you won't get out of your car until I get there?"

"I won't."

"Check your door locks?"

"They're locked," Street said.

"Be there in a few," I said. I hung up.

I trotted down the stairs and out the door with Spot. I ran under the scaffolding, stepping on something hard and painful. I looked down, kicked away another errant bolt, and ran to the car. I dialed the South Lake Tahoe PD as I drove away. I was breaking the law, but I thought the law needed to know about Ned Cavett's abuse more than it needed me not to talk and drive.

Two transfers later, I had Mallory on the phone.

"Commander," I said, "I just got a call from Street about a domestic with Ned Cavett beating on Simone Bonnaire. Did your boys arrest him?"

"We're holding him, waiting on word of whether she'll agree to press charges."

"You don't have probable cause?"

"Look, McKenna, you and I both know that he beats on her. But no, we don't have probable cause. No one witnessed the beating. Just like all the other beatings. Street heard a scream, nothing more. When my officers got there, the man said Ms. Bonnaire fell, and the woman nodded agreement. My boys know that was bullshit. But if the woman won't agree to cooperate, we've got nothing. If we charged him with assault with no probable cause or any witnesses who will testify, then any two-bit counsel with a fake law degree could get him off."

"Street said she's still in the hospital," I said.

"Pro'bly."

"Will you consider putting an officer at her hospital door when you let Ned go?"

"If I can't arrest him, on what basis could I give her protection? I'm short staffed, anyway."

"It's a stakeout on the suspicion that the perpetrator will show up at the hospital. Crime prevention, duty to keep the peace."

"I'll see what I can do," he said.

I got to Third Street, took a left, headed toward the hospital. I went around back, saw a patrol unit not far from Street's VW beetle. I parked nearby. Street got out as I got out.

"No sign of Ned?" I asked.

She shook her head.

We walked together into the ER door.

"Wondering if Doc Lee is in," I said to one of the nurses at the counter.

"Hardest working doc in town," she said. "Seems like he's always in. But he's busy."

"Can you please tell him that Detective McKenna would like to talk to him when he gets a chance?" The logical inference that I was part of official local law enforcement was false in specific but accurate in general principle.

The woman looked at me, no doubt trying to decide if she should follow protocol and tell me that he couldn't be interrupted. But there was always the possibility that I might have some special pull with the doctor.

The woman picked up a phone, pressed some buttons, waited, then spoke. She hung up.

"Please wait," she said.

Ten minutes later, Doc Lee came out. He ushered us down a hall and into a small office. "You're calling about Simone Bonnaire," he said.

"Yes. How is she?"

"Shaken, upset, and bruised. Her facial injuries look bad, but, by great luck, are not severe. There is no fracture and no significant swelling. The facial bones range from very fragile to very strong. The man struck her hard with an open hand across the top of her forehead. He knows how to inflict the maximum pain without breaking bones. The blow split her skin and gave her a major bruise. But the bone is strong."

"A good place to hit someone if you don't want to break the skull," I said.

Doc Lee pointed to his own forehead. "If you are well in from the temporal ridges, here, and substantially above the supraorbital process and glabella, here, then the bone is very strong." He pointed farther back behind the crest of his forehead. "Of course, you have to stay forward of the coronal suture."

"Of course," I said.

Doc Lee made a wan smile. "She is a diminutive woman. Change the nature of how he hit her just a bit, and she could die from such a blow."

Street grimaced.

"In addition to her head bruising, she also has a major bruise on her upper arm as if her boyfriend had tried to crush it in his grip and dragged her by it."

"There is no doubt that her injuries didn't come from a fall?" I said.

"Correct. But it is visceral knowledge only. Technically, this kind of blunt force facial trauma could happen any number of ways. Were I in court, I'd be forced to admit that she could have gotten a similar injury from any number of accidents, in a car for example. The arm injury could come from a range of trauma as well."

"What's her prognosis?" Street asked.

"She'll be sore for several days, somewhat at the bruised area but possibly more so in her neck as she appears to have sustained a Grade One whiplash. Minor, but worth watching."

"When can she go home?" Street asked.

"I'd like to keep her under observation for the next twenty-four hours. If there is no additional pain or swelling, she can go home. The poor girl doesn't have insurance, so she indicated to me that she is worried about the cost. No reason to keep her longer than necessary."

"May we see her?"

Doc Lee nodded.

THIRTY-NINE

There was a young cop I didn't know at Simone's closed door.

"Glad to see you here," I said. "Mallory told me he was short on staff."

"I brought her in. Seemed like I should hang around for a bit." I was pleased to sense a bit of chivalry in his manner. A young woman gets beat up, a young male cop feels protective. At least until he acquires the jaded perspective of some older cops.

"I'm Owen McKenna, this is Street Casey. We'd like to see Simone."

He pulled out his cell and dialed. "A guy named Owen McKenna and a woman are here," he said. "Okay to let them in to see the victim?" He paused. "I'm not playing bodyguard. I was supposed to escort her to the hospital, right? Well, they just brought her to the room." Pause. "No one gave me another assignment, so I'll be here when you need me."

He hung up, nodded, and we opened the door and walked inside.

Simone's shirt sleeve had been cut from the cuff up to the shoulder. There was a large purple bruise on her upper arm. Her forehead was covered with a large bandage, and there was a small bandage on her left cheekbone. Her eyes darted from us to the door and back. She looked terrified.

"Don't worry, Simone," I said. "Ned is currently at the police station. There is a cop outside your door. You are safe."

"I won't be as soon as I leave here."

"You will if you agree to press assault charges against Ned."

"He will kill me if I do! Don't you understand that?"

"If Ned is arrested and if you stay hiding in a safe house, he won't be able to find you. You need only see him when you testify in court. Once he is convicted, he will be sent to prison."

"The trial would last more than a day or two, right?" Simone said.

"Probably."

"Then he won't immediately go to prison. There would be evenings after I testify when he could follow me, find me, and kill me."

"I can detain him. There are ways of making certain that you get to your safe house without him knowing where it is."

"You don't know Ned," she said, and looked away from us.

Street said, "It's my fault, Simone. I came to your house, and that's why Ned got angry. I am so sorry!"

"Don't be sorry," Simone said. "Ned doesn't need any reason to get angry. He probably would have hit me anyway."

Street looked at me, a question on her face. I shrugged. There was an uncomfortable silence.

"I looked at myself in the bathroom mirror," Simone finally said, her voice barely above a whisper. "I don't feel real bad, but the bruise on my face is pretty bad. I peeked under the bandage. My head is the color of an eggplant. Not that I'm not used to it. You probably think I look horrible." She turned and gave us an expectant look.

"You look bruised, that's all," Street said. "The parts that aren't bruised look beautiful."

She paused. "Nothing about me is beautiful."

"Your eyes are," I said.

"You think my eyes are beautiful?" The surprise in her tiny voice was heartbreaking.

"They remind me of Liz Taylor's."

Another pause. "I saw her in A Place In The Sun," Simone said. "I guess part of it was filmed here in Tahoe."

A change of subject. I'd seen it before, an insecure woman who changes the subject when complimented.

"Parts of it were filmed here, yes," I said.

Simone gazed off as if seeing the film set. Eventually, she said, "Have you ever had a dream about something that you would give anything for, and then you realized that it was out of reach? That it was never going to happen?"

"Sure," Street said. "What's your dream?"

"That I can run fast. Ski fast. I think it's about escape. I've spent a lot of my life wishing I could escape."

"From Ned," I said.

"And my stepfather before Ned."

Another difficult silence.

"I'm sorry," Street said.

"My mother married him when I was ten. She was excited that he was going to take us from rural France to Montreal. But she didn't know that he was more interested in me than in her."

Street had been lightly holding the back of my arm. At Simone's words, Street's fingers dug into my forearm.

Simone took several deep breaths. "I never had many friends in France, but I didn't know anyone in Montreal. Not that it would have made any significant difference. But I think the loneliness made me even more vulnerable. I had nowhere to turn."

I waited, thinking that it was better to say nothing than risk saying the wrong thing.

"And I had no way to fend him off," she said. "Ten is awfully young."

My turn to wince.

"You're the first people I've ever told," she said. "I never even told..." she cut herself off. After a moment she said, "My therapist."

"You didn't tell your mother?" Street said.

"She wouldn't have believed me. She thought I lived in a make-believe world, which, I suppose, is true. If I had told her, she would have thought I was making it up to punish her for leaving my father and marrying another man."

Street said, "Is your father still in France?"

"He died a year after my mother left him. They said it was from some kind of blood disease, but I think it was from a broken heart."

"What kind of man was your father?" I asked.

"A good man. Plain and unpretentious, but good. He was a stone mason. He did stone carving for buildings. He even worked on a medieval church once. Like a lot of artisans, he was often unemployed. My mother hated that, hated not having money. She wanted a more exciting life. My stepfather was a salesman. He sold real estate in Paris and then in Montreal. My mother loved finally having nice clothes and a fancy car and traveling. Although she had to travel alone or with friends because he didn't want to travel."

"Did your mother take you on her trips?"

"She didn't like traveling with a kid." Simone's tone wasn't angry, but matter-of-fact. "She left me home with him."

After a moment, Street spoke, her voice wavering, "Do they still live in Montreal?"

"She does. My stepfather died a couple of years after we moved to Canada. A heart attack." Simone swallowed. "He made my life hell on earth. I wish there were a literal hell, so he would know what it's like."

I wanted to learn more about Ned. I said, "How did you meet Ned?"

It was several seconds before Simone spoke. "After high school, I was determined to change my life. I was afraid, of course. Since my stepfather took over my life, I've always been afraid of everything. But I looked at the map and decided to apply to colleges that were a long way from Montreal. After my stepfather died, my mother had no money, so I also had to get financial aid. I found both distance and financial help in a little college in Colorado. That was when I first tried skiing. I was no good, but it was exciting, and scary, to try something where you go fast. It's the opposite of me. I'm not a fast person. I'm not exciting, either.

"Last summer, after my senior year, I went to a high-altitude ski camp. A group of us stayed for three weeks in yurts on a snowfield at thirteen-thousand feet in the San Juan Mountains. The camp's mission was to teach us ski mountaineering. Ned was one of the instructors. All the girls were crazy about him because he was rough and impossibly good looking. But he singled me out. I couldn't believe that he was paying attention to me. But I was too naïve to be suspicious.

"I now know, from talking with Rell, that the reason he singled me out was that I fit the personality type that he could dominate. I was meek, so he could take total control over me. Once we started spending time together, he took ownership of me. I had to do everything exactly as he wanted or he would beat me. I feared for my life almost from the first moment. But I was powerless to do anything about it. It was like my stepfather all over again. My life is ruled by fear."

Simone was breathing hard, traumatized just talking about it.

"I want to leave him," she said. "I can't say how much I want to just slip out in the middle of the night and disappear. But I know he would track me down and kill me."

She looked at me. "You're probably thinking that I'm being melodramatic, but I know it to be true."

"Simone, I'm an ex-cop. I know how it works, and I know you are right. If you believe that he would find you and kill you, you are probably correct about it. However, if you make a plan to kick Ned out of your world, perhaps you can start to rebuild your life."

Simone made the smallest of nods.

FORTY

"The doctor says that you can leave the hospital tomorrow," I said to Simone. "Would you like us to pick you up?"

"Yes, but what about Ned? He'll find me here tonight."

"There's a cop outside your door. I'll tell the nurses at the front counter to keep your room number a secret and to call the police if he shows up. Do you have a picture of Ned?"

She nodded. "In my purse. There's a little photo holder. I wanted to throw his picture away, but I thought he would be enraged if he ever noticed."

Street said, "Ned looks into your private places?"

"I have no private places. Ned always looks everywhere."

We got the photo, said goodbye, and left.

"Any chance you can stay the night?" I said to the cop.

He shook his head. "But I can get Greg to stop by."

"Mallory won't mind?"

"No different than checking bank windows at night."

"Thanks."

We left Ned's picture at the nursing counter and explained that if he showed up, they should call the police. I also requested that they not release Simone's room number to anyone. They understood the importance.

The next day, Street was buried with work, so I picked up Simone at the hospital.

She looked nervous when she saw Spot in the back seat of my Jeep. He wagged vigorously at our approach.

"Don't worry," I said, quoting my standard refrain. "He won't hurt you, but he will want to sniff you. And he will do anything for pets."

"I'm scared of dogs."

"You don't need to be. Here, let me show you something." I opened the back door of the Jeep and took hold of Spot's collar as he stepped out.

"Spot, sit."

He sat, his tail stretched out behind him, sweeping the parking lot.

I reached for Simone's hand. She looked suspicious and pushed her hands into her jacket pockets. So I put my hand on her shoulder and gently walked her toward Spot.

"He'd love to sniff your hand," I said.

Simone's eyes got wide.

"Don't worry. The last time he ate someone for lunch was over a year ago. He hasn't done it since."

Simone cracked a little grin. She took a baby step forward and held out her hand about eighteen inches from Spot's nose. He looked eager, but didn't move, apart from his continuous wagging. Slowly, Simone inched forward until Spot could sniff her hand.

"You can pet him like this," I said, giving him a delicate little pat between his ears. "Or like this." I bent over, put Spot in a head lock and wrestled his head back and forth. When I was done, he still looked at Simone and kept sweeping the pavement with his tail.

Simone gave him a pet so tentative, I didn't think Spot could feel it. But I wasn't getting her to do it for Spot's sake. Once past that hurdle, we got into the Jeep.

"Where are we going?" Simone asked.

"If you have a preference, we can go there."

"I already missed work, so I've probably been fired."

I shook my head. "I called Marilyn and told her that you had another incident with your boyfriend and were in the hospital as a result. She said that you could take a leave for as long as it takes to press charges and get him out of your life."

"You did that on purpose, right?" Simone said. "You manipulated the situation to get Marilyn to join in pushing me toward filing charges, which will get me killed."

"No, I didn't. I merely told her that Ned had assaulted you once again. Marilyn made the generous offer of giving you a leave from your job. Her suggestion that you kick him out of your life didn't come from me."

"Everyone is against me."

"No, everyone is for you."

We rode in silence. I turned northeast on Lake Tahoe Blvd and pulled into the parking lot at El Dorado Beach in the middle of town.

"What are we doing here?" she asked.

"Just a place to park until we figure out your next move."

"You have your job to do," she said. "Why don't I get out here, and you can go help Joe Rorvik find out what happened to Rell."

"I think I should focus on you until we sort this out."

"Why? You have no investment in me. What happens to me has no bearing on you."

"I want to focus on you because it's the right thing to do."

"So this is an effort to help the little wounded woman."

I nodded. "Yeah."

"What's in it for you?"

"Nothing other than doing the right thing."

"Tell the truth." Her words were both biting and pleading.

"I am."

We didn't talk for a minute. Spot got up in the back seat, struggled to turn a circle and lay back down. An old man walked by close to the Jeep. I saw his expression change to worry when he realized that Simone's face was half covered in bandages. He sped up to get away.

"You probably can tell that I don't have a very good opinion of men," Simone said.

"With good reason," I said.

"At times I've hated all men."

"That's understandable."

"But you seem different than the kind of men I've been around."

"There are many others like me," I said.

"I've told myself that, too. Like when I met Rell. I thought, if she is so nice, maybe her husband is nice. But when I met him one day, Rell told him that I was interested in the Tahoe Randonnée Extreme challenge, and he was dismissive. Like he didn't believe someone like me could ever do such a thing. He actually made a scoffing sound. It's really rude when someone dismisses you."

"I agree."

"Even if I could never become a good skier, it is still okay for me to want to try."

"Absolutely. Tell me more about the Tahoe Randonnée Extreme challenge. Is it a competition?"

"Not against others in any specific way. It's more a challenge to yourself. The challenge is, can you do it? Can you bag every peak on the course? Then there is the solstice version, which is like the worst of the worst."

I waited for her to explain.

"The winter solstice is the shortest day of the year. That means that the solstice is also the longest night of the year. So, the Solstice Randonnée is done with the least amount of daylight."

"They don't ski at night, do they?"

"Most do, yes. But even if you don't, you have to know how to survive the cold weather at night. You're up at eight or nine thousand feet camping in a tent. It gets really cold. I heard about one guy who decided to camp near the top of Steven's Peak. That's ten thousand feet. Just to stay warm enough means you're packing a really big sleeping bag plus your tent and a lot of high-calorie food. Carrying enough food for a forty-plus mile journey and then doing it at night makes the challenge that much harder."

"Randonnée is a French word?" I said.

"Yeah. It means trekking and walking. But it's been used for ski trekking, too. The Tahoe Randonnée Extreme event combines back-country skiing with ski orienteering."

"Ski orienteering is where you find your way with a topographic map and compass?"

"Yeah. No GPS allowed. The difficulty with the Tahoe Randonnée Extreme is that it goes through the back-country where the snow is deep and largely untracked. Each person gets a different route through the check points so that no one can follow anyone else. Some routes are a little easier than others, but there is a handicapping system to adjust for that. Compared to normal ski orienteering races, the Tahoe Randonnée Extreme is less about how fast you ski and more about the challenges of extreme terrain. Much steeper slopes than most, some rock and ice climbing where you take off your skis and carry them on your back, and exposed mountains where any weather is more extreme as well. Just finishing the Randonnée Extreme is considered to be a huge accomplishment. If you can document every peak with your phone camera, then you get featured on the website."

"It sounds like there is a risk of getting lost and stranded."

"Yes. That's part of the challenge."

"You said it goes from Donner Pass to Carson Pass?"

"Yeah, roughly. It starts at Sugar Bowl, and it ends at Kirkwood. But hitting all the peaks means that you go a good way off the main route. Like that guy at Steven's Peak. That's a major side trip, but the whole point of the trek is to get our photos from every peak."

I tried to visualize the course. "The course must go through the Desolation Wilderness? Pyramid Peak and those mountains?"

"Right. You have to be in really good shape. If you have a problem in Desolation, there's no easy rescue."

"Have you done anything like this before?"

"Other than the high-altitude ski camp in Colorado, no. That was higher up, but there was a bunch of us, and we lived in heated yurts, and we only went out during the day. This is about going solo, with long nights. So it's kind of crazy for me to be thinking about it. But I've been training for it. Not training like professional racers. But I go out with my gear and try to ski up the mountainside. It's incredibly difficult. Just to participate in something so difficult would be a brand new experience. I've never done anything like it. If I could actually pull off the Tahoe Randonnée Extreme, it would be the most amazing thing I've ever done. I would go from thinking that I'm a loser to thinking that maybe I could do anything."

I sensed Simone turning and looking at me, the big white bandage moving in my peripheral vision.

"It might be true," I said, turning to look at her. "Maybe you could do anything."

Simone's eyes were wet. "Yeah," she said. "Wouldn't that be something."

FORTY-ONE

Simone and I were quiet for several minutes. We looked out at the lake.

"I have a question about Ned."

"What?"

"Ned is capable of nearly any kind of violence, right?"

Simone nodded.

"He could even kill someone, if the impulse struck him, right?"

"I've always known that," she said.

"But could he plan to kill someone? Not an impulsive murder in a fit of anger, but something where he thought about it, took his time, and then carried out his plan?"

Simone didn't hesitate. "Yes. He is impulsive, that is true. And his impulsiveness leads to violence. But he is also evil. If he thought there was something significant in it for him, he could kill someone."

"What if he were paid a fee of ten thousand?"

"Ten thousand dollars?! Ned would do anything for ten thousand dollars. Is this about the man who pays Ned to spy on Joe?"

I nodded. "There were three different people this man wanted out of the way."

"You're wondering if Ned would kill three people for ten thousand dollars."

"Yeah."

"Yes, he would," Simone said with no hesitation.

"You knew Rell," I said. "I'm wondering if you knew the others. One was Manuel Romero, and the other was Jillian Oleska."

Simone shook her head. "I never heard of them."

Snow began to fall, big wet flakes covering the windshield. I turned the heater to defrost and put the fan on high. After a moment, I turned the wipers on intermittent.

"I have an idea," I said. "You said that if you could do the Tahoe Randonnée Extreme challenge, you could do anything. You're interested in it because it represents that, right? It would prove to you that you have the power to take control of your life."

Simone nodded.

"Why not have it represent the ability to leave Ned, too? You could do both at once. Start a new life by pursuing two momentous accomplishments at once."

Simone went still and silent.

I looked back out at the lake so she could think without the pressure of my stare.

I counted up to ten, then twenty, then one hundred.

Simone said nothing.

I was about to speak when I realized that giving her some space to think might be the best thing.

I visualized a map of the U.S. and tried to picture and name every state, starting with Alaska and moving toward Florida. I made a mental list of my favorite painters and then organized them by subject so that I could determine what proportion were landscape artists versus portrait artists versus still life painters versus abstract painters. I did the same for my favorite musicians, ranking the numbers of jazz, classical, rock, and folk artists. I even remembered some country musicians that I liked.

Through it all I was aware of Simone making little movements in the passenger seat. She slouched down low, squeezing herself into the corner where the seat met the door. She put her feet up on the dash, then pulled her knees to her chest in a fetal position. I sensed her chewing on a hangnail, then winding her hair around her finger. She turned away from me and put her bandaged forehead against the cold window glass. She tapped a nail on her front tooth and clenched her hands into fists so hard that her knuckles went white. For a time she breathed slower, then faster, then sighed.

Eventually, she turned to face me. I kept looking out at the lake. No pressure. Let her speak when ready.

She took a breath as if to start speaking, stopped, started again.

"Tell me again what you're proposing I do." Her voice betrayed a little shakiness. To even go near the thought was frightening.

"I'm proposing that you leave Ned by strapping on your skis and pack and making your way into the frozen wilderness. I think you've now learned what you want and how to get it."

I waited. She said nothing.

"Does he know you've been thinking about the Randonnée challenge?" I said.

"I'm not sure. I mentioned it because I was curious about it, but that's all. Mostly, he knows that I've been thinking about the cross-country ski race from Lake Tahoe to Truckee during the solstice. I talked about doing that a long time ago. I wanted to do the race to Truckee to prove to myself that I could finish it. But when I learned about the Tahoe Randonnée Extreme and how it included multiple days of mountain climbing and camping in the wilderness, I thought that it would be a much greater challenge." She paused. "It would be a way bigger accomplishment."

"I think it's a great idea," I said. "Ned thinks you're meek and afraid of the world. He knows that you're afraid of him. Afraid to make a bold change. He would never expect you to head into the back-country. It could be the perfect escape from his tyranny. He wouldn't know where to find you. In fact, the cross-country ski race could work as a decoy. He would think that's where you went. Without the threat of Ned finding you, you would be able to prove to yourself that you could do it. You could show yourself and the world that you're capable of anything."

"But just because I've dreamed of it doesn't mean I could do it."

"Yes, you could. I believe you could. Street believes you could. Only Ned doubts your ability, your strength. This is your chance to prove him wrong."

"Do you think I could do it even during the solstice? Skiing at night?"

"Yes."

"If I could be strong enough to leave Ned, then I could tell the truth about how he beats me."

"Right."

"He would come after me." Simone's voice wavered.

"If you press charges, they will arrest Ned. I could go to your house and leave a hint or two that would reinforce the idea that you are doing the race, while you are actually out on the Randonnée Extreme. Eventually, Ned would likely get out of jail on bail. He would come home and find you gone. He'd look around, see your skis gone, and he'd think he was smart to figure out that you were doing the race to Truckee. If he tried to chase you, he'd look in the wrong place. He'd never believe that you were up in the mountain wilderness at night, skiing alone under the cold moon. It would be the best hiding place of all."

"If I could do the Randonnée, I would know that I could take on other challenges. I could live where I want, alone if I want."

She paused.

I waited.

"If I left Ned, I'd never look back. He couldn't touch me. He wouldn't matter. He would be a... a nothing."

FORTY-TWO

We again sat in silence, Simone thinking, me waiting.

"I would need help," she said.

"I can help. Street, too."

"No, I mean that I would have to learn a lot."

"Like what?" I said.

"Remember how I said that you have to navigate by yourself? They give you a list of check points, mountain peaks and such?"

"You find them with a topo map and a compass."

"But I don't know how to read a topo map. I don't even have any maps of the area. I don't know how to use a compass with a map, either. And even though I've trained some, I don't really know anything about back-country skiing."

"Like avoiding avalanche territory," I said.

"Right."

"So you need someone to teach you all that stuff."

Simone nodded.

"It's December nineteenth. If you were going to go during the solstice, you'd have to learn it all in just two days."

Another nod.

"You won't be healed enough to go in two days."

"Yes, I will. These bruises look bad, and they hurt. But I could still go. I know more about how bruises heal than pretty much anyone."

"Okay," I said. "I know several ski experts, but they all have jobs. They could maybe meet with you for an evening, but that wouldn't be nearly enough time. There is only one person who might be able to teach you all of what you need and do it on short notice."

"Who's that?"

"Joe Rorvik."

While Simone listened, I called Joe and explained what Simone needed and asked if he could help.

He said that she was nuts to consider doing such a dangerous expedition for her first back-country experience. He also said that if she really wanted to pursue it, he would be able to tell her what she needed to know. I asked how long such an intensive workshop would take. He thought about it and said that if Simone was really sharp and if she focused well, he could probably teach her all the basics in a couple of days. But he couldn't get her in shape. That would take months. I said that I'd pass on the information.

After we hung up, I told Simone what he'd said, leaving out the part about her being nuts.

"When would we start?" she asked.

"Now. The South Lake Tahoe police will have let Ned go by now. You can't go home."

Simone and I made a plan. My first call was to Street at her lab. She agreed to meet us at her condo. Because it was surrounded by other condos, it seemed a safer place than my cabin. It was also possible that Ned wouldn't know where Street lived.

By the time we got to Street's, Simone was having second thoughts about seeing Joe. She didn't want to endure his judgment. But she agreed that she needed help from an expert on skiing. I tried to convince her that Joe would respect her efforts and be impressed once he realized that she was going to change her life.

Having already been missing from Ned's life for almost two days, Simone was petrified of what Ned would do if he found her. She knew he'd been spying on Joe, and she believed that he would check on the Rorvik house to see if she went there.

So I called Diamond and asked if he was available for a little off-duty security work. He said he could juggle his schedule and come around the next two days and sit in on Joe Rorvik's impromptu back-country class.

Diamond met us at Street's, driving his ancient pickup.

We tried to hurry, but we didn't get to Joe's until 5 p.m. But the darkness gave us cover. Joe had turned off his front entry light, the Christmas lights on the sculptures, and the motion light above the garage door. We walked from darkened vehicles into a darkened house, and Joe led us into his origami room. It was dimly lit by a night light. The curtains were shut over the big windows.

Joe seemed not to even notice Simone. He turned toward Diamond. "Pleased to see you again, sergeant," Joe said. They shook hands. He looked at Diamond's old sweatshirt and faded jeans and worn running shoes. "Are you a back-country skier?" he asked.

Diamond shook his head. "No. I go into the back-country in winter only if I have a snowmobile and a guide and I never get more than a hundred yards from a house with a warm fire, hot chile on the stovetop, and cerveza in the fridge."

Joe smiled. "Of that list, I only have the cerveza. Would Fat Tire suffice?"

"Sí," Diamond said.

"If you don't ski back-country, you are here to..."

"Security detail. My presence maybe helps Simone relax."

Joe looked Diamond over a second time. "Forgive my impertinence, but does that mean you carry a gun when you're not in uniform?"

"Sí."

"I don't see a holster."

"Sí."

Joe nodded understanding. "I'm a little slow."

Joe and I fetched beers, and we all sat on Joe's big furniture.

"Let's go over the plan," I said. "Tonight and tomorrow, Joe is going to help Simone learn about back-country techniques in prep for the Tahoe Randonnée Extreme challenge, which she wants to participate in during the winter solstice. Come the solstice, morning after next, Simone and I are going to go to the South Lake Tahoe PD, where she will file assault charges against Ned Cavett. I will give Commander Mallory advance notice so that there will be no delay.

"Ned will be arrested and brought to custody. After Ned is gone, Street and I will help Simone gather her ski equipment and other gear. We will leave some evidence at the house that suggests that Simone is going to participate in the ski race to Truckee."

I continued. "With Ned's priors, he will be familiar with the bail process, and he will call a bail bondsman. He is, no doubt, already angry with Simone for disappearing. After his arrest, he will be enraged and will step up his efforts to find her."

I drank some beer. "After Street and I drop Simone off up by Sugar Bowl, I will search their house. I hope to acquire sufficient evidence to charge Ned in Rell's assault and two other separate murder cases. With that we could keep him locked up. But in the event that Ned does get out, he won't be able to find Simone because he will be looking at the race to Truckee while she will have already left on the Randonnée challenge on the Sierra Crest. She'll be in the high country south of Donner Summit, heading on skis toward points south, and attempting to bag twenty mountain peaks on the way."

"A good plan," Joe said. "How can I help?"

I looked at Simone. "Do you want to answer that?"

She looked nervous. "I... I've done some training," she said in a tiny voice. "I carried a backpack. Stuff like that. I've read about the route. But I don't know what else to do."

Joe looked around at the rest of us. "Which of you has back-country ski experience?"

Nobody spoke.

"Who is your buddy on this trip?" Joe asked.

"I don't have a buddy. I'll be skiing alone."

"That is unwise to the point of foolishness," Joe said. "The Tahoe Randonnée takes you through the Granite Chief Wilderness, then on south to the Desolation Wilderness. Most of the time you'll be very far from civilization. There is no cellphone coverage along much of the route. Everyone knows that you always take a buddy when you go into the wilderness." Joe sounded stern.

We all looked at Simone. Her hands shook. I wanted to speak up on her behalf, but I recognized that this was part of the process of taking charge of your life, staking out a position and defending it. If I intervened, it would exacerbate her dependency on others. I looked at Street, my eyebrows raised. She made a little shake of her head.

Eventually, Simone said, "Going solo is part of the challenge. The greater the challenge you face, the more valuable the experience becomes."

"Well put," Joe said.

"I know that I'm small, but I'm strong for my size. I can carry a pack with food and tent. I did a test and walked around the neighborhood with it three different times. It was really heavy, but I could do it. I don't... I don't have skills. But I have lots of endurance. And I've done a lot of cross-country skiing, just not up and down mountains. I believe I can do this. I'm determined to do this."

"Then let me just say that you should call someone every time you get to a mountaintop. The cellphone buddy system. Most mountaintops are within a sightline of a cell tower. At least that way someone will know where you were last, should you fail to come out the other end."

"Okay," Simone said. "I'll call Owen from some of the mountain checkpoints."

Joe took a deep breath. "Simone, have you ever climbed a mountain on skis?"

"No. But I did some hill climb training with skins on my skis. I found some steep slopes to work on over on Tahoe Mountain by the high school."

"You won't want to be on steep slopes of any kind, going up or down. We'll try to keep you on medium slopes or less. Can you ski down medium slopes?"

"I'm not an expert skier, if that's what you mean. I'm a decent intermediate. And I can really make time on the flats. I know I'm little, but I have stamina. I can keep going and going. You probably think this is crazy, but I believe I can do forty miles or more on skis."

"With a heavy pack," Joe said, sounding gruff.

"Yes," Simone said. She looked him straight in the eyes. "With a heavy pack."

"You know that there is no grooming in the back-country."

"Of course." Simone sounded offended. "I've skied on junk snow. I know about traversing and doing kick turns, coming down a slope on bad snow, one traverse at a time."

"Have you ever gone winter camping?"

"Not really. I slept in a yurt on the snow in college."

"Have you cooked on a campstove?" he asked.

"Yes. I got some used camping equipment from a friend, including a cookstove. I told Ned I wanted to try doing dinner on it for fun. He was suspicious as always, but he let me. It was hard. Just one little burner. But it worked. I made stroganoff."

"You have an alpine tent and a heavy down bag?"

"What's an alpine tent?" Simone asked.

"External frame, small, lightweight, but able to withstand high winds."

"Yes, I think that describes my tent," she said. "I got it on eBay, and I set it up in the yard one day when Ned was at work."

"You've never slept in it?"

"No," Simone said, shaking her head. "You think I'm stupid to do this, don't you?"

"I'm just asking questions," Joe said, irritation in his voice. "Do you have experience navigating in the back-country?"

She shook her head.

"Do you know how to read a topo map?"

"No." Simone's voice was getting smaller.

Joe looked at me, alarm on his face.

"Joe," I said, "let's assume that Simone has no qualifications for this other than extreme desire and the need to be safe from Ned. As soon as he gets out on bail, he will come looking for her. If she is in town, in a safe house, he may find her. As you said yourself, he is feral and clever. He has an instinctive sense about these things. I wouldn't trust that he couldn't figure out some way to get the safe house location. If Simone is out in the back-country, he won't easily be able to find her. But the bigger part of this is that Simone has decided to take on a major challenge as the start of a new life. She's dreamed of this for a long time. If she can pull it off, she will prove to herself that she is capable of nearly anything."

Joe nodded. Drank some beer. Made the chewing motions.

"Okay," he said. "Let's start with navigation." He walked across the room to a wastebasket that was filled with rolls of paper. He pulled out several and spread them out on the big origami table. He chose several maps and lined them up so that they made a big picture of the mountains to the west of the lake.

"Come sit next to me," he said to Simone. She did as requested.

"Do you know what topo lines are?"

"No. I'm sorry I'm so ignorant."

"No more sorrys tonight, okay?" Joe said. "We're here to learn." He pointed to the maps. "All these curvy lines show areas of equal elevation. They are called topographical lines because they reveal the topography, the shape, of the landscape."

Joe walked over to the big paper dispenser, pulled off a sheet of paper, and did some folding and bending. In a minute, he had created the shape of a mountain and a sloping valley. He touched the point of a pencil to the mountain. "If I move this pencil around the mountain without going up or down, I've found a line of equal elevation." He drew a rough circle around the paper mountain.

"Now, if I go down a hundred feet and do another line of equal elevation, that would be another topo line." He moved the pencil down a bit and drew another circle around the mountain. He looked at Simone. "Are you with me?"

She nodded.

He held out the paper model of mountain and valley. "If I look straight down at this model of the mountain, I can see what those lines look like from above. If I draw those shapes on a flat piece of paper, I have a topo map."

Joe took another piece of plain paper and set it flat on the table. "This is our map." He drew concentric circles. "Here's a representation of our nice, symmetrical paper mountain. Now let's map our valley."

Joe put the pencil on the origami paper valley and moved it on the level around the top part of the valley. The line made a U-shape. He again moved the pencil down and made another line, taking care to keep the pencil line level as it moved around the origami valley. It became another U-shape, narrower, tucked inside the first one.

"Those are topo lines going through the valley. Let's put those on the flat map." He drew similar lines on the map. Then he filled in more valley lines and mountain lines. He slid his home-made map in front of Simone.

"Look at the result. These lines show the mountain, these show the valley. And I can add more that represent any kind of undulating landscape."

Simone spoke up. "If I were up on this mountain and I walked along as if I were following a topo line, I wouldn't go up or down at all, right?"

"Exactly," Joe said, obviously pleased. "You would be taking a level route across whatever slope you were on."

"And if there's an area with no topo lines on the map?" Simone said. "What would that mean?"

"That would mean that it's a flat area."

Joe pointed to the real map and showed Simone different areas and explained how they went up and down. Soon, it appeared that she had the hang of it and, with a little thinking, could tell the shape of any landform.

Next, Joe showed her how to put a compass on top of a map, then rotate the map until north on the map matched north on the compass.

"Do you know about Magnetic Deviation?"

Simone shook her head.

"A compass points to the magnetic north pole, not the geographic north pole. They are quite far apart. In Tahoe, the difference is over thirteen degrees." He pointed to the map. "See this symbol? This arrow shows geographic north, and this arrow shows magnetic north. So you rotate your map so that the magnetic north arrow aligns with your compass needle. Then your map will match the landscape. By studying the topo lines, you can look at the features on the map and match them to your landscape. That way you will know where you are and plan where you want to go. Do you know your specific route?"

"No. I have to sign up on the website, and then I'll be given all of my mountains to climb. I'm supposed to determine my route from that."

"Can you do that now?" Joe asked.

"If I can use your computer, yes."

Joe pointed to the computer on his desk. "We'll wait."

Street helped Simone work through the process of signing up and requesting a Tahoe Randonnée Extreme route to be started on the winter solstice.

Joe and Diamond and I each had a beer while they worked.

Simone and Street declined. Soon, Simone brought a printout over to Joe.

"Perfect," Joe said. "Each checkpoint is shown in the order they want you to pursue them. This will be fun." I could see that he was intrigued.

Joe pointed to the topo maps arranged across the table. "Here's where you will start on Donner Pass Road. Near the chair lifts at Sugar Bowl. Your first mountain to climb is Donner Peak at just over eight thousand feet." He put an x on the mountain top. "So we'll draw a line that goes up the slope at a gradual angle so that you can climb on skis." He drew with care and precision and just a bit of the wavering common to people of his age.

"Always remember to stay off steep slopes, never ski near the base of steep slopes, and try to avoid any slopes that face northeast."

"Why?" Simone said.

"Avalanche danger. Do you have a beacon or one of those new inflatable vests?"

She shook her head.

"Well, skip the beacon. No one will be near you to pull you out anyway. But get a vest. If you get caught in a slide, you pull the lever and it inflates. Having a big bubble around your neck helps keep you floating to the top of a slide."

"How do I tell if the slope is steep or faces northeast?" Simone asked.

"We look at the same old topo lines. If they are close together, that means the slope is steep. If they orient to the northeast, that means a slope that gets lots of wind-loading and too little sun to help weld the snow layers together. Most people who die in avalanches are on northeast-facing slopes between thirty and forty-five degrees of steepness."

"How do I tell that amount?"

"Those are like Black Diamond slopes at ski areas. Have you seen those?"

"Yeah."

"Okay. You see a slope in the back-country that looks like it would be a Black Diamond run, stay off it. As for route planning, see these lines that are close together?"

"Yeah."

"That amount of spacing represents a steep slope. And these lines that are farther apart represent a shallow slope. We'll pay special attention as we plan your route."

Joe went down the checkpoint list and marked every mountaintop with numbers to show the order. Then he slowly drew a route from one to the next.

Simone said, "How do you know this country so well?"

"I've skied back-country through there."

"Do you like back-country skiing?" Simone asked.

"No, I don't, especially the up part. Doesn't mean I haven't done it. I like to know the territory. And I do like the down part."

"And you remember it so well that you can make paper models of the mountains?"

I interjected. "Didn't Rell ever tell you that Joe is an Olympic medalist in ski racing?"

Simone's eyes widened. "She said that you were a ski racer. I didn't know about the Olympic part. Wow, that's something."

"I don't like Rell to brag about me," Joe said. "Anyway, most racers have good mountain memory. Racers think topographically. It's a bit like a musician who can hear a song and then tell you the key changes. Let me ski a mountain, it gets fixed in my mind."

Joe lifted up the pile of maps and sorted through them. He pulled one out from the pile and drew a curving line across a portion of it. At one end of the line was an X.

"Now we'll give you a little real world experience," he said.

Simone frowned.

"This is a route you can see from this neighborhood. This X represents a viewpoint only two blocks away. I want you to study this route. Figure out which direction it goes and where it goes up and where it goes down. Then we'll go out to the viewpoint and see if you can identify the route in the landscape. It's dark out, but the moon and stars light the snow. It will be very much like what you will do on your Randonnée trek."

Simone studied the map and made some notes on the paper.

Five minutes later, she said, "Okay, I think I'm ready."

We all went out through the dark house and got into our

vehicles, Joe riding in Diamond's decrepit pickup.

Diamond led, with Joe telling him where to drive, and we followed. We stopped at a corner in the road and got out. The snowbank was beat down from snowshoers and cross-country skiers. With only Diamond's steadying hand on Joe's elbow, Joe was able to walk up onto the compacted snow.

The view was out over Tahoe Valley, a vast, beautiful landscape, glowing blue-white under the stars and moon sliver and speckled with a thousand lights of houses, eight hundred feet below the Angora Highlands neighborhood.

Joe handed Simone a compass and stood behind her as she opened the map and held out the compass. She looked out across the valley toward Freel Peak to the east and down Christmas Valley to Stevens Peak to the south. She compared it to the map, consulted the compass, rotated the map, angled the paper to get a better look at it in the dark, rotated the map again.

In time, she spoke softly to Joe. He murmured something back. She pointed to the map and spoke again. He nodded. She raised up her arm and pointed as if following Angora Ridge up to Angora Peak, taking the next ridgeline to Echo Peak and farther.

I understood Joe's mastery as I realized that he had already given her a route into the Desolation Wilderness and had her identify and imagine two peaks that might in fact be on the Tahoe Randonnée Extreme.

Simone made a gesture as if she would go down the southwest side of Echo Peak, opposite the side we were looking at. Then she pointed toward the mountains to the south, her finger aiming directly at Steven's Peak in the distance.

After a time, he patted her on the back, said something else that we couldn't hear, and she folded the map.

"What if it's too dark to see the compass?" she asked. "And what if my flashlight dies?"

Joe turned and pointed at the sky to the north. "Let me show you how to find the North Star." He pointed out the Big Dipper and explained how the last two stars at the end of the pan pointed toward the North Star.

"But that's only useful if you lose your compass," he said. "Otherwise, it's best to dig in and wait until morning."

FORTY-THREE

The next morning, we drove around to buy supplies, an avalanche vest, dehydrated food, extra maps, compass, headlamp, and solar cellphone charger.

When we got back to Street's, before we got out of the Jeep, I tested Simone's resolve one more time.

"You are still solid about this plan?" I said.

"Yes."

"Tomorrow morning we will go to the police and you will tell the truth about how Ned beats you up."

"Yes."

"I'm going to call Commander Mallory and tell him we will be in first thing in the morning."

"Yes."

So I called Mallory to let him know that Simone Bonnaire would arrive in the morning to tell all, and Mallory could prepare for the arrest of Ned Cavett on assault charges. I didn't know for certain, but I hoped that by arresting Ned, Mallory would also be bringing in our murderer.

At noon, Diamond stopped by once again, and we all visited Joe for a final lesson in back-country skiing.

Joe had thought of many more bits of advice over the preceding hours. He discussed a hundred points with Simone, quizzing her at times, explaining the safest approach to tackle the route along with the best escape strategy should something significant go wrong. He even drew on the map the best escape routes from the high country.

As evening approached, Joe announced that he was making a ski racer's dinner. "You're going to need lots of protein and lots of carbs to start off on a trip of this magnitude."

Simone looked concerned, like a vegetarian who worries about being surprised with meat.

"Do you like salad and French bread?" Joe asked.

Simone nodded.

"Baked potato and butter?"

"Of course."

"Broccoli?"

"Certainly," Simone said.

Street elbowed me in my side.

"You like a grilled Porterhouse steak?" Joe continued.

Another nod.

"How do you like it cooked?"

"Medium rare."

"Do you drink red wine?"

"I spent my first ten years in France," Simone said.

"Homemade apple pie?"

"I could eat it for breakfast, lunch, and dinner."

Joe gave her a big smile of approval and went into the kitchen to begin preparations without asking any of the rest of us about our preferences.

Simone again looked worried. She spoke to me in a whisper. "Mr. Rorvik cooks?"

"Lots of men do," I said.

"None of the men in my life have ever cooked."

"Welcome to your new life," I said.

Joe put on a fabulous feast and even cooked a steak for Spot.

While we all ate, Joe paid particular attention to Simone, making certain that she ate seconds of everything.

After dinner, Joe and Simone worked until well into the evening, discussing maps and routes and strategies.

As we left, Simone seemed subdued by the enormity of what she was planning to do. We were getting into the Jeep when Joe's voice called out quietly from the front door.

"Simone?"

"Oui?" she said, slipping into French for the first time, a sign,

I thought, of serious introspection.

Joe walked out to where we stood by the Jeep. The outside lights were still off for security. He reached out his hands toward Simone. Despite the darkness, gold sparkled in his fingers.

"This is my good luck necklace," he said. "I wore it during all of my ski races. I had it on when I won my Olympic Medal. I want you to have it."

Simone stood frozen. "I...I..." she stammered.

"When you are out there in the dark," Joe said, "and the air is very cold, and the distances seem far, and you feel very alone, you can know that I'll be here cheering you on."

Simone shook her head a bit as if in disbelief. She took the necklace and put it over her head. Joe started to back up toward his door, making a little wave of his hand. Simone broke into a huge smile, reached up and gave him a hug, and kissed his cheek.

The next morning, Mallory met us at the police department. He said he already had two men outside Ned's house, waiting for the go-ahead once the judge signed the warrant.

Simone was nervous as we went in. She filled out the paperwork, made her statement, showed her bruises, which, although healing, were still dramatic. They took pictures of her, asked her many questions, then let us go.

I drove to Ned and Simone's house and parked a block down from the patrol unit. I guessed that it would take Mallory about twenty minutes to get a judge's signature on the warrant.

Twenty minutes later, the two officers got out of their car and went up to the door. In about the time it takes to inform and cuff their suspect, they came back out with Ned, his hands locked behind his back, put him into the back of the car, and drove away.

I pulled up to their driveway and parked behind Ned's chinless yellow pickup. Simone pointed out the skis and skins and camping stuff in the garage. I loaded it into the back of the Jeep while she collected her clothes inside.

She had a little list of things to bring, and after we'd loaded everything, she carefully went through the list, checking off each item. It gave me some confidence, seeing her thoroughness, and

I realized that somewhere down in the cellar of my brain I'd been hearing a voice that sounded like Joe's. It said that Simone was nuts to try this with so little experience. It also said that I would be to blame if tragedy should come to her. I'd encouraged her at each step when I should have been telling her to wait, find a skiing buddy, get some experience, go in the spring when the weather was safer.

We drove up the East Shore and picked up Street to join us on the ride. Street has a calming effect on people, and she did a good job with Simone, making conversation that was designed to be casual and thoughtful at the same time.

I could see how it worked as it unfolded. Talk only about trivial stuff, and it communicates that you're worried about the big issues and are afraid to focus on them. Talk only about the major stuff, and it clutters the traveler's mind with too many concerns. Strike a medium balance, and the person knows that you understand the scope of the mission, but you are still relaxed about it. The relaxed manner telegraphs confidence in the person who is about to embark on the big event.

As we drove north out of Tahoe City to Truckee and then around Donner Lake up to the summit and the launch point, Simone seemed more comfortable than at any time since I'd met her.

We parked near Sugar Bowl and got out. Spot ran around exploring while Simone made a last check of her gear. She strapped the climbing skins onto her skis because her very first leg was an ascent up to the top of Donner Peak.

I went to help her with her pack, but she held up her hand to stop me.

"For the next few days I'm going to do all this myself," she said. "I better start now."

We watched as she clicked into her bindings, swung her pack up on her back, adjusted her sunglasses, and picked up her poles.

Street gave her a hug first, then I followed.

"You'll do great," I said. "We'll see you on the other end when you ski down into Kirkwood."

Simone patted her thighs and called out, "Spot."

He came running and jumped around, excited.

She gave him a hug, turned to us and said, "Au revoir."

I held Spot as the tiny young French woman pushed off with her poles and started climbing up toward Donner Peak.

Back in the Jeep, Street said, "She's tough, you know."

"No kidding."

"I watched as Joe marked all of those zig-zag lines to the various peaks. I think it turns a forty-some mile straight trek into sixty or more."

"Probably."

"How many nights do you think she'll be out?" Street asked.

"I'm guessing three nights and four days. She told me that she has more than enough food for four nights and five days. But we'll get a sense as she calls in her locations along the way."

"Do you think she'll make it all the way?" Street asked.

"I'm guessing that the single greatest part of success in this kind of thing is determination rather than skill. She's pretty determined."

FORTY-FOUR

When we got back to Street's condo, I dropped her off, then headed down to the South Shore. I stopped at my office and used my computer to look up the cross-country ski race from the lake up to Truckee. I printed out a couple of pages and left.

The chinless pickup was still parked in front of the drive, but Ned would still be in jail. I parked, put on my gloves, told Spot to be quiet, and walked up to the front door. It was locked. The garage door was up. The inner door was unlocked.

The door took me into their kitchen, as good a place to start searching as any. I didn't know what I was looking for other than some indication that Ned was interested in Manuel Romero and Jillian Oleska in addition to Joe and Rell Rorvik.

The house was surprisingly neat and clean, no doubt a credit to Simone and not Ned. The surfaces were uncluttered, things were put away in their places, laundry was neatly folded in the drawers. I didn't make a mess as I didn't want to enrage Ned any more than he already was.

I went through the downstairs first, then proceeded up to the bedroom. I found nothing revealing except for a white ski jacket and warmups that smelled of sour sweat.

Next, I searched the garage. It wasn't as neat and clean, probably because Simone wasn't allowed to pick it up. As a result, there was more clutter to go through, but I still found nothing.

Over in the corner were several pairs of skis, including small, old downhill skis that probably belonged to Simone. I took the printouts I'd made about the race to Truckee, folded them three times and flexed the folded paper to make it look worn. Then I put it on the floor near the skis. It was a reasonable place for it to fall if Simone had been holding it when she pulled out her back-country skis.

I searched the rest of the garage and was about to give up when I thought of Ned's truck.

I tried the doors. Locked. I went back into the house looking for keys. I found them on a nail by the inside door to the garage.

Once in the truck, I looked in the glove box. It contained the registration and insurance cards and an old Chevy manual. I bent down and looked under the seat. Lined up in a neat row were a dozen unopened cans of Budweiser. Tucked between the cans was a little spiral notebook. Using a tissue, I slid it out and opened the cover. On the first page was writing in pencil with scrawling block letters that were almost illegible.

Mrs. Roarvick
Manwel Romoro
Jill Olesa,
Others to take care of –
Joe Roarvick
Oen Mickenna.

Lines were drawn through the first three names.

I put the notebook back where I found it and called Mallory.

When he answered, I explained that at Simone Bonnaire's request, I had done a search of their house and found a notebook with names in Ned's truck. He sent over two cops who took my statement and then left with the notebook in a Ziplock bag.

That evening, I began to worry when Simone hadn't called by seven o'clock. The temperature outside my cabin had already dropped to 10 degrees. My cabin sits at 7200 feet. Simone's first planned stop was to be at the Sierra Club's Bradley Hut, which sits at 7400 feet. All other things being equal, 200 feet only equates to less than a degree colder. But other things weren't equal. At my cabin, I get a substantial warming from lake effect on cold winter nights. West of the lake in the high country, there would be no such effect. Simone could be looking at a night well below zero.

My other worry was that my estimation of distance had me guessing that Simone would arrive at the hut by late afternoon. If she were still struggling up her last peak... Or if she'd fallen and broken an ankle... The questions swirled.

Spot got up from his bed and walked over to the door, wagging.

I opened it to Street.

"Any word?" she said, coming in, kissing me, and walking over to the woodstove to warm up.

"No," I said.

"Where do you think she is?"

"I don't know," I said. "But it's a cold night. Hard not to worry."

My cell rang.

I picked it up. "Owen McKenna."

"Owen! It's Simone!" she was shouting. I gestured to Street to come close so she could hear. "I made it!" Simone said. "I'm camping. I'm in my tent."

"You didn't make it to the Bradley Hut?"

"No, I went on past it! I'm near Squaw Valley, just down the ridge north of Granite Chief Mountain. I'll be able to climb it at first morning light. That will be my fourth mountain. Isn't that fantastic?!"

"That is great, Simone. Have you eaten?"

"No I wanted to warm up in my tent and sleeping bag. It's pretty cold out here. In a little bit, I'll open the tent door a little for ventilation and turn on my cookstove. I'll be fed and sound asleep in less than an hour. Just like a real back-country skier!"

"Congratulations. We'll toast your progress with a Bordeaux tonight."

"Okay! And Owen, please tell Joe that his maps and his route are perfect. It works just like he says. You turn the map to match the compass, find the landmarks, and away you go!"

"That's great. What's the next mountain after Granite Chief?"

"Squaw Peak, so I'll be looking down at the top of the cable car and a lot of downhill skiers. After that, I head into the Granite Chief Wilderness and then up to Twin Peaks."

"That's near Hell Hole Canyon, right?" I said, trying to remember the route she and Joe had drawn on the map.

"Yeah. I don't want to go down there! That's like four thousand feet below Twin Peaks! So Joe's got me going around it to the east and climbing Twin Peaks. By nightfall, I'm hoping to make it to the Ludlow Hut."

"That's another Sierra Club hut," I said.

"Yeah, up above and behind Sugar Pine Point State Park. It's important that I get a good night's sleep because after that I head to Rubicon Peak, then turn west into Desolation Wilderness and all those mountains. Talk about the middle of nowhere! But Joe did a great job mapping the route, so I'm in good hands."

"I'll tell him, Simone. Thanks for calling."

Street was waving at me. "Street wants to say hi," I said, and handed the phone over.

"Your progress is fantastic news, Simone," Street said. "We'll chart your progress on our map. We're proud of you." She paused and listened, then said goodbye and hung up.

"It's great that she's so pleased with her progress. This gives us every reason to think that she may pull this off."

Street nodded, but her face wasn't bright.

"What's wrong?" I said.

"It's just that on the way up to your cabin the radio report said that the air masses out in the Pacific have started to change. They had thought we were in a stable high-pressure system. But now they're talking about the Jet Stream dropping south of us and sucking moisture into the Tahoe area."

"A potential storm?"

"Maybe," Street said.

"When?"

"They don't know. Everything is iffy right now. But if it keeps changing fast, we could have snow as soon as two days."

"Simone would still be out in the high country," I said.

Street nodded.

"Well, we'll watch it. If it begins to look bad, we can call her in before she gets to the end."

"Where would that be?" Street asked.

"I saw Joe draw emergency exit points on Simone's maps. Squaw Valley or Alpine Meadows. Blackwood Canyon. Emerald Bay. Glen Alpine. Her trail is a long way from any of those, but they would still be better than her trying to press on south."

Street nodded, her face clouded with worry.

I called Joe and gave him Simone's progress report.

He was very glad to hear that Simone was doing well, and I think it sent him to bed with a smile.

FORTY-FIVE

The following day I did catch-up work paying bills, returning phone calls and emails that I'd long neglected.

That evening, Simone called from the Ludlow Hut. She was cheerful, excited, and totally worn out. She said she had blisters on her feet, and she felt like she'd never completely thaw her toes. But she was looking forward to the rest of the trip, and she kept saying that it was the greatest thing she'd ever done.

I told Street and again called Joe to report her progress. He seemed even more pleased than the night before.

The next morning, I headed to my office. As I went south down the East Shore, I noticed the big, chinless, yellow pickup with the overbite tailgating me.

Ned Cavett must have been waiting near the base of my road and followed me as I turned out.

I dialed Diamond.

"I'm talking on my cell while driving," I said when he answered.

"Should I come and give you a ticket?"

"Maybe. Ned Cavett is following me, and if I had to guess, I'd say he's out to vivisect me before he goes on trial for beating up Simone."

"What would you like me to do?"

"I thought you might want to watch."

"The vivisection," Diamond said.

"Yeah. Hold on for a dropped call. Cave Rock tunnel approaching."

I drove through the tunnel. I was surprised that Diamond reappeared in my ear when I came out the other side.

"I'm going to my office," I said. "Ned will follow me there."

"I'll get there as soon as I can," Diamond said and hung up.

I went south past Skyland and headed toward Zephyr Cove.

In another few miles, I came to the South Shore and turned left at Kingsbury Grade. Ned tailgated me the entire way. He wanted me to know he was there. No doubt, he thought it would intimidate me. He was right.

I pulled into an open space and parked. Ned didn't bother to find a parking space. He just stopped in the middle of the lot and got out, leaving his engine running and the driver's door open. Leaving Spot in the Jeep, I got out and walked toward the office entry as if Ned weren't there.

"McKenna! You made my girl file assault charges against me! That's punishable by death."

I got to the office door and turned. Ned was standing in the lot, his hand held out to the side of his belt. He had another knife holster, and he looked like he was imitating a gunslinger ready for a duel.

"You beat on your girl like she's a punching bag," I said.

Ned ignored my words. "You took my girl! You brought her to that Truckee ski race! You think I didn't notice her skis missing? You think I'm stupid?"

They always say not to aggravate a violent suspect, and that instead one should minimize tensions by being calm and reassuring. I said, "Yeah, you're stupid. In fact, there are no words sufficient to describe the astonishing breadth and depth of your stupidity."

"I'm gonna kill you, McKenna. Then I'm gonna find that bitch Simone and kill her. I saw a show on wolves, and there was a lone wolf that ran out of the woods and cut a baby elk out of the herd. No one will know where or when I'm gonna strike."

Without looking down, Ned reached into the holster on his belt, a move that was as practiced as Billy The Kid drawing his six-gun. He pulled out a knife, brought it up above his head and then down behind him in a dramatic, circular swing like a softball pitch. His movement accelerated through the backswing as if his arm were a mechanical wonder, and the knife shot toward me like an arrow from a bow.

I jerked to the right and sprinted toward him. The knife cut the air near my face.

I wanted to do what Ned would least expect, so I kept up my charge.

Ned raised his fists like a boxer in a defensive posture and planted his right foot behind him to brace himself. As he prepared for my impact, I dove through the air toward him, hoping the snow and ice would lessen how much skin would burn off on impact.

My knees hit the asphalt as my arms locked around his waist. He hit the ice with his butt. His upper body went down, and he slid backward with me on top of him.

He pulled out another knife. I shot my arm out, but he raised the knife out of my reach. As he stabbed down, I rolled away. I did a fast pushup and jumped to my feet, staying bent, minimizing the target I presented. He jumped up. I leaped forward, grabbed his throwing arm with my left hand, and put my shoulder to his middle.

We went down again.

Before we stopped moving, I lifted his knife arm and slammed his elbow down onto the pavement. The knife clattered away. His hand came up and clamped onto my neck, fingertips like hooks in my throat.

I swung my right arm and made a solid elbow punch to his face. Ned let go of my neck as his nose turned bloody. I rolled off him and pushed back up onto my feet. He was still on his back. I thought he was dazed, but his hand shot to his holster and pulled out another knife. I kicked his hand hard. The knife skittered away. I stomped the throwing hand. He screamed, rolled, cupped his hand to his body. I stood bent, panting, hands to knees. He writhed in pain, but I stayed focused. I'd been suckered too many times. He rolled partway onto his stomach, but not enough to keep me from seeing his left hand snake to the holster and pull out a knife as a Douglas County Patrol vehicle pulled into the far end of the lot.

I kicked Ned's elbow. He screamed, rolled, and tried to shoot a knife at me from the ground. It was a serious attempt to put me down for good. The knife shot past my shoulder.

I stomped his left hand, then his elbow. I bent down, fumbled at his belt, got my hands on his holster of knives, yanked it off and hurled it toward the trees, the second time I'd disarmed him. Across the parking lot, Diamond was walking toward us, holding a video camera pointed toward us.

Ned twisted and rolled the other way and made an impressive front snap kick up toward my face. His boot caught my jaw and snapped my head back. My vision went blurry. I jumped onto the front of his knee, hyper-extending the joint, grinding the bones against the pavement.

He screamed again.

I turned and walked to my office building, my head lolling. My legs wouldn't work right. My sense of balance was off. I listed to the side, toward the scaffolding. I felt faint.

Behind me came the sound of a vehicle door slamming, then an engine revving. I thought Ned was down for good with crushed and broken joints. Shows what I know. Wheels screeched. The engine roar grew.

I grabbed the scaffolding for support and blinked hard, trying to bring back my vision. The roar grew louder.

Maybe if I jumped to the side at the last moment.

I ducked under the scaffolding and took three fast steps. I grabbed a scaffolding support pole that someone had leaned at an angle.

Ned hit his brakes, then screeched backward, changing his direction to aim at my new position.

I was still light-headed, my visual field seeming to tilt sideways. In my fading consciousness, it seemed like it would be good to have a weapon even though I knew that Ned would still drive over me with his truck. I thought the pole I'd grabbed was free and unattached, but it turned out to be stuck at the top. I jerked the bottom of the pole out from the ground. The bolt holding the pole at the top came free and arced through the air just as I heard Ned's truck strike the first part of the scaffolding.

What happened next was hard to comprehend even though I saw it clearly.

When I jerked the angled pole free, the joint where it had been attached came undone. Three poles simultaneously spread apart. Then, like some kind of magic toy, the entire scaffolding began to come down like multiple, linked, open scissors closing shut, one after another, in a grand design. Every fourth joint popped open, and the rest of the joints scissored closed.

I leaped to safety, but Ned, in his truck, was underneath the collapsing structure.

The scaffold poles came together in a neat pile. As they all stacked up, a significant portion of them landed on top of Ned's truck. The big, yellow, chinless vehicle made a terrific screech and moan as its body panels were crushed to the ground.

I stumbled toward the wreckage.

Diamond appeared, video camera in hand.

We both stared.

"Bad idea to drive into scaffolding," Diamond said.

I was still holding the heavy pole I'd pulled from the scaffolding, the real trigger point for the collapse. But I didn't have the mental wherewithal to explain.

I leaned toward the truck wreckage. "Hey, Ned. You in there? Can you hear me?"

There was no sound. All I could see was twisted yellow metal crushed by thousands of pounds of scaffolding. As I looked down into the metallic morass, there came another screech as more metal under duress finally gave way and tore apart.

I couldn't tell if Ned was squished flat or if he might be alive while contorted into a pretzel by the twisted truck body.

"Ned, did you push Rell Rorvik off the deck?" I called out. "Did you kill Manuel Romero? Jillian Oleska? They were in your notebook, Ned. Was that your murder list?"

But there was no answer.

FORTY-SIX

I watched for a bit while the firemen came and used their Jaws-Of-Life equipment on the scaffolding and crushed pickup. A half hour later, they still hadn't exposed much human flesh. I took Spot up to my office. I made some coffee and drank it with aspirin while Spot lay down near my office door and went to sleep.

Diamond came in thirty minutes later. He pointed at Spot sprawled across the dirty carpet.

"He got tired from watching you dodge Veitsi Mies blades?"

"Looks like it," I said. "I was hoping to get some information from Ned, but no answer. Was he merely reticent, or dead?"

"Ain't no coroner here when the paramedics finally hauled his ass off. But based on what I saw, not much of him was intact. We each have two hundred and six bones. I'm guessing his broken count was in the high one-fifties."

"Was he still breathing?" I asked.

Diamond made a little scoffing noise back in his throat.

"They paddle him?" I asked.

"They're supposed to, but you gotta know where to put the paddles. This was like twisted roadkill. Not clear which end was which."

"You want to take my statement?"

"Sure."

So he asked me the questions, and I gave him the answers, and then Street rushed into my office.

"My God, Owen, are you okay?" she asked.

Spot was suddenly awake. He jumped up, wagging.

Street came around my desk and stood next to my chair, holding my head against her chest. "I heard a big crash from down the street. A minute later, Diamond called me at my lab. He said you'd been in a fight. All the scaffolding on your building has come down! The entire parking lot is a disaster zone. I'm so glad you didn't get caught up in it."

"Yeah, I was lucky," I said, not mentioning that the pole I jerked free started the collapse.

"Is Ned dead?" she asked.

"Sounds like it," I said.

Street looked at Diamond.

He nodded.

"Good," she said.

"I ain't complaining," Diamond said.

"He was going to kill Simone," she said. "It was just a matter of when."

"Agreed," he said.

My cell rang.

I picked it up. "Owen McKenna," I said.

"Owen! It's Simone!"

"Hey, Randonnée Extreme trekker girl. How are you and where are you?" I was still dizzy, and my words were a bit garbled.

"Sounds like you've had some cocktails," she said.

"Just the rush of a hard workout."

"Me too," she said. "I'm on the very tippy top of Rubicon Peak! I did it! I climbed the steepest, rockiest peak around. I had to take off my boards and pack them the old-fashioned way. No skins can get you up rocks. Now I can see the entire lake. If I had a telescope, I could probably see your office. But I wanted to let you know about a problem," Simone said.

"What's that?" I asked. I saw Street and Diamond and Spot all looking at me.

"The solar charger I got for my phone? I can't make it work while I'm skiing. It's supposed to sit on the top of my pack, but the velcro straps don't stick right. It keeps falling off. So I thought, no big deal, I'll just charge when I stop. But that was stupid because I'm skiing all day until night and then some. Anyway, I really have to make my calls short so I can save power to take photos of me at each peak to document my trip. I've already used up a lot of battery power on the mountains I've climbed. So I'll be turning off my phone to conserve power. Not that you'd call me, but I just wanted you to know."

"Thanks for telling me," I said. "Can you hang the charging panel around your neck?"

"But then it won't face the sky."

"It might face the setting sun. You're traveling south and southwest. It might work."

"I never thought of that!" Simone said. "It doesn't have to face the sky. It can just face the sun. I'll try it."

"How's Street?" Simone asked, and I felt a jolt of happiness that Simone had so transformed in her short escape from Ned that she was suddenly concerned about other people.

"Good," I said. "It sounds like you're doing great, Simone."

"I am," she said. "I can't tell you how great this is to be free."

"No doubt," I said. "Where do you expect to camp tonight?"

"I'm still shooting for the Ludlow Hut."

"Sounds good. Call me tomorrow?"

"Yeah. Thanks for your help. Bye. Oh, one more thing."

"What?" I said.

"On my last peak, I was looking out to the west. From up here, you can see all the way to Mt. Diablo, maybe even the coast. That's probably over a hundred miles away, right?"

"Yeah. Something like that."

"Anyway," she said. "There are cirrus clouds in the distance. Doesn't that mean that weather is coming? I thought we were in a prolonged high pressure system. But now I'm wondering. Have you heard anything?"

"There is some talk about the jet stream possibly dropping south. That could bring some weather in a couple of days."

There was a silence on the phone.

"You remember the escape routes out of the high country that Joe showed you, right?"

Another silence. "Yeah, sure. But hopefully, I'll be done before any weather gets here. I'm pretty confident about that," she said.

"Yeah, you probably will," I said. "I also have some news. Ned attacked me in the parking lot an hour or so ago. He drove into the scaffolding at my office building, and the scaffolding fell and crushed him."

"Is he dead?"

"Yes, I'm sorry to say it."

"Oh, wow. That's... that's amazing. After all of this. I don't feel bad that he died. I'm finally free of him. I can't believe it. I don't have to worry any more."

"So I have a question. It'll just take a minute."

"Sure."

"I found a list of names under the seat of Ned's truck. It had Rell's name on it. Another name was Manuel Romero and another was Jillian Oleska. Are you certain you don't know them?"

"You already asked me. I don't."

"They are people who recently died in what looked like accidents that were similar to Rell's fall. Of all the names, Rell's and Manuel's and Jillian's names had lines drawn through them."

"And you think that Ned arranged these accidents," Simone said. Her normally small voice was loud.

"Yes."

"God, that's terrible. Ned is so evil!"

"I asked you once before, but I want to ask you again. Do you still believe that Ned is capable of planning and carrying out murder. Not something impulsive, but something premeditated."

"Yes. I have no doubt."

"Simone, I can close this case if I can find a solid connection between Ned and Manuel and Jillian. Is there any chance you know them by face but not by name?"

"I don't understand."

"Like when you go to the supermarket. You recognize the checkout clerk or the person behind the meat counter, but you don't know their names."

"I see. I could know them by face in that sense. But they could be anybody to me. How would I know that I knew them?"

"I think that if you did, it would be in connection to Rell."

Simone didn't respond.

"Simone, are you there?" I said.

"Yes. I'm just thinking."

"What are you thinking?"

"Nothing," she said.

"Simone, please tell me whatever you know. Anything you know could be helpful."

"What I know has nothing to do with Ned. And it doesn't

matter now with him dead."

"It matters in closing the case. We owe it to Rell and Manuel and Jillian."

Again, she was silent.

"Something is on your mind, Simone. Please tell me what it is. Rell is in a coma. Two other people are dead. If you are in any way connected to all of these people, your information is the one thing that could clear up all the confusion. Tell me, please."

"It's just... Rell and I were part of a group. But I can't talk about it." There was a beep in the background. Her cellphone battery getting low?

"Yes, you can talk about it," I said. "Rell is near death. She would want you to speak."

"No. It would be a violation of the rules."

"Simone, the rules are gone. Rell is near death. It's time to break the rules."

"But I swore an oath."

"Simone, an oath doesn't matter when the people involved are dead. Please tell me. It's the only way I can tie up the loose ends."

More silence. I waited. Street and Diamond stared at me, both frowning.

"It's called No Judgment," Simone finally said in my phone. In the background I could hear the wind whistling. I could visualize the Granite Chief Wilderness, a vast expanse of frozen, high-elevation landscape, covered in snow eight months of the year.

"Is No Judgment the name of the group?"

"Yeah."

"What is the group's focus?"

"Not to judge. I... I told you that I was abused as a kid."

"Right. No Judgment is an abuse group," I said.

"It was beyond horrible," Simone said, not responding to my statement, continuing her thought. "It took away my honor, my dignity, my strength, my sense of self. The group doesn't judge me for what I've been through. None of us judges the others."

"I understand. What was Rell's role?"

"She's the glue for the group. She holds it together. Rell saved me. I could talk to Rell. Anybody could talk to Rell. She had a kind of magic that makes people feel comfortable. People say things around her that they wouldn't otherwise say."

"She made it okay," I said.

"Yeah. Rell was the one who asked if I wanted to join. She started the group. We go hiking. That's our way of meeting. It's about the only thing that Ned let me do. We hike, and we talk about whatever we want. We talk about what happened. When no one is judging, it's easier to talk."

She paused. Again, the wind howled in the background.

"I can't say any more," Simone said.

I shut my eyes and tried to think back. Manuel's wife had talked about how he said that people shouldn't judge. She also said that Manuel liked to hike. Joe had said that Rell tried not to judge. He also said that Rell was a hiker.

"Simone, when you talked about your abuse, you probably focused on what happened when you were a child," I said.

"Yeah." Simone's voice made a little hiccup.

"Did you tell the others about Ned? How he beat you up?"

"Yes, I did."

"Did any of them react? Did any of them know Ned?"

"No, they didn't react. We don't judge, and we don't react. That would spoil it and make it so that no one would talk."

"Did the group have anything to do with the Steven's Peak Resort?" I asked.

"No. Nothing like that."

"Is it possible that Manuel and Jillian were part of the group?"

"I suppose." Simone's voice sounded distant, like she was traveling back in time. "We weren't allowed to say our real names. Only Rell used her real name because the others knew her from other times. The rest of us only knew each other by face and our fake names. We had to pick fake names. I was Serena. Rell also told me that I could disguise my look if I wanted."

"Did the others talk about their abuse?"

"Yeah. We were all abuse victims. Rell, too." I heard another beep. I knew I should hang up, but a deep sense of foreboding was growing in my gut.

"Did Rell say what happened to her?" I asked, suddenly undergoing one of those mental shifts where everything seems different. I didn't want to think about Joe as an abuser.

"Yes. She had to deal with stuff as a little girl. At the same age as me."

My heart made a small thump. "So Joe wasn't an abuser?"

"Joe? Not at all. He may be a jerk sometimes, but as far as Rell ever said, he was an angel to her." Then, after a pause, "But I shouldn't be saying any of this. I'm betraying a confidence."

"The people who joined No Judgment were able to talk about what happened to them," I said.

"Yeah. Rell made it easier. You could say anything to Rell. She made us feel that we could finally tell the truth. Tell what we'd been through. It was cathartic. For me. For the others." Simone's voice was more distant.

"Simone," I said, thinking about the photograph that was on the mantel in Romero's house, "Manuel Romero was a handsome man in his forties with a strong nose and thick, wavy, black hair. He looked Spanish. His eyes sparkled. Was he in the group?"

"Wow. Yes, I think so. Only, we knew him as Robert."

"Jillian Oleska was about thirty, vivacious, pretty smile, very fit. She was a ski racer in college and was still an expert skier. Was she in the group?"

"She went by Miranda. I didn't know about the skiing. But fit. We could all tell that she was fit. That was obvious. If I'd known about the skiing, I could have talked to her about it. But she only talked about..." Simone cut herself off. "So two of the people in our group are dead. And Rell is almost dead."

"Who else was in the group?" I asked.

"Just one more man." Yet another beep.

"Can you tell me about him?"

She was silent.

"Simone, please. Manuel, or Robert, as you knew him, is dead. Jillian/Miranda is dead. Rell is near death. Maybe Ned killed them to get more cash from the man who was paying him. But if not, it could be that the other person in your group is... Look, I don't want to alarm you, but the other man in the group could be the killer. If so, then you could be the next victim."

Simone still didn't talk for a bit.

"He's a nice guy. He went by Cameron. He's kind of a cocky

guy," Simone continued. "Charming in that way. And athletic. Very self-assured."

I was thinking about Michael Paul's tattoos. "Does Cameron have tattoos? Or does he always wear long-sleeves?"

"That's a strange question. Let me think. I don't remember any tattoos. But I don't remember him ever wearing short sleeves, either."

"What did Cameron say?"

"Not much. Just that he was abused as a child. His mother beat on him and his stepbrother over and over. One day, he lashed out and... It would be terrible for me to reveal a confidence."

"Simone, your oath could get you killed. This man could be looking for you."

"No, not Cameron. And I'll go to hell for saying this."

"Simone, you might live if you say it."

"Okay. We were hiking. I still remember where. Up at Marlette Lake above the East Shore. Cameron was kind of loose with his mouth, kind of too casual. I thought he'd been drinking. He had a big bottle of what looked like orange juice. But I wondered if he'd put something in it. Someone said something that made Cameron react in a harsh way. So he told us that when he was twelve, he killed his mother. Just like that. He said that no one ever knew and that even if someone knew, it was justified. Cameron said that one day his mother went crazy and beat him and his stepbrother so bad that he had a concussion from a cracked skull. The brother was non-responsive. So the mother took him to the emergency room and told the doctor that he fell and hit his head. Cameron had to sit through that lie. He said he wanted to tell the doctor, but he was afraid that his mother would kill him. After they left the brother at the hospital, Cameron and his mother were walking back to the car. Cameron saw his opportunity and made like he tripped on something just as they were about to cross the street. He fell against his mother and pushed her in front of a truck. He..." she stopped.

I waited. There was another beep. I wanted to tell her to speed up, but I was afraid she would stop altogether.

Eventually, Simone resumed talking.

"We were all shocked. But No Judgment was the rule. We

understood. I would have killed my stepfather if I could have figured out how. Cameron is the nicest guy. No way is he dangerous."

"What does Cameron look like?"

"Like I said, he's fit and athletic. He's in his twenties. He has long wavy hair and..." Another beep, this one longer, then silence.

Simone was gone.

FORTY-SEVEN

I gave a long look at Street and Diamond, then told them the gist of what Simone had said.

"Do you think Ned isn't the murderer anymore?" Street asked.

"I don't know," I said. "Let's assume Cameron regrets telling people about his personal abuse and how he responded by killing his mother. Does that give him motive for murder? Maybe. But even if he is dangerous, that doesn't mean he can find Simone. She's in the middle of nowhere, about to head into Desolation Wilderness. She just told us that she's at the summit of Rubicon Peak, but that doesn't mean we could go into the high country and find her. She's about as hidden and safe as she can be."

Diamond said, "You could ask Simone to abandon her trip and come down one of the escape routes that Joe gave her."

"Sure," Street said. "But we need to remember her perspective. All this is speculation. Our concerns about Cameron might be legitimate. But they might also be false. If you ask her to come down out of the wilderness and we're wrong, Simone will never forgive us. We'll be destroying her first big effort to take control of her life. She's finally proving to herself that she's strong."

I leaned back in my desk chair and took a deep breath, let it out, tried to clear my head. "I agree. But let's just suppose that Cameron was the murderer all along. If so, then he's very good on skis. He may be the guy I watched skiing after Jillian. If he took out Jillian on the mountain above Sand Harbor, that would show that he is very skillful in the back-country. Tracking Simone might not be much more difficult than tracking Jillian."

Diamond sat on the edge of my desk. "Maybe it has nothing to do with him telling the group about killing his mother."

"What do you mean?" I asked.

"You told me about the sergeant from Inyo County."

"That's right," I said, remembering. "Sergeant Gramercy of the Inyo County Sheriff's Office told Sergeant Bains that Ned Cavett had a younger brother or a half-brother. I think his name was Peter Cavett."

"And Simone said that the man named Cameron had a stepbrother," Street said. "They could be the same person."

"And he could be avenging the perceived wrongs against his wonderful brother Ned," Diamond said.

"Maybe," I agreed. "Simone said that she told the rest of the group how Ned beat on her. The group's mission is to not judge people. But it would be hard to keep an emotional distance if one of the group's members was currently being abused. They would make comments. They'd tell her to leave such a bad person. If Ned's younger stepbrother is Cameron, maybe he couldn't stand to hear everyone talk like his big bro was horseshit."

"I'll call Gramercy at Inyo and see if I can learn anything else." Diamond said. "Meantime, I gotta go." I nodded at him, and he left.

"I should go talk to Joe," I said to Street. "Want to come?"

She looked at me, a deep frown on her face. "I want to think about this. I can join you later."

When Spot and I got to Joe's house, I told him what happened to Ned.

"He died?!"

"Yeah. An hour or so ago, he attacked me at my office. He tried to drive his truck over me. But he hit that scaffolding, and it collapsed on top of his truck. Ned was crushed."

It took Joe a moment to respond.

"Well, that's a damn improvement to this community, having him gone," he said. He looked out the window toward Mt. Tallac. "Maybe there still is a little justice in this world." He looked introspective. "Do you still think he was Rell's assailant?"

"I'd like to think so. And there's more evidence suggesting that. Yesterday, I found a list of names in his truck. You and Rell, Manuel and Jillian. Ned had drawn lines through Rell's, Manuel's and Jillian's names."

"So that does it," Joe said. "He was the killer."

"I'm still not sure about that. After Ned died, Simone called with concerns about the weather changing and about problems she was having charging her phone. I told her about Ned and the list of names. It turns out that Manuel and Jillian were part of the hiking group that Rell went with. In fact, it looks like Rell started the group. Everyone but Rell used a fake name for anonymity."

"Why?"

"Because most of them were victims of abuse at some time in their lives. The pseudonyms gave them privacy." I didn't want to tell Joe what Simone said about Rell having suffered abuse as a child. It was possible that Joe didn't know, and I saw no advantage in visiting that horror on him.

"So Rell's hiking group was really a kind of therapy group?" Joe said. "She was practicing psychology after all."

"Probably, she was just being a supportive friend to people who could benefit from having others to talk to about their problems. Rell knew that people felt so comfortable with her that they told her things they'd never tell anyone else. It appears that she invited some of those people to go hiking in a way that would allow them to talk anonymously. They called their group No Judgment."

"And now they're all dead," Joe said, his face looking hard.

"All but Rell and Simone and a man who goes by the name Cameron. Apparently, he told the No Judgment group that he and his stepbrother were so abused by their mother that he pushed her in front of a truck."

Joe made a little jerk.

I continued, "Also, Ned Cavett was originally from Inyo County. Sergeant Bains talked to a sergeant with the Inyo County Sheriff's Office. He said that Ned had a half-brother or stepbrother."

Joe raised his eyebrows.

"For awhile," I said, "I've thought that these murders were about limiting your exposure to any anti-development perspective on the Steven's Peak Resort. But now it seems that the murders could all be about Ned's half-brother taking out the people who heard Simone talk about Ned's abuse of her."

"So the guy named Cameron might be Ned's brother."

"Right."

"And we don't know who Cameron really is," Joe said.

"Correct. But Simone thought that he's in his twenties and said he's athletic and has long wavy hair."

"Could be anyone," Joe said.

"Yeah," I said.

Joe said, "I think we should call her and tell her to get her ass out of that wilderness. Take the closest escape route on the map. But you said her phone is out of power."

"Right. Maybe she'll try hanging the solar charger sheet around her neck, but for now we can't talk to her. But even if we could, I'm reluctant to call her out of the expedition when our best evidence still makes it look like Ned was the bad guy."

Joe looked skeptical.

"Street says that Simone is in the process of the biggest accomplishment of her life," I said. "Simone is proving to herself that she is strong, that she has self-worth, that she can be independent. We don't want to take this away from her unless we're confident that she is at risk."

"I see your point," Joe said.

"But, let's consider it hypothetically. She called from Rubicon Peak. What would be involved in skiing up there to try to find her and see if she's being followed?"

"It would be very difficult. First, with every hour that goes by, her location becomes harder to predict. Without her calling in to report her location, she's a speck in a huge wilderness."

"But she could have been followed," I said.

"Of course. Following's easy. Finding her is another matter. But an even bigger problem is elevation. Rubicon Peak is almost four thousand feet above the lake. Even if she drops down to the low parts of her scheduled trek, she's still fifteen hundred to two thousand feet up. That's too much to climb in deep snow for most people. And that probably includes you. It's not that difficult for her to come out, because it's down. But I understand Street's caution about asking her to choose an escape route, never mind whether or not she can get her phone charged. There's a lot at stake for Simone. You could save her physically only to find out that she's lost what little confidence and self-respect she has left. From the things that Rell told me over the years, those things are as important as living."

While Joe's words made sense, they also made me feel more lost than ever.

"We need to find out who Cameron really is," Joe said.

I suddenly remembered that Bob Hinton's employee had longish, wavy hair.

"There is a person connected to this case who is around that age and is athletic and has long hair. It might be wavy. When I saw him, it was lacquered up at the back of his head. His name is Benjamin Prattel, and he works for Bob Hinton of RKS Properties."

"The man behind the Steven's Peak Resort," Joe said.

"Yeah. If Ben is the hiker who goes by Cameron, and if he's around, that would remove our worry about Simone. Bob gave me his number. I'll call him."

I walked over to Joe's phone as I pulled out Bob's card with his personal number. I dialed, and it rang, and I got a synthetic voicemail response. I hung up without leaving a message.

"I think I'll pay them a visit."

"Can I come?" Joe asked.

"Sure."

Joe and I headed north to Cave Rock and went through the tunnel, which was very icy from dripping water running down and freezing on the roadway. Just past the tunnel, we turned on the road that switch-backed down to Bob Hinton's house. But as we pulled up to the parking pad, we saw the Beats Working backing away from the dock and boathouse.

We watched as the Predator yacht turned a bit. Then it slowed and began to move forward, turning more. Joe and I watched to see what direction it would go.

The big boat eased forward at no-wake speed until it was a hundred yards from shore. Then it roared. It's pointy bow pitched up, and its stern pressed down into the water as it accelerated forward. The yacht plowed ahead making a large wake. Gradually, the bow dropped as the boat lifted up on plane. The Beats Working made a high-speed turn to starboard and raced north up the lake.

I shifted into reverse, backed out of the drive, shifted forward and drove fast up to the highway. I turned left and sped north up Highway 50.

"You think we can follow it from land?" Joe asked.

"Depends on how she goes," I said. "We'll lose track of her when we turn up the mountain toward Spooner Summit. After we turn north on Twenty-eight, she'll probably go out of sight going around Deadman Point. But if Bob is going all the way to Incline Village, then maybe we can pick the boat up again as we come back close to the water near Secret Harbor."

"How fast do you think that crate goes?"

"I read about the Predator online," I said. "I think it said her top speed was thirty-three knots."

Joe patted the dash of my Jeep. "Whereas this baby probably goes fifty or sixty."

"Funny guy," I said, glad that Joe could still make jokes in spite of the stress he was under. "Problem is, our road winds around as it crawls north. The Beats Working can go straight. So our speed advantage might not make up for the extra distance."

"What if that boat is heading across the lake?"

"Then we're screwed." I pointed toward Joe's feet. "There's binoculars under your seat. Maybe you can see with them."

Joe reached under his seat while I drove. I pushed our speed on the straight sections as we approached Glenbrook, then slowed for the big curve as the road turned up the mountain toward Spooner Summit.

Two-thirds of the way up the mountain, we came to the turnoff where Highway 28 heads northwest, gradually coming back closer to the lake. In quick glances to my left, I could see no sign of the Beats Working.

On my right, Joe had the binoculars up. They seemed to point directly at my face, but I understood that he was looking past me, scanning the lake.

"Any luck?" I said.

"No." But he kept looking.

We went past the snow-covered road that led down to Skunk Harbor, where Leah hid out on Jennifer's sailboat when I investigated the art forgery. Farther north, we cruised above Secret Harbor and the nude beaches. Joe still looked through the binoculars, a difficult thing to do for many minutes at a time and while bouncing along in a moving vehicle.

Our road left the lake as we went by the estate where George Whittell had built his Thunderbird Lodge castle in the 1930s. Then we rounded a curve and came back near the water. The road was high enough up that we could see all the way across the lake. In fast glances at the water, I saw a few specks here and there, boats too far out to perceive easily except by the way the sun reflected off their wakes.

Joe kept scanning with the glasses.

"I think I see her," he said as we approached Sand Harbor. "A large yacht about halfway across the lake. Maybe more. Straight west of us."

"Half way across the lake is five miles from here. Can you tell by the wake which way she's going?"

After a moment, Joe spoke. "She's headed away from us."

"She's going toward Tahoe City, then. It could be a waste of time for us, but I'm inclined to drive around the lake and see if we can see her on the other side. Okay by you?"

"Yeah."

So we drove north to Incline, then followed 28 west around the North Shore and over the state line at Crystal Bay into California.

Joe kept looking through the binoculars. "I don't see her anymore," he said.

We went through Kings Beach, Tahoe Vista, dropped south around Carnelian Bay, went past Dollar Point, and came into Tahoe City.

"Got her," Joe said.

"Where?"

"At a dock. Oh, now she's behind those buildings." He pointed.

"Were there other docks? Did it look like the marina?"

"I think so, yeah."

"Could be she's at the Tahoe Yacht Club." I got in the center turn lane and turned left down toward The Boatworks Mall, the renovated old warehouse-style building. As I parked, I saw the Beats Working at one of the docks.

"Could be Bob wanted to come shopping by boat in Tahoe City," Joe said.

"Or grab a bite at one of the restaurants," I said. "Jake's is the closest. Let's check there first."

We left Spot in the Jeep, went into the Boatworks, and walked into Jake's. They had a good crowd for late afternoon. Skiers who'd quit early as the sun lowered and the temperature dropped.

I stopped at the entrance and scanned the crowd. Bob Hinton and a woman were sitting at a table by the window. It doesn't get any easier.

"Good afternoon," a young woman said to us. "Table for two?"

"Actually, we're here to meet Bob Hinton," I said, pointing at Bob.

"Oh, I'm sorry, I didn't know. I'll grab two extra chairs."

She hurried over to a table near Bob's and began pulling a chair over. We followed.

"Hey, Bob," I said. "Sorry we're a bit late." I took the chair the young woman had brought, and I held it out for Joe. Joe sat.

Bob said, "I don't understand..."

"Sorry. I told you we'd be here first, but we got hung up in the ski traffic." I reached my hand out toward Bob's female companion who was very attractive and half Bob's age. "Hi. I'm Bob's friend Owen McKenna, and this is my friend Joe Rorvik. Bob, I'm sure you know Joe, right?"

"We haven't met," Joe said. "But we know of each other." Joe reached out to shake Bob's hand. Bob didn't stand up. He shook Joe's hand without enthusiasm.

The young hostess brought a second chair. I sat down. I said to Bob's companion, "Joe sits on the Steven's Peak Resort Commission. In fact, he holds the deciding vote on whether Bob's resort gets approved or not. So right now Joe is just about the most important person in Bob's world, right Bob?"

"I don't think this..."

"Of course," I interrupted, "Bob didn't like the idea from the beginning, his fate being in the hands of a single, old ski racer. So Bob decided to try to influence things. Am I right again, Bob?"

"Amanda," he said. "Ignore this man. He's a cheap gumshoe,

sticking his nose in where it doesn't belong."

"Gumshoe," I said. "I love that word even though Bob probably means it as an insult. What I don't get though, Bob, is when you started having your employee Benjamin Prattel pay Ned Cavett to spy on Joe Rorvik, didn't you ever stop to wonder what that made you?" I turned to Joe. "Joe, as a member of the commission, you volunteer for no pay, correct?"

"Well, actually, I'm working for the Forest Service. They pay us. But in charity to the government, I've waived any fee."

"So you are serving as a paid public official overseeing the process of approval on a private business development costing hundreds of millions of dollars. That makes Bob guilty of conspiring to buy influence on a government commission, a serious crime, a conviction for which comes with a long prison sentence."

"Bob," Amanda suddenly said, "What is this about? Is it true that you had Ben pay someone to spy on this man?"

"It wasn't spying or influence buying. It was a simple lobbying effort."

"Ah," I said. "A lobbying effort that included giving Ned Cavett a list of people who were close to Joe. There was Manuel Romero, who just died after his car was run off the cliff at Emerald Bay. There was Jillian Oleska, who just died after someone pushed her into a tree while skiing. Joe has a neighbor who has told Joe that he is against the resort. That neighbor was forced off the highway. And, oh yeah, Joe's wife was thrown off her deck and is near death in a hospital in Reno as we speak."

"Bob!" Amanda nearly shouted. "Is this true?!"

"Of course, not, Amanda. This man is making this stuff up."

"And," I continued, "circumstantial evidence suggests that our murder suspect is in his late twenties and has long, wavy hair. That matches your Benjamin Prattel."

"This is outrageous!" Bob said. He pushed his chair back and stood up. "I'll sue you for slander. I'll take everything you've got!"

I held out my phone and began pressing buttons. "Let me call Commander Mallory of the South Lake Tahoe PD. He will tell you that he has in his possession the list of, quote, influential people, unquote, that Benjamin gave Ned Cavett, the list where

Ned crossed off each name as each person was helped to an early death." Actually, I didn't know if Benjamin had given Ned the list, but it seemed like a reasonable possibility.

"We have witnesses whose testimony might just convict you of murder. In fact, even Benjamin might chime in. It was probably Ned who cut him with a throwing knife. Benjamin might be looking for some justice."

"I'm not saying another word. I'm calling my lawyer." Bob pulled out his phone.

"While you call your lawyer, I'll talk to Mallory. After that, I'll call Agent Ramos of the FBI."

Amanda pushed back her chair, bumping Joe. She stood up. "Bob, I can't believe it! I thought you were a decent man!"

Bob held out his hand. "Easy, Amanda. Take it easy."

"No! I have principles. I don't date just anyone." She grabbed her purse and walked toward the door of the restaurant.

Bob called out, "Amanda, at least let me bring you home!"

She ignored him and left.

Bob moved to go after her. Then he stopped and turned back.

Bob's eyes were a strange mixture of anger and fear. He held the look for several seconds, then waved his hand at my phone. "Stop. Put it away," he said as he sat down again.

"Are you ready to talk?"

"I didn't kill those people. Benjamin didn't either. I can prove it. At least, I can prove he didn't kill Jillian Oleska."

My phone rang. I held up my hand. "Hold that thought."

I answered the phone. It was Diamond.

"This a good time?" he asked.

"Sure. I realized that Simone's description of Cameron fit RKS Bob's employee Benjamin Prattel. So Joe and I are at Jake's in Tahoe City, listening to Bob Hinton threaten me with a slander lawsuit. What's up?"

"Talked to Sergeant Gramercy of Inyo County," he said. "He remembers Ned and his brother Peter clearly. Ned Cavett was older, handsome, stupid, and emotionally disturbed. Peter Cavett looked nothing like his brother, but he was smart and more balanced. Gramercy remembers that Peter worshiped his older brother. They both were athletic. But they looked nothing alike because they were step brothers. Ned from old man Cavett's previous marriage, and Peter from mama Cavett's previous marriage. Gramercy says mama changed Peter's last name to Cavett when she changed her name. After the mom died in what Gramercy said was an accident, Ned went off to his life of crime, and Peter disappeared. Thought you'd want to know."

While I was talking, Bob stood up as if to go.

I snapped my fingers and pointed my finger at his chair. Maybe I flared my nostrils, too. He sat back down like a school boy.

I said to Diamond, "Hold on a second."

I turned to Bob. "What is your proof that Benjamin didn't kill Jillian Oleska?"

"I took him to a ski resort conference at Aspen. We were gone six days. We got back two days before you broke into my boathouse. Two days before that, on day four of our trip, I got a phone call from one of my people about Jillian dying. Ben and I were around people the entire time we were gone. If I have to, I can produce a large number of witnesses who saw us during the panels, in the showroom, at breakfast, at dinner. Here, let me show you some pictures." He pulled out his phone, brought up photos, and scrolled through them. "Here is Ben when we had dinner at the Hotel Jerome with Denise and Denny Uline from Snowmass. We spent quite a bit of time with them skiing and dining. They will verify the dates for you." Bob turned to another photo. "This is Joan Escalante from Miami. She stayed near us at Little Nell. We saw her many times coming and going, and we had dinner with her one night. She'd be happy to talk to you. I can continue like this with several photos of other people."

I raised my hand for him to stop, then I turned back to my phone.

"Diamond, it's possible that Benjamin is not our suspect in Jillian's murder. Not sure about the others."

"Which means," Diamond said in my ear, "that the man named Cameron could be pursuing Simone up in the high country as we speak."

"Right. Let me ask Bob. Bob, where is Benjamin Prattel now?"

He hesitated. "He told me that he was going skiing."

"Where?" I asked.

"He said he wanted to make some back-country tracks. He didn't say where."

"When did he leave?"

"I don't know for sure. But he told me the day before yesterday, when he was done with work. So I imagine he was going out yesterday."

"Is he still gone today?"

Bob shrugged. "I don't know. He has the same two days off every week. He could still be out there."

"In the back-country," I said.

"Right."

I turned back to the phone. "Diamond, Joe and I will head back to the South Shore and reconsider plan B on the way."

"Problem is," Diamond said in my ear, "there's an accident in the southbound tunnel at Cave Rock. Looks like it'll be closed for a couple of hours."

"And the last storm closed Emerald Bay," I said.

"Sí. It will be awhile before you can get to the South Shore."

"Hold on." I turned to Joe. "Humor me. If I wanted to find Simone ASAP, and if I could get back-country ski gear on short notice in Tahoe City, what do you think my chances would be of getting to her from the West Shore north of Emerald Bay?"

Joe was shaking his head before I finished the question. "Small to none. If you try to climb up from Ward Creek or Blackwood Canyon or Meeks Creek, you start from lake level. That's too much elevation gain in too much snow. I don't mean to sound harsh, but you'd have to be a serious back-country athlete to make it. Even if you could get up into that country, she'd be much farther south by that time. You'd have more luck going in Glen Alpine Trail, which is south of Emerald Bay. Not that it's easy, either, because the access from Fallen Leaf Lake isn't plowed."

"Nevertheless, I'd have to start south of Emerald Bay if I wanted any chance of intercepting her."

"Right."

"Keep holding," I said again to Diamond.

I turned to Bob as I pointed out the window toward the Beats

Working. "How long would it take to get from here to the South Shore on that crate?"

He thought about it. "It's about twenty miles. Forty minutes at full speed. But I can't..."

"Diamond," I said, into my phone, interrupting Bob.

"Can you pick us up at the Timber Cove Pier? And can you chauffeur us around?"

"Sure. When will you be there?"

"Forty minutes. Maybe a touch more."

"About the same as it will take me to get there." He hung up.

I stood up. "Let's go," I said to Bob.

"What do you mean? Do you know how much it costs per mile to operate the Beats Working? I can't just flit off to the South Shore."

"No I don't, and yes you can. Get going."

Bob hesitated.

I picked up my phone. "I have Commander Mallory on my speed dial. I can still make your life beyond miserable. The DA has had good results on my past recommendations. You could be facing multiple charges."

"Okay, okay." Bob stood up, tossed a hundred dollar bill on the table, and walked toward the door.

I went out to the Jeep and let Spot out. Bob was startled when Spot came near. When Spot sniffed him, he froze.

Spot soon lost interest, and we went down to the water.

Bob tipped the dock boy, walked up the Predator's port staircase. Joe and Spot and I followed.

Pretty Girl was curled up on a thick dog bed, which was up on the settee in the upper lounge. Spot trotted over to her and wagged. She lifted her head but didn't get up. Maybe she was intimidated by Spot's size. More likely, she only got excited about animals the size she'd naturally eat. She and Spot sniffed noses a bit, then Pretty Girl lowered her head onto her paws. It was interesting to see such calm and remove from a dog that could explode from a standing start to 40 miles-per-hour in about a second.

Spot wagged some more, then turned his attention elsewhere.

Bob looked around a bit, probably checking to see if Amanda was onboard. He sat down on the captain's chair and fired up the big engines. They made a deep, muffled rumble from belowdecks.

Spot explored the boat, no doubt sniffing out the aroma of money.

Joe looked around when we stepped onto the Beats Working, but he played it cool. It took more than a fancy boat to impress him.

Bob waved at the dock boy, and the kid untied the lines.

Bob backed away from the dock.

Once we were out some distance, he shifted into forward and turned the Beats Working around. When he was fifty yards out, Bob said, "Hang on." I held Spot's collar as I sat on the settee where Joe was already sitting.

Bob pushed the throttle forward all the way.

The engines revved up to a low roar, and the boat accelerated fast. The bow raised up, then dropped down as we planed out. When the boat settled in at its fastest cruise, the speedometer showed 32 knots. It was fast, but the size of the boat and our distance above the water's surface made it seem much slower.

Bob called out over the engine noise. "Where to on the South Shore?"

"The Timber Cove Pier."

He nodded.

Spot again walked over to where Pretty Girl snoozed. She ignored him.

The ring of mountains around the lake gradually shifted some as we rocketed south, but we were still in the middle of the lake.

Spot went out the back side of the lounge, stepped over to the side of the boat, and stuck his nose into the wind. Outside of steak, there's almost nothing a dog likes better.

Forty minutes later, we approached the pier. Bob slowed the engines. We dropped out of plane, the stern riding low for a bit. At such an angle, the yacht made a huge wake. We slowed further, and the boat leveled out as we coasted up to the dock.

Bob shifted into reverse to bring us to a stop. As Joe and I walked down the aft stairway to the tender deck, Bob called out.

"I didn't have anything to do with the deaths of those people."

"We'll soon find out," I said.

Bob brought the yacht within six inches of the pier. Joe and I stepped off. Spot followed. We walked down the snowy pier, Joe moving fast considering how slippery it was.

The engine pitch of the Beats Working rose a bit as it pulled away behind us. In a minute, the engines roared.

Diamond was in his Douglas County patrol unit. On the California side of the state line.

Joe sat in front. Spot and I got in back.

"Where to?"

"Joe's house," I said.

Diamond pulled out and turned onto Lake Tahoe Blvd.

"Are you okay with driving a Douglas County Patrol Unit in the wrong county in the wrong state?" I asked. "Against the rules?"

"Pursuit of bad guys knows no jurisdiction in my personal code," Diamond said. "I'll tell the sheriff it was quid pro quo, and we got the cheap end of the deal. Some of your crime-fighting is in our county, and Joe's paying for it."

Joe made a little nod.

FORTY-EIGHT

As Diamond drove, I called Street and filled her in. "Simone said that the man in the No Judgment group named Cameron had long wavy hair. So I thought he might be an employee at RKS Properties, a guy named Benjamin who works for Bob Hinton. Right age, right hair, and proximity to the case. But that hasn't panned out, yet. So I'm back to the beginning. Ned still seems like the most likely murder suspect. Especially now that I found the list of names in his truck."

"But you might never know now that he's dead," she said.

"Right."

"What are you going to do next?"

"Hard to know. I may decide to go into the Desolation Wilderness and see if I can find her."

"How can I help?" Street said.

"You could make a run to my cabin and gather up my back-country skis, boots, clothes, gloves, hat, and such. Maybe grab the small red pack and put some food and water in it. Diamond says the southbound tunnel at Cave Rock is closed due to an accident. But when they get it clear, you could bring my gear to Joe's. Diamond's bringing us there now. Joe's going to pull out his spare maps and help me figure out where Simone might be right now."

"I'll be there as soon as I can," Street said.

I hung up, then dialed 911.

"Nine-one-one dispatch," a woman said.

"Gina," I said, recognizing her voice. "This is Owen McKenna. I'm working with Sergeant Bains in El Dorado County and Sergeant Martinez of Douglas County on a case involving a woman named Cynthia Rorvik and her husband Joe. I will explain the details so you have them on the nine-one-one recording. I recently spoke to Simone Bonnaire, a friend of Mrs. Rorvik's. She is currently someplace southwest of Rubicon Peak participating in the Tahoe

Randonnée Extreme challenge. There is a possibility that she is in danger and being pursued by someone that we should consider armed and dangerous."

Gina inhaled. "You said she's at Rubicon Peak?" she asked.

"She was a few hours ago. She's heading south. At the time we spoke, she was not aware of a pursuer, but I have reason to believe he is an athletic man who has gone by the name Cameron. My last communication with Simone was cut off when her phone battery died. I don't know if she realizes the level of danger, but the man who I think is looking for her has revealed to her abuse victim's support group that he murdered his mother. The other members of the group have died in suspicious accidents. I think Simone may be next. How quickly can you contact Search and Rescue?" I asked.

"We sent the Washoe County SAR up to investigate an avalanche in the Galena Creek Drainage off Mt. Rose. The report was that a slide carried a large group of skiers a long distance. The caller reported that some were not visible under the snow. But others were partially visible. He thought maybe a dozen in all."

"Sorry to hear that. But this is El Dorado County."

"I know," she said. "But you know how all the service agencies help each other out."

"El Dorado SAR went to help," I said.

"Yes. Placer County, too. One team skied in from the side. Another is closer but down below and working up the canyon. The third is trying to access from above."

"So we have no available team near the Sierra Crest."

"Correct. I'll see what I can do about bringing in a team from one of the other counties. Douglas County is closest. But Desolation is hard to get to."

"What about a chopper?"

"Most can't land in deep snow. Even if we can find a bird that can go in, they'd still have to wait until morning light."

"Who called in the Galena Creek report?"

"Of course, that's normally privileged information. But I can tell you that we don't know who the caller was. The caller ID system didn't report the number. Maybe it was one of those untraceable cell phones. Prepaid, or whatever."

"The caller didn't say his name?"

"No. He just said he was out doing some back-country telemarking and saw the slide from a distance."

"He say anything else?"

"Only what I already said about the number of skiers and such. He sounded knowledgeable, if that helps. He spoke of the slide as if he'd had experience, so the information about the location was probably accurate."

"Anything about the call stand out?"

"There was nothing notable about the call. Oh, except he had a real raspy voice."

"A raspy voice," I repeated. I thanked Gina and hung up.

Diamond turned off Lake Tahoe Blvd, and headed up to Angora Highlands.

I thought about Joe's neighbor Michael Paul, the guy with the voice so raspy that it was distracting. Michael could have called in a false avalanche report just to tie up local SAR teams and make them unavailable to search for Simone.

I wondered if Michael had a white ski outfit. I remembered his big black Range Rover, the vehicle that he used for getting into the back-country. When Dwight told me about the person who ran him off the road, he wasn't sure about the vehicle that had swerved toward him, but he thought it was black. I didn't think of Michael's hair as being long, but it was certainly wavy. If Simone knew any guys with buzz cuts, that might give her the perception that Michael's hair was long. The biggest mismatch between Michael and Simone's description of Cameron was that Simone hadn't seen any tattoos on Cameron. But she couldn't remember seeing him in short sleeves or shorts, so it was possible that Cameron was a pseudonym for Michael Paul.

FORTY-NINE

I told Diamond what the dispatcher had said.

"Let's stop at Michael Paul's house," Diamond said. "Which one is it?"

Joe directed him.

"I'll stay here with Joe," Diamond said as I got out of the patrol unit.

"The house appears empty," I said. "The lights are off, garage door closed. I'll probably just be a minute."

I got out and rang Michael's bell, but there was no response. I tried the door. It was locked.

To the side of the garage, there was a narrow trail in the snow. The path ended at a door near the place where an interior wall would separate the house and garage. I tried that door. It was also locked.

The back yard was covered with four feet of untrampled snow. But right next to the house, less snow had accumulated. Hugging the wall of the house, I stepped into the snow and moved along the back of the house to the far corner.

There was a low deck about two feet above the ground. The deck hadn't been shoveled and had three feet of snow on it. I climbed up the short stairs and tromped through the snow to the glass slider. It too was locked.

At the corner of the deck, I could look around the other side of the house. There were no doors. So I retreated and rejoined Diamond and Joe and Spot, and we drove to Joe's house.

Once inside, I asked Joe, "Do you or Rell know anybody who has a white ski suit?"

"I don't ski anymore," Joe said, his words matter-of-fact. If he had regrets about not skiing, he kept them to himself.

"I was thinking about how people in Tahoe often go about their daily errands in their ski gear. They come down off the mountain and head directly to the supermarket, still wearing everything except their ski boots. I thought maybe when you bump into people you know, maybe some of them are wearing their ski clothes."

"But you're only interested in white," Joe said.

"Right. I saw a skier in white following Jillian. I didn't see any indication that she was in danger, but something about it felt wrong."

Joe shook his head and then stopped. He frowned, then angled his head just a bit like a dog trying to get a different take on a sound.

"Come to think of it," he said, "Michael has a white suit. No, not a suit. A white jacket and white ski pants. Not the snug kind. The loose kind with shoulder straps. Ski bibs. In fact, I saw him in it just a couple of days ago. I drove home, and as I pulled into my driveway, Dwight was out for a walk. He stopped and talked to me for a bit. As we were talking, Michael drove by in his big fancy Range Rover. He said he was going up into the back-country to make some turns. He had his bibs on. And his jacket was on the seat next to him. White and white."

"You have a good memory," I said.

"No, I only remember because of Dwight."

"Why is that?"

"Because," Joe said, "every time Dwight looked at Michael he had this worried look on his face. I couldn't help noticing. So at one point when Michael was going on and on about the great snow conditions in that raspy voice of his, I looked at him to try and figure out why Dwight would be worried. The only thing I could come up with was a little mnemonic joke. Dwight is worried about white. White worries Dwight. Like when you get a song lyric stuck in your mind. I knew it was silly, but that's what came into my mind. So I remembered it."

"You never figured out what actually bothered Dwight?"

"No. I even asked him after Michael drove away, but Dwight just got embarrassed and said that he is intimidated by Michael and his cockiness. I told him not to be, that Michael is a bit of a blowhard. Dwight didn't even know what a blowhard is. Different generations, I guess."

Diamond said, "Joe, if Simone is being chased and she realizes it, can you predict her next move?"

"What do you mean?"

"Simone will have been thinking about what Owen said about Cameron possibly being dangerous. She will have been considering the possibilities. She may decide that she's in serious danger. She may also scan the landscape and see someone coming toward her. Either way, she would scan the territory and choose how she runs based on the topography of the landscape, right?"

Joe frowned.

"You could get a sense of her decisions based on your maps."

"I don't know," Joe said. "Tell me how you're thinking."

"Think of it this way," I said, picking up on Diamond's thoughts. "Imagine that Simone has decided to run, to escape. So she thinks about the landscape and she looks at the mountainsides and she visualizes the escape routes that you put on her maps. She'd see things that would make her think that some routes were better than others, right? You'd be much better than me at figuring out where she'd come down. Glen Alpine? Cascade Lake? Velma Lakes to Eagle Lake to Emerald Bay?"

Joe frowned harder. "You make it sound like it's up to me to save Simone's life," he said. His voice had a plaintive quality to it, a tremolo of fear.

"I don't mean to put pressure on you. Just think about it. That will give you ideas. If you come to some conclusions, we'll discuss them and decide whether I should go in and try to find her. If so, we'll figure out how best to do that."

"I don't like it," Joe said.

"Me neither. But it's all we can do."

"Have you decided that Michael is our man?"

"No."

"So you haven't decided to go after Simone."

"It's a moot point unless I know how and where to look for her."

Joe nodded and got up. He was standing more bent than usual. He walked over to the origami table.

"I gave Simone my best maps," he said. "But I might have others. He looked in some bins and pulled out some rolled maps.

He unrolled them on the table, rolled them back up, unrolled some others.

"Here we are," he said, smoothing out old paper and running his big arthritic hands over the maps.

Spot reached his head over the table, investigating what Joe was doing. His jowls dragged across the maps.

"These are older than the ones I gave Simone," Joe said, "and they're at a more macro scale. But they should still be useful."

FIFTY

Joe looked as serious as I'd ever seen him.

"Let me think," he said. He moved his fingers here and there, touching different places. His hands shook when he pointed at mountains.

"You said she was at Rubicon Peak. I remember most of her route from there."

"Great," I said. "Now comes a difficult question, and I'm sorry to ask it."

"What?"

"If a person is following her and he is determined to kill her, what about the landscape would suggest how he might do it to make it look like a accident?"

Joe looked very sad. "I suppose he could just push her off any mountain."

"Well, maybe yes. But I'm thinking that he would want to choose a place where her fall would be certain to end in death."

Diamond said, "Another consideration is that he'd pick a place where other people would be unlikely to see it. A secluded place, less open."

"Okay, let me consider that," Joe said.

He bent over the map, his face a mass of frown wrinkles. I looked over his shoulder, but I was aware that for me, topo maps were something to be deciphered, a foreign language where I knew only half of the words. For Joe, it was like reading the morning paper. He picked up a pencil, wrote numbers on the mountains, drew some arrows.

I left him alone. Because my cell didn't get reception at Joe's house, I used his phone to call Street. She said she had collected my ski gear and checked and found out that the Cave Rock tunnel was open. She would be on her way in a few minutes.

I waited.

In time, Joe straightened up.

"I think this was the order of the peaks. And I think this was her desired route based on what I previously drew for her. Now I have to imagine how she would react if and when she thinks she is being chased."

"Yeah, that would help," I said.

He leaned back over the maps.

FIFTY-ONE

"Okay, I've got some recommendations," Joe said. "I'm worried. I think we should hurry."

"Agreed."

Joe turned from the table to look at Diamond and me. "Tell me, please. You told Simone that Manuel and Jillian had died, and Simone now believes that they were part of her group. But does she know how they died?"

"She understands that their deaths looked like accidents but were likely murders," I said. "She believes that Ned was the likely killer."

"But if she comes to think that the killer is someone else," Joe said, "she'll be wondering how he is going to try to kill her and make it look like an accident, right?"

Diamond said, "She'll be thinking about which routes make a killer's job easier or harder. The obvious choice for the killer is to repeat the process he used with Jillian, a hip-check at the wrong moment to send Simone into a tree or off a cliff."

Joe said, "So if Simone stays away from cliffs and trees and doesn't give him an opportunity, he will look for whatever is the steepest slope she skis near, especially one that faces northeast where the avalanche danger is greatest."

Joe pointed to one of the maps.

"These three red lines are her probable routes from Rubicon Peak. Number one is where she originally planned to go, which, as I recall, is Phipps Peak followed by Dicks and Jacks Peaks. The logical way would be to stay on the Tahoe Rim Trail. It generally follows these ridge lines." Joe traced with his big finger. "Any track off the ridge would be too steep to safely ski. Once she got down to this saddle, the only reasonable direction would be this route up here. Does that seem logical to you?"

Joe looked at Diamond.

"I don't know," Diamond said. "I know nothing about back-country skiing."

Joe nodded. "The second line is her closest escape route. If she's trying to take the fastest way out of the high country, she'd likely veer off the Tahoe Rim Trail at Middle Velma Lake and head down to Lower Velma, then Eagle Lake, and then down to Emerald Bay. But I think she would only do that if she's leaving the high country due to bad weather. If she believes she's in danger from someone chasing her, I think she would behave differently."

"How?" I asked.

Joe pointed at the map. "It's what Diamond said about what makes a killer's job easier. This escape route is a narrow trail through heavy forest. It goes around crags and steep drop offs. A person determined to harm Simone would find a hundred places to push her off a cliff without being observed. Simone will be thinking about how Rell's assault and Manuel's and Jillian's deaths were designed to look like accidents. I think she'll decide to stay in open areas. That way there will be fewer cliffs and a much greater chance that anyone else would see her pursuer. Hopefully, that knowledge will intimidate him."

"There aren't a lot of people in Desolation Wilderness in the winter," I said. "Maybe none."

"True. But Simone will hope that there are some people around, and she will make decisions based on that hope. If Simone is being chased, I'm guessing that when she gets to Middle Velma Lake, she'll turn west and follow its drainage down to Rockbound Valley. That area is much more open. Because there is less cover, anyone pursuing her would be easy to see from a long distance. That will reduce her risk. It also plays to her strength."

"Her endurance," I said.

"And determination," Diamond said.

"Right. Cross-country ski champions are like marathon runners. They're rarely the big, strong guys. They're always the thin, super-fit athletes. While I doubt that Simone is very fast, she might be able to simply outrun someone much bigger and stronger, even if that person is an accomplished skier. But it depends on how deep the snow is. If she's in the lee of a mountain, it will have accumulated deep. She'll have a great deal of work breaking trail.

That will give any pursuer a huge advantage because he can ski in the tracks she made, and he won't have to expend a fraction of the effort. If instead, Simone finds some windblown areas with harder snow, then she can ski much faster and will be on more equal footing with anyone following her. I talked about this with her."

"So she will search out those windblown areas," I said. "But the slopes will still be a problem," I said. "She said she's just an intermediate at downhill."

Joe nodded. "Which is why I think she'll head down here to Camper Flat." He pointed. "She probably won't have time to consult her map for more than a moment, but you can see Camper Flat from up above. Its openness will beckon. From there, she would probably turn south and make the gentle climb along the Rubicon River up to Mosquito Pass. That's a much more dangerous area with cliffs and dense forest, but the long non-technical endurance trek to that point may have given her a substantial lead by then. She could get over the pass to Lake Aloha where its open area would again give her more safety."

I looked over the map, visualizing the areas that Joe had described.

"What if she isn't being chased, yet?"

"Then she would stay on the original route to Dicks and Jacks peaks, which still brings her to Lake Aloha."

"An easy spot for someone to see her and give chase," I said.

"Right. The killer could intersect her at any point," Joe said. "Lake Aloha is a huge open basin above eight thousand feet, with very few trees. The frozen lake area itself would be a great place for her to out-distance anyone chasing her if she can find some windblown, crusted snow."

"I can see your point," I said. "But this route you've outlined is so much longer. Do you really think she'll pass up one of these fast escape routes in favor of a much longer route?"

"Yes. She'll realize that the shorter escape routes are filled with secluded areas that would invite attack. She's quite confident in her endurance ability. She may well believe that she could out-distance her pursuer."

"You say that like you don't think it's true."

"I don't think it matters if it's true," Joe said. "If Simone believes it, that might be enough to get her to choose the more open route."

"If she successfully gets through the Lake Aloha Basin, then what?"

"Then she'd be forced to take the risk of going down to Echo Lakes." Joe traced on the map. "The drop out of Lake Aloha is narrow and heavily forested. It would invite attack. Let's hope we find her before then."

"If we decide to try and intercept her, how do you recommend I go about it?"

"We should go in by snowmobile."

"We?"

"Yes. You and me. Your dog, too, if you want. I'll be driving, so maybe you can hold your dog behind me."

"On a snowmobile. Into Desolation where snowmobiles aren't allowed," I said.

"Right. The girl's life is at stake. We have to choose the fastest way in," Joe said. He sounded irritated.

"I'm not arguing with you," I said. "Just checking."

"We should go in at Echo Lakes and travel from there up to Lake Aloha. Then we go on to Rockbound Valley if we haven't already found her. If you prefer, Diamond could substitute for me, or your dog, for that matter."

Diamond shook his head. "I would be a handicap. I don't know mountain back-country. I wouldn't know what's safe or not regarding avalanche terrain. Other than how to shovel it, I don't really know snow that well."

"Okay, that's settled." I turned to Joe. "Echo Lakes is a long way from where she is now."

"Yes, but that's the way I think she's headed. More important, at seventy-four hundred feet, it's the highest elevation access to Desolation. We would only have to climb seven hundred vertical to get to Lake Aloha. The other Desolation trail heads are a thousand feet below Echo Lakes. We might not be able to make the climb with both you and me, never mind your dog."

I studied the map. "I've been up to Echo Lakes, but I don't remember how long they are."

"Two miles total. And they are well frozen, so we can make

good time before we have to start climbing. With luck, there'll be other tracks we can follow. And Desolation Wilderness doesn't start until after we go through Echo Lakes, so we might find a snowmobile track. That would really make it fast."

"From the far end of Echo Lakes up to Lake Aloha looks to be another two miles. In deep snow, that would take a long time."

"We haven't had a deep snowfall for several days, so a snowmobile would be able to make the climb pretty fast. I'm guessing we could get up to Lake Aloha in a half hour."

"You sound pretty certain about Echo Lakes being the best entry point," I said.

"Of course, I'm certain. Didn't you ask me because I know about snow country? We could go in by the other routes that I labeled as escape routes on Simone's map. But they are mostly too steep to climb on a snowmobile. We'd have to ski. I don't know what kind of back-country skier you are, but I'm not up to that. And while Echo Lakes is high enough, it's most of two miles just to get down the unplowed road from the highway on Echo Summit. That's eight miles of travel to Lake Aloha, which, if Simone is running for her life, is where I think she'll be in about four hours."

"You know where to get a snowmobile on short notice?" Diamond asked.

Joe nodded. "One of the guys in our lunch group. Harry Denner. Works for Caltrans. He's the guy who's always calling me chief. I can't stand it. Doesn't mean I won't borrow his snowmobile. He's got an Arctic Cat Bearcat Utility with two seats and the equipment rack behind. Owen could sit on the rack and help your dog balance on the rear seat."

"And you would drive."

"I'm old, I'm not dead. You think I can't sit on a seat and squeeze the throttle?"

"Not at all. I was just asking. Where does Harry garage this machine?"

"At his cabin up on Echo Summit. It's the reason I thought of this approach. And before you ask, no, I'm not being overly swayed by the presence of the snowmobile. I still believe that Echo Lakes gives us our greatest chance of intercepting Simone."

"And you think that if a killer is out there, and he finds Simone, he won't push her off a cliff before she gets to Lake Aloha."

"That's the beauty of this route. If she makes it to Rockbound Valley, there won't be any cliffs nearby except at Mosquito Pass. If she gets through that, then Lake Aloha will give her a respite from cliffs until she descends to Echo Lake. If we get to her while she's still in the high open areas, we could save her."

FIFTY-TWO

"But this is all still speculation," Diamond said. "We still don't know if she's in danger, right? For that matter, our idea that the killer is motivated by what got said in the No Judgment group is speculation, too. And we have no indication that Michael was a member of this hiking group. He has wavy brown hair. That's all. Simone didn't mention his tattoos, which would be hard to hide if the weather was hot when they went hiking."

"Joe," I said. "Did Rell ever say or do anything that might suggest whether or not Michael could have been one of the hikers?"

"No. But one time she mentioned that many of their hikes were on the South Shore because all but one of the hikers lived close. Of course, Michael lives really close, but I think she just meant the South Shore in general."

I turned to Diamond. "You think there's another motive?"

"Nothing in particular," Diamond said. "But we haven't pursued that idea."

"What else could serve as a motive for killing people like the ones who've died?" I asked.

"This gets back to trying to influence me," Joe said. "A lot of people will make money if the resort is built."

"Like Bob's investors," I said.

Joe nodded. "Also investors not connected to RKS Properties."

"Real estate investors," I said. "People who own land near the resort." I picked up Joe's phone, called information, and got the number for Ira Weinstein, the realtor who sold me my cabin when I moved to Tahoe.

"Weinstein," he answered.

"Owen McKenna. I'll check in with you sometime, and we'll

catch up, but in the meantime I have a quick question."

"Yeah?" he said.

"Do you know if any of your colleagues specialize in Christmas Valley? Especially the properties out at the very end?"

"You're thinking about the proposed ski resort, aren't you?"

"I'm not the first to ask the question, huh?"

He chuckled. "That would be one way to put it. Give a call to Dan Sandoval. I've got his number here someplace." Ira read it off, I thanked him, hung up, and dialed.

When Dan answered, I told him who I was and that Ira Weinstein had given me his number.

"Are you familiar with the proposed Steven's Peak Ski Resort?" I asked.

"Live, eat, sleep, breathe it," he said. "The day they start breaking ground on that baby is the day I never again worry about making my condo payment in Maui."

"I'm calling about properties in Christmas Valley that might benefit from the resort."

"All properties in Christmas Valley will benefit. Not everyone will be happy with the traffic. But when the crowds drive them to sell and move to quieter areas, they'll at least appreciate the price that future vacation home buyers will pay for their abodes, large or small."

"I'm wondering if there's been any unusual activity related to the proposed resort."

"In what way?"

"I don't know. I'm thinking along the lines of someone who really stands to benefit if the resort is built and will lose a great deal if it isn't built."

"Like I said, everyone will benefit dollarwise. But there is one guy who showed up almost before there were even any whispers about the resort. He bought nearly every empty lot left in the valley. Paid cash, too. A lot of people thought he was taking a big risk to dump so much money into a single neighborhood. But he's looking damn smart today."

"Do you happen to remember his name?"

"No, but I've got it in my book. Hold on."

I waited.

Dan came back on the line. "He's from the Bay Area. His name is Michael Paul."

I thanked Dan, hung up, and told Diamond and Joe what he'd said.

"A new motive," Diamond said. "Michael's on the hot seat."

"Right," I said. "Joe, do you have a number for Michael?"

He walked over and picked up his little book from the desk and flipped it open.

"No. I don't. I never had reason to call him. If I want to talk, he's always driving by."

Diamond said, "You call him, he could answer even if he's out chasing Simone."

"Sure, but don't you think I could tell?"

"Wind in the background?" Diamond said. "Breathing hard with exertion?"

"Yeah. It'd be a relief to find out that Michael is currently watching a game at a friend's house or eating at a local restaurant." I turned to Joe. "Can you think of someone who might know him? Or know his number?"

"Dwight knows him better than anyone else around here. They're always talking in the road."

"Do you have Dwight's number?"

"Sure." He opened to a page and pointed at the number as he handed me the book.

I used his land line to dial Dwight.

It rang several times and went to voicemail. I said, "Dwight, this is Owen McKenna. If you're there, please pick up. I need to ask you a question. Either way, please call when you get this message. It's important." I left Joe's and my numbers and hung up.

"Do you have Dwight's cell number?"

Joe shook his head. "But I have an idea. Dwight often goes down to Berkeley on business. Maybe you can reach him there. If not, someone there might have his cell. You could look online and find their number." Joe pointed to his computer.

It only took me a few minutes to find a telephone number for the Physics department at UC Berkeley.

"They're not going to give you Dwight's cell number," Joe

said. "People are careful about keeping personal phone numbers private."

"Right. I'll have to have an angle." I thought about it for a bit, then dialed.

"Physics," a young male voice answered when I called.

"Hey," I said in a voice higher than my natural register, trying to sound younger by ten or fifteen years. "This is John Dalton over at Nanocave Gaming in Palo Alto. We've got a little gamer project going on here that has hit a glitch. I wonder if you can give me a referral? One of our engineers – you probably know him – Bandy Milan?"

"No, I don't know him," the voice said. "You said Bandy, right?"

"Yeah. Bandy. I guess it goes back to when he had to testify at that big hearing in D.C. on bandwidth issues. So Bandy's working on some nano-software modeling. I don't really know about it. I'm in Human Resources. I.T.'s not my gig. Well, Bandy hit some kind of computer trap where everything starts running in circles."

Across the room Joe was watching me, frowning. Behind him, Diamond was grinning and shaking his head. I turned away to make it easier to ignore them.

"Anyway, I made some calls, and this dude told me that there's a nano-modeling consultant who does contract work for you guys. I thought that might be a good fit for us. I'm calling to see if you know who this consultant is and if you can give me his contact info?"

There was a short pause. "Nano modeling? I don't know of anyone like that, but hold on, and I'll call Reginald. He's using some software to try to re-imagine quantum mechanics. He might know what's happening in nano."

The phone went silent. I turned and looked at Joe. "They put me on hold," I said.

Joe nodded. I waited.

Two minutes later came a female voice. "Is this the person looking for Dwight Frankman?"

"Maybe," I said, "if he's your nano-modeling engineer."

"He might be your guy," she said. "But he lives in Tahoe, so I don't know if that affects your needs. We just use him for detail work. We generate a concept to test, he writes the code, we test. It's pretty easy for him to do that from anywhere. He's got a sweet deal, living in Tahoe, working on his own time."

"That would probably work for us. I should tell you that we don't anticipate a lot of big projects, so I don't think our presence would affect his work for you."

"No sweat," she said.

"Do you have Dwight's number?" I asked.

"I do." She read off the number.

"Thanks," I said. Now that I had his cell number, I wanted to get off the phone. "I appreciate..."

"I should warn you that he's expensive," she said. "The only reason we can afford him is that we got a grant from the National Science Foundation. A public university like Berkeley can't throw around money the way Stanford can."

"Thanks for the tip," I said. "We'll try to get some clear numbers from him before we proceed. Thanks again."

"Of course," she continued, "if you need his layer folding software, then he's probably cost-effective even if he's expensive."

"Like I told the guy who answered," I said, "I'm not a tech guy myself, so layer-folding is over my head. I only..."

"Not my area, either," she said. "But I heard an intriguing analogy the other day that makes it more clear. Someone said to think of it like origami."

Now she had my attention.

"What does origami have to do with nano-modeling software?" I asked.

"As it was explained to me," she said, "nature doesn't create blocks of stuff so much as she creates layers. This is especially true in the biological sciences, but it even exists in most of the physical sciences. Many morphologies that look like chunky materials are really just many layers folded and refolded. This is true of huge structures like mountain ranges, as well as the tiniest nano-structures. Layers of atoms and molecules, folded over and over. Understanding and designing nano-structures is a study of micro layers that are folded similar to the way origami artists fold paper. Once I heard that, it made a lot more sense to me. Don't you agree?"

The woman's enthusiasm was great, but I really wanted to get off the phone.

"Yes, you're right," I said. "That makes it much easier to understand. Thanks again."

I hung up and turned to Joe. "Did you ever get the sense that Dwight was interested in origami?"

Joe frowned. "No. I mean, once or twice he stirred through the trash can of origami entries to my contest, but it didn't seem like any significant interest."

"Did he ever talk about origami in relation to his computer work?"

Joe shook his head. "No. Why?"

I was thinking about the scaffolding and how it fell in a neat, controlled manner, a collapse that seemed engineered, origami style. I now had Dwight's cell number, but I wasn't ready to call it just yet.

I turned to Diamond. "When Dwight drove his Chevy Tahoe off the road and down the snowbank, and he used his flare gun to get attention..." I said.

"Yeah?"

"Any idea where the wreckage went?"

"Let me think. I think it got hauled to Carson City Auto Body."

"I'm wondering if Dwight could have used it to push Manuel Romero off the switchback at Emerald Bay."

Diamond was already typing on Joe's computer. He picked up the phone and dialed.

After a pause, Diamond said, "Sergeant Martinez, Douglas County, calling on a Chevy Tahoe you picked up near Spooner Summit a few days ago."

He paused while someone on the other end spoke.

"Yeah," Diamond said. "Wondering if you could tell me the scope of the damage."

Another, longer pause.

"What about the front bumper?" Diamond said, "Was it mangled badly?"

Diamond listened. "Got it. One more question. Did you notice the tires? Did they have good tread? Any chance they had studded snow tires?"

He listened some more, said thanks, and hung up.

"Guy said the tires were bald. When they saw them, they thought, no wonder he went off a snow-covered highway."

"Simone said the man named Cameron in the No Judgment group was athletic," I said. "Dwight's the opposite of athletic. The nine-one-one dispatcher said that the man who called in the report on the avalanche down below Mt. Rose had a really raspy voice. Like Michael's. Dwight's voice is smooth and high, closer to that of a choir boy. The person who hip-checked Jillian into a tree was an expert skier. Dwight doesn't like exercise and said he didn't ski. There's nothing about him that makes him a suspect."

"Except?" Diamond said.

"Except that the woman at Berkeley said that nano-modeling on the computer was like origami. It's a reach, but I'm going to check Dwight's house before I call his cell," I said.

Joe nodded, no doubt understanding that my thoughts were shifting in new directions.

Remembering that my Jeep was in Tahoe City, I said, "Joe, may I borrow your tire iron?"

"Certainly. The cars are in the garage. Unlocked."

"Spot will stay here with you and Diamond."

I looked at Diamond. He made a little nod. "Garage door works best," he said.

FIFTY-THREE

I fetched a tire iron from one of Joe's cars and borrowed a pair of gloves from his front seat.

The street was empty, the vertical snow walls, fresh-cut by the rotary plow, were turning blue in the approaching twilight. I hustled my way down to the end of the block, turned at the corner, went down a steep street, turned another corner, and walked to Dwight's house.

The Subaru was not in the drive. The Tahoe was at a junkyard. Maybe Dwight had a third car in the garage.

I used Dwight's ski binding knocker to rap on the wall next to the door of his darkened house. He didn't answer. No lights showed in any windows. I knocked again and waited. After no response, I considered climbing the snow-walled driveway and trudging through the deep snow to check the doors at the back of the house. I remembered Dwight's fear of everything. I was certain he'd have the back door and deck slider locked.

I walked over to the garage door. Even on homes with heavy deadbolts on the front doors, the garage doors often have no locks at all. The door is held down by nothing other than the lightweight chain that raises and lowers it.

I remembered that Dwight had to turn off his alarm the last time I visited. I hoped the garage door wasn't wired.

I wedged the end of the tire iron under the bottom of the garage door and pulled up on it. The garage door shifted and moaned. I lifted harder. The bottom panel of the door bent inward under the strain. It appeared to be made of fiberglass, light and strong but easy to bend with the leverage of a length of steel. I put more energy into it. The lowest roller slipped out of its track on the left side, and the bottom panel twisted up and in.

I didn't want to destroy the door, so I stopped lifting, lay down on the drive, and snaked my body through the opening. No audible alarm sounded. But it could be a silent alarm.

I stood up in the dark, raised my arms out in front of me like Frankenstein exploring the castle, and hurried toward the back wall of the garage. I moved fast, worrying about Simone. My elbow bumped something that clattered to the floor.

After a minute in the dark, I found the light switch.

There were no cars in the garage, a sign that Dwight was out.

With the light on, anyone from the street could see that the bottom of the garage door was jimmied. I trotted over to where I'd popped the garage-door roller out of the track. I twisted it, and the roller popped back in place.

The hinge that held the bottom door panel to the one above was broken from my prying and bending, but it looked like the door would still work.

On a heavy-duty metal bracket near the garage door hung four heavy tire chains.

The junkyard man had told Diamond that Dwight's tires were bald. But with chains on all tires, the vehicle would have good traction. It would have been easy for Dwight to push Manuel's little Prius off the mountain at Emerald Bay. Manuel wouldn't have had a chance to stop, but Dwight would have stopped easily. His front bumper might have revealed hints of the Prius, but the guy said it was mangled.

The inner door from garage to house looked solid and did have a deadbolt. It could be jimmied, but it would be wired.

It would be better to get in without going through the door.

Sheetrock is great stuff for making walls. It's cheap and strong and fireproof. It's also great stuff for burglars. I punched the iron through the sheetrock on the garage side of the wall, levered it sideways to give some horizontal dimension to my hole, then moved my tire iron a couple of inches to the side and repeated. I went as fast as possible. I panted with effort, inhaling sheetrock dust. My arms got sore. When I hit a stud, I moved back the other direction. I continued until I hit the next stud. Now that I knew where the studs were, I could make a nice opening.

It was a great way to circumvent a burglar alarm assuming that there were no motion detectors or webcams broadcasting to the internet or loaded shotguns set on tripwires stretched across the rooms a foot above the floor.

I'd have to take my chances.

Once through the garage-side layer, I started again on the second layer of sheetrock on the inside of the studs. The destruction went well, and I was inside in a few minutes.

Still no audible alarm went off, a good sign. But I moved fast in case an unseen detector had already sent a signal to the security company.

Rarely were El Dorado Sheriff's officers in the upscale Angora Highlands neighborhood. Assuming the closest patrol unit was down near Lake Tahoe Blvd, I probably had ten minutes before the first flashing lights would come up the streets.

I hurried through the house, looking for anything unusual. There wasn't much. It was a three-bedroom, three-and-a-half-bath, well-made spread. There was a wet bar in the great room that looked unused. The kitchen had the standard island with its own sink. One bedroom had a comprehensive workout station, part of the exercise equipment that Dwight said he was forced to take when he bought the house.

I found what I was looking for in the third bedroom.

It was set up as an office of sorts, a big desk set from IKEA, three computer monitors, two printers, a scanner, stacks of Staples copy paper, and several devices with blinking green lights, internet connections perhaps.

As always, I looked for what was out of place. The room had an armoire, a large walnut-stained, freestanding closet.

Why an extra closet?

I opened the armoire. There were some clothes and some boxes of computer printouts and a stack of old phone books.

I turned to the built-in closet, which had mirrored, sliding doors. I slid one to the side. There were some coats and robes and shirts hanging on the rod. They were spread out in an even fashion. Too even.

I pushed them all to the side. The closet was shallow, the rear wall closer than would be normal. So I pushed at it, and it moved. I realized that it was on a slider.

I slid the right half of the panel sideways and found that it was a large walk-in closet disguised to look like a shallow one.

I reached in, and felt around for a light switch. I felt the other wall. Nothing.

I turned and felt something brush my face. I swatted at it with my hand and felt it move away. Swatted again and found a string. Grabbed and pulled.

A light came on.

It was a bare bulb hanging from the ceiling. When I saw what it illuminated, I inhaled.

I was in a secret shrine.

A shrine dedicated to Nedham Cavett.

In the center was a large framed picture of Ned. He was about thirteen or fourteen years old, dressed in a white football uniform. He was holding his helmet in his hands, and he was smiling, radiating the movie-star looks that were already manifest at that young age.

To the right side of the framed picture was a row of tiny school-picture shots of Ned, stuck to the wall with push pins, each one showing the progression from big-toothed little kid to high school heartthrob. On the left side of the big picture were several trinkets and medals, pinned to the wall. There were Boy Scout badges, a soccer-team group photo, a commendation from a drug rehabilitation program.

Under the framed photo of Ned was a small faded photo of two young boys and a woman. The older boy was Ned, maybe eight years old, looking cocky and insecure and telegraphing a false bravado. The woman looked weary and used-up like a meth-mom cliché of addiction and imploded dreams.

The other boy in the picture was about four. Unlike Ned, the young boy had hints of the mother in his face, but he looked nothing like the older boy. The relationship looked like that of step-brothers, brought together when their separate parents married.

The younger boy looked up at the older boy with a mixture of adulation and worship. Peter Cavett, also known as Dwight Frankman AKA Cameron.

Off to the side were more items on a shelf.

A small framed photo showed a group of young kids. Ned was off to the side. He was beaming at the younger kid in the center.

The younger kid was holding an unusual trophy. It looked like a tiny computer. Written in calligraphy at the bottom of the photo were the words Inyo County Computer Club Champion Peter Cavett.

Another photo showed both brothers at a ski area with Lake Tahoe in the background. Their smiles were infectious, and their bonding was obvious in their matching clothes.

They both wore white jackets and white warmups.

There were other photos taken in a gym. Several showed Ned pumping serious iron. One showed him in a Mr. Universe pose. A smaller photo showed Peter/Dwight/Cameron holding a barbell over his head at the top of a clean-and-jerk maneuver. Ned stood behind him, arms out, spotting him. The barbell looked like it had two 45-pound weights on each end. With the barbell, it would have totaled 225 pounds. It wasn't a lot of weight in weight-lifting circles. But it was a lot for a thin guy whose disguise was pretending to be a skinny wimp. His bulging shoulder and arm muscles were impressive. His abs were ripped, and his legs looked like those of a soccer player. He was as buff as thin guys come.

Yet another photo showed Peter at bat in a baseball game. He looked athletic and ready to hit the pitch out of the park. Beneath his cap, his hair was buzz-cut and dark, nothing like the stringy red mop and stocking cap from when he had introduced himself to me as Dwight.

On a nail to the side hung a wig with long wavy hair, dark brown. Near the wig were pieces of paper taped to the wall. One was a note scrawled in pencil. The handwriting was almost illegible.

> hey littel bro i used that oragamee yu sent me and i won!!!!!! not first place but third and got a thowsand and two hunderd and fifty thats enough to move to tahoe maybe that contest guy has a bunch more money i could take some and put to good use thanks maybe you'll come to tahoe some day!

Another was a piece of graph paper. On it was a sketch of the scaffolding at my office. In neat printing it said, 'Remove these bolts.' There were multiple arrows pointing to intersections at regular intervals. More printing said, 'This piece will serve as the trigger point for an origami-style folding collapse of the entire structure.' Another arrow pointed to the piece of scaffold bar that I had jerked free. Presumably, Dwight planned to wait for me some night and pull that bar free as Spot and I emerged from the building.

The puzzle was beginning to make sense.

Simone told her abuse group about Ned and his continuous assaults on her. Unfortunately, Simone had no clue that Ned's little brother was Rell's neighbor Dwight, who chose the pseudonym Cameron when Rell invited him to join her hiking group. So as Simone told the group about the beatings she suffered at Ned's hands, Ned's worshiping stepbrother was listening and hating the fact that an entire group of people vilified his brother.

Perhaps the worst horror of all was that Ned fell prey to Dwight's devious origami scaffold destruction, a scheme designed to kill the person who posed the biggest threat to Ned.

Me.

Dwight decided to kill the people who believed that Ned was evil. His rage at their perceptions overwhelmed any sense that they might be right. So he arranged murders that would look like accidents. It hadn't yet worked with Rell and me. But Manuel and Jillian were dead. And Simone was likely next.

Now that I knew that the killer wasn't Ned, the threat to Simone went from speculation to emergency. I had to find Dwight before he got to Simone.

I jogged through the house, looking for something that would help me catch Dwight before he could push Simone off a cliff.

In the largest bedroom was a queen-sized bed, the only bed in the house. The bed was made so tightly that it looked unused, but when I pulled the covers down, I could see the wrinkles in the pillowcase that indicated its recent use.

I pulled off the pillowcase, folded it small, and wrapped it in a plastic bag that I found in Dwight's kitchen. I stuffed the bag into my pocket and left the way I came.

The streets were dark as I ran back up to Joe's house.

Street pulled up in her little VW Beetle as I came around the corner. She got out, and I gave her a quick kiss.

The passenger window was open, and my back-country skis stuck out at an angle into the air. I pulled them out. My boots and pack with emergency food and clothes were on the front passenger seat. I set the pack on the hood of Diamond's SUV and carried the boots and clothes inside.

"You've got news," Street said as we hurried into Joe's living room.

"Yes, Dwight is Ned's brother Peter Cavett, as well as Cameron. He's the killer. I found a shrine to Ned in the back of one of Dwight's closets. There is lots of incriminating evidence."

"Dwight is killing the members of the abuse group because they all were against Ned?" Street said.

"It looks like it," I said.

"And Dwight's gone," Joe said.

"Right," I said. "I think we can now assume that he may well be chasing Simone."

"Better hurry," Diamond said.

"We've planned a rescue mission based on a series of guesses," Joe said. "That's not good."

"Best we have," Diamond said.

"You're willing to go along and help?" Street said to Joe.

"That girl who's out there in Desolation Wilderness," he said, "is the best friend Rell has had in years. Now it looks like Rell asked her to join her hiking group, and it's about to get her killed. I'll do whatever I can."

Street gave him a hug. "You take care of yourself." She pointed at me, "and that guy, too."

"Me and the hound," Joe said. "We'll look after Owen, make sure he doesn't get into trouble."

Street turned to me.

"There isn't anything I can do to help, right?" she asked.

"I don't think so."

"So it's best if I leave you to concentrate."

"Probably."

She made a slow, thoughtful nod, and gave me another kiss.

I gave her a hug, and she gripped me hard. Then she nodded at Diamond, and left.

I was pulling on my back-country ski boots when Joe's phone rang.

Joe picked it up. "Hello?"

He listened, frowning. "I can't understand you." Pause. "Talk slower." Then, "Hold on." He handed the phone to me. "Voice is too soft, and there's too much static," he said.

"This is Owen McKenna" I said.

The voice was that of a woman, breathless, crying, and very hard to understand. But the French accent was obvious.

FIFTY-FOUR

"Simone! Are you okay?"

"He's chasing me! It's been two hours since I saw him and started sprinting to get away! Maybe three!" She was panting. Her words were rushed. Desperate. Weak.

"Where are you?"

"Rockbound Valley. He's... kill me! I got the charger... You didn't... cell phone."

She was breaking up.

"We're coming up from Echo Lake!" I yelled.

No response.

"Can you hear me, Simone? We're going in at Echo Lakes. We'll come up to Lake Aloha. Stay on the windblown areas so you can ski faster. If we don't see you at Lake Aloha, we'll continue on to Rockbound Valley. Can you hear me? Simone, you can do this! You have the endurance. Remember what you said, that you can keep going and going!"

I thought I heard a broken cry, a whimper. Then static. I waited.

"Can you hear me, Simone? We're coming to get you!"

More static. Then came a distant scream of terror, muffled by wind. It sounded as if she'd dropped her phone in the snow and kept on skiing.

The line went dead.

I hung up. Joe and Diamond stared at me

"She's alive," Joe said. His face was white. His voice shook.

"For now," I said.

"What can I do?" Diamond said.

Before I could answer, Joe barked out the words. "Drive us to Echo Summit."

"Will do," Diamond said.

"Joe, grab your gear," I said. "We can put our stuff on in the car!"

Joe grabbed his boots. Mine were on but untied.

"Do you have gaiters?" I shouted.

"Forgot," Joe said. He opened a closet, pulled out some items.

I held the door, we all ran out, Spot running ahead. I shuffled out in my untied boots.

I put my skis into Diamond's patrol unit, angling them back toward the rear window. Joe got in front, holding his boots and heavy snow clothes. Spot and I got in back. Diamond backed out of the drive, and we left fast.

The winter night air was unusually cold and humid and it burned our skin. As Simone had mentioned in our last real conversation, wispy cirrus clouds danced in the sky, yet the stars were still visible in most places. The moon was in its first quarter, and it shown bright, but its light came through an ice haze that misted the stars as if they were soft candles flickering inside white paper bags.

Light snow began falling as Diamond drove down the mountain from Joe's neighborhood to the valley floor. I'd seen it many times before, tiny flakes falling from a sky that barely had clouds. But by the time we got down to Lake Tahoe Blvd, the roads were slick. Diamond turned right, and we headed toward North Upper Truckee Road, the back way out to Highway 50.

We now knew that Joe was right about the route that Simone would choose when she recognized that she was in danger. But it didn't bring us comfort. I'm sure I wasn't alone as I contemplated her terror, out in a frozen wilderness, chased by a man who had killed multiple times, a man who was an expert skier and athlete, a crazed man who wouldn't hesitate to kill her once he found the right spot.

There was little traffic as Diamond got to Highway 50 and turned up the long grade toward Echo Summit. The road twisted its way along the ledge carved into the rocky cliff. Diamond pushed his speed.

At one point, the rear end slid out on a curve. Diamond took his foot off the gas but didn't touch the brake, letting the vehicle find its natural traction.

After that, Diamond took it a touch slower, but still drove fast.

None of us spoke. Joe and I laced up our boots and put on our gaiters to keep snow out of our boots.

The falling snow got heavier. It looked cold and bleak outside.

I'd often looked up from South Lake Tahoe at the vast expanse of snow on the Crystal Range, but I hadn't ever made a winter expedition into the wilderness. I thought about Simone, desperate and alone in the Desolation Wilderness Area. If she wasn't already dead, she was skiing for her life.

Diamond crested the top of Echo Summit, drove a short distance, and turned right on Echo Summit Road. It was plowed to the Sno-Park lot, which was about a mile from Lower Echo Lake. The lot had a couple of pickups and a Subaru, but was otherwise empty. Diamond slid to a stop and we all jumped out.

Spot trotted around investigating scents while I strapped my skis into the side tunnels of my pack and put a ski tie at the tips so that they made a stable triangle. I pulled on the pack. The ski tips came forward above my head. Joe reached into his pocket and pulled out a headlamp with an elastic strap. He put it on his head, tested the light, then turned it off.

Joe and I said goodbye to Diamond, then trotted with Spot on compressed snowmobile tracks. Joe did his earthquake version, his gloved hands held out a bit for balance. He moved at a good pace, and was quickly breathing hard. His exhalations became grunts. I couldn't tell if the sounds were his natural exertions, or if they were grunts of worry for Simone.

A hundred yards or so down the unplowed road, we came to an old cabin with a lean-to shed built against its side.

"That's it," Joe said. "Harry's sled is inside the lean-to. Hurry."

I used my boot to sweep away the most recent snow. The double doors to the shed were warped, and they creaked as I tried to pull them open. One caught on the snow. I kicked away the snow and pulled the doors open wide.

Inside was a bright green snowmobile with graphics that accentuated its lines. It was a big, fast-looking machine.

"Looks heavy," I said. "It'll be hard to pull out."

"It's got power reverse," Joe said, panting. He reached inside the upper part of the door frame and felt along the edge. "Here's the key."

Joe turned on his headlamp and moved into the shed, straddling and crawling over the machine's seat. He sat down, put the key in the ignition, and started the engine.

The Arctic Cat seemed to growl. I stepped out of the way as Joe backed it out of the shed.

"You sit here," Joe said. He pointed to the metal cargo rack that projected out behind the seat. "Spot sits here." He patted the second seat. "I drive."

Joe grabbed an old jacket off a nail inside the shed. "Wrap this jacket around the luggage rack to make it easier to sit on."

I took the jacket and did as he suggested.

Spot had ridden a snowmobile before, so it wasn't too difficult to get him onto it. But he was too long to fit on the rear seat facing forward. So I turned him backward. He sat up high, his rear legs straddling the seat and his chest against the seat back, his head turned sideways. I sat on the luggage rack and leaned forward, my arms around the seat back, and held him in place.

It wasn't comfortable, but it was all we had.

"We're going to be very rear-heavy," I said.

Joe nodded as if that were obvious. "It won't be a problem except when we climb. Worst case, you and Spot get off and walk."

I nodded. "How fast does this sled go?" I asked as Joe started off.

He turned his head to talk over his shoulder. "Real fast," he shouted over the engine roar. "But this is night. You can't over-drive your headlights on a snow machine, or you're asking for trouble."

"What's that mean?" I called out.

"On high beams, the headlights shine about two hundred feet ahead. At forty miles per hour, it takes about two hundred feet to stop. So that's our speed limit. Even so, there is always the possibility of hitting an obstruction under the snow."

"A submerged boulder or tree trunk," I said.

"Right. If that happens, we might come to a real quick stop. But it's unlikely on a well-used trail. More likely when we head off into untracked snow." Joe sped up. We were bouncing on the undulating trail.

Echo Summit Road was covered in several feet of compressed snow, packed down by snowmobiles. There was a six-inch layer of fresh powder on top. Joe made good time.

The road twisted through a forest of large trees, some of them old-growth giants. We went past several old cabins and then by Berkeley Camp, the rustic summer hangout for professors and other Berkeley groups.

"What's your plan?" I called out.

"My job is just to get us out there," he shouted. "Because Simone is many miles from Echo Lake, we'll head down the ice in the middle for the fastest travel. When we get to Lake Aloha – or Rockbound Valley if we have to go that far to find her – then I'll pick a route up the southwest-facing slopes to our right of the lake and the valley. Those slopes will be sun-stabilized. And being up above will give us a better chance of seeing her. That's where you come in," Joe said. "I know snow, but I don't know how to apprehend a killer."

Joe was driving faster still.

"If we only see Simone, we come in easy," I said. "We don't want to scare her by roaring up toward her. But if we see them both, then we head toward him. Once he sees us, he'll know we're after him because snowmobiles aren't allowed in Desolation. So the best approach is to aim straight for him. The faster we can get to him, the better. Our approach might intimidate him. And if he tries to make a sprint for her, maybe we can get to her first."

"What do I do when we get to him?"

"Stop when you get close, and Spot and I will jump off."

Joe nodded, squeezed the throttle farther.

"Why did you bring your skis?" Joe yelled over the engine.

"Insurance. Never know when we come to a place where a snowmobile can't get through."

A mile in, we rounded the curve with the spectacular overlook across Tahoe Valley and the south end of the Tahoe Basin twelve hundred feet below. It looked idyllic, the sparkling lights from hundreds of homes dimmed by the icy, filtering haze of snow-filled sky. But all I could see was a vision of Simone trying to outrun a killer.

We went around another curve, then pitched down the sloped parking lot, which is always crowded in the summer but empty now in the winter. At the end of the lot, the road pitched down at a steeper angle. Joe drove us around the switchback at the end and continued down through the powder to the lower parking lot and the old rustic lodge that serves up ice cream cones to summer boaters.

From there, it was a short distance to the lake's edge. Despite the recent snowfall, the snowmobile trail was an obvious cushioned stripe down the moonlit lake.

When Joe got onto the smooth, compressed trail, he throttled up, and the snowmobile growled with power. In a moment, we were racing along. I worried that Spot would bounce off on the many bumps, so I held him tight.

Joe seemed to lean a bit to port. I hoped it was just back pain or a cramp in his arms or his neck and not a heart attack. The machine was too loud to call out and expect him to hear, so I stayed quiet.

Joe's lean didn't get worse, and we made good time.

At the end of Lower Echo Lake, we came to the channel that flows from Upper Echo Lake. Joe took the curves like a pro, slowing only a little. In a minute we came to the upper lake.

The upper lake ended where the mountains rise up, with Echo Peak on the right and Ralston Peak on the left. Straight ahead was the trail that climbs up to a chain of lakes ending in Lake Aloha.

Joe slowed to a stop. "Here's where it gets tricky," he said. "Because we're back heavy, I'm going to have to keep up a good speed to crest the rises without gunning it on each rise. Otherwise, we might pull a wheely and tip over backward. So just hang on, lean forward, and trust me, okay?"

"Got it," I said. "Where do you think Simone will have gotten to by this time?"

Joe pulled up his sleeve, clicked on his headlight for a moment, and looked at his watch.

"I'd guess she will have come to Mosquito Pass at the most.

If that's the case, she'll be coming down the north end of Lake Aloha by the time we get there. It's also possible that she's still in Rockbound Valley. We'll know when we see her."

"Right," I said. Joe's comments were optimistic. We both knew the odds against her.

Joe squeezed the throttle a touch, then backed off. "If we do tip over backward," Joe called over his shoulder, "throw your hound one direction and dive to the other. Your push off him will help propel you both to safety."

"What about you?"

"I crashed in a lot of races," he said. "Hopefully, the technique will come back to me. If not, I'm ninety-two. Not like I haven't lived a long life." He gunned the engine, and we shot up a trail that climbed through the forest, our headlight making a bouncing beam in the trees. Again, Joe leaned sideways.

The trail went up in cycles, sometimes steep, sometimes level. It wound around trees and boulders. From where I sat behind Spot, I couldn't tell if Joe was following the hiking trail or whether he was just choosing the most open path through the forest. The boundary of Desolation Wilderness was a short distance ahead, so if we were benefiting from previous snowmobile tracks, that would end soon.

In less than a mile of climbing, we came to a small open area that was flat. "Tamarack Lake," Joe called out.

He sped up and raced across it. At the far end, the trail rose at a much steeper angle. I held Spot tight as Joe drove the sled at high speed onto the trail. The machine hit the steep incline of slope with a shock. Spot wavered and my foot slipped. But we held on. Joe drove like a fighter pilot. He still listed to port, but he leaned forward and drove hard and fast.

The turns were numerous. On the sharper ones, Joe leaned sideways, helping to carve the sled like a motorcycle, which helped Spot and me stay on. At times, it was like a slalom course, left and right, left and right. We hit a steeper section. Joe leaned forward and kept the throttle up. But I felt and heard the track spinning beneath us, shooting loose snow in a rooster tail behind us. Then the track grabbed, and we lofted over the rise and slammed back down on a flat section.

The next open flat area was Lake of the Woods. After a quarter mile sprint across its surface, we climbed up its far side. We popped over a lop-sided saddle and entered the Lake Aloha basin.

At 8100 feet, the snow was softer and deeper, but Joe kept the speed up, and the machine kept planing on the snow.

Joe angled to the north and climbed partway up the southwest-facing slope as he'd earlier said. The slope was steep, so he only went up far enough to give us a view across Lake Aloha.

The lake, and the Crystal Range on the far side, glowed in the dim moonlight coming through snow showers. With almost no trees around the lake, it was a giant white slab of snow. It made a seamless transition to the angled slab of rock that rose to the three, 10,000-foot peaks on the other side. The three connected mountains of Pyramid Peak, Mt. Agassiz, and Mt. Price seemed a forbidding blue-white monolith whose tips disappeared into the thickening cloud bank.

As Joe coaxed the sled farther up the opposite slope, the mountains, coated in thick snow with no interruptions, were other-worldly, like a landscape one would find in Antarctica.

Joe leveled out onto a traverse near the base of Cracked Crag to the northeast. The machine, less stressed, sped up. I focused on holding onto Spot while I gazed across the plain of Lake Aloha, looking for any movement, any dark speck.

The dim moonlight grew darker. A glance at the bright headlight swath made the moonlight seem non-existent. The snow was brilliant white, smooth and mesmerizing as the machine raced across its surface. Then the right ski tip struck something. There was a shriek of metal on rock as the rear of the sled skidded to the left. The edge of the track caught the snow, the machine tipped, and we all launched into the night air.

FIFTY-FIVE

I landed face first in the snow. My eyes and ears and mouth were packed full. I pushed myself up, arms sinking into the powder. I rolled sideways, got my boots beneath me, pushed them down, compacting the snow beneath me. I stood up, my legs buried up to my thighs.

I spit out snow, wiped it from my face and ears. "Joe?" I called. "Joe, where are you? Joe?" I turned.

A bright blue-white light turned on. Joe's headlamp. I could see no other part of him. He was obviously covered in snow.

"Over here. I'm okay. Where's your hound?"

"Spot, where are you?" I called out.

I heard movement in the snow behind me. I turned. Spot was bounding toward me, his long legs having trouble getting purchase in the deep powder. But he made exaggerated leaps.

"Hey, boy, you're okay, huh?"

He jumped on me, all excited. Flying through the air on a snowmobile was fun.

"Easy, largeness, let me get over to Joe."

Spot leaped around as I trudged across the slope to the buried figure with the headlamp. Joe was in a sitting position, leaning back as if in an easy chair. He reached out his hand.

I took it and pulled him up onto his feet. He was lighter than me, and his snow boots were bigger, so he got more support in the deep snow. He only sunk in up to his knees.

"You okay?"

"Didn't see that rock," he said. "Sorry." Joe sounded stressed.

"Hey, Joe, I was watching ahead. I didn't see it either."

"Where's the sled?"

I looked around. It was behind us, turned on its side, mostly buried. The engine had killed. The headlight was dark.

"Your dog is okay," Joe said.

"Yeah."

"Where are your skis?" Joe asked.

I raised my hands above my head where the ski tips should be. There was nothing.

"They must have ripped out of the pack sleeves when we hit the rock."

"And now they're buried in the snow somewhere nearby," Joe said.

"We've gotta get that sled out and started up," Joe said. "That girl needs us."

I looked around at the dark, snowy slope.

Spot was looking, too, but at something else. His head was pointed toward the north end of Lake Aloha. His ears were focused forward, turning slightly like antennas trying to pick up the best signal.

"Joe!" I said in a harsh whisper. "Turn off your headlamp."

He did so. He too looked at Spot. I turned to study the area that Spot was looking at.

My eyes were still lacking night vision because of our lights. I looked to the side, tried to see with my peripheral vision.

Maybe there was movement a mile away. Maybe not. But all I saw for certain was a gray sky filled with snow. There was no sound, no movement, no indication of anything but a frozen landscape. I figured it was a false sensation, triggered by my concerns.

But Spot knew otherwise. He walked ahead in the snow, focused on something. From behind, I could see his ears held rigid. It was a clear alert, even if I could sense nothing.

Joe stayed silent, understanding that he should do nothing that would distract Spot. I caught up to Spot and put my hand on his back. I squatted down, knees bent. I didn't want to advertise our presence, and in a bent position we weren't so noticeable.

We watched. I still couldn't see any movement. But Spot's eyes and ears never wavered. The silence seemed complete, but only for Joe and me. For a moment, Spot panted hard, four quick breaths to help blow off some excess heat, then he stopped and held his breath to listen. It was obvious that he heard a person or persons coming.

I felt Spot tense. Holding very still and looking slightly to the side, I had the vaguest sense of movement in the distance down below us, a dark speck crawling across the dark, white, frozen landscape. Maybe it was my imagination, but gradually, the movement of the speck seemed to grow more pronounced. It seemed that a distant person was coming toward me, but I had no perception about the person's size. As the speck got a little closer, I sensed that it vibrated. The speck was making frenetic movement as it traveled at an angle toward us.

Then came another movement down below, a second, small, dot on the landscape behind the first. Chasing the first. The second dot was gray like what one would see if the person wore white ski clothes. If it was Dwight, I could scent Spot on the pillowcase and send him after the suspect. If it wasn't Dwight, Spot would probably leave both people alone. But I wasn't certain. While I've put Spot through some police dog training, he's not a professional. He could make a mistake. Like most dogs, Spot is naturally friendly. And like most police dogs, he also has a great deal of enthusiasm for doing his job. The potential problem is if he has too much enthusiasm, and if the likely suspect should act or even smell in a way that would confuse him, then the potential danger to an innocent person could be significant. I was reluctant to give Spot the command until I was certain.

I had an idea. I got out my cell. I expected no reception, but I had one bar. I dialed Dwight's cell number.

It rang one, two, three, four times. Just as I expected it to roll over to voicemail, it was answered.

"Hello?" It was Dwight's polite voice.

"Dwight, it's Owen McKenna."

"Oh hi, Mr. McKenna. What brings you calling?"

I thought I heard noise in the background. He was probably covering the phone, but the wind still howled. His breathing was obvious as well. It still didn't prove that he was the figure following Simone across the frozen lake, if, in fact, the figure in the lead was Simone, and if the two weren't simply a pair of late-night backcountry skiers out enjoying the moonlight. But if I could keep him talking, maybe there'd be an indication. I decided to be direct and challenge him.

"I'm on to you, Dwight. The whole meek geek thing was

a good disguise. I especially liked the bit about being afraid of climbing on the step ladder."

"I don't know what you're talking about," he said.

"No point in keeping up the charade, Dwight. I've been in your lair. I've seen your pics and your notes. What's your plan, Dwight? Or should I call you Cameron? Or just your given name Peter?"

I heard nothing but wind noise over the silence. Then came a raging shout.

"Ned was my brother, McKenna! He practically raised me! He was my only friend as a child. But no one ever gave him a fair chance! Not mom, not the cops, not the teachers. He was hung out to dry. And you know what those jerks always said? They said, 'Oh, Ned is so handsome, life is easy for him. Everybody wants to be with a good looking guy like Ned.' Well, you know what, McKenna? Life wasn't easy for Ned. Life was hell! Ned tried, but he never got credit for trying. If he did something well, people said he got ahead because of his looks. But if he did something badly, they said, 'Imagine Neddy Teddy screwing up his life in spite of looking like a movie star.' I can't tell you how many times I heard that, McKenna."

Dwight stopped to breathe. I hoped that his talking would slow him down and let Simone open the distance between them.

"Ned made bad choices, Dwight. His problems weren't your responsibility." I didn't want Dwight to realize that I was watching him. "Where are you?" I said. "We could meet and talk. I can make this easier for you." I covered my phone, turned to Joe and whispered. "Try to stay low. I'm going to head down there and see if I can surprise them."

Joe nodded at me in the dark.

"Ned tried to do right," Dwight continued, no longer trying to cover up his panting. "But everyone else prevented him from achieving anything. I was lucky and was born ugly. Every achievement for me was credited to my merit, my skill. Not Ned."

"People didn't single him out, Dwight." I was trudging down the slope through the deep snow. I kept my other hand on Spot's back. I wanted to get as close as possible before Dwight saw us.

"Yes, they did single him out. Even the No Judgment group. Talk about hypocrisy. They said they didn't want to judge, but they sure judged Ned."

"They were just supporting Simone," I said.

"Liar! You weren't there. I was! They demonized Ned. They believed every little lie she told them."

In the distance, the speck that was Simone was getting bigger as she skied toward me. Her strides were fast, her arm motion smooth and coordinated. She was skiing like a cross-country racer, her training manifest. But her terror showed in her shakiness. Her strides weren't the smooth movements of a professional. They were the terrified, jerky strides of someone skiing for her life. Behind her, gaining slowly, was a larger figure in white, striding like a pro, the man I assumed – but wasn't certain – was Dwight.

I marched down through the deep powder, lifting my boots high, but moving like I was in molasses.

"I saw Ned abuse Simone," I said. "I saw him grab her, drag her, push her, hurt her. And that was his public, careful behavior. I can't imagine what he did when the door shut. You're defending an evil man, Dwight. But you can stop. Ned is gone, crushed by your origami-design scaffolding collapse. You caused the ultimate judgment to fall on Ned. So let Simone go."

"The scaffolding plan was for you. I hold you responsible for his death! You were taunting him. He was only responding. When I'm through with Simone, I'm coming for you. You'll join the No Judgment group. Manuel, that self-righteous stuffed shirt, and Jillian, the snotty skier who thought she was better than us trailer kids all because she went to college in Incline. Even Rell. Sanctimonious Rell. She's the one who treasured her victim status. She used it to entice the rest of us into the group, got us to tell our secrets. Well, they're all going to stay secret now, McKenna. Simone is the last one before you. Then Ned will be free. His accusers will be gone. Visualize this, McKenna. I'm going to hang up and put an end to that miserable French girl. She's out on the snow, trying very hard. I admire that about her. But her time is done." He hung up.

Now I knew for sure. I fumbled at my pocket, trying to find his pillowcase.

As Simone came closer, she seemed to go even faster. I saw her make a fast glimpse behind her. It was as if she sensed Dwight gaining on her. Her speed and stamina were impressive. But trapped in the snow without skis, I could never even get close before Dwight would catch her. She'd kept her distance from him for hours. But now, newly enraged by me, he was reinvigorated. His speed was way up. I could see him gaining.

Simone was maybe a hundred yards out when I first heard her sounds, terrified, high-pitched whimpers that came in percussive bursts with each stride of her skis. She raced forward, running for her life.

But it wasn't fast enough to outrun the athletic skier overtaking her.

I finally got my frozen fingers on the plastic bag that contained Dwight's pillow case. I tore open the bag and removed the fabric.

"Spot!" I said, excitement in my voice. I grabbed Spot's chest and gave him a shake, vibrating him, transmitting excitement.

"Spot, smell this pillowcase." I balled it up and pressed it against Spot's nose. "Do you have the scent, Spot?! Do you?!"

I got him to smell the pillowcase again. Then I pointed his head toward Simone and Dwight just beyond her. I gave him another shake.

"Find the suspect, Spot! Find the suspect and take him down!"

I made the hand signal in front of Spot's head, then gave him a smack on his rear.

He lunged forward, but his paws sunk into the deep snow. He made impressive leaps, but the powder slowed his forward motion. He still moved five times as fast as me, but he wasn't going to get to Dwight before Dwight got to Simone.

Simone must have sensed us up on the rise to the side of Lake Aloha. She veered toward us. Her whimpers had turned to percussive, desperate shrieks. She came closer, her pace even faster, skis flying forward and back, compressing the snow, propelling herself toward me.

I was marching fast down the slope, but I was still a long way from Simone.

Dwight was striding with fury, his legs reaching, his arms and poles pumping. His pursuit of Simone was ten times easier because she was breaking trail, doing all the hard work of compressing the snow. By contrast, all he had to do was follow in her tracks. And it had been going on for miles.

Dwight stopped poling with his right arm. He was still fifty yards out in the dark. I couldn't tell what was happening, Then he stopped skiing, his arm came up, and he held it out steady.

There was a flash of light and a pop as a flare shot across the frozen lake toward Simone. It went a few feet above her head and landed in the snow in front of her, making a brilliant white glow under the snow. Simone screamed.

Another flare shot out. It caught the side of Simone's jacket, jerking the fabric forward and knocking Simone off balance. The flare stuck to the fabric of her jacket, a brilliant, eye-scorching welder's light that lit up the landscape.

Simone screamed again and clawed at her jacket, jumping and dancing frantic steps of terror as a three thousand-degree flare was stuck to her side. She dropped her poles, got the jacket off, and flung it to the snow. Her scream got louder.

The jacket burst into flame, a huge torch throwing yellow light back at Dwight who was reloading his flare gun.

Simone seemed paralyzed.

"RUN, SIMONE! SKI TOWARD ME!" I kept trudging down the slope toward her as fast as I could, high-stepping my legs in the deep powder. Spot was leaping through the deep powder, getting closer to Dwight, but still many seconds away.

Simone reached down and grabbed her poles. She planted one, made a single stride, and fell over in the snow.

Dwight skied toward Simone. He stopped above her, held the flare gun out, and pointed it down at her.

"DWIGHT!" I yelled, my voice impotent in the huge landscape that was filled with sound-muffling snowflakes.

Dwight didn't respond. He brought his other hand up for support, as if making certain that his aim at the writhing woman was perfect.

As I watched, horrified, I sensed a dark movement at my side. I turned.

Joe flew by me, racing down the slope on my skis. His knees

were bent, his upper body straight. His boots didn't fit into my ski bindings. He was merely perching on the skis, held on by nothing more than amazing balance. He held his arms out to the side for balance like when he did the earthquake walk.

Joe shot past me and then past Spot in the dark. When he came to the bottom of the slope, he had a lot of speed to keep him planing on the powder. He aimed straight for Dwight.

Dwight didn't see him, so focused was he on aiming the flare gun.

Joe was still several yards away, silently racing up behind Dwight when he let forth with a booming yell.

It was a deep alien sound, a resonant, thrusting presence as physical as it was audible. It shook my chest even though I was far away and behind Joe.

Joe's yell rose in volume, a sound like a lion's roar but more powerful for its surprise.

Joe had told me that it was a yell of fear. But its effect on Dwight was as if someone had taken a ship's foghorn and blasted it behind Dwight's head.

He jerked up into the air. The hand holding the flare gun flew sideways. The gun arced through the air as it went off, its little pop inaudible against the bellowing thunder from the old man. The flare traced a shallow arc into the snow.

Spot finally got to Dwight and leaped toward him. But his legs sunk in, and his rise was slow. Dwight saw him and twisted away with athletic speed.

Spot turned his head but was unable to grab Dwight. Spot's shoulder hit Dwight a glancing blow. Dwight went down and crawled for the flare gun. He reached his hand down into the snow, feeling, searching. Spot jumped over, opened his giant mouth, and, like a mountain lion, put his jaws around the back of Dwight's neck.

Dwight froze.

Spot held Dwight immobile.

Simone's jacket was still burning a bright yellow, its light illuminating her face as I reached out for her hand and pulled her up.

She clutched at my jacket, and I hugged her. She cried hard

for a few minutes, but then slowed, her violent jerking shivers calming from the effects of exhaustion more than anything else.

Eventually, she pushed her face away from my chest. Her cheeks were red and wet and reflected the yellow light of her burning jacket.

"He held the gun up," she said in a tiny voice, her French accent more pronounced. "He was aiming right at my face. I could see into the gun barrel. But something happened. Like an earthquake. What was that?" Simone's eyes searched mine. Confusion mixed with the shock of almost being murdered.

I turned and pointed through the dark toward Joe, who was bent over, hands on his knees, catching his breath.

"That was the Rorvik Roar," I said.

EPILOGUE

Late in the afternoon on New Year's Eve, we sat on Street's deck as the sun dropped behind the West Shore mountains and the temperature started to plunge.

"I wonder," Diamond said as he sipped his coffee, "were Ned and Dwight in contact?"

"Dwight hasn't said a word since they put him in jail, but I doubt it," I said. "I think he's been observing Ned from a distance."

Street said, "If Ned had known that his brother Peter had moved to town and was living as Dwight Frankman, he wouldn't have been able to keep quiet about it. Simone would have known."

"Dwight was conflicted about Ned," I said. "On one hand, he worshiped his stepbrother, and he killed his mother in retribution for beating on Ned. He probably wanted to be near Ned. He helped Ned enter Joe's origami contest. But Dwight also knew that Ned was a loser, always in trouble, always broke. If Ned had known of his brother's proximity and success, he would've hounded Dwight for money. He might have even preyed on Dwight to get money. Ned must have been as overbearing on his brother as he was on everyone else."

"Dwight probably changed his name from Peter just to help ensure that Ned couldn't track him down," Street said.

I nodded. "In his closet shrine, the photos showed that when he was still Peter, he was an athlete. When he became Dwight, he adopted a geeky look. When I first met him at Joe's, he wouldn't face the street and he acted furtive. I think that was because he'd spotted Ned in the neighborhood, and he didn't want Ned to recognize him. Later, he told me about how he was careful about keeping his blinds drawn."

Diamond said, "Dwight probably suspected that Ned followed Simone when she went hiking. If Ned saw his brother in the

Cameron disguise with the wig, he probably wouldn't recognize him."

Street's phone rang. She answered it, spoke a few words, and hung up.

"They're ready," she said.

Diamond finished his coffee. "I'll meet you there," he said.

An hour later, we drove the Jeep toward El Dorado Beach in the center of South Lake Tahoe. I had a small box in my lap. Joe sat in the front passenger seat. He held a large box that filled the space between his chest and the dashboard.

Street and Simone sat in back, Street behind Joe and Simone behind me. We squeezed Spot into the little space behind the back seat. Spot sat sideways, his chest jammed between the rear door and the back of the back seat. He cranked his head sideways and hung it over Simone's shoulder. He put on his sad eyes and immediately got continuous pets from her.

We all listened as Joe explained what we mostly already knew, that he'd been to the hospital and had his talk with Rell, and then he'd told the doctors that they could pull the plug. But before they could take her off the life support machines, Rell's heart beat once more and went still.

In my peripheral vision, I saw Street lean forward from the back seat and rub Joe's shoulders.

There was a steady flow of traffic in town, rolling softly through the fresh snow, a hundred thousand ski and snowboard tourists heading to condos and hotels and restaurants after a day on the various mountains.

After a long silence, Joe spoke again. "Simone hasn't been able to find a good place to live. So I said she could live with me if she wanted. It's not like I don't have extra rooms. Of course, sharing a fridge with an old man is not an easy sell. But I think she was eventually swayed by having her own bathroom for the first time in her life. So she's decided to grace this old man's house with her youthful energy. She moved in yesterday. It was a big project, of course, because of all her possessions. You'll be interested to learn that in addition to her small suitcase, Simone also owns a tiny purse."

I glanced in the rear-view mirror and saw Simone smiling.

Street said, "Simone, that's fantastic. I think Joe's house is great. There are quiet woods out every window."

"And you know what happened yesterday after Simone moved in?" Joe continued. He sounded like a kid.

"What?" Street said.

"Molly came back. The other birds, too."

Simone spoke. Her voice, and her alluring French accent, was so small that we all had to hold our breaths to hear it. "Joe said that Rell fed the chickadees," she said. "But when I looked at the feeder, he'd put in dried lentils. Little birds like Mountain chickadees don't eat dried lentils. They're hard as concrete. But then I found Rell's black oil sunflower seeds in the same garage cabinet where she stored her lentils for making soup. As soon as I put the sunflower seeds in the feeder, the chickadees arrived. They were so excited."

"And she met Molly," Joe said.

"Yes. The cutest little bird ever. She only has one leg, but she doesn't let it slow her down."

"Simone," I said, "I think living at Joe's house is a good idea, but that means you'll have to put up with him," I joked. I looked over at Joe. In the glow from the dashboard lights, his face looked stern, but I saw a little tug at the corner of his mouth.

"I know!" Simone said. "He's a strange man, this Monsieur Rorvik. He does things backward. Like wiping his mouth before he eats. And he chews his beer."

"She eats her coffee with a spoon," Joe said. "But I have to add that I've always thought I was a good judge of character, and I thought Simone didn't have any strength, any personal constitution. I was wrong. She's one tough girl. It was her amazing endurance that saved her life."

"And then," Street said with obvious admiration in her voice, "she went back out to Lake Aloha just two days later and did the rest of the Randonnée Extreme challenge. That's impressive."

"Yeah, she's a good skier," Joe said. "But she won't be able to ski at the Steven's Peak Resort because I'm voting against it."

We arrived at El Dorado Beach. I pulled in and parked. Diamond was waiting. He came up, lifted the big box off Joe's lap, and we walked down the steps, away from the sound of traffic.

Down at the lake, the major sound was the gentle waves lapping at the snowy beach. The sun had set, and big white flakes drifted down out of the gray-black sky. The cold air of the winter evening rolled off the mountains, which lurked like giant ghosts, unseen in the dark, snowy night.

Although the main lake never freezes, there were thin ice sheets at the edge where water had pushed in among the snow-covered beach pebbles. As the humid lake air flowed over the shore, long hoar frost crystals grew on the shore bushes. Spot didn't run, but just walked with us, his head turning left and right, nostrils flexing. The falling snow tickled his ears, and when he twitched them, his faux diamond ear stud sparkled in the dark.

When Joe found the spot he wanted, he nodded at Diamond. Diamond held the box while Joe opened the box flaps and pulled out an elaborate origami sailboat made from his big roll of white paper. The boat was a deep-keel design, about twenty inches long with a twenty-four-inch mast and a sail that curved out at a 30-degree angle from the center line of the boat. Joe paused and looked at the sky, sensing, I thought, the breeze. He adjusted the position of the paper sail and the tiller, making some folds to fix their angle.

As with Joe's other creations, it was impossible to see the elaborate boat as a mere sheet of folded paper. The result was much more than one might expect from the components that went into it.

It was like Joe. His life was a grand journey with his wife at its core. No matter how carefully one parsed out the parts, it was impossible to see Joe and Rell as a mere collection of hopes and dreams and plans and efforts and the experiences that arose from them. From hearing Joe's stories, the whole of Joe and Rell seemed grander than any couple I'd ever known, even though I'd never met Rell outside of the comatose woman in the hospital room.

My own life seemed shallow by comparison. My personal boat raced along here and there and provided a few thrills, and, best of all, carried Street along for the ride when our schedules permitted. But it seemed that I spent too much of my time moored at a lonely buoy, listing to starboard, too much water in the bilge, sails luffing or even gathering cobwebs, brightwork getting tarnished.

The man beside me was bent and weak with age, the Rorvik Roar softened. But he was still powerful in his way, a blend of wisdom and glamour and determination and persistence. Despite his claim that he didn't pay Rell enough attention, it seemed that he'd focused much of his life on Rell. He'd put aside many of the Me activities that most men indulge in and replaced them with We activities to do with Rell. Six decades later, the We activities were now done.

Holding the origami boat, Joe used his foot to move some cobbles together next to a piece of driftwood. He set the boat down so that the cobbles and driftwood supported the boat's hull, and the paper keel was suspended, undamaged, a few inches above the ground.

Joe turned toward me and reached his arms out. I lifted the lid off the small box. Joe pulled the plastic bag out, bent over, and carefully poured the ashes into the cabin space on the paper sailboat. I realized that he had planned it so that the ashes would serve as ballast in the keel.

"Simone," Joe said, his voice strong. "The candles, please?"

Simone nodded and pulled two votive candles out of her pocket.

Joe took them and set one in the bow of the boat and one at the stern. They fit precisely into compartments that he'd constructed just for that purpose.

He pulled out a wooden match, and, like an agile young man, lifted his knee to stretch his jeans tight, and struck the match along the taut denim at the back of his thigh. He lit both candles.

Joe picked up the boat, careful not to jar the candles, and waded into the lake. He didn't hesitate even though the water was nearly the temperature of ice. When the water was halfway up his calves, deeper than the boat's keel, Joe set the boat in the water.

He turned his head, sensing the air once again, then carefully pointed the boat and gave it a little push. The boat coasted a couple of feet.

A tiny breeze came up. The candles flickered. The boat leaned a bit, its sail inclined toward the water. It began to move forward under its own power.

Joe walked out of the water. He turned back to face the lake, his hand resting on Spot's neck.

"Okay, Street, we're ready for the poem, if you'd be so kind," Joe said.

Street pulled a small book out of her inside jacket pocket and opened it. She flipped on a tiny penlight and held it against the page.

"This is Emily Dickinson's poem called 'The Humming-Bird.'"

She read the evocative lines.

We watched as the boat moved out into the darkness, its flickering candles illuminating its sail. The boat grew distant and harder to see. After a couple of minutes, we could only see the two points of light. Soon, the lights blended into one distant flicker. After another minute, the single light disappeared.

"Rell and me, we had a deal," Joe said. "We kept it for sixty years." He raised his hand, kissed his palm, blew the kiss toward the lake where the boat had disappeared and said, "I love you, Rell."

About The Author

Todd Borg and his wife live in Lake Tahoe, where they write and paint. To contact Todd or learn more about the Owen McKenna mysteries, please visit toddborg.com.

A message from the author:

Dear Reader,

If you enjoyed this novel, please consider posting a short review on Amazon. Reviews help authors a great deal, and that in turn allows us to write more stories for you.

Thank you very much for your interest and support!

Todd

53737864R00217

Made in the USA
San Bernardino, CA
27 September 2017